Edwin Ahearn

The Arbhal Sequence

DOLVID

The ARBHAL Sequence

The tug of history, often very ancient history, is felt throughout these works. A large amount of information about the past is disclosed in the narrative (and a chronological tabulation is an appendix to ARBHAL*), but for the purposes of these extracts a reader needs to know that long before the land was Arbhal it was Owan, and the Owanil, a gifted, energetic, but often arrogant people conquered and then lost a vast empire on both sides of Arnan, the inland sea.*

After some centuries of obscurity, during which their island-based priesthood, the Atarlum*, was essential to the preservation of the Owani culture and language, the Owanil, through a series of opportune events, were able to regain control of their old realm, imposing themselves as an aristocracy on a numerically superior mixed population of Other Races (their own slighting term for all those without a pure Owani pedigree). Their old speech, however (the Owanilú), has become a scholar's language, surviving mainly for ceremonial and religious purposes, and in titles and proper names.*

Until relatively recently knowledge of the Owanilú was part of the elaborate system, Preference, by which the Owanil maintained control, practically excluding the Other Races from high office, and from many crafts and professions.

For half an age these exclusions were a source of unrest and rebelliousness among the Other Races, while many Owanil came to view the system as incompatible with their people's historic love of justice. At the time when Dolvid *begins, Preference has been abolished for the best part of a century; the exclusive Owani grasp of the realm's rewards has been loosened if not broken. With the extinction of the former reigning house even the* rabhsai *(the supreme, though by no means absolute ruler) has a mixed strand in his ancestry, and a conciliatory Patriarch has moderated the* Atarlum's *dogmatic insistence on the natural superiority and special fitness to rule of the Owanil.*

Nevertheless, the old conflict is muted rather than permanently silenced. The much-intermarried provincial aristocracy still preserves the purity of its bloodlines, and the same is largely true with the landowning class of the Heartland ("the Families"). While, as mentioned elsewhere, Dolvid *is essentially a novel about the childhood and early manhood of its title character, and* Arbhal *an epic adventure, the theme which runs right through the entire sequence is the desire (often the schemes) of this stubborn Owani minority, with the support (often the covert assistance) of reactionary elements within the* Atarlum, *to reestablish their former unchallenged dominance, and beyond that to somehow bring back the supposed glories of a legendary Owani past.*

Among the important people Dolvid meets when he's allowed to go to the Residence with his father is the head of the powerful Teaching Order of the Atarlum, *known only by his title,* Menadhi. *His frightening suggestion, that Dolvid come to the* Mankh' *for an education commensurate with his obvious gifts to the boy's relief is quickly declined by Vidukh, Dolvid's father.*

When, four years later, Vidukh suddenly falls ill and dies, Dolvid is virtually abducted and taken to the Mankh' *by* Menadhi, *where he becomes his personal pupil.* Menadhi, *generally expected to be the next Patriarch, is a leader among those who seek the restoration of exclusive Owani privilege and power. These opinions are at first embraced by Dolvid, who had begun to think his father's notions on the equality of races quaintly out of touch with the real world, but in time the very zeal of* Menadhi's *advocacy, together with the evident fraudulence of* Atarlum *history where it deals with the Other Races, begin to change Dolvid's mind. He gradually becomes, in his own view, the silent adversary of a man who still regards him as a disciple.*

Dolvid finds his own interest in the languages, lore and customs of the Other Races is tolerated so long as there's no open clash with the patronizing attitude proper to a true Owani scholar. At fifteen, to supplement the scant available written material on the Froghul, one of the little-assimilated minor races of Arbhal, he's permitted to spend a few midsummer days with a Froghuli clan now camped near Kadon Dinul...

The interim state of peace attained by the protagonist at the end of DOLVID *as he turns thirty is a personal victory, oddly incongruent with objective circumstances: he is unsuccessfully married, pessimistic about the future, and, after some triumphant years, out of favor with a new* rabhsai *who seems determined to restore all the ancient injustices, or wreck his realm trying.*

ARBHAL *opens after the elapse of six years, with Dolvid living alone in enforced exile, and the realm at the brink of civil war.*

Edwin Ahearn

DOLVID

i

2912

This could not be a city; it was a painting. The boy had never seen a painting to fill his whole view; still, so much was new, what was impossible in night being a tunnel, and dawn at its far end a softly-lighted hall? where wall to wall and floor to ceiling were covered with the tawny tints of a vast picture, quietly glowing at the center where walls rose beyond outer walls, an air-founded edifice, silvery and shimmering.

"Kamanta light," his father said. "You have seen it along the road, *ga-ôthu*."

Dolvid was silent, resenting the tone of voice, not one his father often fell into. There was an aunt with a sickly-sweet smell who behaved as if children were half deaf or half idiot, speaking always in that overclear, grotesquely gentle manner. Whenever she explained anything it was with many boring questions (`And you know what a billy-goat is, not so, Dolvidh'?'). He had expected better of his father. But nothing was the same since the death, since his mother's swelling, supposed to promise a new brother or sister, but instead taking away the woman herself, comfort, safety, an ear he could almost always rely on to listen.

The horse's gait kept jamming Dolvid's chin down into his chest, then jerking up and back, eyes opening as his head came against the big leather-covered button on his father's riding-coat.

And of course this was not dawn, but evening, the light cold because the sun on its way west had slid behind smooth, unspeaking clouds. Dawn had been journey's start, long talked about, delayed till now, when weather here in the Heartland

(Surely, this must be the Heartland) would be tolerable to travellers from the distant south, and there would be no chance of roads blocked by something Dolvid had never seen; snow. Dawn had also been other settings-out, his half-waking as misery itself, outshirt buttoned against chill air, dogs barking as they left the place called Bathrâd, just as barking dogs had greeted them, a muddle of days before, as they rode into the town called Kir with its broad hill.

Then they had still been riding with others, numbers for safety crossing the dangerous emptiness named Ní-Tilagh, where there were no towns or hostelries; they rested in bags on the ground, and Dolvid's father had to get up in the night and go from the fire, a blade in his hand. All but the youngest and the few women took turns watching, and Dolvid had been told not to move if anything happened, to lie still no matter what noises came, what feet, what voices.

A woman there had said the Ní-Tilagh would be safe once more, 'Now we have a new Banak at Kadon Dinul.' Dolvid knew this was a joke, and did his duty by smiling, although he did not understand, and hated the woman, who had bad teeth, and called him 'little warrior.' She meant well, but he kept close watch as she tried to take possession of his father, often talking as if Dolvid were not there, making much of how the little warrior must miss his mother, poor mannikin.

That evening in the Ní-Tilagh she hugged Dolvid tearfully, as if her jarring stench of rancid and decayed was anything to him but insult after the warmth and comfort of his mother with her fresh-bread, laundered smells. His father's patience could be a trial for Dolvid. Happily the woman with her black teeth seemed to have gone away sometime after Kir; Dolvid at first made no conscious note of her absence. At six, the comings and goings of the chance-met are unordered; big people arrive unaccountably, and then vanish into an elsewhere of untested extent.

The new Banak, he found out from his father, was a

baby, who lived in a big thing called Residence. But where he lived was also Kadon Dinul, where they were going, a great city. This Banak was grandson of Great Banak, who had been *rabhsai*, but was dead; his son Lambarr ruled. But the new Banak should never become *rabhsai*, because he had an elder brother. There was also a sister; Lambarr had fathered three children in just five years of marriage.

A lot, Dolvid gathered. "All with the same mother?"

"Yes — " a sad smile coming. "Saëdhu." She was young and pretty, daughter of someone else famous, and her title was *rabhsayu*.

He never connected his distant view of the walls with the dark gateway they rode through, halted by men with lanterns, breastplates gleaming yellow. For a moment, as the horse toiled up a steep rise, banging his head against his father's chest, Dolvid was fully awake.

"When are we coming to Kadon Dinul, father?"

"This is the city. This is Kadon Dinul. The arm that kept the boy from falling off squeezed tighter. "Didn't you see the Residence?"

His eyes would not focus up and off to the right where his father tried to point him. It was all without sense; Kadon Dinul was a painting spread against the sky, not this enveloping jumble of shadows and lights, loud voices and strange smells. A dog barked, and that should be the place called Bathrâd.

More tunnels, the next one called hostelry, and he was shoved down it feet first. Swollen, yellow-lighted faces moved about him, meaningless voices surged and distanced, the world was a complicated misery with no space for him. The light was flickering; something was on fire, that must be the meaning of the farther shouts. He wanted to tell his father, wanted to escape the flames. His legs could not be moved, and none of it mattered, they had to let him sleep, even if everything was burning, even gripped by this scratchy bed.

One of the swollen faces, abruptly, was his father. Dolvid tried to ask about the fire, and about why they had not ridden on to the painted cityscape, already melting from his memory, its loss a sorrow past bearing. All these questions he managed to put into three cleverly-made words, but no one understood.

Between Deaths

High above the Estuary gulls were winding. The day was streaked with cloud, patches of sun dappling and gliding over the grey-green of the hills beyond. Back pressed to the uneven stone of the house, Dolvid squatted on cobbles, looking out over the roofs of Old Kadon. Distantly, northward, he believed he could just make out masts of the ships, craft built for long voyages, resting at the wharves of the royal port, Owan Sai. Though he could not see anything of them, there would also be long, low barges, oar-driven, that carried goods and travellers up the great Paowan River, bringing back other travellers and other goods; fleeces, furs (it was said) from the far Northeast, weapons and tools forged on the Upper Dakbân where the best steel came from, tar and other ores transferred to barges up past the Angle, after their long overland journey from dry Asekh, the desert province.

"Four hundred years," his father came outside, wiping his face with a worn towel.

A challenge, having to do with the far uplands, Dramal, where the Treaty of the Wind Caves was made. "From the Return, 2477, when Plakhat Gabh'Owan became first *Rabhsai*, to when Great Banak took the Bronze Sword."

His father nodded. "If you get started on your tasks, you'll have a chance to practice your scripts, and read from the *Song of Tales*."

"My tasks can be finished this morning." Not exactly a lie; he was not saying who would do the work. Esodra, who came later to cook their meal, never said anything if she found bowls unwashed, floor not swept, but quietly did it herself. Her uncomplaint could sometimes shame Dolvid into whole weeks of dutiful service, but today he had plans for meeting other boys at the Gardens, for some hard campaigning.

His father went to the corner of the house to take in the morning sun. Southward was the soft bowl of the fertile Heartland, coming alive in varied green, after long months of drab earth and slow-thawing snow.

Dolvid kept farmlands and the roll of hills hemmed at the edge of his vision, preferring to look down on Market Way, past the Disc of Aëlovoi, where the incline steepened to the wide opening of the paved square inside Market Gate, an exciting place, where farmers brought their grumbling wagons, and stopped to trade and barter, and to swap news. The city walls were mellowed in sunlight, and breastplates shone on the Household men at the gate. Farther left were newer houses, many with flat roofs, all well built of clean-cut stone. That was the Residence Quarter, where the important lived, south of the magnificent Avenue of Treaties. Kadon Dinul was a true city, grander than anything ever imagined in the narrower times of the South. After nearly two years, those memories were dwindling, yet Dolvid had never lost the tremulous excitement of being here in the capital, with its long, proud history, its size and beauty.

"Think of it, half the grain for all the realm will be reaped within sight of where we stand."

"Aye — " the hard, young voice of Darborr, whose house was the other half of the low building where Dolvid lived with his father. "And again, I shan't be reaping any of it."

The man, really not much beyond a youth, had come out into the day, still chewing at his breakfast. Dolvid stared at the flat, always angry face. He never quite trusted the man.

"Aye," Darborr said, "it's your Old Race, Master Vidukh, who'll be doing the reaping, and the selling, as usual."

"Come." Dolvid's father was soothing. "That's all in the past, before Great Banak. Anyone, today..." He gestured a little vaguely.

"If decrees buttered the bread of folk not lucky enough to be born with the right shape nose." Darborr's own, flanked by darker eyes than Dolvid had been used to, was broad-bridged, nothing of the slender arch Dolvid would some day inherit from his father.

"Oh, Darborr, nonsense. The *rabhsai* himself is Mixed, Banak's father was half-Gabhani."

"And the *Rabhsai* Lambarr," Darborr, as if winning a round, "took care, didn't he, after his father, to wed into Old Blood." He saw coming affront, and hastily added, "Not to say anything against the *rabhsai*, nor his lady."

"Nor his mother, I would hope."

"Well, Laluvoi *Asayu* is honored by all."

"And surely — " not to be placated by less than a complete roster. "Surely you don't mean anything against the descent of the *rabhsai*'s lady?"

"Oh, Saidhan and his house have been good friends to ordinary folk," Darborr agreed, in his grudging way. "That's not to be denied, but he's there in the West, and here we are. If what you say's true, and all the exclusions belong to old times, how is it my suit never comes to a hearing, hah? A plain case; the land is mine by any reckoning."

"We should have right to compensation." Radis, her hair hanging loose, came to the open door to call a shy good morning. She was even younger than her husband, though she tried to be motherly to Dolvid, telling him when his face was dirty or his breeches torn. Dolvid trusted her better, and her face was nearer what he had been used to in infancy, light eyes and a curved nose.

"Compensation! I've a right to the land, that's what I've a right to."

"But Dar, you don't want the land." Radis rubbed at a dish with a piece of blue cloth, trying to scour away the threat of being wife to a farmer. "You say yourself, breaking your back from first light to last, old before your time..."

"Land is land," Darborr said. "Still, things are

changing, that's so, Vidukh? Money will breed of itself, without putting it in seed; your money-planter has it all over your little farmer, as things are — and what race is it plays that game best, hah? Still, if I was lettered like you, I could put my plea in proper form, the right phrases..."

"Oh, if that's what you want," Dolvid's father said, "I'll be glad to frame a plea for you. It will have to wait till evening, I must be off. Your proper course — " Vidukh moved his hand to stroke at the beard not there since he was a young man — "is to enter your case in the Court of Grievances. Any suit can be heard there, no matter what language it is argued in."

"There, see what you should do, Dar," Radis agreed. "Though why we would ever want a draughty farm-house, three days from news — "

"I've told you; that's not what I want. Having the land, we can raise a loan, and buy a share in my uncle's fleece business. I'm not spending my life north of the Avenue, neither. The Court of Grievances." He turned back to Vidukh. "That's what it is; Banak made the laws, but who's there been to show us how to go about it, plain folk who never had a suit at law in the clan? That's how Owanil keep the realm in their soft hands."

"Now, Dar," Radis, embarrassed. "There are good lettered men in plenty like Master Vidukh, always ready to lend a hand."

"Oh, I'm not saying no, and I thank you, Master. Except most of the time we poor Others wouldn't even know the questions to ask. See?"

Perversely proud of this wisdom, he went back into the house, leaving Radis, the blue cloth over both her hands as she conveyed apology. Vidukh merely smiled.

"Had your breakfast?" Radis asked Dolvid.

"Yes I have." He had not followed the dispute, except Darborr was pretending to be poorer than was true (really poor people could not live where they did), which had to do with his love of blaming everything on the Owanil, Dolvid's race.

"There's honey," Radis wheedled. "You always find room for bread with honey."

"I thank you, but I've got my tasks." He would not mind sitting down with Radis, but Darborr showed no signs of leaving. He did not see why the man was allowed to speak to his father so. Dolvid's friends had respect for a father whose work was at the Residence, and who spoke with Lambarr *Rabhsai*, with Laluvoi, *Laluvoi*.

Vidukh, having gone inside for his outshirt, came into the sun again. "Privileged Owani I may be, but if there's a book needed and I am not there to find it, I'll be begging my bread with any." The little smile with this was to say it was only a way of speaking. He hurried off before Radis could answer.

In the evening Dolvid's father spoke again about Darborr's claim. "Any such suit can get a hearing, no matter what that son-in-law of yours says about Owani ways."

Esodra, cooking, shook her head as a comment on Darborr's ideas. She was mother to Radis, and that was strange; while the daughter might have been taken for Owaniyu, the mother's broad, padded face proclaimed her Mixed origins.

"Being Great Pledging year, it might be judged by Lambarr *Rabhsai*, or even Laluvoi," Vidukh went on. "Pledgings, now, they're no Owani custom." He turned to Dolvid, who squirmed. A lesson was coming.

"Banak, Banak-*rai*, as we say, knew long ago the people of his father's father governed themselves, and had midsummer meetings where all the men took new oaths, and clan-chieftains in turn renewed their allegiance to the high chieftain — that's so, Esodra?" He caught at the woman's loose sleeve.

"No use asking me what the old Gabhanil did," she sniffed. "My grandmother always said they had no history anyone could be proud of. She would never speak of that side."

"There!" Dolvid's father struck the table with an open hand. He was (as even Dolvid could tell by now) a small man, and mostly placid; that made his rare shows of anger the more frightening. Though his present annoyance, clearly, was with no one present. "That's the worst of it! What we're taught causes Gabhanil themselves to repudiate their past. Some day — " he clenched his fist, to bring it down on the closed volume left on the small board table, the *Song of Tales*. "Some day we shall have a book to give them justice, instead of this so-called re-translation. If you knew the tale of Pir Perus as was first told — well. The question is, the Pledgings." Abruptly he was his mild self again.

"You've never seen a Great Pledging here at Kadon," Esodra, a warning note in her voice. "Seven years comes round too soon for my liking. Last pledging — "

"I can remember when Banak and Laluvoi came to the Sword," Vidukh interrupted.

"Aye, and I can too, though I was no more than ten. Who here at Kadon could ever forget it, end of the killing, and how lovely she was, Laluvoi *Asayu*, all robed and with the baby in her arms, that's Lambarr now, and all the girls my sister's age going moon-eyed over how handsome Captain Saidhan was —"

"In the South, where I had then been two or three years, many called that day the darkest since the Night of Owan. Oh, yes — " as Esodra murmured disbelief — "the Old Blood is strong there, and they saw the end of the realm they had called theirs, a tanner's grandson robed as *rabhsai*. When we talk, when your son-in-law talks, of injustice, he should be taught how it was then, and how bitterly this realm was divided. Three civil wars, and it took the coming of Banak and Laluvoi to end that. Many of the Old Blood hoped openly for Kargul to triumph, and some urged the then-Patriarch to refuse all part in the investing of Banak. Only Laluvoi's being from the proudest of the Great Families made that day possible at all."

"Proud? Well, there's proud and proud. I've never seen Lady Laluvoi not to have a word and an ear for any, Mixed or Gabhani, just the same. Not changed a bit, is she?" Dolvid had seen women speak about babies as she did the Dowager, head to one side, eyes brimming with tears.

"Indeed," Vidukh agreed. "Her spirit, as much as Great Banak's, brought change. That's what Pledgings stand for, chance for any grievance to be heard, and new laws made public. There'll always be some, of course, for whom it's just a midsummer holiday."

"Soaking themselves in wine and beer! Is that how to show honor to the realm? Mad dancing in the Avenue of Treaties, to say nothing of the women." This last called for a dark glance at Dolvid.

"They'll be coming," Dolvid's father told his son, glad-faced, "farmers, dyers, workers in weave and wood and steel, from every corner of the realm — "

"So they will," Esodra chimed in. "Hostelries filled with the dregs of Six Provinces, the Avenue alive with week-wives and worse. I'll be glad when it's past. A decent woman, it's a fact, doesn't dare stir from her house between dusk and dawn."

"Happy, then, it is when they're closest, one to the other." Vidukh preened. "A pairing for a song! I must remember that, when I see the Poet Nilradh."

"He's been dead for years," Esodra said. "Or is this some other Nilradh? It could never be the one who made the song about Banak and Laluvoi? He wasn't young then."

"The same. I saw him just yesterday, when he came seeking — well, never mind. Some slight tale."

"Some filthy tale, you would say. All the same, your song-makers, musicians and such." Esodra was ready to launch into a tale of her own, but her words had made Dolvid's father frown. A set speech was coming, one known very well, about song being mirror and memory, our best treasure. Other fathers had rougher tongues, and few could boast of being at the Residence unless as mere servants; some beat their sons with sticks or leather straps. Still, none Dolvid had seen spouted things other boys could so easily mock.

Quickly, he said, "Father, they say there is money to be made, Pledging Weeks, running errands for, for those who need errands run. Who don't know the city."

"He's too little," Esodra objected.

"We have never been servants," Vidukh said.

"Only for a fortnight."

"There may be tallow-boilers in our descent, chandlers, but always their own masters. This is our own roof we sleep under. At the Residence, I run no one's errands."

"Your father," willing to use anything, "has his position to maintain." She had been steeping nettles and other herbs in hot milk. This she poured into blue mugs and brought to the table.

On the borrowed horse, they came to the brow of the rise. Less than two miles away was Arnan, the inland sea. Westward, beyond sight, was the Island, Kamanta, where Owan had its beginnings.

The strangest of days, and not only because Dolvid had no idea why they had ridden this way. They set out in brilliant sunshine and a friendly, inquisitive breeze. As they came down to Harbor Gate, there were silvered clouds on the horizon, dark-hearted, while the wide square with its slender column of natural rock, the Spear of Yoëlladhu, the Old Bronze Residence on the far side, seemed to purr in the sun. Then, on the westward road, stinging spatters of rain, icy gusts of wind from a new direction brought sun and cloud in rapid alternation. At Treaty Stone, the massive squared block that stood for concord between *rabhsai* and Patriarch, a cool drizzle spun scintillating in sunlight, and now, with bright patches moving on the broad surface of Arnan, Dolvid and his father looked down into shadow. Almost at their feet was the wall, strong and forbidding, enclosing the inner grounds of the Patriarch's chief Mainland residence, temple, shrine, school, home on these shores of the *Atarlum*.

"There." Dolvid's father motioned with a hand. "The *Mankh'*."

Sober and ponderous, the edifice was impressive more than beautiful. Two wings reached from a squat central block, and a shaft of sun struck but did not illuminate somber stone, heavily worked with carving. It was a big, dangerous animal, dozing beside the Inland Sea.

"Where this stands is the very spot where Yoëlladhu Founder first set foot on the Mainland. There is an older *Mankh'*, the True *Mankh'*, as the *Atarlum* call it, at the foot of the Mountain, Karg' Kamanta."

"Have you been there, father?"

A laugh. "Not I. The Island is *ga-dazhu*, holy and forbidden. Since they closed the road across Kamanta, only the *Atarlum* can go there. And, naturally, the *Adanum Plakh'*." As with the day, Vidukh's features quickly clouded, and Dolvid felt the slight shiver. He had heard that name before, always spoken in fear.

"You can work out what it it means, Golden Brotherhood. They are the bodyguard of the Patriarch. Down there at the gate."

Dolvid saw soldiers, quite similar to Household or General Cavalry, except their tunics were longer, and had yellow facings. The helms, too, had yellow crests.

"We're on estates of the *Atarlum*," his father warned. "That is generally permitted, though you could not pass that gate, not the *rabhsai* could, without a token from the Patriarch. But now or ever on *Atarlum* lands, if riders of the *Adanum* come to challenge, make your answers short and courteous. Those men have sworn the death-oath, and you can't joke with them, as you can Household. Here on their own ground, they are outside the laws of the realm."

"Father, are we going home the same way we came?"

With a keen look, his father chuckled, thinking Dolvid meant he wished they had not come here. That was true, but chiefly his mind was on the food-shops in Harbor Way, where they sold cooked things and a variety of sweet and interesting drinks. One could enjoy them while looking at the windows and crowded counters of shops belonging to the Craft Guilds, built up against the city's westward wall, or while exploring among cheaper goods on stalls and wagons in the Way.

"You must learn the powers of this realm. Many can see no good, Darborr I am sure would see no good, in what this stands for, the *Mankh'*, the *Atarlum*, the long story of the Patriarchs. But we have to believe something about our beginnings, and the *Atarlum* teaches it all begins with the Will of Raëdh'." Here, Vidukh made a pious sign, touching his right thumb to his breast, then closing the hand, so thumb rested at the root of his little finger. "With Aëlovoi Giver, He fathered Zhôl, but our time begins with the Descent, after Yoëlladhu had climbed the Watch-Rock, where he had surveyed the boundaries of the realm that would be."

A fresh spatter of rain came, bigger drops, wind-blown. Vidukh glanced up at the sky, where heavier clouds were rolling in. "It seems Zhinzhappa would have his say," only half-humorously. "If this nag of Arvus's can raise a canter, we may stay ahead of the worst."

As they wheeled, Dolvid again considered the heavy, near topheavy sprawl of the *Mankh'*. Power was there, as well as menace, and yet he had met some of the *ramidul*, the Healing Order, as they went about in the city, and they were mild men who brought comfort, perhaps cure, to those who sickened, summoning back life with chants and medicines. This was their home, too.

iii

Menadhi

Once before, he could not remember when, there was this feeling of being passed hand-to-hand into the mouth of a tunnel. He was struggling, and the arched entranceway really was a tunnel, though not a black one; a double row of *ôdul* gave light enough to see many doors on one side, a single more ornate double door on the other. Dismounting from the wagon (from where, swathed in blankets, Dolvid had just been handed down), *Menadhi* said, "All is well, Dolvidhai. A bed is waiting for you."

Dolvid threshed with his imprisoned feet. As his kicks started unwinding the blankets he was half free from the soldier in the long tunic. But the *ramidu* holding his shoulders had a firm grip, and *Menadhi* himself bent to catch up a trailing corner of blanket; the ankles were seized again, and the windings made secure.

"He is distraught with grief, and no wonder," *Menadhi* explained, though the soldier had not been about to question any orders. Surely not; he was of the *Adanum Plakh'*, and Dolvid did not want a bed here. Here at the *Mankh'*.

"You can't — " his throat was already hoarse with this shouting — "I don't wish it. The *rabhsai*, the Lady Laluvoi won't permit this." He swallowed down a flood of spittle.

One of the lesser doors was open, and at-Sepivadhi, who had also climbed down from the wagon, bypassed the clump around still-struggling boy, and slipped inside. At once he came back with several rough-dressed youths, who took the bundle containing Dolvid from the others. They smelled sweaty, and held him so he could not do any more kicking.

He had been handled in this way since *Menadhi*'s invitation had hardened into insistence, and Dolvid's refusal into fight. He had been asleep, and that had to do with the musty taste of the drink he had been given. Wakening in the back of a feed-wagon, rumbling slow under a blue sky aswim with white clouds.

When, from where he was lying, he recognized the top of Treaty Stone, and shortly the black pillar marking the beginning of the Sacred Precinct, he began his shouting, not much use on this lonely road. *Menadhi* had reappeared, and through all cries and struggles continued to speak in a soft, soothing voice, as if he could believe the tale that had begun this abduction, so he could be safe, best for him to come to the *Mankh'*, where *ramidul* could watch over him till certain he had none of the fever that had killed his father. Only the *Atarlum* could give the care he needed. He was to be wise, and trust to the *Mankh'*, home of life and hope.

Dolvid's shouts were, he did not want to be cared for, or need to be cared for, at last that he wanted to die. Now, as he was borne rapidly inside, there was no more shouting. His throat hurt, his mouth was sour and utterly dry, and he was swiftly awed by the agelong hush of this heavily listening place.

Even now he could tell it was less grim than on the outside, with *ôthu*-lighted corridors of warm-colored stone, doors of burnished wood or wrought bronze with a subtle sheen, many-tiled ceilings of glowing gold. Wasn't it the kind of beauty to come from long handling? But *Mankh'*, it sounded like the scrape of an iron gate, and *Atarlum*, that was the thud of a heavy door, shutting behind him forever.

The bed was in an alcove, he worked that out. He was squinting through the gap left by soft hangings into what must be a small chamber, sparsely furnished, but not comfortless. On the floor there was a roughweave the color of brown-green moss, and he could also see part of a low, wide chair. It all seemed lighted by one or at the most two *ôdul*; he could not see any window, nor tell whether this was night or day. In the bed there was linen over as well as under him. It did not seem he could still be at the *Mankh'*; while he slept, perhaps, Household soldiers had come, and he had to be given up to the *rabhsai*. He must have been brought to the Residence, to be the Heir's sword-partner.

His father was dead, that was certain. All thought had to begin after that fact. If this was the *Mankh'*, they could not keep him here against his will, that was law, part of Plakhsila's Code. They must let him go.

Where? He had kin in the South, in Ninkufu. A vast distance away, seven or eight dayrides with the best horses. Travellers waiting to buy spaces on wagons could take as much as a month; he could save time as well as money walking it. But he would need food; he would have to earn enough money before starting such a journey, south through the Paowan, then Upper and Lower Nîv. South of there came the Ní-Tilagh, and Dolvid shivered: he could not walk that, but if he found other travellers to take him, could come in the end to Ninkufu, and to the town of Thenimala on its bay.

What sort of welcome would be there? He was not sure he would find home, or even shelter, with his mother's kin, who would by now have forgotten his existence.

Surely he had friends at Kadon Dinul? though Esodra had left long ago. He did not know why he thought of her, a Mixed woman of no standing or wealth. His mind turned to Kheval, a harsh old man, to Rhunsilakh, who knew who he was, was going to promote his apprenticeship to the enameller. But Rhunsilakh had his own son, big enough to come and watch the swordplay. Besides, Dolvid could not ask for help from Rhunsilakh, whom the discerning did not respect.

There was Faëdhal, but he no longer had any use for Dolvid. In the roster of Kheval's pupils he could think of no one who might speak for him — and did not know just what that meant. The long-limbed, rowdy Bradhinal of Ân, near friends with Dolvid, except for the disdain of his elder brother, Brodhai. The Heir, with his big, unobeying hands and feet in the end was not so bad; lately he had exchanged a joke or two with Dolvid, and everyone had laughed long and loud, except Banak-loi, who did no more than smile briefly. He never laughed, regarding the world with stony eyes, his shoulders always hunched-seeming, but only because his neck was so short. Something about Banak-loi frightened Dolvid, who shocked himself by deciding he would very much like to punch the *rabhsai*'s second son, very hard in the middle of that sour face. Banak-loi was only seven.

But real, one doorway into the real, and Dolvid let despair come. There was nothing princelings would or could do for him, nor any of the lads of Family who came to Kheval's classes. Not unless he was going to be taken in as a servant. At the Residence, all he could hope for was service as a groom, a kitchen lad, at best a copyist in the library.

If he could escape the *Mankh'* and avoid service, all that was left was the apprenticeship. Boys without parents were occasionally taken on before the twelfth birthday, and the master-enameller, Rhunsilakh's kinsman, could surely make room in his household for Dolvid; that too was common. It was what his father had wanted.

Nevertheless, he did not want to be a maker of fine enamel. It was years and years before he could start to be a soldier, and he no longer wanted that, either. What he wanted was for everything to be as it had been. For his father not to be dead.

Waking again he heard a voice give a small, birdlike cry, and feet go scuttling away. Next, *Menadhi* was at bedside, looking down gravely. Once more he said, "*Bi namakil shudal yi-butraghal ul.*"

"*Y'olagh am, Menadhai.*" Wary, Dolvid this time made the proper response. He felt some of the tautness go away.

"This no mere rote mouthing, Dolvidh." The change to ordinary speech was smooth. "Your father is a heavy loss, to the realm, as well as to those who loved him. We weep with you, as much as for you."

For the moment he was far from tears. Outrage was his

chief sense with a mixture of curiosity, but all feeling was happening somewhere else. He was unnaturally alert; his ear could catch tiny settling sounds in *Menadhi*'s grey robe, softer and finer than the one he wore on his visits to the Residence. On the right side, part of the neck opening was tucked under, as if he had dressed in haste. There was a brown mole on his right cheek, level with the earlobe — Dolvid might have become all senses, with no room left for a self.

"The *ramidu* has the opinion you have not caught any fever — at-Sepivadhi has consulted in this with *Ramidhai* in person." That was to say, head of the Healing Order; *Menadhi* signed with third finger extended to touch his breast. "No *rabhsai*, not the Patriarch, has ever been observed with more concern. Hradhi is good."

"Hradhi is good," echoing dutifully.

"Now you must be hungry."

"No, not very, *Menadhi*. Or, yes — " he was, rapaciously. "That is, I thank you, yes."

Menadhi was smiling, eyes rather than mouth. He indicated the low, curved seat next to the bed, where clothing was folded. "Dress, and we shall take a little food together."

Dolvid discovered he was in plain underlinen, not his. While *Menadhi* drifted a few steps back into the main chamber, he swung his legs out from under the covers. He stood, and *Menadhi* came darting back to catch at his upper arm. "There, you will be a little unsteady. Sit, Dolvidh, sit." The small hand was quite strong.

Dolvid did sit, on the bed, resenting life. A slow turning in his head; his senses gave a lurch, and slowly seeped back into their proper places. He could stand without aid, knees not altogether certain.

The main clothing on the chair was a parchment-colored smock as were worn by youths, apprentices of the *Mankh'*.

"Come, dress yourself."

"*Menadhi*, my own clothes — "

"Are being cleansed, and must wait for an east wind to

purify them. It is the rule with a fever. Come."

A simple thing, to put on a smock. Yet as reason accepted *Menadhi*'s reassuring tones, something else, superstition or wisdom, fought against assuming this emblem. Reluctantly, Dolvid took the garment. It went over his head, again a tunnel, and at the end was *ga-ôthu*, Kamanta light. *Menadhi* made an affirming sound.

"This is how we tie the cord — " he came and showed how to make a double bow, so the two short loops were the wings of bees, bees in memory of Yoëlladhu. Looking up from this task the eyes were filled with good humor, and he quickly put arms behind Dolvid's shoulders to give the slightest of hugs, breath warm on his collarbone.

"*Menadhi* — " He had discovered another and urgent need.

After using the small side-closet, where there was a covered night-jar, as well as warmed water and a large, rough towel, Dolvid came back to see this chamber possessed a low table, where two chairs were drawn up. Farthest from the table was a clear window. It was light outside, the sky a rich blue. From where he stood there was no view, so sunlight striking the window gave little clue to the time of day. He felt strong aversion to asking, that or anything else; it would too readily admit *Menadhi*'s complete control.

"Sit, Dolvidh, sit." He came padding back from what must be the entrance door, where he had been giving soft-voiced instructions to someone unseen. "We shall have more light soon."

If he meant from the sun, just striking the bare margin of floor by the window, it must be afternoon, and this a west-facing room.

"Come, no ceremony till you have broken your fast." He took one of the two chairs, and Dolvid, after half-deference, sat in the other.

"These are part of my own quarters," as Dolvid continued to look about him. Not a single book in sight. Shelves let into the wall had only a small, intricately worked bronze vessel with a spout, set on a bow-legged little stand. Dolvid tried to make out any breaks in the walls that might be hidden doors; common belief held the *Mankh'* was riddled with secret ways. One legend insisted on a tunnel all the way to the Old Bronze Residence. If that was improbable, the version that had it going beneath all the miles of Arnan to emerge on the Island was ridiculous. Anyway, anyone could see the wharves behind the *Mankh'*, where, in all but worst weather, ships of the *Atarlum* came from and departed for the Island. That was how *raminat* and other Patriarchal goods were brought to the Mainland.

A knock at the door, and a boy dressed like Dolvid shuffled in. He was carrying a single *ôdu* in a kind of metal cage making it into a hand-lantern, and its light struck upwards to sharpen hard boning of a face that appeared far older than its owner.

Above the table was a brass hook at the end of a chain, and after deference to *Menadhi* the boy hung up the cage with the *ôthu*-globe. They had their light, and it was still uncertain whether this was morning or evening. The creases down *Menadhi*'s face had softened, and as he shifted back in his chair he seemed quite benign. "You may bring food, Dravadhi."

"At once, *Menadhi*. It's just outside." The words sounded strange; this must be the Island accent. Dravadhi could not be above a year or two older than he, but the face was amazing, eyes set deep in chiselled sockets either side of a curved knife-thrust of a nose.

When he brought in the food, it included a wheaten loaf, butter, a big wedge of yellow cheese, a dish of pickled and spiced fish. On a second journey the awed-seeming Dravadhi carried in bowls of preserved fruits, radishes and spring onions no fatter than grass-stems, and a tiny plate of what turned out to be a costly delicacy from the Island, smoked eel, also a Patriarchal monopoly. After he had finished by bringing in two cups and a jug of what might be barley-water, Dravadhi withdrew.

Deftly he filled a plate for Dolvid and urged him to eat.

For himself he took only bread, fish and a tiny piece of eel. Dolvid did try not to cram his mouth with food, small two-tined fork not adequate to his hunger.   Besides, his hands were trembling.

"A good boy, Dravadhi," *Menadhi* remarked after a while. "He'll make a good *atarlai*. Not, however, of the *Manadilum*. Our Order calls for a special aptitude."

Self-conscious, Dolvid said, "Is that the reason why, of all Orders, the *Manadilum* has given the most Patriarchs?" His father had told him that, discussing the possible future of this very man.

"*Betufi la Rhuva ki-lodakhi ôl.*" Complacently, *Menadhi* raised a hand to illustrate these words, evidently an established saying, `forefinger is closest to the Thumb,' Raëdh's Thumb.

"You could go farther," he continued, "and say the *Manadilum* has made more Patriarchs than all other Orders together. Each of the Orders has its virtues, gifts to bring the realm. Healers, Growers, the bringers of pleasure and of rest — these all serve the body, and the body must never be despised or neglected. But the *Manadilum* is the Mind of the *Atarlum*, and only with mind can we learn the body — know the past, so we can dream at a different future.

"Or make it," he added.

Dolvid was puzzled and uncomfortable. This man spoke as if he, Dolvid, was being asked to approve, as if there was a choice to be made. Yet he had been brought here by force, against his will. He tried smoked eel, and liked it. The barley-water was subtly flavored with mint and something fruity.

Menadhi stood, putting down his drinking cup, and Dolvid hastily did the same. As they ate, that it was afternoon had become obvious; sunlight, always reddening, had advanced more than a pace into the chamber, and where it came the roughweave glowed, green turning to dark gold.

Menadhi went to the window, beckoning the boy to stand beside him. Puddles of writhing light swarmed on the slow swell of Arnan. The Sacred Precinct took in a bulge of coast too slight to be called a headland; behind the *Mankh'* the ground fell sharply away to where the stone wharves were, a two-masted vessel tied up. This place must be at least halfway up in the *Mankh'*, and he could see stonework of broader lower levels, slopes of leaded roof, jutting rain-spouts.

But *Menadhi* pointed westward, so they were both squinting against the lowering sun. "Arnan, *Arnanai Owani, Ul'Arnanit*, our sea. We are looking towards Kamanta. On a clear day, when the sky pales, it is good at least to believe we can discern dawn sun glinting on the yearlong and age-long snows of Karg' Kamanta. Our beginning is the Island, and the Island is our being, where else would we turn for our renewal?" Dolvid was a half-step nearer the window, and when he turned the man's face had taken fire from the sun.

"You love history, so I am told. What is it we call our one story?"

"*Menadhi*, the Annals, *Kezhul baRadhum.*"

"And what else?"

"*Menadhi*—" hesitating; his father did not approve of this title. "*Menadhi*, it is *ga-Keghu Owaniyu.*"

"Yes, and that is also the style and title of *Manadilum, ga-Keghu Owaniyu*, the Blessed Memory of Owan."

"Of Owan, *Menadhi*?" That name for the realm was passing from use. Since Banak's reign in law, as long before in usage, the inclusive name was Arbhal.

"Of Owan. Here at the Paowanu *Mankh'*, as everywhere on the Island, no other name is ever used. Our memory goes back before there was a *rabhsai*, before *Nim'raibakim*, before Yuvakh Martyr, to the beginning of time, and Owan was the name Yoëlladhu gave. Think, Dolvidh, the *rabhsai* himself does not set foot in the Sacred Precinct except with *g'Asalladh's* permission. That is the Treaty, where the *Atarlum* forever relinquished any claim to govern. We rule only over our own, and have no realm measured in land, except for the Island. Who could wish for more?"

A last time, he gestured to the west, before taking Dolvid's arm to lead him back to the table, the light of the *ôdu* sickly against the sun's.

He sat, not inviting Dolvid to sit, contemplating him. "There are realms that are not field and mountain, forest and stream, empires more glorious than the one the Shâl' made. Our *Nim'raibakim*, if you will, is knowledge, a world with no frontier."

His face was made of two distinct halves, gold and grey. Dolvid had felt a start at mention of the First Empire, as if *Menadhi* somehow knew or had guessed his favorite dream. Even stranger was the near-echo of his father's last words. "*Menadhi*, the same was said by my — " His voice trembled, and he could not finish.

"Your father's love and respect for learning are well-known. It is no secret he was not fond of the *Mankh'* — perhaps with reason. He very much wanted to come here."

"Not so." It was impossible.

"But it is so. When he was the age you are now. But your grandfather, Dolvidh, an honest man and good chandler, needed an apprentice, and wanted his late-born only son, your father, to have a useful trade. I marvel your father acquired the learning he did." A fragile smile. "It must have meant burning a lot of his father's stock, night after night. A pity those who find their knowledge outside fail to see the good within the *Atarlum*. Master Faëdhal is another such. Though he had his start with us."

How this man could know so much about his father's life Dolvid could not say, nor how much was true. Faëdhal's distaste for the *Atarlum* was also no secret. But a new idea was creeping in; for himself Dolvid knew nothing about the *Mankh'*: all his fear and dislike came from the opinions of others, from Darborr, who had hated everything Owani, from Esodra, not the cleverest of women. Even his father was not infallible.

"As I told you once before, though you have probably forgotten it, there may be good men, clever men anywhere, but it is only here at the *Mankh'* the best scholarship can thrive. I recall you have kin in the South?"

"Of — of my mother, *Menadhi*." Taken by surprise, and

suddenly afraid of being sent off to an uncertain welcome among strangers.

"But none here in the Heartland, where you belong."

"None I know, *Menadhi*."

"There are choices. Here, as my personal pupil, you can have your own room, with a window facing on Arnan, as mine does, on Kamanta. You would have duties, too — here, we all work, and there are enough tasks for us all. Still, in summer there is good swimming. The Estates are spacious, and the *Adanum Plakh'* can perhaps be persuaded to lend a mount, to a friend. As for books! Not only histories, Dolvidh, and the great songs, but every kind of lesser book; journals and diaries, learned treatises, marvellous tales told in every language, written in every mode ever used on the shores of Arnan. We have hundreds of books never properly examined; there are few alive I would attempt to teach the older scripts, much less the glyphs."

"My books, *Menadhi*, and my father's — the household goods?"

"We'll see to it nothing is stolen. Indeed, if you decide to stay with us — "

"My father believes — my father believed — "

"He made his views plain to me. I shall sadly miss our debates. Your father was not an ignorant Deniant filled with hatred of what he does not understand, but a man who could buttress his opinions with learning, no easy opponent. And a man who could be trusted to speak his true mind — you are tired, I see." He swiftly stood to grip Dolvid's upper arms. Tears had started, and he could not look in the face of the man, who was murmuring he must have more rest, for tonight, at least, he was to stay here.

The boy Dravadhi was summoned again, and next came at-Sepivadhi, the *ramidu* (who could not heal Dolvid's father). Many hands again were tugging him to bed. He wept, ashamed of weeping, his chest painful with the effort of trying to stop. *Menadhi* was saying soothing words, the sheets were cool, slippers making a soft slap as they dropped to the floor. The world began slithering aside, but like a sharp rock in rivers of mud, the thought stayed in his mind he had not agreed to be here, had yet to choose.

"Shortly, I must go," *Menadhi* said. The day before, the Family had removed to Tan Lughsai, and *Menadhi* was going by water, for discussion with the *rabhsai*; *g'Asalladh'*, the Patriarch Himself, would be there. The subject would once more be reopening the *manal*. Dolvid, having heard that Laluvoi, for the time being, was staying at Kadon, remembering her old debate with this man, wondered if *Menadhi* believed the *rabhsai* might be easier to persuade without his mother near.

In conjecturing the *Atarlum* might, after all, have been slandered, Dolvid had forgotten or avoided thinking about Laluvoi, whose opposition was not easy to explain away: she was not untaught, could have no personal bias against the *Atarlum*, and was of the Great Families, the best blood of Old Owan. Suspicions came back, turning to dread at the notion of *Menadhi*'s absence. He was afraid of this man, but much more of the unknown *Mankh'* without him.

They were in a different room, with rows of books and a broad work-table, as well as a smaller table, where they sat. Again they were sharing a meal, with pastry and butter and goat's milk, cold meat and eggs cooked hard. The bronze pot from before was between them on its bowlegged stand, part-filled with warm *raminat*, a small blue flame burning beneath.

"More than ever, you could join us at a dawn of brightening, when the *Manadilum* needs the best of our youth. The reopening of the *manal*! Their closing was — no one questions Banak's greatness in war, but that was a dark day for the realm."

"I had heard, *Menadhi*, my father said, the Patriarch ga-Owan-Alladh shut the *manal*."

"Ga-Owan-Alladh XIX. Undeniably, by his command the *manal* were finally closed down. A man takes the pen you write with, and trims it so you can do nothing with it but make blots. If you then throw the pen away, who has destroyed it? You understand? The conditions Banak tried to impose would have made the *manal* worse than none at all."

"I thought — your pardon, *Menadhi*."

"Come, you thought what?" He was very nearly jocular this morning.

"Well, I didn't think the *rabhsai* had changed about this." So he had heard Faëdhal report to his father.

Menadhi leaned forward confidentially. "The *rabhsai*, and what Laluvoi *Asayu* says of the *rabhsai*, may not always be the same. No, no, she is very rightly loved by all; Laluvoi has added chapters of her own to the long tale of Owani glory — never forget her blood, Dolvid. But — how can this be said? You will come to understand — yes, you'll understand this very well — when a man who has been loved dies, the ones who are left may jealously guard positions he, living, would have altered with the years; what was meant only for an overnight resting-place gets turned into a granite shrine. The Banak-rai preserved by Laluvoi cannot change, as the living Banak might have. My true conviction is that he would have come to see learning and language cannot be torn apart." He displayed his small right palm, spreading the fingers. "How do we speak of the Four Counsellors, Ministers, Guides — there is no word in ordinary language. In the Owanilú, Dolvidh'?"

"*Menadhi*, is it *Radh Baëdhral*?"

"It is *Radh Baëdhral*, and speaking that you contemplate that they are also *Radh Bôdhal*, the Four Directions — " He closed the hand so only the thumb projected. " — and *Radhit ga-Raëdhi ôl*, the Four are Raëdh Himself, as He looks east or west, north or south." He closed down the thumb to make a tight fist. " — and again, *Radhi Radhum dhanol*, Four is Wholeness. Words in themselves begin with Raëdh; *Owanai Oladhu ôl*, Owan is All Being — how can this be taught, except in its own language?"

Using a small piece of folded kidskin he took the handle

of the intricately worked bronze vessel, to pour small cups of
raminat; the pleasantly musty smell came. "Is it not odd — "
becoming lighthearted after his passion for words — "at the New
Residence, where the banner shows a bronze border, the *rabhsai*
can serve from a golden pitcher, while here at the *Mankh'* our only
gold is in emblems?"   Carefully, he touched the worked surface
of the pot with admiring fingers.   "Yet bronze, with former
craftsmen, was a noble metal. Time and patience bring their own
riches." He passed a cup, and indicated golden honey for the
taking.

After knocking, a boy came in and made deference. Not
Dravadhi of the carven face, a much smaller boy, but in the same
rough smock. At first he seemed perhaps seven.

"Yes, Zhâlai?"

"*Menadhi*, by your leave, I'm to say the boat is waiting."
The accent was less strong than Dravadhi's, but with the same
peculiar rhythm. This boy must also be of the Island. The custom
there was to give names of ancient heroes and rulers, and *Zhâlai*
was probably a version of *Shaël*.

Menadhi sipped quickly at his *raminat* as he stood. "Yes,
the wind can often change mid-morning. We thank you, Zhâlai."
He gave the boy's shoulder a small passing pat as he vanished into
an inner room.

Solitude came flooding back. Zhâlai, whose eyes had met
Menadhi's with near-adoration, watched Dolvid with suspicion
and envy under half-lowered lids.

The man came back, pulling on a wide-sleeved travelling
cloak. He drained the rest of his *raminat* standing. "Dolvidh —
" who stood, half-thinking and wholly wishing he might be asked
to go along. "I shall be away a week at most, and then we can
speak further about your future. For the present, you are warm
here, and safe. Zhâlai!"

"*Menadhi*?" Face eager for service.

"You may take Dolvidh to at-Aval, who knows about
him." He turned again to Dolvid, putting hands on his shoulders.
"Everything will be arranged when I come back; do not despair,

nothing is to be forced on you. Till then, *aragh ido Hrafi, Dolvidhai."*

"Y'aradh Hrafit ke-ido am, Menadhai."

Dolvid's care to use a deferential form met with a nod of approval. Both of them were committed to the protection of Hrafi 'the Encompasser,' and both had made sign with the little-finger. *Menadhi* briefly, sleeves flapping, clasped each boy, and when he put a hand to his cheek Dolvid achieved a faint smile; it was necessary to be cheerful. But when he had vanished through the doorway, and Zhâlai was ready to lead him away, he felt drowned in mournful terror.

Clutching the satchel which contained his pens, a small flask of ink already mixed, as well as half an ink-block with its scraper, and a sheaf of parchment ends, Dolvid paused by the Disc of Aëlovoi.   Along the Avenue nothing in particular was happening; his view down the broad sweep of smooth stone, deep rose in color, was all the way to Harbor Gate, to the spike of the Spear and the Bronze Residence beyond. A few lone or paired riders, a small knot, a half-file of Household lancers, many men and women on foot, but nothing to suggest imminent arrival of anyone important. Only the day before two *nimul*, provincial overlords, rode in with their trains, Vinilat, just succeeded to the Great House in Dramal, and Laënakh of Nîv. A province Dolvid had traversed on their journey from the South two years ago, but his memory muddled its two chief cities, Kir and Nivu Din, and he was no longer certain of anything he had seen.

But each of the two *nimul* had ridden the length of the Avenue escorted by detachments of their provincial cavalry, each met and joined by squadrons of Household, brave under the banner with the Bronze Sword depicted; such shows were worth lingering for. Someone had said today the most eagerly-awaited of all would arrive, Saidhan, Great Banak's faithful falcon, chief vanquisher of Kargul in the War of the Widowed, friend to Laluvoi for nearly forty years. For him and his wife Doleni, this would be first sight of their newest grandson, Little Banak, a solid child of four. The *rabhsayu*, Saidhan's daughter Saëdhu, was with child once again, last year having given birth to a girl who, sadly, lived only days.

There was general regret there would be no sight of Saëdhu's brother, Sebhal, needed where he was soldiering and winning renown, at the Frontier, in the farthest west of the Colony across Arnan, where his father ruled. Before Saidhan, Great Banak himself had once been Captain of the West. The turmoil and hard campaigning of the borderlands had for generations bred the toughest soldiers and most famous commanders; Dolvid loved tales of battle at the Frontier, though they also made him fearful. The streets of Kadon Dinul filled with peaceful holidaymakers, it was strange to have in mind that not in a far heroic age but at this very moment, hard-faced soldiers were riding out into the bleakness of Landegh to challenge hunger and thirst, heat and bare rock, dust-storms and wild men of the tribes — and other enemies, worse ones.

Impatient with lingering by the Disc, Dolvid went galloping down the incline to Market Square, and across to its city gate. Not far outside, having been waved through by an affable guard, just up the opposing slope of the Burantal road he came to the hostelry often used by farmers bringing their goods to Kadon Dinul. It had a wide walled compound where wagons could safely be left, and where for these weeks a number of tents had been put up to accommodate an overplus of visitors.

In the main building, the common-room Dolvid entered had a higher ceiling than the cheaper hostelries inside East Gate, but was plain-furnished in brick and stone, wood used sparingly. It was filled with loud talk and laughter; there were very few women, and one or two of those Dolvid knew at once as week-wives, without being certain of what that meant; one had dyed lips and a loose robe of a purplish shade.

He stood a while unnoticed amid the holiday boisterousness of others, before he found courage to do what he had come for. Choosing one sitting alone, not much different from most there, a rough-dressed man of the Other Races, he asked in a clear voice, "Your pardon, master. Are there letters or messages you want written?"

His father had in the end allowed a son of his could act as a scribe, since it entailed a skill, and so was Craft, not Service. Besides, it would be good practice, and that (Vidukh said) was more important than any money he might earn. They had agreed his services would be free to those who could not afford even his small fee, though privately Dolvid had made up his mind to avoid any like that.

"What? Joking with me, boy?"

"Master?"

"You a scribe, then? A thatcher myself, from Lower

Province, down south of Shemugrân — you know the country, lad? So you're a scribe, is that it?"

"I can write you a letter, master." Dolvid had not thought much of his ability to write fluently in the common letters. Using the same mode, he could also put down what he knew of the Owanilú, and had begun to master the Script of Shâl, an older way of writing, invented, his father said, when war-captains of the First Empire (very long ago) made too many mistakes using or reading the yet-more-ancient Syllabary, which had funny marks above and below the line to help fix meanings.

Still staring down at Dolvid the thatcher paid for barley-beer, and had a deep swallow. "Well," he grunted at last. "My wife. She might take a letter you wrote to the magistrate, or my cousin Nelutt, they could read her what it says. We'd best tell her so in the letter."

Dolvid sat on the bench beside him, tongue curled back against his upper lip, while the man dictated a plain tale of his safe arrival at Kadon, all the time watching, with a blend of wonder and envy, the boy's hand moving across the parchment. Having soon run out of news, he said, "Now, say to her she's to take this to Nelutt, or else to the under-magistrate — "

Dolvid stopped writing.

"Put it down, boy, put it down."

"But, master — "

"How, but? You're scribe, my letter. Your own letter, you put in and leave out what you choose. This is mine. Write, boy."

Dolvid sighed. "Master, it is not sense."

"How, not sense? My cousin reads, aye, writes, too — well as you do, boy. Not so quick, maybe, but loops as round as any man could ask. Put down what I tell you, boy, don't keep me from my business."

"But master, if your wife, your lady wife can't read the letter, she can't read the part telling her where to take it to be read. When she can tell what that says, she'll have already found one who can read it all."

From the thatcher there was a long pondering, while at the

far end of the table three or four herders from Dramal sat down, bantering hoarsely over the value of their sheep. Dolvid saw light come into his client's face, quickly masked with unconvincing guile. "Thought I'd see how sharp you were, lad. All my letters, I tell them to write that. You'd crap to see how many scribes just put it all down, good scribes, older heads than yours, lad. Many a good laugh I've had over that. Aye." He achieved not a very good one now.

"All right then, we've had our little joke. Just write my name down there at the bottom then, lad."

"What name is that?"

"Asdron, of course, my name — did you think you were to write your name, then?"

"No, master." Thatcher watching over his shoulder, Dolvid wrote again.

"Asdron, that's it. Well-written, that is, lad, well-written." Taking the pen, he put a meaningless flourish next to his name, and then went back to alter part of it. Dolvid asked him for a bronze coin, and went to a serving man to buy a plain seal stamped out of tar. At the next table men had been toasting bits of cheese, and there Dolvid borrowed a candle. He folded Asdron's note, heated the seal carefully on the flat side, and when tar began to bubble, slapped it down on the overlap. Asdron then dictated an address that seemed sketchy, but was, he said, adequate.

"Now what is it I pay you, boy?"

"For the parchment, two tobhai. Your lady wife has money, master, to pay the carrier?"

"Oh, aye, she will. Left her money, I did. Not like some who take it all to spend on drink and — and the other."

"Then, two more bronze pieces for the man at Market Gate, who'll give it to one riding south."

"Not Market Gate, East Gate!" Generous now he could score, Asdron slapped a silver half-keshai on the table. "Road goes south from here, lad, you're right, but why would I want my letter dawdling by way of Burantal? Royal Way is always the

fastest road for Kanzan Tâl, for all it sets out eastward — don't
you know even that, then? Nay, never mind changing the piece,
have a honey-pear. Very obliged to you, lad." He never did
discover Dolvid's name.

    On the Avenue of Treaties, crowds were swelling. For a
short while Dolvid joined a small throng gathered about the large
booth belonging to the Marionette Guild of Burantal, where life-
size figures were being put through dances and sword-fights. He
was too early; the real shows, mainly scenes from history and
myth, would not begin till later. The marionettes were elaborately
costumed, with face-masks lovingly done by the Master,
Nettumar, who, with his two sons, was most of the Guild, by far
the most famous in the realm. According to Dolvid's father their
tales were not to be trusted for historical truth, but no one cared
much about that, so long as they were exciting or stirring. The
tradition was scenes from long ago, but the Burantal Guild was
enough honored to dare depicting men and women still alive, or
only recently dead: years ago Saidhan and even Great Banak had
allowed themselves to be represented, and episodes from the War
of the Widowed were often played. Fragments only, and many
felt they lacked point, since Banak had forbidden the making of
a Laluvoi-marionette, but, according to Esodra, Saidhan's famous
victory would be cheered till the city resounded with it. Dolvid
hoped he could see that scene.
    Household men and special levies raised for the Pledging
helped patrol the streets, riding in half-files, not many with lances.
By night, when drink and dancing could cause unruliness, a few
of the horse-soldiers went with drawn swords ready, but the
commonest weapon was a long, thin cane for persuading obstinate
crowds; once, people remembered, they had carried whips, till
Banak (or Laluvoi) forbade it.
    He took an indirect way to East Gate. From the first he
had loved the alleyways of the city, mysterious winding passages
that came out at unexpected spots, cobbled narrows that ran past

deeply weathered walls and sudden patches of green garden, leaping across spurting rivulets, crossing lower ways on tiny, uneven bridges, or curling blind down rough steps of brick or cut limestone, often worn hollow. In parts where aged walls on one side or both had bulged out, only a child could wriggle through, and others in summer needed to be pushed through where bushes overspilled their garden plots. Dolvid had done days of exploring; knowing the bypaths as he did could go a cunning way, crossing only four real streets between the Avenue down below the Disc, and the final, shadowed stretch of East Way, just inside the gate. He had traversed the city.

Two miles eastward was the *margú*, the hostelry maintained by the *Nôdhilum*, one of the Four Orders of the *Atarlum*. The *Nôdhilum* was devoted to pleasure, to rest, and to homecoming; their patron was Hrafi "Encompasser," whose sign was made with the little-finger, and whose direction was West. Priests of this order wore red-brown robes, and were not feared.

This one was a *doni-margú*, a town-hostelry. Not understanding all the difference, Dolvid gathered it was not quite the same as *zhani-margú*, one of the way-hostelries that in some parts were the only resting-place between town and town. Both kinds of *margul* could be known by a stand of small, light-limbed trees, always to the eastward side, so the rising sun caught their luminous leaves, palest yellow in spring, and never darker than the fresh yellow-green they were now, at midsummer. In autumn the leaves would change to a delicate pink-gold, and at last a warm parchment shade. On the Island, these same leaves, dried and cured by a secret method, were used to make the thick, sticky-brown *ga-raminat*, a medicine the *ramidul* administered with much success. Simply dried and lightly kilned, the leaves were infused to make *raminat*, a restoring drink, taken cool in summer, warm and spiced in winter, often mixed with honey or sweet wine. Not that the leaves came from trees grown next to the *margul*, which would not have been nearly enough; on the Island were said to be wide plantations of *ramminal* trees, and harvesting was done by convicted criminals. These the *rabhsai* turned over to the Patriarch in exchange for goods in *Atarlum* monopoly; one such was *raminat* itself, and the price was high.

Here at the *doni-margú* he hoped to find more clients, having failed to do so at the meaner lodgings inside East Gate, where he had gone after leaving off Asdron's letter. No reminder of the brooding *Mankh'*, this low-built structure of mellowed limestone with its many windows, its central doors opened wide to the warm day. Travellers here, standing beside their horses or clustered by the entrance, were better dressed, and their talk was in gentler tones.

Inside, Dolvid turned left down three broad steps into a flagged common-room, softly lighted. The windows, facing south and east, were many-paned, with rounds, squares, and lozenges of glass, some tinted. At a wooden table by one of the windows a man somewhere about his father's age was reading in a small, calf-bound volume. Seeing his interest the man turned the book so Dolvid could see the title.

It was in the Owanilú. Aloud, Dolvid read, "*Kezhul Plezhinaleyi baBanak-rai Rabhsayit.*"

On his long face, the man's eyebrows went up. "Which means?"

After all, he must be older than Dolvid's father, or perhaps it was just that he was so lean, Owani nose jutting like a bird's beak. Its high cheekbones and pinched cheeks gave the face an expression Dolvid was unsure about.

"A Tale," he began, "A Record — "

"Record is good, yes."

"A Record of Pledgings of the *Rabhsai* Great Banak."

"Exactly."

"Only *plezhinal* isn't a word in Owanilú. It's made up."

"Ah, then we are conversant with every word in the Owanilú. It is, in point of fact, what is called a transliterated borrowing, a loan-word. Clearly, no existent word of the Owanilú could be employed to describe a practice initiated in the reign of Great Banak."

"But my father — " wanting to tell this man about Pledgings not really being new.

"What is your name, lad?"

"Dolvidh, *Asai.*"

"Ah."   The pale eyes gleamed interest.   *"Frelagh', Dolvidhai, shilavi lamal n'ola wedro lal?"*

Dolvid touched brow in half-deference. *"Asai, udh' lamal vekh'an' efradhal ô wedro —* " and then deciding it was fair, with his birthday quite near, to claim almost eight years: *"Laëdhi lamal vekh', Asai."*

A chuckle. "Not bad, not bad." With the tips of long fingers he touched Dolvid's hand. "But you do not call me *Asai.* And here comes — " the keen eyes flicked to the steps as a broader, fleshier-faced Owani paused there " — another you do not call *Asai."* Dolvid's companion rose as if to greet the newcomer, and went on rapidly in a low voice, "I don't say he would not love to merit that mode of address. He's Zhival, a very well-connected man. Make him half-deference, Dolvidh'. Ah, Zhival." He himself sketched half-deference.

"Master Faëdhal." The beefy voice suited the man. "What brings you here? What about my boy? You find him apt?"

"What brings me here, sir, is the answering of such questions. But it is such a fine day, and an idle one for me; all my charges are about the ceremonies and amusements. As for your son, Zhinladh is, ah, steady. Here, sir, is a new friend, Dolvidh. Dolvidh Vidukhat', I fancy."

Dolvid repeated his hand-sign and bow, not astonished Faëdhal had guessed whose son he was, but all of a sudden shy, having been speaking the Old Tongue for one called the greatest master of languages outside the *Atarlum.* That, indeed, was Faëdhal's title at the Residence, Master of Tongues. Dolvid's father always praised Faëdhal.

"Your father is Vidukh, boy, the little Keeper of Books?" Zhival said. "A fine fellow, a good head on those shoulders. But it seems you'll have the broader shoulders, eh?" As he spoke, he squeezed Dolvid's upper arm between fat thumb and two fingers.

"Sir," he managed to say, reddening with what would be taken for bashfulness, but was truly anger.

The newcomer, convinced he was witty, had a gift for annoying. In talk it came out he had large lands across the Paowan River in southern Dramal, but kept a house at Kadon Dinul. Zhival had further questions about the tutoring of his son Zhinladh; Faëdhal's answers were bland and rather evasive. At last the father said, "Well, Master, if the boy isn't as far ahead as might be, perhaps after all I should have given him to the *Mankh'* for a few years."

Dolvid could see Faëdhal's lean body stiffen. The face, too, was rigid, as he answered, "As you wish it, sir, as you wish it. However, it is generally acknowledged my own pupils, at comparable age, display a more flexible command of the Owanilú than those taught by the *Atarlum*. This, let me stress, is only what others say."

"But with our history — "

"History, sir, may I remind you, is not among my learnings, but if a boy has a bent for it he may read all for himself, given a proper command of language, and its modes of writing."

"At the *Mankh'*, our history is taught."

"To my mind, sir, it is their history, with no room for any dissent. The aim of the *Atarlum*, I mean no disrespect, is not thought, but obedience to the One Way."

After this came other cool exchanges, but Faëdhal's irritation was scarcely masked, and as soon as he could he asked leave, going to a distant table to be greeted by another prosperous-looking man. The Master of Tongues was taller than he had seemed, very long in leg and neck, though he went with somewhat rounded shoulders, chin forward.

"A cup of cool *raminat*, boy?" Zhival motioned to a serving-man. "Well, boy, what is your business here?"

When Dolvid said, he first was dubious, then with the air of a joke decided he must send word to his brother-in-law at Dônshei. Dolvid saw Zhival was deliberately choosing long and difficult words, watching to see how the boy dealt with them.

Listening carefully there was no need to panic: the marvel of the letters now used, as Dolvid's father often said, was that for either of the main languages one could write what was heard, and reading, sound what was seen. You did not have to have learnt a word, or what it meant.

"My boy Zhinladh," Zhival said, when the letter was done, "is near twelve — you know him? No? I wish he had your head for learning. Do you ride, Dolvidh'?"

"A little, sir."

"Oh, well, Zhinladh is a splendid rider, a solid lad. He may yet make a fine officer of the Household. How's the *raminat*, boy?"

The cup was tiny. "I thank you, sir. I believe I like it."

"Haven't you had it before?"

"Once, sir, I had some, I think. But this I like."

That a boy Dolvid's age hardly knew *raminat* amazed the man. Reading over the letter, passing it back for folding, he muttered two or three times, "Never had *raminat*."

When Dolvid said he needed money for a seal, Zhival said, "No, boy, not a plain seal." In a pocket of his outshirt he found a blue-colored seal of hard wax, with his device, evidently meant as a hunting dog, molded on the front side. Letter sealed and addressed, Dolvid said he would leave it, as before, at East Gate.

"Hrafi go with you, my boy." Zhival pressed a small coin into Dolvid's hand.

"I thank you, sir, and with you." He seemed to have been paid no more than a quarter-dabhai, a fourthing, but that was reasonable with the customer furnishing his own seal, and with the price of the *raminat* put in the bargain. Dolvid made up his mind to go back to the city; it had been foolish to come here, where many would be able to pen their own letters. Besides, for those who could not, a real scribe was standing just inside the doorway, and had given Dolvid increasingly baleful looks.

Not seeing Faëdhal to say farewell, Dolvid went out into

warm sun, and the faint sourish taste of the drink lingered in his mouth, an unfamiliar mingle of pleasant and repellent, yet reminding him of something forgotten but once familiar, the taste of a drink that satisfied thirst better than any he could name; what his mouth yearned for after hours of parched campaigning in the Gardens.

Amid eruptions of grasshoppers and the panic of butterflies, he cut across unused land to the Royal Way, the Great Stone Road, no foot of it unpaved all the distance to Kred' Bakali, half of that lined with spheres of *ga-ôthu*, so in all weathers night travel was no hardship.   On his big, purplish *pefrai*, a fast-messenger of General Cavalry went thundering eastward, overtaking a small cart and then a slower rider, meeting and passing a laden hay-wagon rolling for the city. Dolvid waited in the shade of a horse-chestnut, and when the wagon came up was permitted to clamber up at the tail. There were many riders, two-and-a-half families from the Talbronu country. It was a happy ride among holiday-minded people, the sun filtering through dust rising from the road, his legs swinging over the dropped tailboard, *raminat* live in his veins, so he felt ready to leap mountains or wrestle wild boar.   Next to him, a farm-lad of not less than thirteen, together with a younger, shyer sister, listened respectfully to all Dolvid had to say about what was worth seeing at Kadon Dinul, his lengthy, familiar descriptions of the *rabhsai* and all the Family at the Residence. East Gate arrived too soon.

He was late starting for home. The sun had not yet set, but here in the low-lying northeast part of the city shadows were deep and long. He had been fed by his last clients, a man and his wife from the Paowanu Loi. For help framing a plea concerning recovery of past taxes they had enlisted an old man said to know law, but unlettered. Dolvid had never run across half the words he had been hired to write out, spelling everything by sound, hoping it would be right. Or at least understandable.

At the end of the tedious task and some food, the couple

had asked if it was safe for him to return alone through the dimming streets. Being midsummer, Dolvid answered, it would not be truly dark for some hours, adding proudly that Kadon Dinul, anyway, was never as dark as lesser cities.

True. At Pledging flares and lanterns were carried by late travellers and the patrols, but even without these, on the blackest night of winter, the city had few corners of absolute black. Open squares, gates, the crossings of major streets were lighted; important buildings such as both the Old Residence and the New, the Treasury, Zhôl's Shrine, and the big houses fronting on the Avenue were always lit by softly glowing *ôdul*, clear glass with light trapped inside. They were used by well-off people for indoor lighting as well, but had to be taken outside by day, for the sun to renew them, and they dimmed gradually over weeks and even months, till they had to be replaced. Each gave a lot less light than a lantern, but they were far more beautiful than any flamelight. The globe was *ôdu*, and the light it shed, *ôthu*, *ga-ôthu*, as was usually said: *ga* went in front of many words to do with the Patriarch and the *Atarlum*. It meant 'blessed.' With *raminat*, the *ôdul* came from the Island, and were a Patriarchal monopoly, their making a mystery.

Even so, there were streets of Kadon dimmer and less frequented. Dolvid knew very well he should take the long way by main streets, but instead turned up the narrow lane that started steeply for the Residence walls, afterwards curving to run almost straight for home. He went briskly, and it was very quiet, except for distant rumblings that came and went, not deep enough for thunder; crowds over on the Avenue making merry or acclaiming their favorites. At this distance it was hard to tell which.

In a narrower part, between sets of ascending steps, he walked harder, feeling the chill absence of sun, hungry despite having shared in a pie, his uneasiness over what his father might do or say deferred to a tremble of immediate fear. Behind him were heavy, shambling footsteps, clattering on the steps just climbed. He quickened more, fearing to run, and the steps behind also picked up pace.

"You, boy," a rough voice, the accent new to Dolvid.

"You, there — " Just as he made up his mind to run, his shoulder was grabbed from behind. He turned with a small sob of his breath.

Two youths, broad-shouldered and unkempt, grinned at him. Their hair was long and matted, their cheeks stippled with straggly beginnings of beard. One was taller, the other a little stouter, otherwise they were much alike. Dark eyes, small mouths, uneven teeth and lumpy faces, and each carried a wooden stave.

"A soft Owani brat," the taller one told his companion.

The other put his face so close to Dolvid's his breath was hot. "You! Who's Father of Us All then?"

Dolvid's tongue was curling to the roof of his mouth, and without any command his body was shrinking from this pair.

The shorter, his questioner, shook his shoulder. "Who? Who? Your Patriarch, is it?"

Terror told Dolvid either agreement or silence would make things worse. "No. No," he said, trembling.

"Then who would it be?" Joining the interrogation, the other made his voice horribly bland. He bunched his fist, middle knuckle jutting, and gave Dolvid's shoulder a short, vicious punch.

He cringed, not trying to twist free. There was no one else in the street; he was alone in the world with these two monsters. A deeper roar coming from the crowd on the Avenue was no more use than memories of being safe in his own bigroom, Esodra busy at the stove.

A mistake to let his eyes wander about. "No one minds what we do with you," the first questioner, jerking at Dolvid's outshirt. "Who, then? Who? Who? — " with a jerk for each.

"Well, then?" the tall one demanded. Dolvid looked from one pair to the other of near-black, eager eyes. He swallowed much spittle.

"Raëdh," he said. "Raëdh *Toladhi*." That must be right. Raëdh mated with Aëlovoi, and she was moon and tide, the

Mother.

"Rard!" the thicker, shorter one snarled in scorn or anger, shaking Dolvid to and fro, neck snapping painfully. "Rard! You maggot."

The shaking stopped. "What are we going to do with this?"

"Give him a clout," the taller one said. "Break his shins and let him go. The Watch might come."

"Let him go?"

"He's nothing but spawn."

"Aye, let him go. He'll soon be toad enough, sitting on his horse, saying his Rard gave him the right to all our land. Knock him over the head, and drop him in the water to drown. There's water here."

True, the next short set of steps led up to a narrow, railless bridge across Rekhsepa, the small swift stream which came gushing from the bank beneath the Residence walls, and rattled down through the city in a narrow cleft.

The taller youth's hesitation seemed to add to the other's anger. "Rard be fucked, there isn't any Father of Us All!" As one tamping earth, he lifted his iron-footed stave, and brought it down hard on Dolvid's foot.

Shocked and numbed, he tore free. He was up the steps and on the bridge before his foot began to recognize injury. With a muddled clatter his tormenters started after him, and the noise, with curses, suggested a mixup where the bridge began, with the iron post set in the middle of the way, to warn night travellers. Not looking back to see, Dolvid was across the stream. Rightward he bolted into a narrow, shadowy hole between close-set houses, made another turn, and leapt down a short set of steps. He knew his way well; where the alleys branched he took the left-hand way, squeezing quickly through a tight space, rough-cast wall in front, bowed brick behind. He heard fragments of decaying mortar trickle down as he brushed by. His foot was very painful, and once past the strait he stopped and shut his eyes, sniffing back the start of a wailing sob. Heavy boots paused and made baffled half-steps, and there were voices, swallowed in a fresh storm of cheering from the Avenue; someone or something, a new decree, perhaps, had found favor. Dolvid trembled, shoulderblades pressed to the wall taking much of his weight.

So close he jumped, certain he was found, there came a bawling shout: "Hoy, spawn! There's no Father of Us All. Remember, there is no Father of Us All." Then the feet, falling into a step. Receding, surely receding. Up leftward, at the head of a long, uneven stair, the roof of a building was glowing with a weird, coppery light, and seconds passed before he realized it was the last of the setting sun. He hurt, and his thudding heart did not think he was safe.

He was hobbling when he came home, but did not begin to weep, not till Esodra, after his father's curt demand where he had been, left off wet-brushing of clothes to come and hug Dolvid, murmuring comforts that were hardly words.

The story came out in spasms, often prompted by the grown-ups, and held back less by tears or reborn terror than a senseless shame. Not in how he had behaved, but just because it had happened, the episode was in some way to his discredit, as if the very existence of such roughs was for him to be guilty over.

"Filthy *jinzal*." Esodra brought warmed water to bathe the bruised foot. "The filthy *jinzal*."

"*Jinzal*?" Fear came back in force, and Dolvid reached for his father's firm arm.

Vidukh put a hand behind his son's neck. "Now. Esodra means only to say these youths behaved like *jinzal*. In some ways like *jinzal*."

"There's no real *jinzal* any more," Esodra soothed. "Great Banak, he killed them all. Don't fret, Dol', there aren't any *jinzal*."

"Yes, in the West, beyond the Frontier."

"No, no."

"Father — ?"

"Perhaps a few. They are seen now and again, but they're

all killed by the Army of the West."

"And in the other, where we slept on the ground." The Ní-Tilagh was one of the few things about the journey to Kadon Dinul he still genuinely remembered.

"Some say. But it has been years on years since a *jinzai* has been certainly sighted there. And *jinzal* could surely never come here to Kadon Dinul. There are provincial soldiers, General Cavalry, Household, to keep them away. You'll never see one. I never have."

"If I saw a *jinzai*, I would shoot it with my bow." In the Gardens, when other games went stale, boys would play hunting *jinzal*, but that was never as comfortable as Saidhan-and-Tobhsila, or Shâl against the Tribes. Some bigger boys would imitate what they had heard about the shuffling, head-swinging charge of a *jinzai*; the youngest would scream shrilly, and more than one of the mimics did it too well, the glaring eyes, menacing noises in the throat, clumsy mowings of clawed hands, bared teeth. Other games had moments of fear, but *jinza'dazhai* was a terror belonging to night's lumpy shadows, darkness that could tear and swallow you.

"With my bow," Dolvid repeated.

"So you would. But hear your father; you'll never see one."

"It takes lots of arrows to kill one *jinzai*."

"So they say, so they say." She was patting his foot dry, and thought he did not see the look of despair she gave his father, who answered with a small, resigned shrug.

Then Dolvid gave himself to the rare luxury of being babied, fed soup, face washed by Esodra, who must, he thought vaguely, be going to spend the night here. Bundled in blankets, though the night was warm, he was bedded down in the alcove next to the cooking stove. As if he had been pressed down, he sank into sleep. Dreams could not be grasped, above the question of *jinzal* all at once troubled most by whether or not there was really a Father of Us All.

Drying his hands behind the wooden door that closed off the washroom with its earth-closet, he overheard their voices.

"No help for it," his father said. "But it's a pity you brought in *jinzal* last night."

"Vidukh, I ask your pardon. With all his weeping, my brain must have been addled. Don't we have enough bad dreams? Why must there be *jinzal* to plague us, even if they are all driven into the West. I must blow up the cooking fire."

"He has had bad dreams, too, these past two years."

"And no wonder, the poor — hush!" Going to the stove, Esodra must have sighted the empty wall-bunk.

" — Another fine morning for the Pledging," Dolvid's father was saying, as the wooden door swung open. A sheaf of lists had been grabbed in haste; Dolvid could see his father had them upside-down. The two grown-ups had a quick glance for each other; many years later it came to Dolvid one day how Esodra, a widow, had been there so often to give them breakfast. His father, plainly, never contemplated a second marriage.

"Deniants," his father said. "They were Deniants." With no work being done at the Residence, he had come home in the afternoon, and there was chance for real talk. "Were you on the Avenue when Saidhan *Asai* rode in with his following? Those Army of the West men look real soldiers."

"He came while I was at Market Gate hostelry." Not to surrender to fear, he had gone scribing again this morning, instructed to keep to frequented ways; he did not need telling about staying out too late. "What are Deniants?"

A sigh. "Those who deny," without trying another unsubtle change of subjects. "Not only the dominance of the *Atarlum* — many, even Laluvoi, for one, would wish to see that curbed. Deniants also reject all teachings of the *Mankh'*, the whole Tale of our being. Few of Owani descent ever go so far, but not all Others, by any means, are Deniants. But there are good men, honest men, who are — Arvus, son of Ardirr, at the Treasury, for one, he's a good friend, the one who lent us his mare." Vidukh chuckled. "I did not tell him we wanted it for a ride out to see the *Mankh'*. But the *rabhsai* himself knows Arvus is a good man. Those lads who hurt you, they were nothing but louts; any war-cry does for that kind to do mischief by. We must respect honest belief, even when bullies claim to share it."

After perplexity, Dolvid asked, "Then is Raëdh not Father of Us All?"

His father took as long to reply. Touching a thumb to his breast, he said at last, "To my mind, there must be a Father, and Raëdh is the name we have for Him. Others may see Him in other ways, and perhaps no one sees clearly what He may be."

But that satisfied nothing. If Raëdh wasn't Raëdh, why need He be anything? It was not as if `Raëdh is Father of Us All' described what he could see or touch, like `the mug is on the table.' It had to be the beginning, the start of names themselves. "But Raëdh — " he tried again.

"Such questions aren't for us." Esodra had just come in, carrying a head of cabbage. "The grand folk, and those of the *Atarlum* and such can fret about that. We've got our work, and what we're taught as children. That's enough, say I."

"But if men and women are to live in cities, such questions will have to be for them."

"If they're to live in cities? Where else, then? Your pardon, but I've lived all my life at Kadon. Are you thinking of making some move, then?"

"No, no, no, no — " Vidukh waved it away. With his own remark, it was clear he was not going to explain, and perhaps did not know himself what he meant.

"I did see Tobhan of Kargul ride in, but he wasn't much cheered."

"I should think not. Rebels and traitors, killing our best men."

Dolvid was puzzled. Kargul, too, was one of the Six Provinces, and Tobhan's riding had been honored by Household troops, the Lady Laluvoi on the Residence steps to welcome him. He was a *nimu*.

"Not yet," his father corrected. "He's Heir. Tolvan is still *Nim'*."

"Too wicked to die. He must be near the hundred."

"He is certainly past ninety," Dolvid's father agreed.

"Is he Tobhan's father?" To Dolvid's eye, the lord he had watched ride in was elderly.

"His uncle, in blood."   Vidukh went on to explain. Tolvan's real son had been Tobhsila, who in 2876 was Great Banak's rival for the hand of Laluvoi. That was the War of the Widowed, ended two years later when Saidhan killed Tobhsila in single fight, as was shown in the puppet-play. Then Tolvan adopted as his heir his nephew Taran, who changed his name to Tobhan.

All these names were muddling for Dolvid, but from knowledge of the Old Tongue he guessed why they began so much the same: *tolvu* was bronze. Though greying, the hair of Tobhan had been a deep reddish color.

His fears having ebbed, Dolvid recounted the rest of yesterday's adventures. Mention of Faëdhal brought a nod from his father, who then asked several questions about the encounter with Zhival.

"A rich man, a very rich man. He's to take that house in the Residence Quarter, with the peach tree in the roof garden."

"He did buy me *raminat*, though he paid me only a fourthing for writing his letter." Dolvid had not yet displayed his earnings. When he turned out his outshirt pockets, Esodra gave a cry, pouncing on the smallest of the coins. "Is this your fourthing, then? Two hundred fourthings, nearer. What, can't he tell gold from common copper?"

Vidukh took the piece and nodded. "A half-plakhi," he confirmed. His smile kept broadening. "What were we to have for dinner?"

Cabbage with minced mutton, and Esodra insisted, the weather being what it was, the meat had to be used. But next night, Midsummer Eve, they had a piece of beef rump, roasted, and there was wine, Dolvid's heavily watered.

Without ever considering it, he had imagined going into the Residence the front way, up the central course of the broad main steps, passing between twin rows of gilded figures, emblems of the Six Provinces, the Colony, and even Ninkufu, the southern enclave where Dolvid was born — that was the leaping Dolphins, lowermost of the statues on their marble plinths. First disappointment came when his father led the way past the foot of the steps, to a small gate in the wall next to the Residence. A pair of Household pikemen greeted Vidukh, letting him pass with hardly a glance for Dolvid.

So far, the grand day had been very tame. Plied by other boys with questions amounting to taunts, Dolvid had never stopped asking, when? When would it be fulfilled, the promise he could spend a day with his father at the Residence? This morning Esodra had been more fidgety than Dolvid, telling him several times what he did not need to be told, to be on his best behavior, to obey his father in everything.

Passing through paved courtyards and rounding a jutting bastion of the Residence, they came to the Court of the Ram, with the main stables on its far side. Quite a narrow stair led up to doors, and at the head they were once more passed by guards, and came into the clean, tinted world of the Residence, where polished stone and glowing metal gave back soft white light of *ôdul*, many set in niches, so the globes were not seen, only the quiet radiance they threw on pale green or pinkish stone, on rich wood.

It was far too much to take in, woven hangings and brilliant mosaics, shining windows and varied ceilings, the sibillantly echoing hush. They turned several corners, going up or down short stairs, passing silent guards, making a half-deference to someone of importance, and Dolvid's father explained they were making their way around the big central block, where the audience chambers were, and the chair of state, as well as the Personal Suite, where the Family lived, and no one else went without good reason.

The library was on the second level of the north side. Its main chamber was long with a high ceiling. There were tables and reading stands, and the shelves lining the walls had more books and rolls than Dolvid could ever have imagined. Two copyists were already at work, pausing long enough to greet Vidukh and nod to Dolvid as they came down the steps from the entrance. Dolvid saw how piles of manuscript at the copyists' elbows were criss-crossed in small sheaves, ready for the sewing.

He was soon near tears. He could not have put in words what he had been looking for — ceremony, surely, glimpses of the great, echoes of the thrill when crowds gathered on the Avenue to see the *rabhsai*, or any of the Family. Certainly not to be seated by his father at a heap of books, and told to separate them, first by language, and then according to whether they were history or romance, treatise or song.

He was sighing over the task, feeling his face already beginning to swell with boredom, when a man arrived, tall, careful on the steps, then coming forward with a long stride, nose well to the fore, Faëdhal, clad in a long robe of unbleached stuff, an enamelled belt of many links drooping where hips might have been, if he'd had any.

"Ah, Vidukh. Splendid morning, a little cooler, you would say? Um — Laluvoi *Asayu* was enquiring of me last evening whether I knew anything of a *Rok'olul b'Akhi* in the general tongue. I have read it, you may be sure, in the original, but..." Ever so slightly, he pursed his lips.

"There is a rendering, if you will credit it, in the Script of Shâl — " Vidukh took one step.

"Yes, yes, that I know of, a mere curiosity. Laluvoi *Asayu* recalls Banak *Deghi* at times read from the *Rok'olul*, and Banak, as I remember, had only the letters."

"I have seen an *Atarlum* translation, somewhere — " Another even more doubtful half-step.

"Oh, please! Spare me *Hearthside Lyrics*, Vidukh; that is, if I recollect, what the barbarian who produced that mangling took for his title? No, this would be a respectable version made outside the *Mankh'*. See what can be found, and — ah! Here's

Dolvidh, without whose ready pen the Great Pledging could scarcely have been conducted at all. Well met again!"

"Master," getting to his feet to make half-deference.

" — and whom you have taught your Ninkufu mouthing," Faëdhal told Vidukh, but unseriously. "One had only to hear his `la-ëdhi lamal vekh`' to be aware whose son he was. *La-yedhi*," Faëdhal exaggerated.

"My father says," Dolvid was hot, "it is in the south the most perfect Owanilú has been preserved."

Faëdhal gave him a long, considering gaze, at length choosing debate over reprimand. "Well, the same claim is made for the Western Karguli sing-song, while in the south of Kamanta a form of Owanilú remains an everyday speech — they allege it is the Owanilú, and its adherents that it is the only pure form, although those of the *Atarlum* who have dealings there cannot follow one word. Not one word."

He came back to Vidukh. "You should leave off those rough-written romances and your plain histories, and give the boy poetry to read — to read aloud, as all poetry was meant to be. Epics, that is, not little songs. Reading a *frela'olurai*, the sounds of the best Owanilú, as one might say, pronounce themselves."

"The best Owanilú?" From the doorway, a newcomer was ready to dispute with Faëdhal. A short man, the height of Dolvid's father, but broader, so it appeared, though the robes of an *atarlai* made it hard to be sure. Grey robes, those of the *Manadilum*, the Teaching Order, but this could not be an ordinary *manadu*, because both Vidukh and Faëdhal made half-deference, and Dolvid quickly did the same, remembering to touch his breast with the forefinger (of Maëdhi the Wise, whose direction was North, for clarity and far vision).

"*Menadhi*," Vidukh confided. That meant this man was head of his Order, one of four with only the Patriarch above them in the *Atarlum*. Coming down into the chamber, he puzzled Dolvid with how old he might be. Older than Dolvid's father, yet with the *Atarlum* it was always hard to tell: they were trained against strong emotions, and that made their faces mask-like.

Vidukh had said they tried to foster among the ignorant a legend of unending, unchanging lives.

But this face, nonetheless, had many things in it; humor was there, and what might be a quiet flame that could flare up. Dolvid had no notion what the fire was for, but could feel the man's confident sense of command.

Faëdhal was not overawed. "We were speaking, *Menadhi*, of the several forms and dialects, all quite different, calling themselves the original Owanilú. My view, if I may be permitted, is that allowing for the long break in general vernacular tradition, we must aim for a purer form of Owanilú — "

"A perfect language never spoken anywhere," *Menadhi*, complacently. "But, Master, where is this break in tradition? I am not aware Night ever came to the Island."

"Ah," Faëdhal said, "but as a living tongue, in the mouths of ordinary people — "

"Were we Owanil ever ordinary? On Kamanta, as we are taught, they kept their age-long heritage of language and custom, with no break or seam. The Patriarchal Succession has been uninterrupted for twenty-two long centuries; *g'Asalladh'*, our present Patriarch — " he touched a thumb to his breast — "made the same oath, in the same words, as the eighty and more who sat in the Golden Seat before Him."

Blandly, *Menadhi* gazed at Faëdhal, who decided not to continue debate, turning away with a faint mouth of having tasted something sour.

Vidukh asked, "*Menadhi*, is there a book we can find for you?"

"And this is Dolvidh, your boy?" *Menadhi*, moving to where Dolvid stood by the table, momentarily took the boy's face between very small hands; the palms were dry and cool. "We have heard of you, Dolvidhai, and not only from your excellent father. Zhival would wish his Zhinladh exchanged for you, or so he implied, in a mood of exasperation. You belong with us, Dolvidh, with the *Mankh'*. But then — " wheeling on Vidukh (they were indeed of a height, or a shortness) — "we are all to be worldly scholars, isn't that so?"

"*Menadhi*, the realm is changing — "

"Give us Dolvidh, Vidukhai, we need boys of promise, and only with us can such promise be fulfilled. You think this a library?"

Late, Dolvid realized the question must be for him. "*Asai*, I have never — " he heard Faëdhal cluck at his mistake.

"Not *Asai*, Dolvidhai." *Menadhi* was gentle. "Only One of the *Atarlum* could be so addressed; *g'Asalladh'* has not often heard an *Asai*, but it would not be wrong. But I am called *Menadhi*, nothing else."

He waved away apology, to go on about libraries. "At the *Mankh'*, there are ten times as many books and rolls as here. For the history of the First Empire alone, before Night came to the Mainland, there is a collection to equal this in size."

"There was a volume you were lacking, *Menadhi*?" Vidukh's face was quite innocent.

"A treatise, merely. It seems you have the only extant copy — a moment..." he was dismissive. Returning to Dolvid, he said, "Will you not come with us, and learn more than you can yet have dreamed? You might yourself become a writer of histories."

Uneasiness about treatment of his father had lessened, as he saw Vidukh, for all the head-bobbing, had no fear of this man. Still, he could feel the strong attraction of *Menadhi*'s personality, the soft voice that could unfold entire new landscapes.

"*Menadhi*," Dolvid said. "I am going to be a soldier."

His father made a startled sound (it was an ambition Dolvid had just acquired), and Faëdhal snuffled a laugh in his nostrils. Soon, *Menadhi* was making a smile, too. "There is time," he said, and to Dolvid's father, "Even the most promising boy does not seriously begin *Atarlum* studies till past his tenth birthday. As for Dolvidh, he might be my personal pupil. It's a worthy life, a life of service to good, as you might see, if only you could — well. Our victories," to Dolvid, "endure, perhaps, longest of all."

Dolvid had no words. He did not want to enter the

frowning *Mankh'*, and yet *Menadhi*'s words, or the air surrounding them, held obscure possibility, as well as reasons for awe, as if the *Atarlum*, this man, might have answers to questions that came without seeking them, as when looking up into a night sky alive with stars, and thinking about words such as `forever.'

"It has already been discussed, *Menadhi*," his father was saying. "That Dolvidh might well be a writer of history."

"Well enough," *Menadhi* approved. "Deprived the disciplines of the *Mankh'*, however, his possibilities will be somewhat circumscribed?"

Faëdhal murmured, "A new generation of scholars, if one may venture, might hold those taught only by *Atarlum* are, in their own way, circumscribed."

By his father's face, mainly, Dolvid knew Faëdhal had been quite daring. *Menadhi* was not done, but before he could continue, the door above was flung wide, and the gleam of a Household breastplate could be seen. All turned that way, all making deepest deference, ending with the hand-gesture called the Royal Salute. The new arrival was a woman, a tiny woman, and Dolvid did not need to be told who this was. He had last seen her from a distance on the final day of the Pledging, next to her lofty son, the *rabhsai*. She had bent over her stocky second grandson, Banak-loi, trying to get a smile from him, as the crowds in the Avenue gave acclaim, most often shouting the name of the Dowager, Laluvoi.

Seen close to, she was still beautiful. The straightness of her slender back was emphasized by the fitting of the pale green robe. Her walk, both graceful and dignified, was youthful, and her face was not just kind, but had fun in it, too.

Dolvid was not presented, and was relieved not to be; he would have drowned in shyness. But Laluvoi had purpose there, and all her graciousness did not hide her habit of making things happen. Nodding to Vidukh, she began at once. "The *Rok'olul b'Akhi* from which Banak would often read; I have recalled it was a small book — " she measured with her hands — "Not the entire text, but a selection. It is not in his personal collection, where it should be. The cover was a dull yellow. Banak made some interlinear notes I wished to see again."

"*Asayu*, this would be a single volume, or one of a set?" Vidukh was on the scent now.

"Ah, now you remind me, it did belong with a set, the others mainly law-commentaries and so forth, dry and not accurate. Banak, I remember, was astonished to find the Lyrics there. The books were from Plakhsila's time. There was history, too."

"Indeed, yes, *Asayu*. They are exercises in various skills and learnings, done by Filat Plakhyali, who was nephew to Plakhsila." Vidukh was moving a rough set of steps into place by the shelves.

"Filat." The look Laluvoi gave was like those Dolvid had seen on the Avenue during Pledging, when young women told men to go away, but did not really want them to. "I am amazed he had leisure or strength left for anything resembling scholarship."

Vidukh descended, cradling a clutch of small, dusty volumes. He nearly echoed her smile. "These writings were done, *Asayu*, in later life, what might be called Filat's decline." He put the books down on a small table, and took a piece of linen to wipe them.

"For now, only the yellow one, I thank you, Vidukh." Laluvoi received the little book. "The others can be sent to our suite in your own time. Banak, it may be, had comments to make elsewhere."

She was about to leave. Dolvid had just noticed how *Menadhi* was watching Laluvoi, lips slightly parted. The unblinking eyes, and something about the nostrils, were like a cat, when it sees a thing move, and waits to decide whether it is enemy, or prey, or neither.

"I thank you again," Laluvoi said, and turning was face to face with *Menadhi*. "The Residence is honored."

"I have spoken, madam, with Lambarr *Rabhsai*," he said

in a quiet, even voice, "with regard to reopening of the Schools."

"The *manal*."

"*Asayu*, of the Schools."

The tension here could not be missed, but Dolvid did not understand why Laluvoi insisted on, and *Menadhi* wanted not to use what was only the Owanilú word for school, *manai*. He had heard from his father that once the *Atarlum* had schools for teaching the young, not only at the *Mankh'*, but throughout the Six Provinces. They had long been closed.

"Tell me, what was the *rabhsai*'s answer?"

"Lambarr *Deghi*, as ever, *Asayu*, has many concerns. We had thought you, *Asayu*, might keep the matter in his view."

"You, *Menadhi*, thought I, Laluvoi, might speak up for reopening of the *manal*."

"Madam, *g'Asalladh'* Himself charges me with this question."

"How odd," Laluvoi showed amusement in her eye. "When we saw Him, only yesterday, *g'Asalladh'* mentioned nothing about it. But you would say *g'Asalladh'*, also, has many concerns, while those of the *Manadilum* are particularly your own."

"Exactly. We have much to do in the realm, much more to give the realm, *Asayu*."

"Have you forgotten whose wife I was?"

"Times have changed, *Asayu*."

"If so, that is largely because of what we built, Banak and I."

"Madam, everywhere in this realm there are children denied learning, even their letters."

"Teach them, Teacher. Send out your *manidul*, you do not need *manal* for that. No — " she signalled for his silence. "Ask for General Cavalry for escort and protection, and it is yours. If you want messages and instructions carried by the fast-messengers, that can be done. That is, I can urge it on the *rabhsai*. But you must teach in ordinary language, not the Owanilú."

"As was our intent, *Asayu*, in speaking of the *manal* — the Schools."

"Yes. To come to the widow of Great Banak, and ask her to approve setting up a little *mankh'* in every corner of the realm? Banak was always willing for the Schools to reopen, on three simple conditions." Laluvoi ticked them off on her fingers. "Any child of any race, taught in ordinary language, with no forcing of belief. Give those assurances, and the Schools may open next week, if you want. Master Vidukh, our thanks again. Master Faëdhal."

She went, straight-backed, up the steps. *Menadhi* did not want the debate to end. The door was already closing behind Laluvoi, as he gathered his grey robe unceremoniously, and went after her.

The door banged shut, and Faëdhal sniffed expressively.

"Father, why is Laluvoi not still *rabhsayu?*"

"*Rabhsaëyu*, rather."

"Isn't it the same?"

Esodra turned from cooking to say, "Master Vidukh has answered enough of your questions for today, twice enough. If you don't give him some peace, he's not going to want to take you to the Residence very often."

"It is well, Esodra."

"But so many — "

"Hush." Vidukh's firmness was mild but not doubtful. "Questions are how we learn." He came back to Dolvid, and explained *rabhsayu* meant wife of a *rabhsai*, as with the present Saëdhu *Rabhsayu*. But when a woman reigned in her own right, as with Thral-Sivu, last in the Gabh'Owani line, her title was *Rabhsaëyu*. Though Laluvoi had been Banak's wife, they were joint rulers, and that was the only occasion when there had ever been a *rabhsai* and a *rabhsaëyu* together.

"Then why does Laluvoi not still reign?"

His father paused, as if wondering what sort of answer to

give. Then, "When Lambarr reached an age where he could rule, Banak's health was failing; he and Laluvoi proclaimed that as they had ruled together, they would abdicate together in their son's favor."

"But Lambarr was unwed, then," Esodra put in.

"Oh yes. Saëdhu could not have been above thirteen or fourteen. Banak did not live to see a grandchild."

"Should never have given up the Sword," shaking her head. "A man as he was — how would he ever sit doing nothing all the day?"

"I wish Laluvoi could be *rabhsaëyu.*"

"You should not speak that wish aloud, if you come again to the Residence," his father warned. "Though, truth told, you wouldn't be alone. Even the *rabhsai* might agree."

"What's wrong with Lambarr *Rabhsai*?"

"No — never ask such a question. The *rabhsai* is *rabhsai.*"

"When there's peace," Esodra said. "It's good to have the *rabhsai* so taken up with his family."

"He is certainly taken up with Saëdhu *Asayu.*"

"They love each other, anyone can see that. Of course they do."

"There's no `of course' in it." Vidukh did not please Esodra. "A ruler can take his wife for policy, beget children as his duty: the wife might have married for position, then submits as her duty. When the son of a great warrior takes the daughter of a captain who was that warrior's friend and right hand, it need not be for love."

"A fool could see — "

"As in fact it was, in this case. For policy, it might have been better if Lambarr had found his wife in less friendly parts — among the baKargul, it might have been; that niece of Tobhan's who's become wife to the *Nim'* of Ân."

"Kargul? Our Lambarr marry into those rebels and murderers? What was it his father fought the war for, if not to keep Kargul' riding boots out of the New Residence?"

"Many a rebellion has ended with marriage and new alliance. As Dolvid tells us, Kargul is one of our provinces."

She did not soften. "And what about the farms they burnt, down south of Shemugrân, the good men they killed, the women they — well, you know, the filth. Banak might be alive and well today, if he hadn't worn himself out fighting Kargul. And you yourself say — " lowering her voice, Dolvid could not tell why — "they were leagued with your *Atarlum*; we'd have the Residence filled with them, everything in the Old Tongue, no justice for Others, still less for the poor than there is..."

"Father, the *Menadhi* — ?"

"What about him?"

"He can't make me go to the *Mankh'*, can he?"

"Course he can't," Esodra soothed belligerently. "See him try!"

"Not now," Vidukh said. "*Menadhi* is, and is to be, a power in the *Atarlum*, but that no longer means what it did in the wider realm. For long years no one not a lord would have dared deny the *Mankh'* his son, once spoken for. Nor his daughter."

"Aye, and girls, the filth." Dolvid had seldom seen Esodra so wound up. "Putting them there to lead good men astray." This stayed obscure.

"He said I am of promise."

"But never promise for being one of those. The *Atarlum* has nothing for ordinary folk."

"You're forgetting the *Edhrodilum*." Vidukh named the green-robed Order dedicated to Growing.

"Mumbling their sorceries over the fields."

"They do more than mumble."

"Aye, they do," grudgingly. "My cousin out by Abfekh might still be waiting for his first apple, if they hadn't shown him, what is it?"

"Grafting?"

"No. Grafting? Oh, aye, the grafting it is. Well, one of four has a bit of good to it, then."

"And the *Ramadilum*."

"Well, but let me and some rich, pardon me, but it's truth, some rich Owani, let us fall sick the same day, and see who the *ramidu* comes to soonest and comes to most often." She sniffed.

"You talk as your son-in-law does, about what was and is passing. You should have heard Lady Laluvoi today, telling *Menadhi* the Schools must be for everyone... "

"Ah, well... "

Esodra's face had taken on the doting expression Laluvoi's name always brought, not strange to Dolvid now he had been near the Dowager. But in his mind he went over the list of those there in the library to hear that debate, all about the rights of the Other Races, yet both the principals were of the oldest Owani blood, with Dolvid's father, and Dolvid himself.

"Father, is Faëdhal Owani?"

Esodra enjoyed that, but Vidukh said, frowning, "He's of Arbhal, as we all are."

"Yes, but — "

"Of the Families, isn't he?" Esodra said.

"Is Faëdhal related to the *rabhsai*, then?" Dolvid was instantly embarrassed; he had made that mistake before. Patiently his father again explained the difference: the *rabhsai*, his mother, and the *rabhsayu*, with their children, they were the Family. They were also related, through both Laluvoi and Saëdhu, to the Great Families, provincial rulers and their near relatives, who claimed to be the oldest Owani aristocracy. The former rulers, the House Gabh'Owan, belonged to that dense web of intermarriage and tradition.

Then there were the Families, untitled, but equally interconnected, and just as proud of their pure Owani blood. The chief servants of *rabhsayum*, counsellors, leading officers of the Household, usually (before Banak, always) came from the Families, which also included most big landowners and food dealers. Especially of the Heartland; there were people from Dolvid's birthplace in the far south, and even on the Island, who said they were of the Families, but the word was used mostly of those here in the Paowan, with their estates in the Arbhu Hills, their grand Kadon Dinul houses, in the Residence Quarter or (best of all) fronting the Avenue of Treaties.

"They are not lords," his father said, "but the Families and Great Families are not unmingled. Your friend Zhival is both at once, a cousin to the *Nim'* of Dramal, as well as a corn-dealer."

"Aye, and they keep most of the money in their fists," Esodra said. "And do their best to keep the other bloods down."

"Not all," Vidukh, mildly. "Master Faëdhal is proud enough of his bloodlines, and can tell you descents and connections for all the Families, but he is one with Laluvoi against the old exclusions."

This constant return to the question of the Others was making Dolvid impatient. Esodra was a good woman, but her daughter was married to the oafish Darborr; anyone could see the Owanil had the fine speech and gentle ways, and knew how the world began.

"Those Deniants, father — "

"Now don't you fret any more over any Deniant louts," Esodra urged. "There's no Deniant and no *Atarlum* going to harm you in Laluvoi's realm." She was ladling barley soup, with the usual high flourish that seemed like ceremony, but was only to let drips fall back in the pot.

"Dolvidh," his father, joking, "is in any case to be a soldier. He'll have no fear of either."

It had rapidly become a serious ambition. Lately he had been reading about the First Empire, when the realm west of Arnan had been not merely Colony and the Protectorate as they were today, but lands vaster than all the Six Provinces together.

That was so long ago its tale was legend rather than than history, except for a few settled dates sticking up, hard rocks in a shifting sea. There was more than a thousand years before even the Age of the Shâl', which began with Lord Shaël, later called Shâl I. Rulers then were not *rabhsai* but *nimúrai*, great lord, and the fourth Shâl had changed that title to *Nim'raibaki*, Emperor.

He had ruled an empire stretching from the Eastern Ocean

at Naëni to the wide lands of the West: Kufshei, Minshei, Tufani, Froghushei, just the names were enough to make blood race in the veins. Westward again, many dayrides beyond where the Frontier now was, were tributary tribes, and savage nations kept in check by the might of Old Owan, the swift deadliness of its armies, led by Larghai, most famous captain under Shâl IV. Larghai was `Nim'raibakim-dhanai,' Mason of Empire (though his master was sometimes given the same title). Leader of horse, mighty in war, brave in battle, generous in victory, Larghai Unconquered was a hero without rival, and Dolvid's thoughts, half-dreaming as he let sleep take him, were often of those broad days, when the cavalry of Owan was counted in tens of thousands. He could see himself put at the head of such an army, riding lightning campaigns to carve out a new empire in the West, spurring to the top of a hill after routing the last enemy to look down on the Western Ocean no one living had seen.

The Gardens of Kamzhinu, south of the city wall, were a wonderfully tumbled and rocky landscape within a narrow confine, a kind of ravine (once a deep moat) where, out of sight of roads, houses, hostelries, it was easy to keep up a pretence of being in the wild. Boys played games of hiding and battle there, and one who often joined with Dolvid was Shumat, his own age, though bigger-framed and a little taller. True he was a Mixed, with funny, dark-eyed looks, but he was always eager to hear Dolvid's tales (usually what Dolvid had just learnt for himself) about the First Empire and its wars. Being of poor family and having many tasks, he could not come to the Gardens as often as Dolvid; he would be absent for a whole week, and then one morning would come galloping down the steep slope, a colt untethered, flatnosed, serious face lit up with eagerness for adventures.

In the wars fought over the broken lands of the Gardens, Dolvid was always impatient to begin, while Shumat insisted on understanding of the rules, an agreement about how territory was to be captured or an enemy made to give up. Oddly, when it came to those afternoons, quieter, but just as thrilling, when they shared dreams, it was the other way about. Shumat was perpetually sending armies on forced marches of eighty miles to the day over waterless terrain, Dolvid forever reminding him about supplies, the barriers of river, mountain and desert. Then Shumat would press lips together and make a growling noise in his throat, punching at Dolvid's shoulder. After a while he would find an answer.

"We'd build a bridge," Dolvid having checked his advance with an impassable ravine five dayrides long.

"What of?"

"Wood. What, did he think I'd sit there a year, while the stone-masons measured and cut? Wood's as common as stone in the West."

"There aren't any trees on Landegh. Everyone knows that."

"There's a big forest at Kamsilat."

"Everyone knows that. That doesn't put trees on Landegh." Kamsilat was the Arnan port and capital of the present Colony: Saidhan had his Great House there.

"I'd send to Kamsilat for huge big logs. No, I wouldn't have to. I'd bring big huge logs with the army, in case a bridge was needed."

"Carried how?"

"Wag — pack-animals — " making a quick change, anticipating fresh difficulties about roads. "Big ones could be dragged behind draft-horses. You see that when they're clearing land."

"Now you'll need more water again. Water and feed for the horses."

Again the growl from behind the flat lips. Then: "These tribesmen come along, men of the Froghul' or such. They tell about a secret river that flows under the ground, except this one place where you can go through like a cave, and lead horses down to drink. There's a hidden city," he expanded, growing happier. "A city where no one ever dies. They have fruit all year, and bears for servants, and the swords are gold."

"Not bears, on Landegh," Dolvid objected.

"We could be greatly honored there, and come back after winning the war. They make me ruler over the city. You — " He faltered.

"I shan't stay in the West. I'll ride in triumph through Kadon Dinul, and stand on the Steps to be acclaimed."

"I'll have a breastplate all of gold."

But they usually stayed allies when causing submission of a new tribe, or when, cut off from their armies by the daring of their charge, they had to fight their way back through masses of enemy, just as Larghai once did.

That was an unending summer of few shadows. They were together, too, when one of them (most often Dolvid) had a coin to spend, and they cut across the broad square by the Spear of Yoëlladhu to where the shops were, on the slope of Harbor Way, and they could buy fruit drinks or herbal infusions, ice-cold from deeps under the city wall. Even by the standards of his people, Shumat, who was a good part Gabhani, had an ugly face, and it was perplexing to Dolvid how men and especially women took instantly to his friend, with the sprouting hair, low forehead, and lopsided smile. When there was a special favor to be begged, extra honey in a sour batch of fruit drink, or two cups when they could afford only one measure, it was always best to let Shumat do the asking. More than once a woman winked and ladled out two measures for the price of one, or slipped him a free piece of pastry. Shumat's grin would widen, with a sort of rue, as if to say he could not explain, but this had been going on all his life.

At the real Frontier, Sebhal, son of Saidhan, not yet twenty, was winning renown, giving Dolvid and Shumat feats to relive and elaborate. Any tales about fighting *jinzal* they kept away from without ever needing to mention it, riding instead against well-armed, fierce and cunning but routable human enemies, Dolvid and Shumat, warriors whose names were spoken with awe throughout the realm.

"By way of *Menadhi*," Faëdhal observed wryly, "His Enlightenment sees fit to complain to the *rabhsai* — I had this from Rhunsilakh, who was there — about pleas and offerings at the Disc of Aëlovoi, and likewise the Shrine of Zhôl.   An extraordinary affair."

Dolvid's father said, "But there have always been votive bags at the Disc, particularly at this season of the year." Though winter had started mild, daylight hours were shortening; Fire Days were not far off.

"Ah, but formerly, those who tied them there had been properly taught to make their pleas to Raëdh Himself." Never a pious man, he nonetheless signed with his right thumb. "So Raëdh can choose which should come to Aëlovoi. Raëdh, too, should receive the offerings; Aëlovoi, to whom we owe gratitude for all, is not to be thanked for particular favors."

"Master, I had not known you to be such an adept." Rare for Vidukh to risk irony with Faëdhal.

"Nor will you again. These, to my blunt wits, are cases to be cackled over by *atarlal* of the *Manadilum*, when their brains are too worn out for anything weightier." Gathering up the book he had come for, Faëdhal pretended he would leave.

"Pardon, but what then is he supposed to do about this, Lambarr *Deghi*?" Vidukh asked.

"What, that's just the question. Can he use soldiers of the Household to see pleas properly directed? His goal, *Menadhi*'s — or, one should say, *g'Asalladh*'s, always, as merely presented by *Menadhi* — " ponderously sarcastic — "his object is to show again what this realm suffers, deprived of guidance the *manal* could give. But the *rabhsai* — "

"Yes?"

"Um, took note, as Rhunsilakh has it, of the complaint, and asked whether *Menadhi* had a good name for the new baby, should it be another boy." Saëdhu was expected to give birth once more, soon after year's turn.

Dolvid said, "*Menadhi* says a man can be both scholar and

warrior." The small, deep-eyed man had renewed his arguments for Dolvid's entering the *Mankh'*.

"Once, so it seems, that was true," Faëdhal said. "The term, *uzh'-freladhai*, poet as we say, formerly meant historian, a maker of great songs, and it was said he would have pen in one hand, sword ready beside the other. He who wrote the *Frela'olurai Larghayi*, for instance, also rode as one of Larghai's captains, or such is the tradition."

Vidukh was carefully considering his son. "Many boys of Family would be flattered by *Menadhi*'s interest. What he says is true enough, there are learnings for which only the *Atarlum* can furnish texts. If I had my way, the *Mankh'* library would be open to all."

"To all, my good Vidukh?" Faëdhal was shocked.

"All who want to be scholars, anyone who needs to learn about law and custom as well as history."

"Better. I feared you meant to throw open the Sacred Precinct to any garlic-muncher seeking a romance unread."

"Yes, but as things are, unless a boy's in love with all the *Atarlum* stands for, that's a high price to pay for a good library. Safe enough, surely; no one ever heard of an *atarlai* going hungry, except for some fast. Yet, as Master Faëdhal would tell you, if our *rabhsai* doesn't turn aside from the course set by his father, this may come to be the age for scholarship outside the *Atarlum*."

"A renewal, rather, if one may put it so. There were past eras when learning was not property of the *Mankh'* alone."

"Still, books can't make you rich." Dolvid had never heard his father so expansive in Faëdhal's presence; that and something about the tone of voice wakened suspicions, he could not say of what. "If you can win a place as tutor in one of the Great Houses, well and good, but in the meantime, I would have you master one of the useful crafts."

"Touching that," Faëdhal said, "when I was speaking with the good Rhunsilakh — we are, by the way, related through my mother's sister — he was mentioning other kin of his, a very old Craft Family, makers of fine enamelware. The man, Khazubran, is looking ahead to a new apprentice. He has one now, his son, soon to have half-standing in the Guild."

"It seems all the ages when you're young," Vidukh said. "But it won't be so long before you turn twelve."

"When Rhunsilakh asked me if I knew of any likely boys, Master Dolvidh's name, as is natural, came at once to mind. Very graciously, he promised he would speak for that apprenticeship, if you tell him of your interest." Faëdhal was addressing Vidukh, and Dolvid knew what he had heard in their voices; conspiracy. All this had been talked over before, behind his back.

"At sixteen," his father was saying, "you would be half-master, and could always find work in that line, even if you didn't go on for your full standing."

"Enamelling!" saying it like the names of foods he disliked. Endless stretches of time before he would be even ten, and this mapping out of all eternity filled him with a fearful despair.

"Burning a few candles," his father said, "learning a craft would not mean leaving your histories. But it is good to have a trade in reserve."

"And, Master Dolvidh, enamelling is a fine Owani craft, ancient and honored." Faëdhal spoke with unusual severity, fingering the small enamel links of his costly belt. "You, pardon me, have nothing to wrinkle your nose about, where Rhunsilakh, *bôdh'loiki* to *Rabhsayum*, is proud of his Craft kin. Even I, Master of Tongues, am not entitled to be called *bôdh'loiki*." It meant, lesser counsellor, and there were never more than about a dozen in the whole realm.

"Learning, sad to say, can't be all." Vidukh was not altogether to the point. "You have made some good friends, and there's no shame in knowing men of good position."

Dolvid hugged his empire in the West, and kept anger quiet. Rhunsilakh, fleshy and pompous, though younger than Faëdhal; his well-known father, Rhunat, had been *Bôdhrai*, Chief Counsellor, to Banak and Laluvoi, a very clever man. But the son was something of a joke; it said a great deal that Lambarr

Rabhsai, when Rhunat retired, then died, had never filled his post.

As often, Vidukh had to stay late at the Residence (there were times it became overnight), and Faëdhal said he would walk with Dolvid as far as the Disc; his house, in his family for generations, was just off the lower Avenue.

Not needing special leave to pass through part of the central block, his way through the Residence was more direct than Vidukh's. In a west-running corridor with a window at its end they saw a figure approaching, black against the sun's red. The legs were a little bowed, but the walk light-footed for a large man, shoulders very level. Faëdhal just had space to inform Dolvid, "Kheval, Master of All Weapons," and the man was up to them. They both made him a half-deference.

Dolvid was thrilled: here was one who had fought next to Banak in 2876, and since then had been tutor to warriors, having invented a whole new system of sword-fighting.

He squatted easily next to Dolvid. His face was deeply scored, lines about his eyes like cracks in parched earth, though the body was a young man's in how it was kept and carried.

"So this is Vidukh's boy, Master? Anyone would recognize that brow, eh? Eight, is it, eight-and-a-half?" With strong and well-kept hands he was measuring Dolvid's hips, then felt his calves like a buyer considering a horse, but too practised and expert to give any offence.

"What weapons might you know, Dolvidh?"

"Master," he was shy, "staves, a little. I have a bow of my own."

"Gabhani bow? — no, one of our little toys? As I thought." Without effort he straightened. "I've more than half a mind to take Dolvidh and put a sword in his hand, what would good Vidukh say to that? There's a shortage of princelings about the Residence. Brodhai of Ân and his brother are snowed in this time of year, the Heir's going to be tall as his father, and come summer I'll have to match him with one who has at least the beginnings; Zhinladh's too grown for him. What say, young

Dolvidhai? If your learned father can spare you mornings, you'll be a help to me, and it may be I'll be some use to you."

Dolvid could not speak. Eyes bright, he nodded; it must be. He could not wait to tell Shumat.

"The gist of Dolvidh's intended speech," Faëdhal said. "Is, if I may conjecture, that he is honored beyond words at this invitation from so renowned a master — " they bowed gravely to each other — "And that should his father, who, if I may offer my own opinion, will be at least equally honored — should he approve, then Dolvidh accepts with deepest gratitude. Is that well?" He was only half-joking.

"Yes. Oh, yes."

Kheval, grinning, slapped him on the back.

Shumat listened glumly to the news. A grey day, the one before Midwinter Eve, and at fourth hour this afternoon the great fire would be kindled up on the heights across the Estuary, where the Wind Caves were, with other fires, to be kept burning through four nights and three days. For this, shiploads of wood had come from the Colony, the poorest wood, twisted branches, splintered stems. There were those, Esodra was one, who thought it a terrible waste when poor folk were going cold.

Shumat shoved hands deep in his pockets, and shivered. "Will you be going to the Residence every day, then?"

"Most days."

Some of the other boys were gathering, mainly Mixed, like Shumat. The place, at the western end of the Gardens, was called the Grottoes; besides several small pockets, one wide, shallow cave had been cut, in the face of a big, chalky baulk that rose to look out on Harbor Gate and the Spear of Yoëlladhu. Here Dolvid and Shumat often gave out instructions for the day's campaigning.

"Dolvidh," Shumat announced, careful with the aspirate he usually left out, "Is to be sword-partner to Tholat the Heir, and other lords."

A murmur, frankly incredulous.

"He's to wield a fine blade," becoming wilder: "There are

to be servants to bring him *raminat* and wipe his brow."

Other times, alone, this mood of ridicule had come on Shumat, and he was as if snared in his wish to destroy, echoing and mocking everything said, till Dolvid's irritation was a tearful sneeze blocked behind nose and eyes. Then Dolvid had come back to his house with the same senseless guilt as on the day of the Deniants, as if all the world's unloving was his fault. But when he next saw Shumat, not for a week perhaps, all misery would go, and he would pick up their games again, happiness deepened by gratitude Shumat's mood had passed.

"Not so," Dolvid told the other boys. "It's only — " and then came complete betrayal.

"Dolvidh — " once again with the exaggerated aspirate, and that was mockery Dolvid did not understand; even the Heir was not unmixed Owani. "*Dolvidh* is going to win back Empire in the West. He's going to find the grave of Lost Plakhan, and come back to be cheered on the Steps. He's to be a hero."

"But you — " Dolvid started to stammer.

"He is the new Larghai," Shumat sneered. His face was flushed. Dolvid struggled with memories of Shumat's equally lofty imaginings, but it was no use. Jeers were breaking out among the boys. He fled, not turning back when a voice, perhaps Shumat, called out his name.

In the murk he stood chilled on the knoll. Tiny sharp pellets of snow were coming steadily. Lanterns at Harbor Gate glared in the gloom, the *ôdul* lighting the Residence a vague shimmer, but towards the Estuary was black.

Not many were gathered here on this drear afternoon; most were silent, simply waiting.

"Soon," a woman close by whispered. They were all blinking snow from their eyes, trying to peer through dark and mist to where the heights of Dramal must be. Was there a flicker, a spark? The watchers stirred.

"Aah — " a collective sigh, as far golden light struggled

and then steadied, a brave needle of fire too low for any star. It was a cry of hope nearly snatched away by the wind, a plea, a desperate promise. Bodies around Dolvid were straightening, and there was scattered clapping of hands.

Closer, at the Shrine of Zhôl, flamelight broadened and danced, thrown on the stones of the nearby Treasury, though the actual fire could not be seen from here. There a denser crowd would be gathered, and their cry, swelling to a loud cheer, reached the knoll.

Smiles, but not any face Dolvid knew. In spring, Shumat would be leaving Kadon Dinul, going back to the country of the Angle, far up the Paowan River. Shurri, his father, had some importance there, before he had left to join an elder brother in the harness business, now failing. Shurri would go back to farming, and also to surveying of lands and drawing of boundaries, arts Shumat would be taught.

Shumat! what did he matter, a Mixed of no standing, when Dolvid would be among lords and heirs? His mockery was worse in remembering there had been boys, mainly of Craft Family, who would not join in any game with those of Other Race. Faced with that, Dolvid had chosen Shumat as his friend.

The fires were safely burning, the sun was not going to leave them forever. Dolvid rubbed his nose with the back of a hand, shook cold feet, and made for home.

Still grumbling about his lost farm, Darborr, having his compensation-money for a share in his uncle's business, also left in spring, taking his wife to the ancient city of Dônshei, which had been the first capital of Old Owan, so long ago Kadon Dinul was then only a clump of huddled hamlets.

Near Dolvid's tenth birthday Esodra went to live closer to her daughter. That was a strange leave-taking, with strain between his father and the woman Dolvid felt but did not understand.

Yes, Esodra ought to stay, but she too was a Mixed, and he had learnt not to put trust there, even if she had been as near as he could remember to a mother. She was only at the edge of his life, the Residence, and his growing skill with arms.

His father bleakly promised another woman or other women would be found to do Esodra's tasks. But in the flat, toneless talk, the long pauses of their farewell, both grown-ups behaved as if it was not all decided, as if one magic word might change all plans. How silly, Esodra's remark, "When all's said, a woman has to look to herself." Of course that was true, when she did not have a husband.

Simple as it was, it nearly became too difficult for Vidukh. Though he assented, "Indeed, indeed," he also said, "You'll be missed, much missed," in exactly the tone Dolvid knew from his own voice when he tried to be offhand just mentioning something he wished for too much to ask outright. That passed, and so did Esodra's gush of tears over parting with Dolvid; she presumed to give his father a number of reminders about care of the boy. The final farewells were lifeless on both sides.

Quite soon, he realized more than Esodra's wonderful fritters had gone away. Her going left him face-to-face with his father as never before. Not wishing it, Dolvid had not done much lately but wrangle with his father, and he began to see him plainly as an adversary. A well-meaning man, yes, but with a world too narrow to hold his son's dreams.

"Are we to move south someday, father?"

A blink. "Leave Kadon? While Master Kheval puts such reliance in you?" This was mildly sarcastic, Dolvid having twice told how that morning Kheval had called out to Brodhai of Ân, "Watch the Vidukhat lad, he'll show you how the feet go."

"I mean, south of the Avenue."

"We are comfortable here, not so? We've got a view to the Estuary. Even the Residence Quarter can't boast that. Besides, it's a fine healthy spot." This was a side-reference to Old Town, the low-lying quarter north and west, once notorious for plague, although the great Plakhsila, who had also built the Avenue and the New Residence, had done much to improve drainage of the city.

"But we're north of the Avenue." When one of Kheval's pupils asked him where he lived, Dolvid found it hard not to blush — or lie.

"Between Avenues," his father corrected. "Where, also, lives Arvus of the Treasury, now raised to *bôdh'loiki*. For that matter, Khelagh lives north of the Avenue."

This was one more annoying joke. Khelagh (a kinsman to Dolvid's teacher, Kheval) was an important landowner, magistrate over wide lands, and one of the richest among the Families. His costly and imposing Kadon Dinul house faced from the north side of the actual Avenue, not far below the Disc. That was even better than the Residence Quarter, although best of all was to not have a city house at all, because you were certain to stay at the Residence when visiting Kadon.

"If we lived in the Residence Quarter, you wouldn't have so far to walk each day."

Vidukh laughed. "If I took a house there, I would have no distance to walk at all. I'd have to hide at the Residence to escape my creditors."

Dolvid swallowed back a bold offer to make money by working every day as a scribe. The provincial Pledging brought crowds every summer, but not the size of the Great Pledging, and for much of the year hostelries had few guests, most of what there were farmers up for market, with no money to waste on letters. Besides, he dared not imagine what it would do if Kheval's class were to hear he toiled as a scribe. Even as things were, he had to suffer through unspoken comments on the distinction there was between being son to the *Nim'* of Ân, and to a Keeper of Books.

A part of those veiled sneers must be revenge for how quickly he learnt, and how often Kheval held him up as a model. But the Heir, Tholat, had not spoken one word beyond absolute necessity ever since the second time they had met. Then, between bouts, he told Dolvid to fetch him his cold drink.

Dolvid just stared. Two years younger, but as tall as Dolvid, Tholat reddened, but Kheval took Dolvid's side, saying, "Nay, by your leave, *biRabh'loi*, a man you cross blades with can't be your servant. We're all our own stewards, here."

"My father — "

"Lambarr *Deghi* would say the same. He would, I had the teaching of him. Why, Great Banak, your grandfather — " He left the thought unfinished. In shade under the archway to the Rose-Stone Wing, Tholat's brother, the five-year-old Banak-loi, became more sullen. In the end, Lambarr, perhaps, had been asked to rule, and ever after a servant came with the royal brothers to the gravelled court in the Residence grounds, or to the Winter School when the weather was bad; Dolvid had not again been asked to fetch. His father called this 'a true Lambarr answer,' adding quickly he meant no disrespect. But he heartily approved of what his son had done, or declined to do.

Vidukh did not have much use for warriors, unless, like Saidhan, they were statesmen as well. Even Banak, he said, in a rare criticism, could have been even a better ruler with more learning. Learn, learn, was his cry, the persistent note piped by a marsh-bird. Dolvid, hungry for knowledge but often daunted by its drudgery, found by gritting his teeth, putting his head down, and doing the duller work he could sometimes have his way elsewhere — and more readily escape sarcasms, when his swelling muscles would not let him be still, and he would go posturing about the bigroom, defeating shadow enemies with Kheval's sequences.

He went on yearning for his empire, but it became harder as he knew more. Ability with weapons might give him his half-file if he could get into the Household. Closest to the power, the Household attracted many of the most ambitious, and yet there was hardly a man left in the saddle who had ever faced an enemy fiercer than unruly drunks at a Pledging, and promotion, in the absence of wars, was very slow. Sons of influential families could come in at file-leader or even half-squadron level, and one such, Kizhunai, a quiet-spoken young man, told Dolvid what he would do for quicker advancement, if he did not have plans for marriage here at Kadon; serve out his initial six-year enlistment, but instead of renewing for another twelve, make his way to Kamsilat in the Colony, and get into the Army of the West. He would most likely have to lose a bit of rank, as well as his six-year start towards the small farm that came with eighteen years' service. But there was action in the West, chance of deeds to win a command. He did not add that space was made by officers there being killed each year, or wounded into early retirement.

This rewoke old dreaming. In times such as these, no big wars in sight, the hardest part was getting command of troops. Kheval was not always an easy master, often rough-tongued, expecting his pupils to be able every time to do what they had done well once, a taskmaster still dogged after perfection at the end of a long career. At times Dolvid was near tears with Kheval's weary and wearying "Again." If others had been his real friends he might have been wounded less when Kheval called him fool or blunderer, but while he could have pleasant words with fellow-pupils, there was always the gulf made by his father's lack of standing, and he knew they saw him as an upstart, secretly rejoicing in his mistakes, the certainty of Kheval's sarcasm or wrath.

Plainly, the answer was to rise so far above boys of Family and even sons of a *nim'* they would all beg for his friendship, like those who had formerly despised Banak, a Mixed, grandson of a tanner. As the dream grew harder to accomplish, it became more necessary.

He needed a horse, or the use of one. That summer both the Heir and Brodhai of Ân would begin learning lance, and without that it would never be possible to captain cavalry.

"An ordinary horse would be no use," his father said. "And certainly we'll never own a *pefrai*."

"If you would ask Faëdhal, father, he could speak with

Rhunsilakh, and Rhunsilakh could ask the *rabhsai* to allow me use of a *pefrai*."

"Yes, I can see the decree: 'We Lambarr *rabhsai* deem and stipulate that for the better welfare and enhanced glory of this realm, our servant Dolvid Vidukhat be permitted to ride a *pefrai* of our Household...'"

"But I must have a *pefrai* to ride." This was not for joking; the others all would be riding. A *pefrai* was a warhorse, different from a saddle horse as a wildcat from a house tabby. Because trained cavalry mounted on *pefrai* could easily rout three, five times its numbers on ordinary horses, breeding of the warhorses was controlled by the *rabhsai*. Many years ago the *Atarlum* had discovered a certain substance added to the feed of a *pefrai* foal, while affecting neither fighting qualities of the grown horse, nor its urge to couple, prevented it from siring. Since then, no untreated stallion was legally allowed to pass outside control of the *rabhsayum*, which was thus able to limit the numbers of *pefrai*-mounted cavalry permitted provincial overlords.

Or so it should be, but formerly Kargul had been traditional breeders of horses, and after long squabbling the *rabhsayum* had not regained its hold on the breeding stock without fighting the War of the Royal Stud, second of the three conflicts in which Great Banak had captained the victorious forces of *rabhsayum*. Nevertheless, it was widely rumored defeated Kargul had not given up all the untreated stallions, and to this day still bred illicit *pefrai* in its isolated mountain valleys.

Vidukh was frowning. "Dol, I have never studied arms. But isn't there a law, or a rule, it might be, that except for a common trooper in his training, a man must have his own mount when practising with lances?"

Dolvid pressed his lips together, only legacy of his friendship with Shumat. His father was right; lance-work, it had been explained to him, was too dangerous for horse for anyone to risk someone else's, too dangerous for the rider except on a mount he knew entirely.

"Brodhai of Ân rides a *pefrai* not his own, a yearling."

"Aye, borrowed from the Heir, you mean? And he's Brodhai of Ân, not Dolvid Vidukhat. Well, you'll all go on meeting for swordplay, not so? and fighting with knife, and bow and staves? If you have to spend a forenoon alone, now and again, while the Heir is riding with lances, you can use the time on the Script of Shâl, in which you're not yet perfect."

"Perfect! Shâl himself wasn't perfect in his script."

His father gave a long regard, and Dolvid wished away the shrillness of his tone, ready to say, `all I said was — ' and then the same words spoken calmly.

"Also," Vidukh said, "these floors, lately... " Not waiting for the ending, Dolvid went for the broom.

"I wish," he said in the soft-lighted library, "we might have nothing but *ga-ôthu* at home."

Faëdhal was there. "No doubt," he agreed. "So do I, and so does the *Nim'* of Asekh."

It was a joke, and Dolvid did not take the bait; Asekh, distant, poor, barren, mainly unpeopled, had long ago lapsed from full provincial standing, and had no *nim'*. The very name was connected with *asikhu*, empty, though Dolvid believed it must come from *seghu*, blood, because of blood-red mineral pools there.

"Which reminds me," turning to Vidukh, who was using a thin-bladed knife to scrape moisture-spots from the pages of an old history. "You have heard the matter of Arvus? He has been accused, not to blunt words, of stealing, some six *ôdul*, among other treasures. Not to mention a quantity of gold."

"Who accuses him?" Vidukh hardly looked up.

"As you would suppose." The tone became confidential. "There are people of my own kin, I fear, among them."

Dolvid's father gave a small grunt.

"As I have said to Rhunsilakh, it is quite out of the

question. Arvus, a thief?"

"He's Deniant," Dolvid said. He knew the Master of Revenues only by sight, a small, dark-haired man, always hurrying, but with a quick, knowing glance.

Now Vidukh stirred, and Faëdhal turned slowly, showing gradual astonishment. "That, indeed, is the true nature of these charges; there speaks the voice of the Residence Quarter. He is Deniant, what crime might he not be guilty of? I myself — " he made Raëdh's sign — "while by no means of their number, cannot see why men may not be both Deniant and honest, more honest, perhaps, than those who affirm pious belief only to gain advancement, which was very common not many years ago. And, Master Dolvidhai — " he swung back — "you are acquiring, forgive my words, Vidukh, too lofty a regard for your own views. You are not yet to be our Captain-General, even if you do swing a better blade than the Heir."

"As who might not?" Vidukh said slyly.

"Hush — " but Faëdhal too was giving way to a smile. Tholat, true, had inherited all his father's height, and much more than the *rabhsai*'s hint of awkwardness. With half his reach, eight-year-old Bradhinal of Ân could beat Tholat in swordplay.

Seeing the men had all along been making fun of his boasts about outdoing the Heir made Faëdhal's reprimand all the more offensive to Dolvid. His face reddening, breeches clinging hotly to his thighs, he thought sullenly of how Faëdhal could speak as he did, never having been set upon in a back street by brutal Deniants. Faëdhal, meanwhile, explained the *rabhsai* had yet taken no action, but Arvus, angrily demanding immediate hearing on these charges, had suspended himself from all duties at the Treasury.

"And Lambarr...?"

"Is, you will recall, setting out for Tan Lughsai, with some of the Family. His departure is not to be delayed. The case of Arvus is to be heard by Laluvoi *Asayu*."

Vidukh nodded satisfaction, but mention of the departure for Tan Lughsai was fresh despair for Dolvid: he would never be taken there.

Arvus won complete exoneration, and yet before summer was out was obliged to fight a duel with his most persistent accuser, Ladh-Sivai, from near Kred' Bakali. They fought with swords, and to the shocked wonder of the Residence Quarter, the Deniant, formally untrained, beat the man of Family. Arvus gave his man a wound in the face, far from fatal, though leaving a scar that would stay. Dolvid was more envious of this feat so near to hand than of the larger but remote triumphs of young Sebhal. Duels were forbidden under a law of Plakhsila, but the excuse of intolerable insult, here as before, made the law look away.

Most of Kheval's pupils saw the outcome as a defeat, though the Heir had no comments; his father may have warned him to say nothing. Dolvid was not sure. Arvus was friendly with his father, and praised by fair-minded Owanil, while even his own people called Ladh-Sivai mean-spirited and sour. But when some of the Old Blood blamed Others for thrusting themselves forward, helped by the changed climate, into posts where they lacked, if not the needed skills, then desired graces, the Owani sense of what was proper, Dolvid did not altogether disagree. Not to mean the Family, because there the mixture of bloods was diluted by three or four generations of good marriage, and they behaved like Owanil of the best descent. It was not that Dolvid hated the Other Races, as many did; Esodra he remembered fondly, and had he not made Shumat his friend? But he did not see why they wanted to be in places they were not suited for. Their own history, the *Song of Tales*, showed them as followers.

Yet in the Army of the West, where Dolvid's fortune might be waiting, he had heard many squadron-leaders, and at least one under-captain, named Nolimas, were Mixed. If they had an Owani among their troops, how did he feel, obeying men who properly should serve?

In this Dolvid saw he was avoiding the hypocrisy of others; to him it was clear who ran things at the Residence:

Laluvoi, men like Rhunsilakh, even Faëdhal. Though Faëdhal he had come to dislike, a self-important pedant, and exactly what Others meant when they complained about the pompousness of the Old Blood. His father was well-meaning, but Dolvid thought he was rather easily taken in by fine-sounding phrases and his own impossible beliefs.

This year summer seemed brief, and a hard winter set in early: six weeks before Fire Days the heights of Dramal were white above the Estuary. In the new year the port of Owan Sai was briefly closed by ice, and Entun Shelum, the lake of Lower Paowan, was frozen shore to shore as it had not been in years. For weeks the Heartland was a white almost without features.

Since his long years in the south, Vidukh had always suffered in cold weather, and Dolvid too shivered; there was a general shortage of fuel for fires. Nevertheless, he wished for spring never to come. In the chill, echoing cavern of the Winter School, partly hollowed from the limestone eminence where the New Residence stood, no day went by without mention of Tan Lughsai, where, at first sign of warmer weather, the *rabhsai* and most of court would remove for an indefinite stay. Happy while he still had a sword in his hand, Dolvid wished mountains of snow from the skies.

Tanu in the Owanilú was cape, or headland, and Tan Lughsai was the name given, originally to the tip but eventually to all of a small peninsula, due south of Kadon Dinul, where Arnan swept back to cut out a great bay. In its exposed position, winters were sharp at Tan Lughsai, but a freak in the currents of Arnan gave the cape a spring earlier than many spots southward. Certainly earlier, sometimes by weeks, than at Kadon Dinul, only a dayride to the north.

Though there was good growing-soil idle, Tan Lughsai had long been deserted. It had become part of the royal estates during the lengthy reign of Plakhsila, but Lambarr was first to begin any building there, having in mind a home where his growing family could escape the formal life at Kadon Dinul. That notion was generally admired, but his choice of sites was not: for reasons no one could remember, Tan Lughsai was considered a place of ill-omen and bad luck. Lambarr had occasionally had difficulty recruiting workers for his expanding schemes.

This year at last, there were buildings and beds enough, the road southward, never a main one, was in repair, and a new cavalry post had been built at the hamlet of Rhutalai, near halfway, mainly to furnish fresh mounts for the fast-messengers who would keep the *rabhsai* in touch with his capital.

The whole Family would go, and so would the brothers from Ân, and others of Dolvid's companions and rivals at arms. Kheval was going, so none of the important pupils need miss lessons: Faëdhal was travelling south for the same reason. But while he was working with Faëdhal to help select the books to be taken, Vidukh would be left in Kadon Dinul.

"Because there will be no need for me there," was his answer to Dolvid's wailed *why?* "I would not prevent your going, if Kheval asked, or one of your highborn sword-partners. Although... " He made a resigned face. In winter their life was not easy, and Dolvid helped, both by scavenging for fuel, and in saving them the need of a real housekeeper; a Mixed girl came two or three afternoons a week to cook their evening meal, and carry off soiled clothes for washing.

But Kheval said, "Nay, Dolvid lad, you've enough polish on you so's you aren't going to rust away in a few weeks, and we'll be doing most work outside, with lances and bows, I fancy. Best stay and keep your father company." This verdict might have been changed by a word from one of the princelings, but that did not come. A few weeks! in itself all eternity, and among the others there was talk that even if the *rabhsai* had to come back to Kadon, they could spend all summer and well into autumn at the Cape.

The feeling of being singled out for misery was increased when his father became sick. Having walked to the Residence through a bone-freezing mixture of hail and icy rain, he took to his bed with alternating fever and cold shudders. It was very vexing; most of the nursing fell upon Dolvid, and he had to miss some of the last precious days with Kheval at the Residence. The bigroom, with fuel scarce and very expensive, had to be kept warm day and night, and all Dolvid's knowledge of the alleyways no longer got him many scraps of wood.

Each morning he woke expecting his father to be making a clatter with the breakfast bowls, but a fifth day came with Vidukh still dull-eyed and flushed, breath creaking, face hot to the hand's touch. It was as if he was staying ill on purpose to thwart Dolvid.

That day Vidukh told him to send word for a *ramidu*; he could either leave a message at the Old Bronze Residence, or else go to Faëdhal, who would arrange it. Wrapped thickly against the bitter wind, which had come back after two days of somewhat milder weather, Dolvid walked down to the Bronze Residence.

After his father had shifted and muttered through the night, a *ramidu* came in the morning, at-Sepivadhi, a round-faced man with a thorn of a nose, scrawnily built, but with a pot-belly his blue Healer's robe did not hide. Squatting next to the wall-bunk where Vidukh lay, he chanted a brief *kolukezh'*, and advised Dolvid to leave a plea at the Disc of Aëlovoi. In addition he dosed Vidukh with thick, brown *ga-raminat*, telling Dolvid to keep the room warm, and give warming drinks. This he had been doing, and he did not argue, though beginning to believe the opposite course might be better; several times in the night his father had thrown off the blankets, the under-bedding soaked with sweat.

Later, he felt enough restored to sit up and swallow mouthfuls of gruel made of oatmeal and beef marrow. The *ramidu* had vowed to return.

Another morning came, and Vidukh was livelier, freer in the chest. Again, he took a little food, asked what day it was, and urged Dolvid not to miss his weapons-class.

"We're short of fuel, father. There was talk of a wagon at Market Gate today."

"You have money?"

Dolvid nodded, pulling on his outshirt. The day might be a little warmer. As he went to the door his father wriggled up in bed. "That apprenticeship of yours. Rhunsilakh says his kinsman has asked to see you. Your twelfth birthday is less than a half-year away." Before that day the indenture would have to be signed.

Dolvid felt his heart thump, but said quite coolly, "I want to join the Household. As a common trooper, if I can't learn the lance before then." In the saying, it was untrue; he had grown out of his dream and omitted to discard it: he would never conquer a new empire in the West.

His father finished a lengthy cough. "Then be a common trooper. It's an honorable trade, soldiering, only as bad as the men who may follow it. If you want, be the scarecrow who follows after the squadrons and collects their droppings to sell as manure — " growing excited — "Do what pleases you to earn your bread. Your grandfather kept his own shop, and none of us ever wore livery. You will never be any man's servant, so long as you keep to your learning. It never stops, Dol, never."

Dolvid was numb from loss of his heroic imaginings, gone with nothing left in their place. He went out into sun and a kinder wind.

Before making for Market Gate, he went scouring once more through the alleyways, picking up a few sticks and scraps of wood. Gleaning firewood always reminded him of the Ní-Tilagh, but that was not exactly true; he had no real memory left of the journey, five years ago, and Ní-Tilagh was mainly a horror in history, where Thral-Sivu, last of the Gabh'Owan rulers, had died, when Laluvoi first became a widow. Gathering wood brought back instead the many times he and his father had reminisced about their long, hard journey, the fire built to huddle near in the middle of emptiness, a tradition of words binding Dolvid and his father together, despite all their skirmishings.

When he returned to put what he had collected on the fire, his father seemed to be resting quietly. From behind the loose brick in the wall Dolvid took money, and went out again. At Market Gate he found peat-wagons had indeed come in from southward. With elbowing, he was able to buy a short sack of turves, at twice the usual price for a full one. With care, if the weather was no colder than this, they could have several days of grudging heat, with wood for a brief blaze, to heat drinks, or if his father felt chilled.

He came back with his prize, and there was a difference. He stirred the fire to heat water. In the quiet, with only the odd sound of a voice or a heavy footfall coming from outside, Dolvid stilled his own breathing to listen for what he had stopped hearing, his father's long breaths, rasping these past days, often close to a soft snore.

He never thought of calling out to his father. With distaste rather than fear he came near the bunk. The left hand hanging outside the covers was cold as nothing alive could be. The eyes were shut, mouth open, the forehead cold, after so many days of burning heat. Under the covers the chest was still, and there was no breath in mouth or nostrils.

After long emptiness, squatting beside the fire, watching bubbles form in the bottom of the pot, he went back. Everything was just the same, except the escaped hand was stiffer.

Before loss, he was flooded with a muddle of incapacity, even guilt. He was sure someone should be told. He would go away not saying a word, and let others who knew what to do find the body. Having at the fourth try succeeded in folding the dead left hand up under the blankets, he stayed next to the bunk. A corner of blanket was trailing on the flagged floor, and by its bent edge there was a fluffy little accumulation of dust. Ashamed of his housekeeping, he gathered it with the side of his hand, and used his fingers to roll it into a tight twist of grime. When he went to drop this into the fire the water was simmering. He decided to make a warm drink.

After the infusion of nettles and comfrey was made, Dolvid began to weep. He had set out two mugs on the table.

Later the outside door came open. The short, robed figure standing there against the light Dolvid took for at-Sepivadhi, the *ramidu*.

"I think my father is dead." It was longer than should be; in front of him, the drink was cold.

The *atarlai* made a short exclamation, and went swiftly and more lithely than ought to be possible to the wall-bunk. Rapidly, using tiny, clever hands, he tested for warmth, heartbeat, pulse, breath.

He turned with a huge sigh. "Ah, Dolvidh, I am afraid you are right." He was not the *ramidu*, he was *Menadhi*. Unthinking, Dolvid touched forefinger to his breast, and made half-deference.

He, however, made the left-hand sign of death. "*Bi namakil shudal yi-butraghal ul*," he intoned, "Would we could meet again in happier times."

Learning

At-Aval was still another Islander, squat with a long upper lip, and a high-pitched, creaking voice. He knew who Dolvid was, but whatever instructions had been given, soon made plain he would be treated as any other pupil. With those of his age he was set to study scripts and letters he had known half his life.

Among boys having unbounded awe for the various *atarlal* who taught them and ordered their lives, memory of breakfasting alone with *Menadhi* soon lost any power to make him feel out of the ordinary. He kept to the supposition he was being set some sort of test, and made up his mind he could endure a week of these baby-tasks.

He found the custom was to give new arrivals the most unpleasant of the work to be done about the *Mankh'*. Dolvid did not so much mind the scullery with its huge tank of steaming water and ever-renewing pile of used cooking-pots and eating-bowls, though his hands became sore and rough from harsh yellow soap. Far worse was the emptying of night-jars into deep pits dug to the southward side of the *Mankh'*, which meant much handling of heavy, foul-smelling and often slimed jars. He was never sent to the laundry, and those who helped the cooks were chosen from among the same few each day.

Boys of good family often came to the *Mankh'* for a year or two of study, but rarely became candidates for *atarlum*, and kept mostly to themselves. They could wear their own clothes, and had private lessons, private sleeping quarters, and even their own table for eating, where they were served by ordinary boys.

Dolvid was not used to having his food with a crowd of others. Talk was allowed at table on most days, but he had little to say, and ate with hunger but no appetite. Mornings always began with a hot mash of oats or barley, too stiff to be called porridge, occasionally with a trace of preserved fruits. The same mash came back at midday, stirred into a soup made of trimmings from meat eaten by the privileged boys and grown-ups. At both these meals there was no lack of coarse bread in big loaves. Once in that week there was meat in the evening, tough beef boiled to chewy strings, but mostly there was plain yellow cheese or eggs cooked hard; another day there was fish cooked in oil. At most meals there were large containers of barley-water, and once warmed milk; the red apples springy from winter storage at Dolvid's first midday meal did not appear again. Before, he had never given much attention to food, but now half-waking hours were spent dreaming of roast meats or forcemeats, even of despised things, lentils, carrots, pickled cabbage, all winter fare. Thought of butter, or the fritters Esodra used to make could bring him near tears.

He was also unaccustomed to sleeping with many others. His bed, a stuffed mattress, was in a long chamber with about a dozen boys, mostly from the Island; Dravadhi of the amazing face was one, and so was the tiny Zhâlai who, after all, was almost the same age as Dolvid. For three days he was nearest a friend Dolvid had, less rough-spoken than most, proud of kinship with one of the big Kamanta landowners, Pedhivan. Whose daughter Petakoi, Zhâlai proudly announced, would soon be married to Tovakh, Heir in Kargul, son of that red-haired Tobhan seen riding in for the Great Pledging, what seemed hundreds of years ago.

Zhâlai told a little about the Island, its cliffs, the famous City of the Bridge, Drin b'Afon, where the Patriarch had his Summer Palace, the animal hunts through stands of man-high Kamanta grass, found nowhere else. In return, Dolvid incautiously spoke of visiting the New Residence, his father's post, weapons-classes with Master Kheval.

Zhâlai was also friends with Dravadhi, who showed a quite different face here from the timid one he had for *Menadhi*. He liked to give orders, and was allied with Yubhai, oldest and

largest of the dozen, heavy-limbed, heavy-browed, very backward
with his letters, his face shadowed by the start of downy hair. On
the evening of the fourth day, Yubhai, sitting cross-legged on his
mattress, told the others all about Dolvid.

"He's friends with the Family," he recited in his thick
Island accent. "He has learned talks with Laluvoi *Asayu*."

Dravadhi asked, "In which language?"

"Jinzalú." Yubhai bared teeth and rolled his eyes. All the
others laughed; *jinzal* were well-known to have no speech.

"Nay, Yuv," Dravadhi said. "They'd do nothing as
common as talk. They *write* to each other, in the Script of Shâl."

"The Script of Banak," someone else suggested.

As with the long-ago day Shumat had turned sour, Dolvid
suddenly knew why these boys mocked him. Some of them, from
the south of Kamanta, had spoken from their cradles a kind of
Owanilú, but so altered that if anything it would make their study
of the formal language all the harder. His command of the best
Owanilú must annoy them. Understanding did not bring
forgiveness; after being up at dawn to help empty the night's
harvest of waste, he had been reprimanded by at-Aval for dozing
through a lesson on *yi*, which he had known about since he was
seven. Nevertheless, with his chambermates, it was a mistake not
to see the joke.

"Dolvidh's father," Yubhai said, "worked at the Residence,
taking care of all their boots."

"Books," Dolvid said.

Another voice said, "Dolvidh Bootmanson."

"Dolvidh Cobbler," Dravadhi improved.

Dolvid came thrusting into the babble. "My father," he
told Yubhai, "was Keeper of Books. That's better than an eel-
salter."

To an Islander, as he well knew, especially from the south
of Kamanta, this was a deadly insult. The eels were slit and salted
by the worst of the convicted criminals *Rabhsayum* turned over to
the Patriarch.

Yubhai scrambled up to glower down on Dolvid, who

refused to flinch. "Boot Keeper," he said, flicking out with his fingers.

Dolvid hit him once hard in the chest. Immediately, they grappled, Yubhai furious. Toppling, they rolled over mattresses, out onto the pathway of hard, bare floor. In the fierceness of their holds, Dolvid felt this was not the same sort of fight as in the Gardens, where also tempers had sometimes blazed up. Here there was nothing to stop them; it would have to be fought out to the end. He was conscious of watching faces showing interest, excitement, grimacing with imagined blows.

He was using knees and elbows to defend himself, knowing he must not let the heavier boy pin him down. Catwise, he twisted suddenly aside, helping Yubhai down with a wrench on his shoulder. The boy went thumping to the floor, and turned to answer with a kick, or what, standing up, would have been a stamp of his shod foot. The heel caught Dolvid above his knee, but he hardly felt pain, bringing a bunched fist down into Yubhai's belly, causing a grunt and a whooshing cough.

About to follow up this success, he was gripped from above, and dragged backwards onto his feet. He jerked his shoulders, nearly coming free, then noticed the others had fallen silent and quieted their faces. He was being held by at-Dhanurai, one of the younger teachers. Besides instructing in making of maps, he was the *atarlai* who gave out the various household duties. Dolvid knew him only in that function, and did not have much reason for liking him.

After Yubhai was back on his feet, at-Dhanurai had to find out who had begun this brawl. He threatened both boys with extra bouts of the most unpleasant tasks. Yubhai mumbled, "I can't say, *at'ai*."

Dolvid, warring between pride and shame, kept silence. At-Dhanurai's face was like a hunting dog, not to be turned from purpose.

Dravadhi offered, "Dolvidh was first to strike a blow." A general ripple of assent, and with a decisive nod the *atarlai* abruptly left the sleeping-chamber. A boy murmured a word, and his neighbor nodded in agreement, lower lip pushed out. Feet were shifting, and Dolvid did not find any eyes meeting his.

At-Dhanurai came back, carrying a short, supple thong, perhaps a length of stirrup-leather. At his command Zhâlai and Dravadhi, each two-handed, held Dolvid's wrists. The smock was pulled down from his shoulders, and at-Dhanurai, feet wide apart, laid four hard blows of the leather across the bared back.

Never having been beaten, Dolvid shrank from its insult to his body, the shock of pain dealt out with this measured deliberation. When he was released, and turned to face at-Dhanurai, the man's face was flushed, eyes glowing. "I am reducing your punishment, since you are new to the ways of the *Mankh'*."

He was waiting for the right response. As Dolvid stayed silent, the *atarlai* appealed to the others. "Must we teach him gratitude as well?" The hand holding the thong swung to and fro.

Dolvid's mind agreed he would not be beaten further, not before he was overcome, and exhausted from struggling. He would punch the first who tried to take a wrist, and kick out at the *atarlai*.

Very near his ear, Zhâlai whispered, "Say, `I thank you, *at'ai*.'"

The obsequiousness of it revolted Dolvid, and there was obscure loss in taking this way out of doomed resistance.

"I thank you, *at'ai*," indistinctly, his mumble making it impossible for the *atarlai* to be certain about his contempt.

After, Zhâlai said, "He's given twenty before now." The next boy bid that up to an indefinite "More," beginning a general discussion of past floggings. Stiff-necked, Dolvid declined to yield to the tug of fellowship there was in this, where bitterest complaint was also proudest boast. In whispers the debate went on after the light had been taken out, and he tried to arrange two separate sets of bruises, from fight and punishment, not to interfere with his sleep.

The voices in the dark took on a tense, tremulous note, just as when they speculated about the *nôd'yanul*. That was a baffling affair. For some time Dolvid had known the chief difference between the *doni-margul* of the town and *zhani-margul* of the highway, both of which offered food, rest, *raminat*, stabling for horses. Only *zhani-margul* had also the *nôd'yanul*, girls trained by the *Atarlum* in many skills. Sensible enough they should be taught singing and dance, and the art of massaging weariness from the legs and back of a traveller. But the accomplishment most discussed by the boys, 'pleasures of the bed,' was both vague and puzzling: Dravadhi had given forth with many improbable details, but even if they were true, they merely swapped one mystery for another, a *what?* for a *why?* In spite of which there was a feeling that took up residence in Dolvid's belly, dread or anticipation, not truly desire, not yet.

Not to be disputed was that on the farther side of the *Mankh'*, twenty or so girls between the ages of thirteen and seventeen were being instructed by the *Nôdhilum*. Mainly they were Island girls. Unlike poor families of Mixed origin here on the Mainland, Dolvid learned, poor Owanil of the Island were not necessarily dismayed by the birth of a daughter. If she turned out to be pretty and teachable she had a good chance of entering the *Mankh'* for training. Not all would ever become *nôd'yanul*, but the training alone gave any girl a better chance at a good marriage. Those who did well enough to go to one of the *zhani-margul*, just like an apprentice, served six years, and then were free. According to Zhâlai, those always married well, not only because of their accomplishments, but for their *Atarlum* dowries; over their years of service payment accumulated in the form of farming lands in Patriarchal grant.

What the other boys most relished in the night was the prospect of being fifteen, when they would be permitted a visit to one of the *nôd'yanul*-to-be. This was a part of the girls' training in their last year: many fathers of family took their sons to the *zhani-margul* to be initiated, so bedding of an untutored youth was a needed art for any *nôd'yanu*. Dolvid heard boys telling what older boys had told, and was sure they must have it wrong.

Women, he knew, were mostly gentler than men, and he had never disliked girls except when they tried to join activities for which they lacked the necessary strength or daring. He quickly missed the bright, soft gowns of Kadon Dinul, the prettiness and grace of women, but he could not imagine wanting to fit his body to a fragile girl's.

Yet there was the sign made when speaking of Zhôl, right thumb folding across the swell of soft flesh to touch at the base of the little-finger; Raëdh mating with Aëlovoi to bring about their son. His father had explained fathering, but not that it was sport, and now it was all muddled up with giggles and smug grins. Nothing would reach the suffocation of knowing he could not turn to his father for help; no use saving up his questions, he would not do that again, not ever.

Hungry, always dishevelled, soot-eyed from shortage of sleep, harried for not paying attention when they taught baby things, he began to plan escape. Rather, in the midst of misery like a howl unscreamed, escape seemed to think of him, one day as he was scouring at a vast pot used for cooking the barley-mash.

Once past the wall of the Inner Precinct, it should not be hard to get out of the *Mankh'* estates. Southward the lands were rough and empty; half-files of *Adanum Plakh'* could be glimpsed riding there, but so long as *g'Asalladh'* was not in residence the soldiers were too few for a large-scale search — if, indeed, they considered it worthwhile looking for one vanished boy. Again, supply-wagons were constantly coming (it could only be from Kadon Dinul) and going, not closely examined by guards at the gate. If he could hide in an empty one he could certainly reach safety.

If it was safety; *what then?* was the question delaying his plans. He had an idea that under the Treaty, unless he had the *rabhsai's* protection, he could be seized and brought back. Even Household or General Cavalry soldiers would hand him over to the *Atarlum,* just as they did convicted criminals. That was even likelier with provincial troops, if indeed *Atarlum* had stronger influence with the Great Families than it had at Kadon Dinul.

Bands of outlaws, it was said, lived by theft in remote parts, but if he could ever reach one he did not see why they would want him, a boy, as recruit.

There was the West. If he could get to Owan Sai, hide away on a boat, and cross Arnan, he did not think he would be sent back from Kamsilat. Saidhan ruled there, and his father always said the *Atarlum* did not approve of Saidhan, partly because of his success in the War of the Widowed, but also because he gave high rank in the Army of the West, and even magistracies in the Colony to men who did not speak a single word of the Owanilú, many who had no trace of Owani blood.

He could not yet be a soldier, but could do something in the Army of the West, and then might get a chance for distinction. He had read an old tale where a lad taken on as a cook-boy overheard plans of the enemy, and gave timely warning to save the army.

Or he might suggest a successful strategy. Dolvid could see himself at the elbow of Sebhal Saidhanati, offering wise counsel. If he could hide aboard a ship, the next difficulty would be admittance to the Great House at Kamsilat, where —

"What worm-tracks are these?" at-Aval demanded behind his shoulder. Dolvid was beginning to see this *manadu* must be very stupid; this same scene was played whenever they did the Script. Like anyone who had used it for a time, Dolvid had departed somewhat from book forms, writing swiftly and fluently with a style even Faëdhal had complimented. As a soldier, at-Aval would have been the captain who complains a squadron-leader's shoulder-guard was not properly polished during the charge that won a battle. He saw himself as a sort of military figure, wearing an old sword-belt over the grey robe. In the scabbard he always kept a couple of hazel-rods, used both as pointers and for keeping discipline. One of the rods was tapping at Dolvid's piece of slate. "Is this how I showed you?"

Dolvid's breathing slowed and deepened. "No, *at'ai*."

"Then why do you not write as you are shown? Are you too stupid?"

As Dolvid said nothing, the rod began tapping on his shoulder.

"Answer me, boy."

"*At'ai*, I already know the Script of Shâl, very well. Also — "

"Oh, certainly. You could also read the inscriptions at ga-Tembúrai, not to mention the glyphs, ancient and middle. But you cannot write three forms in the Script of Shâl as you are shown. There is a mystery!"

Boys nearby laughed. He despised them. He at least knew what glyphs were, while these dolts were just cackling at words they did not understand, so as to please the bigger dolt. Dolvid said, "I shall learn the glyphs, *at'ai*, and also to interpret the inscriptions."

"Aye, every donkey has dreams of flying, when he has not yet learnt to walk on command." That gave at-Aval another general laugh. "Stand then, donkey."

Quite slowly he did so, knees beginning to shake. But his mind was calmer than his body, and he was quite clear he was not going to submit to a beating so unjust.

"Now, for a last time. Dolvidh, why can't you ever write as you are shown?"

If at-Aval reached for his arm Dolvid would swing his piece of slate two-handed, aiming for the elbow. "Because, *at'ai* — "

"Tell us. We are all waiting to hear."

Dolvid gabbled, "Because I write the Script much better than I'm shown." The gasp that only showed in the man's face was sounded by the boys. At-Aval's eyes squeezed narrow, knuckles where the rod was gripped going shiny-taut.

Then all the boys rose, touching forefingers to their hearts. Quiet-footed, *Menadhi* had come into the lesson-room. At-Aval hurriedly lowered his weapon and made half-deference, but *Menadhi*'s quick eye had taken in the scene.

He was carrying a browned, half-coiled piece of parchment. "At-Aval," pleasantly, "an excess of policy is bad for scholarship. This was given me by *g'Asalladh'* Himself, Who graciously wishes to know what can be made of it."

Obviously puzzled by this, at-Aval took the parchment, and peered. His mouth, very distant from the nose, twisted in concentration. "It is in the Owanilú," he reported, voice becoming squeaky. "Written in a form of the Script of Shâl, a form of it."

Benignly, *Menadhi* nodded.

"Here, in fact, is Shâl's own name. Yes, here too is the figure four, so it would be to do with Shâl IV. This is a rare and difficult style, *Menadhi*. A military report, might it be? These figures, here, and — yes. Here is *kímukol*, hundreds. As the boys should know, the armies of Shâl fought in *kímukol* — don't we still call a leader of paired squadrons a *kímukan*? *Konu kímukol*, five hundred troops... "

"Here is Dolvidh Vidukhat," *Menadhi* said agreeably. "Perhaps he can tell us something about this."

Thinking this was more of at-Aval's kind of humor, the boys laughed, though rather uncertainly in *Menadhi*'s presence. Dolvid stepped out, and took the stiff, crackling parchment in both hands.

The style was quaint, but nothing that should baffle *Menadhi*. There were words needing some thought, but Dolvid saw at once what he was looking at. "It is a bill of sale. Not, pardon me, *kímukol*, but *kímuko-frei*, *konu kímuko-frei*, five dry hundreds — it was a measure once used, but I can't say what it would be in our weight. They are dry hundreds of *fegha*, salt, and here's the price, given in silver and gold."

"Perhaps if you could give it more consideration, Dolvidh'. You can spare me this pupil, *at'ai*? There are other, similar leaves, and as I say, *g'Asalladh'* Himself — "

They both made the sign. "As it pleases you, *Menadhi*."

"Come then, Dolvidh." To leave a perplexed *manadu* and a stunned class, *Menadhi* guiding him from the room with a hand on his shoulder.

Outside, he took the parchment back, and walked a few paces down the long, silent hall, frowning slightly. "Our good at-Aval was astray, was he not, with his Shâl IV?"

"*Menadhi*. It is a sum of money, *radh shaël'*, four *shaëlil* — the gold coin of the First Empire."

"And for centuries after on Kamanta, where Night never came. It had a portrait head of the reigning *Nim'raibaki*, just as we have the plakhi, and the first showed the profile of Plakhat Gabh'Owan."

"But also *plakha* is `golden.'"

"True.   Gold coins for the son-of-gold.   Well."   He resumed walking. "It is good you did not draw attention to at-Aval's error. Positions, stations have to be preserved."

Up a stair, under a gilded archway with a representation of the Patriarch's Seal, saluted by a man of the *Adanum Plakh'*, *Menadhi* led the way to a room not seen before, low-ceilinged and restful, with a peat fire gleaming. On the wide, flagstoned hearth were several covered dishes, and the bronze *raminat* vessel, steaming softly on its tripod. Beside the fireplace were big leather cushions or hassocks. *Menadhi*, pulling off boots and shuffling into brocade slippers, waved Dolvid to be seated.

He did so without relaxing his wariness; the contrasts were too abrupt for anything approaching ease. Nine days had gone by, nine, he counted them again, trying to find more, since he had last taken food with *Menadhi*, since being told about the special position he could have here at the *Mankh'*, if he chose to stay.

Moreover, the scene in the lesson-room, or something near it, had clearly been anticipated by *Menadhi*, who must have brought the sheet of parchment with him only to humiliate at-Aval; how could Dolvid put full trust in a man who pretended to need help with a document he obviously could read with no difficulty? He was here and friendly, but could vanish again, leaving Dolvid to lash and rod and demeaning tasks: these comforts and confidences were not to be read as any sort of promise.

The *raminat* was spiced, and beneath the covers were

succulent things, a whole roast chicken, pickled green beans, a
sweetish mash, near-white with almost translucent and a few
purple-veined fragments. The last was identified as chestnuts,
rubhinul, which Dolvid had often heard of. He made peaty toast
from a fresh wheaten loaf, and there was pungent heather-honey
from Dramal. For a quarter-hour there was not much talk, what
little there was about food. *Menadhi* pretended not to notice
Dolvid's wolfish appetite.

He, slowing, asked about the success of *Menadhi*'s visit to
Tan Lughsai, and whether the *manal* were soon to reopen.

"Discouraging, in every way — " the response, almost as
to an equal, greatly relieved Dolvid. "The weather was hardly
warmer than at Kadon Dinul, and Lambarr *Rabhsai* was taken up
with his children." The youngest, Sai-Nivu, was three, but
Saëdhu would soon be giving birth again.

Menadhi picked toast-crumbs one by one from the lap of
his robe. "We must be patient. The *rabhsai* says he won't object
if the question of *manal* is raised in the Council of Thirteen, and
there the *Atarlum* has its good friends. In a long game, the tiles
always favor the *Mankh'*. Do you play *zhabhu*?"

"*Menadhi*, I have watched it played." A complicated
game, with a board where rival banners were set out, and skill was
needed to enclose conquered territory and capture enemy
standards. Luck came into it, too, with a bag of small tiles from
which players, at certain junctures, could choose to or were
obliged to draw, bettering or worsening their positions according
to markings on the tile.

"I may be able to teach you the beginnings, but *zhabhu* is
also the study of a lifetime, and never entirely mastered, good
training for the mind — and for the temper, too."

That gave Dolvid a small stab, wondering how much this
man knew about events here in his absence.

"We in the *Manadilum*," he went on, too casually,
"dedicate our lives to patience, in learning, in teaching. A long
line of men have been *Menadhi* before me, but above titles and
positions, we inherit the thoughts of our forerunners — and their

tasks. Actually, Dolvidh, I was much the age you are now when the *manal* were closed, and the then-*Menadhi* took me for his special pupil. He guided this Order through a stormy period, but he never doubted, not only that the *manal* would flourish again, but that the true Owan can one day be fully restored, and a new Empire, broader even than the Empire of Shâl IV, taking in all lands from the Eastern Ocean to the Western."

Dolvid felt the skin of his forearms tingle. "Is there an ocean in the Farthest West?"

"Oh, yes. And wide lands southward of the Kufshei, where there is gold and ivory, honey-sweet fruits and unimagined animals. They all could be part of a restored Empire. To conquer that new Empire would be the most stirring of adventures."

Eyes shining, he looked straight at Dolvid, who almost blushed. As always, *Menadhi* knew too much about him.

"But no more than an adventure. Holding it would be the task for serious men. With our Six Provinces, little toeholds in the south and the far northeast, the toy empire west of Arnan, we need skill just to hold this as one realm. Then how are we going to keep the Empire, once won?"

"Soldiers."

A smile. "Yes, they will be needed. But the soldiers will have to carry with them a faith in one realm. Can they? What if armies fall out among themselves, as has happened in the past? What is needed is acceptance by all of the Gift Yoëlladhu foresaw, a single mind, the Mind of Owan, encompassing not only written law but our customs and courtesies in how men and women deal with each other. All this is held in our Memory, *ga-Keghu-Owaniyu*. To speak about reopening the *manal*, Dolvidh, is only one part in the growth of the One Mind; it is the *Manadilum* that will be husbandmen to a new Owan." It seemed he could no longer sit still, and jumping up he paced and gesticulated excitedly. "To be *Menadhi, manadubalaki-manadul*, Teacher among teachers, is a burden of honor, and of duty to the realm that is to come, as well as the realm that is. You understand me?"

Dolvid, swept up with this tide, only nodded.

"All need to be taught, but my responsibility is to seek out the young with special gifts and special promise, who can share my larger work. And so, Dolvidh, you are here. You know our great Larghai is called *Nim'raibakim-dhanai*, the Mason of Empire. Not in my tenure, but a *Menadhi* to come is going to earn a prouder title, *Nim'raibakim-manadu* — and the Teacher of Empire will make that empire one."

It thrilled Dolvid to hear *Nim'raibakim-dhanai* again, and moved him more to be told (it seemed) he could be even greater. *Menadhi*, he saw, was the only one to have a true picture of his worth. How splendid, here with a grown-up, to see a better dream come from ruins of his old, discarded one. Obviously his father and all the others could never have said sarcastic things about the *Atarlum* if they had ever understood its aims. He wanted to be part of big deeds — and still he could hear the iron-door sound of *Mankh'*.

Menadhi read his face. "Service, Dolvidh, not servitude. But I do not believe you have learned to love the life here."

"No, *Menadhi*." In only an instant the noble vision of future empire was driven out by the terror, tedium and hardship of the past nine days. Injustice endured was swelling up inside him like a bubble.

"You must reflect," he suggested, "you remain saddened, as is natural, by the loss of your father. These losses may never lessen, but you must trust me, they do recede in time. In other circumstances — "

"I have hated it here."

The scorings deepened in the earnest face. "Your studies — "

Ever since mention of his father had supplied an acceptable reason, Dolvid's lower lip had been trembling. He sobbed out, "I haven't got any studies, except what a baby knows. The others, they can't write *ól*, they can't add seven to seven, they say I've never had sword-fights with the Heir, and then they mock me for my learning."

Menadhi sat back down on his hassock, waiting for this to subside. He leaned forward. "Dolvidh, did I not — Dolvidh, listen to me. Have I not promised you your own quarters, and that you would be my pupil?"

"Yes, you have, *Menadhi*."

"We have to have trust between us. It is unfortunate if the instructions I gave about you were misunderstood, but you will find even a very bitter rind can have sweet fruit clinging to it. You have sat among beginners, and see the hard task we face, teaching; a good lesson in itself, for one who might come to be *manadu* — or anyone else."

"*Menadhi*, I don't have anything that's mine."

"Not many have, here. But you have not taken an oath, and cannot, for long years yet. I want to show you a room that can be yours to work and sleep in, and you'll find your pens and others of your household goods have been brought there. Finish your *raminat*, and we'll go and see."

A bare little room with a wall-bunk, two rough chairs and a table; the window-seat turned out to be the lid of a deep chest. The view was westward, and Arnan was dull and heavy under a clouded afternoon, no sail in sight.

On wall-shelves Dolvid greeted familiar things; he caressed one of the blue drinking-mugs, picked up pens and touched his ink-block, opened his scribe's pouch to find inside the same used scraps of parchment, some partly sponged clear, where, at the time of his father's sickness, he had been trying to draw signs from the Syllabary. Tears began again, unbitter now, genuine grieving. There was no remedy for loss.

Menadhi said, "Despite our care, someone was before us at your house. No books were found there."

"No books?"

"We can't tell what else might have been taken. The blankets on your bed, here, are your own, the bowls and platters, the eating tools. Your bow is there, though it seems you will need new darts soon."

Dolvid felt duly ashamed of the mangy flights and untrue shafts of his five much-used arrows.

"That reminds me. We all have duties here besides learning, but I can't come back from a lengthy journey with a few hours to spare for tutoring, and find you are squeezing out laundry or some such thing. You have not yet seen the library? Well, at-Oradhai there has asked me to find him a new helper. He expects an *atarlai*, but you may know a little about the work; there will be books to mend, pages to clean and restore, perhaps some copying — "

"*Menadhi*, my own books, my father's books — " In control of his weeping, Dolvid was becoming angrily suspicious.

"A search is being made. We cannot command at Kadon Dinul, Dolvidh, only enquire and request. Let us keep hoping; they'll be known if they come to light, and there are not many places where such serious works can be offered for sale." He appeared truly concerned, perhaps as much at the failure of his powers as loss of the books.

"Shall I be allowed to leave the *Mankh*?"

"Tonight, if that is your choice." The disappointment in his face could not be mistaken. "Or tomorrow morning, you can be taken back to Kadon. But where in Kadon, Dolvidh?"

"No, *Menadhi*, I mean, if I stay here."

The head went to one side. "Leave, you mean, the Precinct? That is a privilege to be earned. You will have freedom, within reason, of the Estates, although — " he was smiling — "I'll set you tasks, yes. As with arms or legs, the talents you have need challenging into growth. Are you going to try us?"

Dolvid at last realized he was being treated with extraordinary consideration, even kindness, as this room stocked with his belongings showed. He found a towel, his own, and wiped his itching face, then made deference. "*Menadhi*, it is not mine to say I shall try the *Mankh'*, as ancient and holy as it is."

"Very good." *Menadhi* approved of this return to the proprieties, and in noting that, Dolvid was aware his trust was not yet given; with this man, even in submission he felt the need for strategy.

"You will find respect and even love grows, as fear of the unknown lessens. Welcome, Dolvidhai." Briefly but warmly, he was hugged.

V

Service

Not forgetting the miseries of that first week, he moved warily into his new life at the *Mankh'*, a cat nosing into risky sunlight. Exempt from the most menial tasks, from all but a few lessons with the others, he could sit up late with his books, so long as he remembered at-Oradhai expected him early at the library. *Menadhi* in person was to instruct Dolvid in ritual and what he called Inner History, and for mapmaking and measuring there was at-Dhanurai, far from stupid and surprisingly easygoing when he had neither a roster of duties nor a piece of stirrup-leather in his hands.

Of the others, Zhâlai, while not hiding envy, kept offering to do small favors; Yubhai would give a slow grin when he saw Dolvid, but Dravadhi kept his head down when passing in a corridor. Dolvid did not see much of them; he had his midday meal with at-Oradhai, and at other times was allowed to fill a plate in the kitchen. He had to wash his own clothes and keep his quarters clean, but those were things he was used to. Remembering hateful tasks, he would never make use of his night-jar, but even when the *Mankh'* was chilliest went padding along the hall to where there was an earth-closet. If it had been *Menadhi's* plan to teach him something with those first nine miserable days, in one sense he had succeeded; Dolvid never forgot he was of the privileged.

The *Mankh's* general library was far larger than the one at the New Residence, yet dreary, with its dank stone walls, and comfortless tables of the same discolored stone, a sprawled cavern with dim and dusty corners where no one, probably, had gone for years. Light came from tall, narrow windows high up, and from many *ga-ôdul*.

At-Oradhai was a gentle old man with blackened teeth, and the habit of plucking with thumb and forefinger at his chest, or shoulder, or thigh, as if his robes made him itch or prickle. His memory was prodigious but unpredictable; he could go hobbling with his stiff joints to the very spot where some unheard-of roll had lain unread for a generation, but then might fail to recall a commonplace and much-copied volume. He knew about Dolvid's past, and when he assigned a task calling for special care, "as it is done at the Residence" was his normal, mildly ironic instruction.

Offhandedly one day he mentioned he was kin to the present Patriarch; his grandnephew. Dolvid had not yet seen the aged Kamanasalladh, except distantly, being assisted from a ship at the wharves, but though at-Oradhai explained he was eldest son of the eldest son of the Patriarch's much-older brother, it was hard to imagine anything living could be two whole generations older than this venerable, creaking man.

No less muddling was to see familiar history from a new direction, that of the *Mankh'*, to hear *Menadhi* turn his world upside-down. There was Plakhsila `*Kímukoi*,' longest-reigned of all Gabh'Owan rulers, who had taken Sword (under guidance of a Protector) at the age of twelve, and held it till death in 2831, a few days short of his one hundred and sixth birthday. Once full-grown, he had been a strong *rabhsai*, father of Kadon Dinul as it now was, loved by the people, a hero to Dolvid's father. He was first to appoint a magistrate of Mixed descent, and had decreed that except for the few words in everyday use, the Owanilú would no longer be a required language for officers in royal service.

Though Dolvid had come to doubt the wisdom of putting the Other Races in positions of authority, that had not yet caused him to reconsider Plakhsila's reputation. But he was brought to that, learning the assault on the *manal* had begun with the *Kímukoi-Rabhsai*. "Now," *Menadhi* charged, "men rode under the colors of *rabhsayum*, untaught in what that banner stands for, or whence comes the right of the *rabhsai* to rule, to judge. Plakhsila, no doubt, had intentions he saw as noble, and his person commanded awe, but is it any wonder after his death the realm fell into dissent? Within less than half the years he reigned, his line, the House Gabh'Owan, was called extinct."

To Dolvid, taught strife had come largely from the ambitions of Kargul, the desire of the Families to regain waning influence, this too was a new way to see those years.

"Who is Sender?"
"Raëdh is Sender, Who is also End."
"Who gave the Land of Owan?"
"Aëlovoi is Giver, She the Earth, Moon and Tide." The room was lighted by a single masked *ôdu*. Their language was the Owanilú, with responses scarcely louder than the soft questions.
"To whom was the Gift?"
"To Yoëlladhu Founder, whose laws we obey."
"Whence came Yoëlladhu?"
"From the heights."
"When can the Gift be whole again?"
"When the Four are obeyed in all."
"What is the Number of Wholeness?"
"Four is the Number of Wholeness. Wholeness is Raëdh, Who is fourfold, Whose Beginning is beyond all ends."

The moment for the lamp to be uncovered, and for *Menadhi* to pour *raminat* from the bronze pot. "You are pale," touching Dolvid's cheek. "Now the weather is better, there might be duties to take you out into the air. You admire good horses, I've heard. What would you say to carrying water for the stables?"

"*Menadhi*, the stables of the *Adanum*?"

A grunt. "The men of the *Adanum* are as other soldiers, men who drink and swear, laugh and sleep, take wives and get sons. Only enemies of g'*Asalladh*' have anything to fear from them. I am told they have been known to lend a mount for a canter about the Estates — this is not my business to command, you understand, but they are good to lads they take to. Do you want the task? There may be cleaning out to do."

"I would like that, yes, *Menadhi*." He was still shy of the dreaded *Adanum Plakh'*, but was ready to face *jinzal* for a chance of riding again. After his first week at the *Mankh'*, mucking out after horses was nothing to scare him.

The rednosed Silnath said, "Fetch me my practice sword, lad, so I can teach these louts a few things." He was a senior file-leader, a brawny Islander, looking forward to being part of the escort when the Patriarch went to the Summer Palace. Silnath was not a young man, but his bride of less than a year was waiting for him there, at Drin b'Afon in central Kamanta.

The louts were four young apprentices to the *Adanum*, inexpertly clashing their practice swords together in the sunlit courtyard. Skirting them, Dolvid went to the weapons rack, remembering Kheval, trying not to display contempt. The ungainly fighters were all between sixteen and seventeen, the age when some of the pupils at the *Mankh'*, instead of continuing to study as priests, chose the *Adanum* — or were chosen for it by their aptitudes and failings.

Silnath's blade under his arm, Dolvid started back. The nearest apprentice, tall and slender with a flat face, bounded in his path with a snarl, flourishing his own guarded blade.

"Yield, dog," menacingly.

Hardly thinking, Dolvid whipped Silnath's weapon from under his arm, and disarmed the youth, whose grip had been careless. Frowning back over his shoulder, he stooped for his sword, and, rearmed, lunged overlong. Dolvid parried, stepped in to lock hilts, and disarmed him again.

The sword was retrieved once more, and Dolvid had to defend against a wild, whistling attack. In the absence of any counter, it drove him to the center of the courtyard, though in not the slightest danger of being touched. Angered by the ease of Dolvid's parries, and trying to use superior height, the youth, when they again locked hilts, pressed down with all force. Dolvid set his back foot, feinted to hold, then whipped away his weapon, skipping back and aside. His adversary went face-first into the sand and gravel.

Of the other apprentices, the one left without a partner, then the other pair, had stopped to watch. Two thoroughly enjoyed the baffling of their comrade, but the third, a beef-faced lad, came in a pikeman's charge, sword-arm stiff. Dolvid turned him and sidestepped, to find his original assailant waving a weapon again. Blocking crude swipes, he circled nimbly to prevent the two dividing, and with a rapid double change of direction had them stumbling into each other. When the rawfaced one shook free, going right to make a mow from the flank, Dolvid made use of Kheval's favorite and most startling disarm, sword flung back over the swordsman's plunging shoulder.

"Ho, now — " Silnath came lumbering up, a smile on his battered face. Taking his blade from Dolvid, he made the earliest challenger give up his sword, and had Dolvid tie on the straw-packed throat-guard before continuing. Even with its guarded edge, a full stroke of the practice sword could lacerate unprotected flesh.

Not by a long mile Kheval, nor anything resembling his pupils, Silnath was a plain, experienced fighter, his big advantages in height, weight and muscle offsetting Dolvid's better teaching. The apprentices watched in fascination, clapping each exchange, cheering for a hit, and soon Dolvid, though his arm was tiring, let enjoyment show. There was one long moment when he was dizzied by the strangeness of it all, the bright sun, the stables shadowed, gravel crunching beneath his feet, as he clashed blades with an officer of the *Adanum Plakh'*.

Silnath panted out little comments in his Island accent; "Pretty," or, "No, too clever — " when Dolvid tried a trap that might have worked with an opponent near his own reach. At last Silnath said, "Enough for a young arm, say?" They saluted each other, and lowered their points.

After taking off their guards they sat in the sun, and Silnath gave Dolvid his first half-mug of beer, having allotted Dolvid's afternoon tasks to another lad so they could sit and talk swordplay.

"What about the edges, lad?" He meant the cavalry sword, used more for cutting than thrusting. "Well, you're a bit small for that, say? Give you a year's growth, you can take on all comers. Plenty of time — you'll come with us, when? Two years? More — three?"

"Four years before I can speak the Lesser Oaths."
"Mainland boy? Kadon, say?"
"But I shan't be coming to the *Adanum*."
Silnath sought sense in this. "You — your pardon. Family? Should've known, sword style straight from the Residence, old Kheval to the life. Pardon, you're not son to the *nim'* of anywhere, are you? Not the Heir."
"The Heir is only nine."
"Tall, though, for his age, so they say. No, they'd never have the Heir down here shovelling dung. What?" Face filled with disbelief, Silnath found the only remaining answer. "Not *atarlai*, never, not you. Waste that pair of wrists? Don't mistake me, wonderful folk, the *atarlal*, some of them, and where would the realm be without them, eh? But, Hrafi, it's a waste; not six men in all the *Adanum* know swords to say they know swords. All that muttering, never a tobhai to call your own. Listen, I could have a word with my squadron, and he could speak to the under-captain, say? we'll have you out of the robe and into a tunic before we leave for the Island."

"I thank you — " flattered, though if he still wanted to be a soldier he would not choose the *Adanum*, jogging in companies to escort the Person. "But it would never be permitted."

"You'll see them ride in tomorrow," Silnath, wistfully, trying to breed wistfulness. "Three squadrons, under the Gold. Ride yourself, say?"

"Not *pefrai*, I mean, I never have." Dolvid's speech was beginning to go with the careful step of a Dramali rope-walker seen long ago at the Great Pledging.

Silnath cackled. "The *Adanum*'s not anxious to lend out its *pefral*. There's the piebald there, not much for looks, but been a steady saddle-horse in his day. Good riding in the Estates, you don't go too far south, where it's an ankle-breaker. When you're free, say."

"I thank you, File Silnath." He wished he could go at once, for the renewed joy of being on a horse's back.

"Just the same, I'm speaking to my squadron about you. Tonight."

"No, don't." Dolvid put down his mug, leaving a little beer.

"Too good for the *Adanum*, is it?"

"No, no." When it came to taking easy offence, Dolvid saw an uneducated Owani was not much different from the uneducated Others he had met. With painstaking care, he explained just why he would never ride with the *Adanum Plakh'*.

Silnath listened, shaking his head. "*Menadhi*. I thank you, sir." He made the forefinger sign. "You'd been *Edhrodilum*, *Nôdhilum*, even the *Ramadilum*, though a boy who has the healer's voice, they don't like to lose him. But *Menadhi*, oh. Sooner ask *g'Asalladh'*, I would, for a loan of the Seal."

Zhâlai came cautiously to the door of Dolvid's room.

"Yes?"

"I have strawberries, Dolvidh." He was carrying a small wooden bowl, two-handed.

"Not from the plots of the *Edhrodilum*?"

A nervous laugh. "No. They're from Kadon Dinul. One with privileges brought them back with him."

A puzzle here; food-smuggling was a thriving business; pupils in their last year before taking the Greater Oaths were allowed weekly journeys to Kadon Dinul, and most brought back as much food as they could conceal. Almost all of it ended up in the hands of certain younger boys, who could get out of the most unpleasant duties by trading fresh fruit, sweets, pastries, meat pies. Easy to guess the original smugglers obtained these supplies by acting as scribes, or helping small shopkeepers add their accounts, but the mystery was the middle step. Except with the few boys of family, who kept to themselves, there was no money at the *Mankh'*, and Dolvid was sure the bigger boys did not give the food away for nothing. What was their return for all the trouble and risk?

"You don't want these yourself?"

"There's more — I've had lots. These are yours, only I must have the bowl back — oh, it doesn't have to be now. There was no need." Dolvid had rolled the yellow-tipped strawberries out onto his table, blocking the runaway escape of some with his free hand.

"Good," trying one.

"Dolvidh...?"

"Yes?"

"You often have *raminat* with *Menadhi*..."

"Yes?"

"Nothing. Dolvidh, do you understand measuring the height of a tower?"

"Don't you?"

"Almost. But the rod you use — must it always be the same length?"

With a sigh, Dolvid slid a torn piece of parchment through the throng of strawberries. He dipped his pen. "Here, then, is the tower," drawing it.

"My father — " Dolvid swallowed, and tried again. He had to go warily, testing accusations he had grown up with. "My father said at the end of the Night, when the plague, when *Konúrai* came, the *Atarlum* withheld healing from the Others, till they would accept the overlordship of the Owanil." It was out.

"Strong words." *Menadhi* was unruffled. "There are other ways to say it: Patriarchs of that rough era could not send the *ramidul* among the Other Races without assurances they would not be attacked. We think of the Gabhanil as a hospitable people, but in those suspicious years they did not always welcome strangers. But what is this about accepting Owani rule? Had they not already sought out Owanil to lead them in the Wars of Cleansing?"

"Pir Kallikuk was not an Owani." The most famous hero of those triumphant years leading up to the Return, 2477.

"Well, Pir did have Owani blood on his mother's side — the Gabhanil, of course, kept records of descent only in male line. And then Kallikuk journeyed to the Island. Not as a warrior; that soil has never been stained by an invader. He went as one day you shall go, as suppliant, and bowed to the guidance of g'Asalladh'."

"The Other Races say he was the father of Plakhat Gabh'Owan."

"Yes, I have heard the tale," smiling. "Do you believe after keeping Memory unspoiled for six centuries of exile, the Patriarch put the Sword in alien hands? He — "

"Ga-Kamanasalladh VI." Dolvid responded to a gesture.

"Yes, ga-Kamanasalladh; He Himself named Plakhat, who took the surname *Gabh'Owan* to proclaim his intention, to be *Gâvu Owaniyu*, the Shield of Owan. His blood could be traced back to the Shâls, and they first met on Pir Kallikuk's second visit to the Island. In age they were as father and son, but unrelated by blood."

Dolvid had been taught Plakhat's surname, Gabh'Owan, was taken to signify he meant to be *rabhsai* for both peoples, Gabhani and Owani. But *Menadhi*'s version was much more plausible, considering how Plakhat had worked to restore the Owani aristocracy.

Though distant doubts lingered about the fairness of Owanil methods, he was gratified to hear these new versions of old events; it truly did not damage memories of his father to find these explanations that fit so much better. The Owani race was best by far, and must always have been the leaders.

Menadhi had been pondering. "Tell me, Dolvidh, if I gave you themes in history to write about, would you seek out books and rolls for yourself? This would be your own work, not mere copying. A question, for example, never settled, is whether Old Owan had the keystone arch for itself, or borrowed the device from architects of Ancient Vrobhan. But for that, I'm afraid, you might have to visit both the Island and the city of Dônshei, where the leading Vrobanil captives came, after their defeat."

"The fate of Lost Plakhan." This excited Dolvid, and he was eager to show there were puzzles in history he had heard about.

"No, no, not the Bride-Quest." *Menadhi* was very grave. "It brings in too many things that have bewildered the best scholars — for that one, you will have to wait till you are older. I would choose a smaller test to begin with. One thing that has never been certain, for instance, is whether a second child was born to Plakhat II and Tinalu during their exile in the South — in your birthplace, was it not? — and, if there was indeed a daughter, what became of her."

Dolvid tried not to show the let-down this was. Plakhat II, known as *Arnaël*, `Exile', the deposed *rabhsai*, was about as far from a hero as was imaginable, with his many futile years at Thenimala, trying feebly to claim back his realm by sending messages demanding submission. The chance of adventure had quickly turned to boredom.

His feelings were not well enough hidden; *Menadhi* saw. "This question should not take long to satisfy. Afterwards, you could, after all, look into the development of the keystone arch. There might be records, it occurs to me, in the Old Library."

"At the Bronze Residence?"

"The volumes there are, to our inconvenience, joint property of *Atarlum* and *rabhsayum*. They would be better cared-for here at the *Mankh'*, where we have ample space, but..." The tone conceded even his powers had limits. "Well, you'll have to study them there."

Dolvid was incredulous. "*Menadhi*, only last-year pupils — "

"Do not instruct me in the rules, young friend. Do you suppose I cannot have that set aside?"

"Your pardon."

The face stayed stern. "If I permit this, would you spend

the time wisely? We can't have boys in the tunic of the *Mankh'* loitering in Harbor Way, or romping in the Gardens of Kamzhinu."

The names, and that he would see those places again, increased Dolvid's excitement, and he started to stammer his thanks, and vows of good conduct all at once.

"Here is a token," going to a chest to take out a small disc depicting the Seal, hung on a fine chain. "Wear it about your neck. It will get you past the Precinct gates, and the doors at the Bronze Residence." Having put the chain over Dolvid's head, *Menadhi* left small hands resting lightly on his shoulders.

"Go when you have no other duties. I shall expect to see some writings in ten days. Your token can also get you a ride on one of the wagons." He took away his hands. "Or perhaps by now you have made friends at the stables."

"*Menadhi* — " making deference. This time, the small cold tremor of feeling this man knew everything that happened was swamped away in happy anticipation: he was going to see the walls of Kadon Dinul once more.

The piebald's name, Nuril, meant `Smiles,' and he had, truly, the face of a good-natured tippler. His gait, however, was anything but drunken; on Nuril's back it might be possible to pen fine manuscripts while riding for Kadon Dinul, and never make a blot. Once over the rise, out of sight of the *Mankh'*, he did urge Nuril into a canter, but there was a reproachful toss to the blunt head, and Dolvid soon let the horse settle back into his bland walk.

Even without the feeling of release from imprisonment, without the luxury of being unwatched, the day would have been a glorious one; full summer, with bees scrambling over the meadow-flowers, a light breeze out of the southeast. Small beeches were glossy, lindens full-fleshed, grass rich. With a more mettlesome mount Dolvid might have ridden cross-country, but even on or near the road, where there was little human traffic, he saw many rabbits, a pair of busy hedgehogs, the sharp face of a fox who peered out from bushes long enough to remind Dolvid of

Menadhi, flickering away as the horse approached. A plodding wagon piled high with sods came into view, neared, and rumbled on for the *Mankh'*, its driver not answering a raised hand. Farther on, he overtook a pot-man pushing his handcart with its ribbons of bright solder, forms of baked clay for hammering out dents, a bundle of tinder-cord hung along the side. The man, a leathery Mixed with a friendly face, must have been working at the *Mankh'*; there were no houses out here.

So blithe he had not noticed his own impatience, Dolvid climbed the last curving rise. His heart leapt as he looked down to where the western walls of Kadon stood, and the sharp Spear of Yoëlladhu next to the grey-green cornices of the Old Bronze Residence. Away to the right, wagons and horsemen were raising dust on the Tan Lughsai road, and beyond, the fields of the Heartland, more different greens than could be numbered. The seagulls had come back to Arnan shore after last month's gales, but above the city walls swallows were darting and flashing, and the distant New Residence was fresh and brave in the sun.

Yet this was not a homecoming; he would not ride up the Avenue to Market Way, then on up to the house to wait for his father to come home full of tales about Residence doings.

He left Nuril at small stables partly cut into the grassy mound of the Bronze Residence, but did not yet go up the nearby steps to the side entrance. Remembering his pledge, he would not enter the city, but surely he could risk a few minutes looking at the shops where Harbor Way began. There was a jeweler near the end of the row, and goldsmith, both shop and forge, like a cavern of marvels, where half-naked, shiny men worked with crucible and tongs, or others bent over work at benches, blacksmiths in little, using magically tiny hammers and punches, pliers and files. An apprentice who recognized Dolvid missed a pump of his bellows to wave greeting. The lifetime away from Kadon shrank down to the reality of not many weeks.

Up by Harbor Gate was a murmuring; a small crowd was gathering there. Tipsy with freedom, he ambled that way. Three boys his own age came at the run behind, shouting and giggling, dodging merchants and their customers. One, an Owani, jostled Dolvid in passing, turned back with a look to take in the short summer tunic. He gave a hard laugh, saying something about `*Mankh*" to his nearest friend. They ran on, and a seller of smoked meats grumbled about declining manners, while Dolvid fingered the disc *Menadhi* had hung round his neck.

To acclaim from the watchers, a crisp half-squadron of Household, breastplates dazzling, came into the Square from southward. Wheeling by the Spear, they trotted in through the opened gate. Behind them came a looser knot of riders, also cheered. Dolvid worked out the *rabhsai* must be returning from Tan Lughsai; he caught sight of several of the court functionaries, Rhunsilakh a sack in the saddle, small Arvus riding with long stirrups, gesticulating in all directions. Then he saw Faëdhal, dignified, very upright except for the round of his shoulders.

At the same time, Faëdhal noticed him. He spoke a word to Rhunsilakh, and turning his dark mount, rode to where Dolvid stood, all at once overcast with despondency, not certain why. He reached to take the horse's head, and Faëdhal dismounted somewhat cumbersomely.

"My dear, dear Dolvidh." Faëdhal took the free hand between his long-fingered ones, and pressed it. "My dear Dolvidh, *bi namakil shudal yi-butraghal ul.*"

"*Y'olagh am, dhanakai.*" Surprisingly, he was very glad to see the Master of Tongues.

A small boy was gazing at the horse, and Faëdhal, beckoning him over, gave him a small coin to lead the animal through the gate and give it into care of the guards. Faëdhal then took Dolvid's arm, and conducted him to the nearby pie-shop. They came out with a cup each of sweet fruit-drink, and a finger-scorching mutton pie for Dolvid.

They crossed the Way, to sit on the green bank, backs to the low, wavy wall of the Bronze Residence. Faëdhal's first words then were, "The *Atarlum*, Dolvidh? How is this? I have known you were taken to the *Mankh*'; that much the *ramidu* would tell me."

"At-Sepivadhi."

"The same. It was just before court left for Tan Lughsai. I had resolved to make enquiries as to your present whereabouts and condition, just as soon as we returned — judge my astonishment when yours is the first face I glimpse at Kadon Dinul! Are you well? The Treaty, still our guide, forbids the *Atarlum* to take any boy or girl against the parents' will. The *rabhsai* is coming back by water, and should be here tomorrow; it would be simple to place before him this matter of your, um, your abduction." Faëdhal made a dubious lip at the *Mankh'* tunic.

"Master, *Menadhi* has been very good to me. I am not a captive."

"As it would appear. *Menadhi*, of all — not that he is not, let me say, a man of real learning; there is little even I — well, let us say, little anyone could teach him about forms of the Old Tongue. We need not worry about the soundness of his instruction in that. I myself, in point of fact, began at the *manai* near Kred Bakali. Indeed, I was among the last pupils there, before the closing."

Dolvid heard a hint of blame. "The *Atarlum* had no choice."

"I have small doubt," after a sharp glance, "that would be your teacher's view of it. Are they turning you into *atarlai* then, Dolvidh? That, if you will forgive plain speaking, would not have been your good father's wish." Now he seemed indignant. "The realm cannot afford such losses; Vidukh was scarcely older than I. Younger, perhaps."

Dolvid had never supposed otherwise. He said, "I couldn't take any oaths, till I'm sixteen."

"True enough. If that was all of it, if, as you say, you are treated well, it would not be a bad thing, till you are able to make your own way in the world. But the *Atarlum*, Dolvidh!" He fingered the tunic. "Livery, livery, as your good father would say."

"But my father — " There was no finish.

"He was his own man. A man, let me say, of

extraordinary strength, in ways you might not guess. He was beyond question the only one in his position ever to maintain a separate house, instead of sleeping under the roof of the Residence. Largely, I would venture, for your sake, despite the hardship it also entailed."

"I don't understand."

"It was, if you will forgive me, his salary. With his stubbornness, he won the right to his own house, but the salary for his post assumed otherwise; he had to pay for food and lodging, his and yours, out of moneys meant only for clothing and the few added comforts of one living in the servants' wing at the Residence. Small wonder his furnishings and books were less than he would have liked."

"His books and mine are lost."

After a pause, "Not so." Faëdhal struggled. "My dear Dolvidh, I am afraid I have played thief. When I came to your house and found things as they were, yourself gone and the *Atarlum*, as it were, in charge, I contrived to have the *ramidu* called away to an imagined illness. In his absence, I had Vidukh's few books carried to my house, where they still are." He raised a hand to prevent Dolvid speaking. "They are, need I say, yours for the asking. A careful inventory was made."

"But why?" Faëdhal's unexpected tactical resource was a quite separate question.

"There is also a sum, a small sum of money. Your father honored me by sharing the secret of its hiding-place, and to it is added his final salary. When he was lying ill, I had intended to bring that money to him, in case it was needed. As for the books — " He searched for a way to say what he meant. "They include several works where the *Mankh'* has often expressed a strong preference, a very strong preference for its own versions. To the extent, I may say, of wanting to have all other editions destroyed. Your good father's leaning toward histories unblessed by the *Atarlum* led me to the opinion, mistakenly, perhaps, that his library might be better kept in safety, till you are able to, um — to make your own determination."

"*Menadhi* has had men looking for my books."

Complacent eyelids predicted it would be a long search. Then the face became shrewder. "Ah. Well, if you are certain, the books can be sent off to the *Mankh'* for you tomorrow — today. My only thought was to forestall condemning them to the fire. Or, shall we say, to imprisonment."

"*Menadhi*," Dolvid persisted, "said I could have my own books. He wants me to study everything." Faëdhal's level gaze was disconcerting. Dolvid displayed *Menadhi*'s token. "He is letting me come to the Old Library. Just the same as my father, he says history has to take in many other studies, letters, dispatches, even contracts and bills of sale. He tells me to read everything I can."

"Forbidding nothing?"

"Nothing. That is, except what is too near our own, our own eyes to be seen in perspective." He remembered the Bride-Quest. "Or a few things he says I am not old enough to study properly."

"Ah."

"It hasn't got anything to do with things my father used to say, about the *Atarlum* keeping down the poor Other Races and all that."

"Well, then," the face did not change. "You would want me to send your books along to the *Mankh'*."

After coming near annoyance with Faëdhal's skepticism, Dolvid was abruptly reluctant. "There's not a wagon for the *Mankh'* every day."

"True. And if you are going to be allowed to come here, there is no need, if I may venture, to settle this now. You know my house? — certainly you do. You can always leave a message for me there. Or a written message would get to me at the Residence, humble as my position may be." Faëdhal seldom forgot a Master of Tongues did not rank as *bôdh'loiki*.

"My father never said anything about refusing to live at the Residence." He did not doubt Faëdhal's word, but it puzzled him.

"One might assume he guessed you would fail to

understand the choice he made. To embrace, as one might say, some degree of hardship."

"Nor do I understand." Doubly: there would be more sense if it had been the other way about, and his father had been paid for giving up the glory of the Residence. "What didn't he like about living there?"

"To my mind? May I answer as I believe your father might? He would say, as I surmise, for the lowly, as for the highborn, there is no danger in living among great lords, and being at their call; neither has a standing that can be harmed. But for those of us who do not rule, but want to avoid being, as we may say, owned by those who do, four walls and a door, and a table for meals — that is more than a place to live. One might without being unduly fanciful call them one's title."

"My father had a title, Keeper of Books. If we had lived at the Residence — " and Dolvid, out of all the imagined benefits, startled himself by nearly blurting he would not have been taken to the *Mankh'*.

"It is likely you would have become an apprentice at the library. In due course, no doubt, succeeding to your father's post. But that, if I may say so, remains easily within your reach. The Treaty of the Wind Caves, as far as I am aware, is not yet a discredited document. Practically speaking, your *Menadhi* could never refuse to produce your person, if the demand were to come from the Residence." Faëdhal grew avid. "If, indeed, you, at this very moment, were to ask for refuge there, the *Atarlum* could never lay hands on you. Come with me, Dolvidh; I can assure you you will be safe."

Ridiculous how much he was tempted; the dreary prospect of one day following his father, as against the vast visions *Menadhi* held out, Keeper of Books instead of Guardian of Empire. He shook his head, and felt pain in refusing the familiar. "Master, I am trusted at the *Mankh'*. I have no reason to run away."

"I would be the last — " watching his face, "to urge a course that might not be in your best interest. I am certainly no seer, and it may be, after all, the *Mankh'* is your best refuge for the next few years, if you can escape, shall we say, its infections. Are you sure, Dolvidh?"

"Infections?"   Faëdhal could not mean exactly that. "There are the *ramidul*."

"Would you not rather come to the Residence with me?"

It still pulled at him, and he had to remember his father would not be there, either. "I wish," he fumbled. "I wish it would not be for ever, if I say no."

That brightened Faëdhal. "Nor is it. Not in the least. Your whereabouts are known for certain, and the law will not change. At any time, should you, ah — " He became fastidiously delicate. "I would regard any help given as a duty owed to your father's memory, should you ever turn to me. If I may, as with your books, I shall hold the money till you need it; there will never be impediment to your claiming it. Although — um..." With a small cough, he went to his pouch, and took out a handful of small change. "It might be as well, might it not, for you to have a little ready money, if only for cooked food when you come here to the city." He passed over about the equivalent of a plakhi.

"I thank you, Master," brushing pie crumbs from mouth and chin.

"Very good, but thanks are not needed; the money is your own, and you can call on me again when you need more. Also call on me if you need any advice. True, perhaps, I have small knowledge of the world, but I shall try to give answers your father might have. That little man had a large heart, Dolvidh, a heart that knew right, no matter, you will pardon me, what the *Mankh'* might say. Not enough of us have worked to keep alive the dreams of Banak-rai. I, for one, am proud, proud — "

A fresh shout from Harbor Gate, and Faëdhal could turn away, clearing his throat noisily, putting a long finger to the corner of his eye. Another detachment of Household was crossing the Square, and under the white banner Laluvoi was being escorted in, tiny, straight in the saddle.

The horses vanished through the Gate. "Master," with peculiar reluctance. "I should be at my work."

"Yes, well, duties, however unimportant, are waiting for me, too. You are quite sure, Dolvidh, you will not come with me instead?"

The battle was still a mystery. "I thank you, Master." Dolvid broke away from troubled eyes. "I can't."

The *Mankh'* had its rhythms, like Arnan, slow and steady, measured in seasons and years instead of hours and days. High summer was slowest of all; *g'Asalladh'* left for his summer home, and except for enough to guard doors and gates, the *Adanum* went to the Island with Him. The four Heads of Order came and went, crossing and recrossing the glassy Arnan; messengers arrived and departed without urgency; pupils of high birth had gone home to their families, and boys of no rank yawned at their lessons and were beaten by bored teachers.

Deprived of a horse now Silnath was absent, Dolvid walked to the Bronze Residence over the baking road, or sat impatient in a crawling wagon, coming back dry and drowsy, dust clotted at corners of mouth and eyes.

Inside the *Mankh'* there was always cool, a quiet chill seeming to press from the huge stones of the building itself. In the long centuries that were the Night of Owan this had stood empty, when not used as a storehouse or fortress for this chieftain or that warlord. There had been several attempts to burn it down, but nothing had harmed the bottommost courses of massive stonework, and after the Return the newer *Mankh'* had been raised on the stump of the old. How the heavy blocks of the original structure had ever been set in place was a mystery, but Dolvid, wandering in their shade, concluded it must have been simply many strong arms and backs, slaves, after the defeat of Vrobhan and absorbing of their empire, lashed into a thousand-legged machine for lifting.

Most of the carving on the early stonework was weathered to a blur, but in one inlet of the building sheltered from wind and rain, an arched entranceway closed in the rebuilding, Dolvid discovered a frieze where the sculpting kept its sharp detail. In particular, one caught his eye, a head in profile, wearing the tiered crown of the Vrobanil. It could only be Shaëlai, Shâl I, conqueror of Vrobhan, yet the features were like someone else, and at last he recognized who; eyes set deep in pits above iron cheekbones, nose a curved wedge above planed lips — exactly the face of an older Dravadhi. He remembered first sight of Dravadhi, the disturbing impression of age, and Dolvid laughed, thinking he could start a legend that instead of dying Shaëlai had retired to the Island, and at last came back to the *Mankh'* after eighteen centuries in the albeit dull-witted shape of Dravadhi. All the same, such a joke, frowned over by the heavy walls of the *Mankh'*, made him shiver just a little.

As summer passed and the sun lost its force, the cool inside, welcome at first, became a clinging chill, in winter a nagging cold, to change hands into clumsy bundles of dead flesh. Dolvid's room had a tiny grate, and he was allowed to take smoking sods from the kitchen fires, and carry them to his quarters in a battered bucket. While wind moaned outside, he would move his table next to the half-hearted gleam, and sit reading, his eyes smarting from the sour smoke. An oil-lamp was, after all, in some ways better than an *ôdu*-light; he could wrap his hands gratefully around the hot earthenware base, before plunging under his blankets to lie rigid and shivering, shuffling off his clothes only when he stayed awake long enough for the bed to lose a part of its chill. On coldest nights it was hard to believe there was not an actual source of cold under his bunk, sending wave after wave of burning cold through mattress, cover and blanket, making his feet into dead, alien things.

When *Menadhi* summoned him, it was a reprieve. In winter they always met in the room with the flagstone hearth, and there was a good fire, which might be wood, but as often the rare and costly sea-stone, a shiny black stuff like a softish rock, which burnt many hours with yellow and blue flames, and later with the fierce glow of a smith's charcoal huffed up with bellows.

There was usually food, too, dates, perhaps apricots, or either baked in pastry, honey-cakes or a crumbly wheat bread with apples at its heart. All this would wait, and the *raminat*-pot sat on its stand, steaming softly, while *Menadhi*, room dimmed, took Dolvid through the Responses once again:

"*Shilai Toladhit ôl?*"

"*Raëdhi Toladhit ôl, ai embi Ofrat ôl,*" Dolvid answered.

"*Shilai Owani-aëbhu an yaëlo?*"

"*Aëlovoi Yoëlu ôl, o Lukhu, Aëlu, Finnal n'ôl.*"

"*Shilai-ne ga-Yalit yaëlo wa?*"

"*Ne Yoëlladhu Yoëlladhai, b'ai ga-Koëlul inawal ul.*"

"*Shibani Yoëlladho laro wa?*"

"*Bi teghil lai laro wa.*"

"*Shil'shu ke-daradhi Yoëlut owan?*"

"*Amshu ga-Radh' la rava inanol owan.*"

"*Akshi ga-Radhumi-ridho ôl?*"

"*Radhi ga-Radhumi-ridho ôl. Ga-Radhumit Raëdhi ôl, b'ai ridho radhizan ôl, b'ai akhadu kinaënit bi ravul nedhul ôl.*"

"*Olagh am, Dolvidhai.*" At last *Menadhi* uncovered the *ôdul*, and reached for a plate of oat-cakes. "Soon we can begin the *ga-Rakul*. Some of that is kept from you, till you take Lesser Oaths, but the *Lalaru* you can learn." When he dropped from Owanilú into ordinary language, it was the shedding of a ceremonial robe, handsomely ornate, but stiff and restricting.

He questioned Dolvid about his researches, and heard Plakhat *Arnaël* had indeed fathered a daughter, who had died young. The dullness Dolvid felt vanished when they turned to the other question, and he happily recounted how, after conquest of Vrobhan, Shaëlil had invited the nobles of that shattered empire to come and learn the ways of Owan at Dônshei, then the capital. This, Dolvid proudly pointed out, was no later than 1190.

"Yes, and?" *Menadhi* prompted.

"Ifbleni the Scribe says Shâl XIV wanted records of old Vrobani building, and sent learned men there, before their ancient cities and shrines fell into complete ruin. They found both corbelled and keystone arches. But that was three centuries after Vrobhan had been restored within the Empire, in 1480, so there is no proof whether architects of Vrobhan taught the Owanil, or learned from them. There are very old buildings with keystone arches at Dônshei, in the Schools there, but no one says they're from before the Vrobanil came in 1190."

"An open question, then?"

Dolvid was just warming to his subject. "Well, but on the Island, where there were never any Vrobanil captives, the arch at the head of the Sacred Valley, Lunu Midhi, was built long after 1190, and it is corbelled, or so it is shown in the drawing."

"That drawing, as you will see with your own eyes in due course, is correct."

"Well, then..." turning up his palms.

"What is your opinion?" *Menadhi* demanded, startling Dolvid, who might have been flattered, except for worry about how his ideas would be received.

He swallowed. "The Dônshei Schools have a central Shrine of Zhôl," he began. "The chroniclers agree, the Vrobanil always claimed Zhôl as their own god. As we do, they celebrated Spring Halving as the day of His birth. In this they all agree." A nervous point, when Zhôl was called Son of Raëdh and Aëlovoi; how could He also be a foreign god?

Menadhi was encouraging. "Many peoples love Zhôl," he agreed.

"Then the Schools could really be the work of Vrobanil builders. If at the time they were conquered, they had just then invented the keystone, they would have brought the knowledge with them to Dônshei — Undaëni Shei, as its name was then. Naturally."

"You must never be over-sure." Having started embarrassment, *Menadhi* bestowed his smile. "Nevertheless, you have done well. When you write your treatise, by all means give your conjectures, but call them such. And do not forget to name the chroniclers who write about Zhôl, and His importance to

Vrobhan. I expect us to read it through a week from today. When it is perfected, we shall have it recopied; it should be in the Library, it seems to me, beside what has already been written."

Dolvid was deeply thrilled. The recorders he had consulted, named and nameless, were as much legends as the events they dealt with, and now he would have a little place beside them. Mixed with pride was a good part of relief; after all he was allowed to praise accomplishments of races other than his own. With Ancient Vrobhan, anyway.

The next prescribed venture caused fresh flutters of fear, an account of the abdication of Kanavakh, which came very near the edge of a subject previously forbidden. Not because too recent; if, next to the depths of time Dolvid had been diving in, Kanavakh was only yesterday, he had still been dead more than three hundred years. But *Menadhi* had told him to stay away from Plakhan's Bride-Quest, and Kanavakh was Plakhan's younger brother. He would never have been *rabhsai* but for Plakhan's disappearance, and everyone would have been better off. Kanavakh was notorious as `Vakh'biSegh,' Blood-Red, his nine-year reign crowded with killings and cruelties.

"It would be interesting," *Menadhi* suggested, as he prepared to pour *raminat*, "to determine whether his forced abdication was only agreed-to, or, as some say, brought about by the Patriarch of that time..."

"Ga-Owan-Alladh..." trying hard to get the number right. "Owan-Alladh XV."

Menadhi nodded. He was pleased, and his manner as they sipped the spiced *raminat* together was pleasantly unawing. Dolvid wished in every vein he could get rid of misgivings the encounter with Faëdhal had renewed, wished he could stop watching for traps. So much here he was coming to love: the grand feeling of riding to Kadon Dinul with a Patriarchal token at his neck, these talks, when things he would have studied just for the pleasure of knowing also became accomplishments to win the praise of *Menadhi*. It was good to be near the treasuries of learning, and be able to plunge hands elbow-deep into rich hoards of stored wisdom. Best, the sense of alliance with an enfolding permanence, where what he did, much of the time, was prescribed, not by his teacher or the needs of now, but by rules and customs tested through centuries. He would love to belong completely, accept the sunlit future *Menadhi* mapped, let himself be carried by this giant, safe river flowing through all ages. To surrender to that would be so easy, but for the silly, nagging doubts.

"You will find Kanavakh a challenging study, I think." What was in that to make Dolvid look for more than one meaning?

South and east of the *Mankh'* there ran a long, low ridge, man-made, with small garden-plots on the farther side, where the *Edhrodilum* taught its pupils secrets of growing, and made trials in cross-breeding and grafting of plants. Came a day when sunshine went beyond mere promise of coming warmth, and Dolvid climbed the ridge. Arnan was sparkling, brown earth was dusted with palest green, and the air flowed sweetly out of the south, life returning to the Paowan. He opened his outshirt, and wished he could open his skin, so sun could drive out the cold that had burrowed into his bones.

The nearest wing of the *Mankh'* was where the *nôd'yanul* were, and behind there was a walled courtyard, where (said the knowing) girls took fresh air and exercise. Dolvid was not high enough to see down into the court, but his eye was held by fluttering that came and went. Soon he realized he was watching, not girls leaping in a dance, but a line of drying laundry, swinging to and fro in the same breeze that lifted the clothes. Bright blue, primrose yellow, pale orange; women's clothing, and acutely he wished he was back at Kadon Dinul, where there were women and girls, whose walking or riding made their cloaks and gowns flutter and ripple, and whose hair swayed gently against soft faces. A novel wish, connected to the idea of new growth the wind set stirring, a pressure, a pleasant dread, a looking-forward.

"What else can I teach you?" The usual question at the end of a lesson.

Oh, so much! The Bride-Quest, all the events of 2876, whether the *Mankh'* still sought outward power to rival *rabhsayum*. "The *nôd'yanul, Menadhi* — "

The smile threatened to become a chuckle. "I have been expecting that. But I am afraid there is a good deal you cannot yet understand, not till your body and your feelings are ready for it."

"But — "

"It is a puzzle. I know," but Dolvid did not see how he could ever know that: the mysteries of his own body unpicked in the emptiness of night, hungry, parched, unjoyful pleasures.

"One of the peculiarities of this generous gift," soberly. "Is that we could mate long before we are ready to, ready in our persons. If we could teach mating, not just the act, but all the muddlings of body and mind, even heart, if that could be taught, these waiting years might vanish. But I am dubious. It is a huge force, Dolvidh, and can crush us like ants as easily as turn us into giants. Besides, we are Heirs of Raëdh and Aëlovoi; it is a large-hearted gift to us, but brings duties with it, too."

"Mating does?" — wondering if he meant marriage.

"Life, as men and women. A kitten can learn in a few short weeks all it needs to be a cat — to hunt, to clean itself, sleep warm, fight its enemies, run from those it can't fight. Before its year is out, it is a cat, and can father or conceive kittens of its own. But cats remain cats; the ages go by, and they do not learn much more than to hunt, clean themselves, run from danger, bury their leavings, and sleep warm. Dogs can be taught a few tricks, but cannot pass them on to their sons and daughters. If Raëdh had decreed men and women would be ready to mate so soon — in five years, or even ten — perhaps we would never have learned more than any animal does."

Dolvid did not quite see why. "Could we not mate first —"

"And then learn? Learn letters and language, history and lore, counting, measurement, law, the skills our hands can master?

Dolvidh, there is a best time for learning. Oh, we can learn at any age, but the foundations must be laid before our heads get cluttered with the day's needs, or our blood is muddled with soft lips and tender words. If that chance goes by, it is lost. If we mated as children we would soon be struggling to provide for children of our own. It is good we are given a respite, and can learn what can help us provide, but beyond that, far beyond, the belief that built this *Mankh'* is in knowledge much deeper than what is needed simply to live and make new life. Maëdhi asks us not only to obey, but to grow in wisdom, and leave a legacy of growth."

"*Menadhi* — " Dutifully, Dolvid had made Maëdhi's forefinger sign, but this was nothing new, except as set off, rather obscurely, against mating.

"Patience. The long wait between thirst and drinking needs to be understood. Now — " He interlaced the very tips of his fingers, and regarded Dolvid with an approach to humor. "Take my word, many of your questions are going to answer themselves, as time passes. As for the *nôd'yanul*, you know they are maintained at the *zhani-margul* everywhere in the Six Provinces — and there is also one in the Colony, west of Banakit. Formerly, long ago, *nôd'yanul* were found in cities; once there were more than a thousand. The number of *nôd'yanul* is far smaller today."

"Why are they not at the *doni-margul* now?"

"In those days they could also go to the houses of the highborn. But some — " he leant hard on that word, so it was understood he meant the Other Races — "said they ruined good marriages. A lie; even of the week-wives or a common town-whore, the opposite is often true. Marriage, with us, is from Aëlovoi, Whom we most honor; our *nôd'yanul*, seen without bias, can strengthen its ties. In later years this will be plain to you."

It was unclear his question had been answered. "If so —
"

"The *Mankh'* must occasionally make concessions, even to what the unwise say and believe. As things are, only travellers can enjoy the *nôd'yanul*, and a *nôd'yanu* is not permitted to see the same man so often as to form an attachment. No reasonable wife can complain about that — no Owaniyu wife does, so far as I have heard."

Dolvid knew marriage was different, in ways he did not comprehend, for Others. "*Menadhi*, are men of Other Race forbidden to visit *nôd'yanul*?"

"Not at all, many do. Nor is there anything to say their women may not be trained as *nôd'yanul*. But the superstitions descending from their Gabhani past are quaintest when it comes to mating; what Island families see as an honor, they call a disgrace, and their pretense no daughter of theirs could ever please a man outside marriage means girls of Other Race become town-whores, untrained, unlettered, despised, living in danger, instead of sharing in the education and high standing enjoyed by our girls. At the end of her service, with her accomplishments and the dowry-lands she earns in the six years, any *nôd'yanu* can make a good marriage."

"When men of Other Race visit *nôd'yanul* — " trying to untangle his bewilderment — "aren't they pleased, then?"

By the shake of his head *Menadhi* was no less baffled. "A wise question, my friend. As near as I can perceive, an age-long habit of thought with a Gabhani man is to divide all womankind into two sorts; one kind for play, the other for motherhood and the hearth. This second kind they revere, even while, to an Owani mind, treating their wives as goods to be owned, and this reverence makes the other kind all the more necessary to them. That, perhaps, is why they despise the women that give them pleasure; those we need are a danger to us."

"But women of Other Race — they also despise them —" remembering how Esodra's nose would wrinkle up when she mentioned such women.

A sigh. "Don't ask me to explain; with you I can only observe and wonder. The Others do not even make the elementary distinction between one of their town-whores and a fully trained *nôd'yanu*. That is as if your friend Master Kheval could be lumped together with a street-brawler. But the Gabhani mind resists change, though there are not many left who could claim unmixed Gabhani blood. In Upper Ân, more than once we have needed troops to prevent a Gabhani mob from burning down the *margú* on Luskran Bay. In cities, by their nature, blood is admixed, and feelings do not run as high; the Others have more chance to learn our ways. At Kadon Dinul, even a man calling himself pure Gabhani could no longer force his wife to take sash, though not many years ago it was their sure sign of a married woman. Married, or spoken for."

"But there are women of the Owanil who take sash, too." His mother had, though he was not sure what it meant.

"Choose to, there is the whole distinction," gazing earnestly at the low ceiling. "Where Yoëlladhu Founder speaks about wedlock, He says not a word about ownership of another person, or of that person's pleasures. We, I mean the Owanil, have long seen it as a sign of the uncouth, that a man in some way owns his wife, or she him. Yoëlladhu speaks elsewhere about the act of mating, but marriage He deals with as a question of sharing — of property, to be sure, but also the upbringing, welfare and inheritance of children, comforts, oneness of beliefs. Earlier, when any mating might bring about conception, there was reason to keep that, too, within wedlock: women feared being left to care for a child alone, and men wanted to be certain the sons that came were theirs. But even now there are no doubt many who prefer to keep their beds and their most intimate pleasures only for a husband or wife. Some of our own women, as you say, to signify this, have borrowed the Gabhani custom of wearing the marriage-sash. But should it be a badge, Dolvidh, chosen and proudly worn, or the mark that brands cattle? The Gabhanil have not refused the *Atarlum*'s gift of sport without conception, but have never outgrown the primitive notion a man's honor demands imposing the sash on his wife. In backward, country parts, to this day there are women killed, yes, *killed* for an hour with a man not their husband, and unmarried girls said to have sported with a man may never find a lifelong mate. Here at Kadon, and in other cities, with the protection of our Owani law, the women of Other Race are beginning to enjoy increased freedom."

"Isn't the law the same everywhere?"

"As written, yes. But in a huddle of farms the other side of Yuvakh Din, *Rabhsai*'s Law, I fear, may count for less than what is decreed by an ignorant head-man, out of his obsolete customs. That is the ignorance our *Manadilum* has to fight against, Dolvidh, with ancestral ways as our stubbornest enemy."

"Is that why — ?"

"Yes?"

"I was about to say, going against their old customs must be why the Others, many of them, hate the *Atarlum*." Not saying he had been stopped by the thought that his father, or Faëdhal, who also had small use for the *Mankh'*, were not Others.

"Indeed, and not only the *Atarlum*." *Menadhi* was grave, but still showed his pleasure in Dolvid's perception. "A question I have pondered more than half my life, and cannot do better than to say that somewhere in their past, perhaps before they ever came across the Eastern Ocean to our shores, the Gabhanil were poisoned with the notion all mating is in some way evil. Strange, when no race who kept to it could go on existing, but you can see if we held enjoying food was a wrong, we would not stop needing it, and might end by scorning our best cooks much as the Others despise the *nôd'yanul*. But it goes beyond that. Hating the need and ashamed of the pleasure of mating, they also despise the Owanil for lacking those feelings. Never forget that, Dolvidh. A lot is said in this realm about making all races as one, ending the so-called privilege enjoyed by the Owanil and those who follow our ways. We all have, and should have, the same rights in law, but that does not make the customs of any race as good as any others, and do not forget you will always be hated by some, just for being a son of Yoëlladhu, and an heir to his Enlightenment."

"But *Menadhi* — " not ready to let go of the original subject. "If women enjoy mating, too..."

"Why should there be *nôd'yanul*? Or you might put it the other way, why are there no *nôd'adanal*. Once again, I can only speculate. I chose very early to marry the *Atarlum*, and know little about the minds and feelings of women. That is also a choice; more than one Patriarch has had a wife, and there are married *atarlal*, especially in the *Nôdhilum* and the *Edhrodilum*; we have women among the *ramidul*. But many of us, and especially in the *Manadilum*, do not expect to marry. The paths we take are seldom part of living as such, and can not be understood by most women, whose life is life, Aëlovoi's Gift. That Gift might hold an answer to your question. Surely there are women who enjoy the game of mating as an end in itself, as men do. But usually a woman, I surmise, wants other things; companionship, lasting tenderness, a father for her children.

"Yes — " catching the question before it left Dolvid's mouth. "Men want companionship, too, tenderness, a mother for their sons. Sometimes. Men are divided creatures, at war with what is, while women, to my inexpert eye, are often more singleminded in their wants; they desire the very haven of rest, the settled state, some men see as an enemy. Many women, so I am persuaded, wish it was their nature to enjoy bedding just for the sport, but always find themselves trying to take a captive, unwilling to move on from the partner once picked. Then, too, though they surely enjoy the sport once begun, most women do not have a man's overmastering urgency to mate; that is what allows them choice."

"But the *nôd'yanul* can't choose who they bed with — " taking up the only part of all this he clearly understood.

"Good." A nod of approval. "Very true, they cannot, although, as I told you, having served their indenture, they can find their husbands, and have a much wider choice because of their service. Are they such a long way, then, from a boy who would wish to be, as it might be, a maker of history, but who becomes apprenticed to, let us say, a craft of little interest to him, so he can make his way in the world, until better chances come along?"

Dolvid answered by dipping his head, as always confused by how much *Menadhi* knew about him. Actually, he supposed, anyone who could speak with Rhunsilakh at the Residence might have heard about the enameller. But that did not explain away the double meaning in *maker of history*.

"For their first two years here," *Menadhi* went on, "the girls we accept, but for being trained additionally in dance and song, learn the same as boys their age, things they otherwise would never know; to read and write in ordinary letters, to speak the Owanilú acceptably. But the following two years are, I venture, what you are most interested in."

"The other boys talk," Dolvid complained. "I can't tell how much of it is true."

"Well, we could satisfy their curiosity earlier, except for the foolishness of boys who are not ready to accept the mystery and the power of this gift, along with the pleasure. With you, there is hope."

"Is it true last-year boys can visit the *nôd'yanul*?"

"The *nôd'yanul*-to-be. The custom has double value. The *Nôdhilum* can teach a great deal, but doing is the only way to learn some things. Such as 'breaking the colt,' as it is called, which as *nôd'yanul* they will need to know. In many good families it remains a tradition, when a boy is fifteen or sixteen, for his father to take him on a journey, so they can stop at one of the *zhani-margul*, and the boy can receive pleasant instruction for his manhood, and are so made the better teachers themselves, should they find for wife a girl as-yet unschooled. On the other hand, youths with the *Manadilum*, just when studying for the Greater Oaths, may lose capacity for work, because of their unruly bodies. Some, not all, and many make different choices. We do not let any boy go to the girls whenever the mood strikes him, and no one is allowed to go back to the same girl again in a month. Still, the visits are a high privilege. After their training, the young women would be lovely, even if all you wanted was to pass an hour or two in cultured conversation, sharing *raminat*, listening to music or witnessing dance in the pure forms of Ancient Owan.

"As for the bed, the *Nôdhilum* possesses wisdom of the body, and can teach skills that you can hardly imagine; those joys may be transient, but they are fierce while they last..." Small fingers rewoven, he sat silent, and Dolvid half-expected a personal reminiscence, a small gap in the armor of generalized fact and settled opinion. He was not altogether sure he wanted that from *Menadhi*, not on this subject. He had found there was always foolishness when mating was talked about in detail, and did not like to contemplate *Menadhi's* cool world overlapping into the taut and overheated speculation of the general sleeping-quarters.

He ventured, "But there are boys, you say, *Menadhi*, who do not want that?"

"You have heard of men called *anib'anul*?"

"I have heard the word. My father said they're the same as what the Others call Changers."

"Perhaps — " but he was not pleased. "Words we use bring with them a legacy of feelings, and this is another of the subjects where we of Owan can never defer to the ignorance of Others. Changer: their word can hardly be spoken without also borrowing their contempt for what they call unnatural ways. Unnatural — the Others are farmers, and before that were hunters and trappers, and must have observed everywhere in nature, horses, dogs, cats, rabbits, everything that mates, has been seen also to mate like to like, so what can *unnatural* mean — ?" This had a force not displayed before; he checked himself, and put out a hand to test if the *raminat* was still warm, but did not pour any more.

"I have said," he made a new start, "service, complete devotion to Maëdhi, can mean not having a wife. But yet there are needs, for affection, companionship, understanding. Two men, both in that service, can join together, and their love need not compete with their devotion; it can become part of it, and each will be a better servant of the One Mind for what they give each other. This is especially so where one of them has experience, judgment, even wisdom it may be, and the other has the eager hopes, the energy and the beauty of youth; each then increases the other."

"But — " Dolvid heard the start of a stammer. Puzzled beyond anything before in his life, he sensed there was a flaw somewhere in *Menadhi*'s explanation, a sidestepping. For one thing, Dolvid did not see what the fierce hungers he had felt, or fierce future joys *Menadhi* promised, had to do with the other, with companionship and tenderness. But beyond that, it was Raëdh mating with Aëlovoi whose union brought forth Zhôl, not like to like, but unlike parts forming a perfect Whole; day's gold, night's silver, rain on thirsty earth — all this came in the *kolukezhal* they chanted to the Sender and the Giver, and must be more than just words.

Menadhi leant to pat his shoulder. "I said there would be a lot you could not yet understand. Nothing is wasted; it is good to store away mysteries, fruit picked green to ripen in the dark. Patience, always patience is needed."

"For yours with all my questions, I thank you, *Menadhi*." In the smile that was his answer could be seen the faint tint of condescension, and had the painful feeling he had come out very stupid today.

He became almost-friends with Zhâlai again. The small boy, no matter how rudely sent away, kept coming back, and while Dolvid was too proud to confess being lonely, he had to admit he had begun to welcome the nuisance. Grateful for company, he could still be led to say more than was judicious, and later cursed himself for telling Zhâlai about seeing Dravadhi's face carved in an ancient frieze.

Dravadhi heard about it in an hour, and came to see Dolvid, but only to ask exactly where the carving was. After that, he was proud of the nickname `Shâl-face,' and Dolvid, the inventor, became as popular as his ways allowed, occasionally giving up his kitchen privileges to share a meal and gossip at the long table with the others.

Even large, slow Yubhai became cordial. He had, or was allowed to boast, a vast store of information on the subject of women, the main ways a girl's body between shoulder and thigh differed from theirs, the various methods there were for having sport, most sounding very silly to Dolvid, and none of them promising much pleasure.

Yet, since having the urges of his body in part explained in the long session with *Menadhi,* a faint light had dawned. Now he could understand the special friendships between older and younger pupils at the *Mankh',* although recalling *Menadhi's* words he could not see much wisdom on one side or beauty on the other. Among the tangled terrors of his earliest days here, a young man wearing the belt to show he had taken Lesser Oaths had come up to ask, "Are you spoken for?" Seeing he was not understood, the last-year pupil had laughed and walked away; now it was clear, and clear how gifts of smuggled food came to certain boys — to Zhâlai, for one.

But new knowledge went beyond where it was learned. The Gabhanil — the Mixed, that was, who clung to the ways of the Gabhani component of their ancestry — they not only had different noses, eyes, peculiar customs, they really were different. Stupid. *Menadhi* had said *ignorant,* but to call mating evil when they enjoyed it and would soon die out without it, was stupidity. Now Dolvid could stop being puzzled about the *Song of Tales.*

Though assembled by the *Atarlum,* the *Song* was Gabhani history, their own account, and the only one for happenings on the Mainland during virtually all the Night of Owan, when most of the Owanil were in exile on the Island. There, chroniclers meticulously recorded centuries almost without event, but for the momentous doings that became the Wars of Cleansing, and led to the Return, there was, regrettably, only the muddled and muddling Gabhani history. In the *Song of Tales* the war-captains of the Gabhanil were courageous and worthy, but their fights never were with any clear objective, nor, till they found Owanil leaders, much planning or persistence. But once see them as brave but stupid men, struggling with what they could not govern, warriors who occupied rather than ruled, and the picture emerged, through all half-told tales and contradictions, of a people made great by events too large for their understanding, suddenly within reach of a prize beyond their grasp.

Yet for all that, the *Song* was an assembling of fragments, tantalizing and exasperating, rather than a real, coherent history; always a relief to get back to periods covered by the orderly chroniclers of the *Mankh'*. Such as the task set by *Menadhi*, the abdication of Kanavakh.

He must begin by firmly setting aside the mystery of the elder brother, Plakhan `Rhaëli,' The Lost. Well after the famous Bride-Quest, he had suffered some unexplained tragedy to do with the birth of his first (most probably only) son, and had gone away, out of history, into the Farther West. This cryptic event, together with the later horrors of his brother's reign, had revived and attached to the name of Plakhan an older legend (told also of his grandfather, Plakhat I), *Rekh'Rabhsai*, the True *Rabhsai*, who, at a time when hope was dead, was to return out of the West to reclaim his realm.

Kanavakh, who became Heir with the disappearance of his brother, acceded on the death of their father, a dozen years later. No worse catastrophe (the Poet Nilradh said) befell the realm between Night and the Ní-Tilagh; Kanavakh's nickname, `Blood-Red,' once said to refer to the color of his hair, very soon became far more sinister.

In all history, even of Ancient Owan and certainly since the Return, execution of criminals had been rare, kept for traitors and the most callous murderers, but during Kanavakh's reign death was an ever-more-usual penalty, beginning with bandits and robbers, but as the *rabhsai*'s appetite grew, those accused of ever more trivial crimes. In the final year, the hanging of both men and women accused only of slighting the *rabhsai*'s dignity became so common the city gates were called Kanavakh's Orchards. But he also studied slower and more painful ways of killing, and descriptions of these revolted Dolvid, in whose vivid imagination everything was inflicted on him. He was relieved beyond words to get to where, after rioting at Kadon Dinul had brought a big new batch of gruesome executions, the Families, the Great Families and the Captains combined to depose Kanavakh, winning over the Household, which killed or disarmed the *rabhsai*'s personal guard, and seized the Person. He was given to the Patriarch's custody, and his son, Plakhval, became *rabhsai*.

The part played by the Patriarch, ga-Owan-Alladh XV, was not very clear. Certainly, He had not declined to keep Kanavakh a prisoner, and had seen to the swift proclaiming and investing of the new *rabhsai*. That suggested He was also part of the deposing, but a guess was not good enough; Dolvid needed documents.

At the *Mankh'* library, the best place to look, old at-Oradhai helped guide Dolvid's researches, even bringing him a pile of texts: to have a kinsman of the present Patriarch as his clerk, however briefly, was a heady experience. But very soon Dolvid began to think he had been set an unreal task. With no shortage of writing on the subject, for the *Atarlum* there was hardly a moment's doubt ga-Owan-Alladh had been not only a participant, but instigator and chief architect of the alliance forcing Kanavakh's abdication. One chronicler approached the boastful in recording the meeting at Treaty Stone, not far from where Dolvid now sat, where the Patriarch satisfied Himself Plakhval was fit to rule; all writers of the *Mankh'* betrayed satisfaction when *Atarlum* was in the ascendant over *rabhsayum*. Another gave supposed texts for the Patriarch's letters to the provincial overlords and the Captain of the Household. All Patriarchal correspondence was kept secret, but the chronicler, working in living memory of these events, clearly knew such documents existed, and their gist.

Lately, *Menadhi* had begun to touch on the importance, to a faithful son of the *Mankh'*, of "knowing and not-knowing." Dolvid did not quite grasp what this meant, except it had to do with humility, and winning battles against pride in one's own cleverness; there were occasions, *Menadhi* said, when accepting belief could serve a truth larger than petty victories in disputing what was agreed. Not clear, but, without understanding how, he sensed this meant every task was a test, not only of ability, but reliability.

Irritated, he wished he could simply write about what

happened, instead of trying to guess what was wanted. He surely was not expected to challenge the general view of Owan-Alladh XV as an indefatigable champion of Patriarchal power; what more was there to say? Through long days of a summer slow to die, his search went on, bent over faded texts while others lucky enough to be fairly stupid were splashing in the cool waters of Arnan.

Then, one afternoon in his dim alcove, a dream-bridge of sunshine thrusting through windows above, Dolvid noticed among his texts a book he was not permitted to read, a small volume stamped on its calfskin cover with the Seal, which meant it was restricted to those who had taken all their Oaths. It ought to be handed back to at-Oradhai unopened, but the librarian was at the far end of the hall with his own tasks. Not yet deciding what he would do, Dolvid slid the small book under a pile of loose parchments, where it was completely hidden by drooping edges.

Opening a larger volume he was in the company of a familiar and always enjoyable acquaintance, a nameless *Atarlum* chronicler of the 2600s, whose penmanship was as recognizable as his chatty style, a few habitual spelling errors, and his weakness for picturesque digressions from the main narrative.

Turning back to the years before Kanavakh's accession, Dolvid could not find a word to support a wild conjecture the future tyrant had somehow helped cause his brother's disappearance. A little later, as always, the writer led him into unexpected territories:

> `Although all agree the surname* Red-as-Blood *was amply earned in Kanavakh's deeds, the name had been bestowed long before, only to describe his appearance. His very name, Kana-vakh, supports the assertion he was born with a full head of copper-colored hair, as has been seen in the Gabh'Owani House, and is common among the baKargul'. Some later claimed to have foretold from this his blood-craving nature.*

> *On the other hand, I have spoken with a*
> *learned man who says the name* Red-as-
> Blood *was acquired later in boyhood, when*
> *began Kanavakh's lifelong habit of flushing*
> *deeply from neck to scalp, particularly when*
> *he was thwarted or contradicted, be the*
> *matter never so slight. As a young man he is*
> *said to have made all effort to maintain a*
> *reputation for a mild disposition, being*
> *constantly betrayed in this by his sudden*
> *coloring.*
>
> *I find many still alive can well recall the*
> *`blood-flush' in Kanavakh's face when he*
> *was condemning some unfortunate man or*
> *woman to die. In addition, his death at Drin*
> *b'Afon, on our Blessed Island, in 2580, four*
> *years after his deposing, was caused by an*
> *apoplexy.*
>
> *For all these reasons, I am inclined to the*
> *view that the name* Red-as-Blood *had not*
> *one but several meanings, in the earliest*
> *instance with reference to Kanavakh's*
> *complexion.'*

Here, then, was new information, including the cause and exact place of Kanavakh's death. Other sources said only Kamanta, but Drin b'Afon proved the Patriarch had kept the deposed *rabhsai* closely confined; the city where the Summer Palace stood was also famous for its impenetrable defenses. Perhaps they feared that Kanavakh, once free, might repudiate the forced abdication, and find fresh supporters.

Dipping his pen and reaching for unused parchment, Dolvid uncovered the little book with the forbidding Patriarchal Seal on its front. What his punishment might be for opening it Dolvid had no idea, but no one was anywhere near his alcove.

Inside, a flyleaf depicted a *ramminal* tree in full leaf, with the rays of a rising sun behind, a book from the *Ramadilum*.

It seemed small reward for the risk he was taking, a treatise on healing, recopied this century in ordinary letters, most likely from an original in the Script of Shâl. About to close the book and forget he had ever seen it, his eye was caught by a word, not very common but recently seen, *bikradhapaghai*, apoplexy. After a quick look from his alcove to be sure at-Oradhai was still busy, he began reading.

A quaint text and meant for those of the *Ramadilum*, but Dolvid made out it dealt with herbal remedies for choler. An extract compounded from various plants, several of which he did not recognize, was advised for acute attacks, `when the sufferer makes complaint of buzzing as of bees in his ears, or if flesh of the face is darkened by much blood beneath the skin.' It went on to warn this remedy, given too often or in doses too strong, had been known to bring on apoplexy and could cause the patient's death. The conclusion was an invocation to Hradhi, `Who teaches His servants how to divide strong poisons that they may bring His healing.'

Dolvid shut the book, and his hands were trembling. He heard a brisk, shuffling step, and slid the volume out of sight under parchments again, as at-Keliukh, who often worked here as a master-copyist, went wheezing past, with a nod of many chins for Dolvid.

Who sat in fierce thought, doing nothing. Plainly this book of healing had not come to him by accident; *Menadhi* might have said it was the Will of Maëdhi, but then he would also say Kanavakh's death had been the Will of Hrafi, and that did not have to mean no one had worked that Will.

Because Dolvid had discovered, had been meant to discover, that ga-Owan-Alladh XV, hero of this story, had duped and betrayed Kanavakh, in the end murdered him. `*Vakh'biSegh*' of the face that flushed was not to be mourned, but by the Treaty the Patriarch could judge and condemn only those of the *Atarlum*, and could not take any life. Nevertheless, while poisoning a captive was a cowardly act, it could not be called altogether an evil one, if there had been chance, however remote, that Kanavakh might have attempted regaining the Sword.

Then what was expected of Dolvid? Finding the book of remedies on his table meant he was not the first to see its bearing on Kanavakh's death, so the test for him was somewhere else. Was it whether he would admit to making use of a forbidden book? Perhaps, and beyond that, whether he would dare call ga-Owan-Alladh XV an assassin; it was all about discretion and his, Dolvid's, loyalty to the *Mankh'*.

Knowing, not-knowing. Service to Maëdhi the Wise meant learning everything he could, but Maëdhi was only one of the Four, Who together were Raëdh Himself. And serving Raëdh, *Menadhi* had obscurely hinted, might mean being able to forget part of what was evident. All the same, there would be no point if Dolvid pretended completely; *Menadhi* had to be aware he was choosing to forget, all preparation for Oaths that would one day be taken, acceptance of the *Atarlum*'s higher purpose, the renouncing of any right to judge, or even to see, an act in isolation. *Menadhi* himself must want to know, not-know, what Dolvid meant to forget about Owan-Alladh XV. This was not an easy test.

Zhâlai sat on the window-seat, legs folded under him. "There's an uprising at Narn." This was how news from the wider realm often came, one boy telling another what he had heard. The truth, at sixth or seventh hand, was always hard to judge, when everything else became flickering and unreal in this setting, the timeless *Mankh'*, wide Arnan, inviolable Kamanta, where nothing changed, out beyond the edge of vision.

"But the *rabhsai*," Zhâlai expanded, "is not going to send any extra soldiers to the West."

A resigned face. "Narn is in the farthest Northeast, beyond Yuvakh Din, not the West."

"No, Yuvakh is in Kargul."

"You must be thinking of Yuvat. Yuvakh Din is on the eastern borders of Ân."

"Well, if Narn isn't in the Colony, why have Lambarr *Rabhsai* and Saidhan *Asai* fallen out over troops? Saidhan is in the West."

Scorn increased. "Who told you the *rabhsai* has fallen out with Saidhan? Saidhan is Lambarr's father-in-law, and Laluvoi's oldest friend."

"But Saidhan wants a bigger army, and it's against the law."

"Where did you hear this?"

"From *Menadhi*."

Dolvid did not let jealousy rise. Probably Zhâlai had only been bringing *Menadhi* his *raminat*.

"Also, there are these Deniants near Kred Bakali saying they won't pay their taxes, unless they are allowed to nominate their own assessor. *Menadhi* says in all these events we see what happens when men who forswear the One Way are permitted — " Zhâlai's recall faltered, and he ended lamely, "— to be important."

"To aspire to high office in the realm — " drawing some consolation from being able to supply the measured phrasing. But it was usually with him *Menadhi* discussed such events, and besides he was anxious to find out how his treatise on Kanavakh had been received. *Menadhi* would soon be leaving to visit Tan Lughsai, and if he went before reading the work, Dolvid might have to wait weeks to hear anything. And he had not yet been given a new task.

Well, if *Menadhi* had time to talk with Zhâlai, he would have time for *raminat* later, and would send for Dolvid. In the library, helping, under at-Oradhai's painstaking direction, to restore faded old manuscripts, he looked up whenever the door swung open. Morning went, and he decreed *Menadhi*'s message would come about the second hour.

Near that time, the main doors opened, but it was only at-

Aval, hazel wands rattling in his scabbard. He gave a nod, as always nervously conscious how well Dolvid could define the limits of his learning.

By late afternoon at-Oradhai was making clucking comments about Dolvid's frequent use today of blade and brush to take out errors, while he, having gone from self-pity to lofty dismissal of *Menadhi*'s friendship, settled deeper into angry gloom.

Shâl-face, Dravadhi, at last came with the summons. "If he can be spared," the boy quoted to at-Oradhai, but Dolvid was already out of his seat, wiping stained fingers with a damp cloth.

The *raminat* was ready, and *Menadhi*, standing by the window, gave a westward wave of the hand, "A pity this golden autumn brings such a harvest of evils. Let us sit in peace, while we may." As on the first time, Arnan was glowing gold.

"Well," *Menadhi* conceded, as they sat, "it is not all bad news. Our Zhâlai has added kin. Petakoi has given Tovakh baKargul a son."

Dolvid half-smiled at the reference to Zhâlai's supposed relationship, and saw that news must be the only reason why *Menadhi* had spoken to the boy this morning.

Menadhi went on to speak about Petakoi as true daughter of the Island, with bloodlines from nobles of the First Empire. "Blood of the purest. Thus the *Atarlum* keeps the best of Owan alive — not least at Kadon Dinul."

In answer to a raised eyebrow, Dolvid nodded; the meaning was plain. Great Banak was of Mixed descent, but had married Laluvoi, of the best southern blood. Again, their son Lambarr's wife was from the Great Families; over generations, *Menadhi* was saying, the Gabhani strain in the Family would become insignificant. Still, while that might be happening, Dolvid did not see how the *Atarlum* could have influenced Lambarr's choice of Saëdhu, much less Banak's of Laluvoi, a match they had certainly been against. Then he remembered his father's friend Arvus saying, long ago, the *Mankh'* claimed credit when sun and rain came at the right season, but drought and floods were the unfathomable Will, "and fools swallow it." But Arvus was a Mixed, and a Deniant.

Menadhi gave approval of Dolvid's long and detailed work on the matter of Kanavakh. "You have done very well. In speculation, one might have wished for a little more daring — " he lingered a moment on that word. "But this is sound work. Tell me, what do you mean by — here it is, `*Kanavakh died at Drin b'Afon in 2580, but that does not mean that in helping to bring about the events of 2576, ga-Owan-Alladh saved the realm from only four more years of Kanavakh's tyranny. Famed for his choleric nature, Kanavakh, reigning at Kadon Dinul might have lived far longer.*' Explain."

This rope was trodden with care. "*Menadhi*, it is said Kanavakh's choler rose when he was thwarted in any way. Seeing himself deprived of *rabhsayum* would surely have hastened his death."

"I see." A long pause. "We do not condemn this, Dolvidh, but such matters might be better left to the *Ramadilum*. No doubt they could tell us much."

"Yes. No doubt." Eyes met, and everything was understood; here on both sides was perfect knowing, not-knowing.

Disappointingly, *Menadhi* did not set him any new tasks, only saying vaguely he could go on studying the epic poets of the Island years, whom Dolvid thought longwinded, imitative and boring.

"With the realm as it is, my journey to Tan Lughsai takes on new importance." This was introduction to an account of the events Zhâlai had muddled, without being completely astray. The *rabhsai*'s authority was indeed being challenged in three widely separated parts of his domains.

Farthest was Narn, remote port of the Northeast, lying several dayrides beyond the borders of the realm proper. Reports were not reliable, but there had been some sort of revolt against the Council of Elders that governed the port and its small hinterland.

Also true, there was a dispute between Saidhan and his son-in-law the *rabhsai*, over the size of the Army of the West. Plakhsila's Law regulated the numbers permitted for provincial armies, but Saidhan asserted the law had never been meant for the West, with its job of guarding a long, hostile frontier.

"In this," *Menadhi* sourly commented, "he follows an ancient tradition. Every Captain of the West sees a skirmish fought in the dust of Landegh as a dagger-thrust at the heart of the realm, needing the immediate raising of twenty new squadrons. Never a war-captain who did not want to ride at the head of bigger armies. But Saidhan *Asai* has never been greedy for his own glory. His son must be behind this."

"But Sebhal Saidhanati — " too eager, and he had to sober up. "Isn't he best of the new men? Winning his own fame so early?" There was a tale Sebhal, all alone, had gone into the midst of a hostile tribe and disarmed the head-man.

"He is young, as you say, and there is not much to choose between *bold* and *rash*. Saidhan is past sixty, no age for one of his blood, but he is perhaps looking ahead to retirement. If the Army of the West is permitted its new squadrons, a man whose judgment is yet to be proven may command forces stronger than any other in the realm. The *Mankh'* sees this as unwise."

"The *rabhsayu* is Sebhal's sister."

"As history shows, over and again, for the powerful and ambitious, kinship hardly means what it does to most of us. You know how — "

A soft tapping at the door interrupted him. Most who knocked then came in, but here there was a wait, and the tapping again.

"Yes?" *Menadhi* called.

The door was thrust open by an arm sleeved with the yellow piping of the *Adanum Plakh'*, but the knocking had been done by the old, robed man who came in, wisps of fine white hair fringing a squared, close-fitting cap. In haste *Menadhi* stood to make deep deference, thumb touched to heart, and Dolvid, amazed, did the same. He had seen the man at a distance, but not expected to be in the same room with Him, the Patriarch, ga-Kamanasalladh XI.

"*Yi-gatagh am Raëdho, Menadhai.*" Fogged by age, voice matched the blotched and worn face, gentle, filled with peace.

"*Yi-nampagh Raëdhi, g'Asalladhâo.*" A new bow from *Menadhi*. Only the Owanilú had cases for addressing the Patriarch, and Dolvid had his memory groping for forms learnt but never used. He did not want to be sent away, but hoped he might be overlooked.

Waving the guard to shut the door and wait, *g'Asalladh'* came to the middle of the room, slowly but not haltingly. He had been a big-framed man, and memory of His robustness still clung, thinned and faded, like His hair.

Staying in the Old Tongue, *Menadhi* said, "Would He graciously see one I have spoken of, this Dolvidh, son of Vidukh?"

"Ah, yes." Peering eyes came on Dolvid. "He knew thy father, a very good man."

"He is gracious, *g'Asalladhâo.*"

The Patriarch hummed wistfully. "He counsels thee, youth: study is good, but eyes must rest from close work, lest thy brain outlive its windows. Swing thy sword with Our *Adanum*, bend thy bow; no history was ever worse for being undertaken with sound wind and strong shoulders." Seated, He reached forward, and before *Menadhi* could move, served Himself with a small cup of *raminat*. The broad, spotted hands were still very capable, as they must have been when He was of the *Edhrodilum*, out in all weathers, advising and showing farmers how to improve their crops. Easy to imagine those hands, large now for their wrists, wrapped over a smoothed spade-handle, or thumbing soil.

"The lad may stay." *g'Asalladh'* forestalled the dismissal by *Menadhi*. "This is to be no lengthy council. Would there were no need to interrupt thy tutoring."

"His Enlightenment can never be interruption, High One." This, to Dolvid's ear, was a hair more than effusive courtesy, as if *Menadhi*, while flattered, nonetheless disapproved of a Patriarch who went padding about the *Mankh'* instead of summoning His servants — as all were.

G'Asalladh' insisted Dolvid sit also, and he did, placing his chair just outside what he felt to be an oval space belonging to the two men. Intent, he tried to appear simply unbored, alert for any command.

"Having chanced to encounter Laluvoi *Asayu* at Owan Sai this morning," the Patriarch resumed, "He wished to see you before your departure, to counsel what matters should be raised with Lambarr *Deghi*. Our good Laluvoi believes there is no difference between *rabhsai* and the West that cannot be resolved in discussions, face to face." A small smile. "Face to face in her presence, the meaning was."

"Yet, by His Graciousness, the excess troops, and the future Captaincy in the West, these matters must be raised, must they not? So that views of the *Atarlum* may be conveyed to the *rabhsai*?"

"The views of the *Atarlum* — " He gave a little grunt. "Unless at a meeting of the Council, had We offered Great Banak Our views as to the composition or command of the realm's armies, Our Enlightenment would have been lucky not to find Our blessed backside on the Residence steps."

Menadhi started a glance in the direction of Dolvid. Kamanasalladh waved a hand airily. "It contributes nothing to the blessed dignity of His Blessed Patriarchate, to enter into a quarrel between the *rabhsai* and his wife's father, on a question which, by the Treaty, is *rabhsayum*'s alone to decide, unless a change in actual law is sought in Council."

"By His Gracious leave," *Menadhi* said. "Has the *Mankh'*, then, not always stood ready to offer its reading of law?"

Another grunt. "Of law, yes. As Laluvoi observes, however, it is by no means clear Plakhsila's Law applies in this case, the Colony being no province, Captaincy of its armies the *rabhsai*'s to bestow, just as with the Household."

"*G'Asalladhâo*, by His leave, does it not remain true the *rabhsai* alone must judge what forces are necessary to the safety of the *rabhsai*'s realm?"

"As you say, the *rabhsai* alone, taking advice where he may seek it. It is no one's part to thrust counsel at him unasked."

"Does His Enlightenment then not wish me to undertake this journey to Tan Lughsai?"

A slow rubbing of the shrunken chin. As with hands, the ears and jutting nose seemed too large for the face. "No, not so, *Menadhi*, you must go. The question of these Deniants by Kred Bakali needs your attentions."

"There is also, by His leave, the question of Narn."

"Oh, Narn. As Laluvoi *Asayu* asks, where can Narn sell the goods it takes in, if not to this realm? What counsel could be offered to the *rabhsai* as to Narn, if not, patience?"

"Dignity, *g'Asalladhâo*, the sovereign power — " As he had twice before, *Menadhi* put a rein on himself. "Of this realm, of which Narn, by His Graciousness, has long been part."

This realm, Dolvid took note. In their private sessions it was always Owan, and long ago *Menadhi* had lied to him, saying that was the only name ever used here at the *Mankh'*.

"Better to reign in ten willing hearts," the Patriarch quoted, "than over ten thousand slaves." This was from *Zhanu ba g'Ati*, the Sayings of Zhôl. "Yet, *Menadhi*, if it is your desire, you may speak to the *rabhsai* of this. We do not believe Lambarr is willing to send large armies so far, for the sake of adding expense to his treasury. As for the *Atarlum*, We know of no sons or daughters eastward of Yuvakh Din. Now, as to this matter of the Deniants — "

This seemed a dull business compared with the others, but for *g'Asalladh'*, perhaps to the masked annoyance of *Menadhi*, clearly the most important. In the beginning, everyone had paid an *Atarlum* tax, till Banak-rai refused to oversee its collection, saying instead the *Atarlum* must ask for direct fees for actual services performed. But after a few years, it had been this very Patriarch who had made Banak change his mind, arguing that those who most needed the healing of the *ramidul*, the farming advice of the *edhradul*, were often those least able to pay.

The restored portion for the *Edhrodilum* was what the Kred Bakali Deniants were refusing to pay, and *g'Asalladh'* was unwavering on the point: all must contribute for the Growers, whether or not they believed themselves aided by them, just as everyone was taxed to help maintain the Army of the West, even if they felt no threat from beyond the far western frontier. Whatever his wishes that the Patriarch would bring the same decisiveness to the other questions, *Menadhi*'s warm concurrence here was real enough.

The interplay fascinated Dolvid, who had never had any notion there might be variances, even clashes of viewpoint, within the *Atarlum*. That *Menadhi* might not always speak for the entire *Mankh'* was a new idea, but in this talk he obviously saw far fewer limits to the powers of the Patriarch than the Patriarch did.

Not that there was anything contemptible in the milder views of this man, who had debated endlessly with Great Banak, and ended by calling him a friend. On the contrary, in conciliation there was hope; it might be possible to join what he had been taught by his father to what he now belonged to; in *g'Asalladh'*s gentler world, Plakhsila and Great Banak could be heroes again.

A word often heard at the *Mankh'* was *mai*, meaning both a certain quality, and the rapt emotions it aroused, the feeling of sacred places and things, the air surrounding chanting of a *kolukezh'*, contemplation of Raëdh, the presence of His Ministers as seen in a sunset, the Arnan at dawn, heard in thunder or a note of music echoing to silence. *Mai* was found in the serene beauty of Aëlovoi, goodness of Hrafi, thoughts of the inviolable Island; it was source of *ga-dazhai*, blessed dread, joy as well as fear for those devoted to the service of Raëdh. Decaying body, abrupt informalities, in every way a plainer man than *Menadhi*, Kamanasalladh was nevertheless surrounded by *mai*, and Dolvid knew it was not entirely due to of the office He held.

Ending *Menadhi*'s tentative attempts at getting Him to reconsider the question of Sebhal and the Army of the West, *g'Asalladh'* mentioned that Saidhan's other child would soon be leaving for the South. "Some have said," He offered slyly, "a large family is intended."

Menadhi smiled at the standard Lambarr-and-Saëdhu joke. At midwinter, but in the milder climate of Ninkufu, the *rabhsayu* would give birth for her seventh time.

"There can be seen the future. It may be this is only the old habit of hope when the harvest is seen to ripen, but He has hope, this old one. Can it not be seen as a measure of prosperity, of peace, that our troubles are such as they are, when once to speak of troubles was to say war and pillage, cruelty and dearth. We Ourselves have lived in six reigns — nay, it is so, youth — " He had noticed Dolvid's startled face. "We remember little of the *Kímukoi-Rabhsai*, but were born near the end of that reign."

This was dizzying; Plakhsila *Kímukoi* began building the New Residence a century-and-a-half ago. Clinging to his wits, Dolvid worked out the death of Plakhsila, after all, was not yet ninety years ago; Kamanasalladh was old, but part of the natural world. Many men and women of unmixed Owani descent lived to be a hundred.

"What the young call history," *g'Asalladh'* said, "can be someone's yesterday. What wouldst thou hear of, youth, of all He has witnessed?"

Though shy, Dolvid thought he could risk one question that had given him trouble. *Menadhi* had forbidden study of events as recent as the War of the Widowed, but was smiling indulgently at the Patriarch's indulgence. "*G'Asalladhâo*, by His Graciousness, would He remember if the harvest of 2876 was a good one?"

"When Banak's last war broke out? We spent much of that year on the Island, and later were in Nîv, as also the Colony, and do not remember it as is recorded in the Annals, cold and wet; it was, we think, not worse than many another year. Too often — " He turned to *Menadhi*, "the annalists have judged the whole world by what might be seen from a small window of this *Mankh'*, is it not true?"

"As His Enlightenment says — " again smiling, but *Menadhi* had flashed a furious glance at Dolvid, who wondered what this small bit of knowledge might cost him. In official history, poor harvests in 2876, making for general unrest, were blamed for helping bring about the war.

After the Patriarch, bestowing blessings, had left, there was an unquiet silence. "His Enlightenment is kindly." The return to ordinary language was like cold water in the face. "You should heed His advice about your eyes."

"I shall, *Menadhi*." As the door closed Dolvid had lost what he had not known was there, a feeling of protection. Evidently he was still afraid of this man.

The voice remained cool and exact. "These years have demanded kindness, a watchful conciliation. The *Atarlum* has been fortunate in His Enlightenment. The *Mankh'* stores up many kinds of virtue."

On the third afternoon of *Menadhi*'s absence Dolvid was eating a cold meal while reading in his room when Zhâlai came to say at-Dhanurai wanted him for work in the kitchens.

Dolvid stared at the small boy. "He's aware — you know I don't do those tasks. Tell him I have duties at the *Adanum* stables." When there, actually, he seldom did stable work now, but helped Silnath drill the apprentices in sword-fighting. Dolvid was losing part of Kheval's cultured style, but his strength was increasing.

"At-Dhanurai said you were to come, never mind what other tasks you might have."

"Tell him, *Menadhi* gave me my duties, and they are approved by *g'Asalladh'* Himself."

"Dolvidh, I'll get beaten if I come back with that story."

"No you won't. Don't be silly."

Zhâlai hovered. "You are sure to be beaten. He's getting fonder and fonder of the lash. You get five strokes just for being half a second late to a task. On the backside," he clarified helpfully, rubbing his own in reminiscence.

"At-Dhanurai knows very well — "

"Come and tell him yourself, then."

"It's been a year-and-a-half since I've done those tasks — " not wanting to give Zhâlai the chance of telling others how he came running to set things right. It was a mistake, or else an elaborate joke by the other boys.

He saw that must be it. Zhâlai was often turned into a bringer of false reports, sometimes knowingly, often in trusting good faith, as a double joke. If the others told him at-Dhanurai wanted to see Dolvid, he would never admit the order had not come direct from the *atarlai*. In the end, he got rid of Zhâlai, mouthing on about doom.

Having pushed the incident aside, Dolvid, washed after his afternoon at swordplay, was back with his books when two boys came. One was Yubhai, growing even beefier, getting a bull-neck early. The other Dolvid did not know, also big-limbed and broad.

Yubhai said, "At-Dhanurai sent us for you." Dolvid could not tell whether he was getting used to the Island accent, or whether this one was fading.

He did not get up. "The joke's finished. Zhâlai told me all about it."

Yubhai looked puzzled. "No, Dol. At-Dhanurai sent us."

"Tell him *Menadhi* — "

"We are not to come back without you." Yubhai was possibly half-apologetic, but he and the other one had moved one to each side of Dolvid. This at last seemed too much for a joke.

He closed his book. "He knows, at-Dhanurai knows. Why do I have to go and explain what he already knows?" He stood, and his knees were wobbly, but he was not going to be seized and marched there. "Come, then. But he knows what I'm going to say."

"He sent Zhâlai to fetch his thong," the stranger said.

What was baffling was that at-Dhanurai's anger was quite real. They were in the general sleeping-quarters, and the *atarlai*, swinging the length of stirrup-leather to and fro, listened hard-mouthed to the claim of immunity from kitchen tasks.

"*Menadhi* is away," he said, no glint of the pleasant teacher of map-making. "When he comes back, you may complain to him. Now, get ready."

Trapped, too proud to struggle, Dolvid took off his tunic and was held down over a rolled mattress by Yubhai and the other boy, for a severe beating. He did not make a sound, although the last, loud few of the sixteen strokes he got were agonizing, and when he put the tunic back on it seemed lined with thorns. This time at-Dhanurai did not expect any thanks for his leniency, but only dismissed Dolvid, who went back to his room on feeble legs, and lay on his bunk, throbbing with bruises and choked with humiliation. He had always known about envy among the other boys, but never guessed the *atarlal* might also resent his privileged position with *Menadhi*.

For an hour he soothed himself with imaginings of what would happen to at-Dhanurai when *Menadhi* came back and heard. Then he began to doubt. Surely, at-Dhanurai would never defy *Menadhi*, or even risk going against what might be his wishes. Then, though punishing Dolvid for refusing a task, he had not given him another. That might yet come, but so far it appeared an excuse had been created for beating him.

Impossible once in his head to dislodge suspicion this had to do with his rash question for the Patriarch, forbidden curiosity about the events of 2876, connecting this with the terrible nine days when he first came to the *Mankh'*. Then, the lesson had been that he needed *Menadhi*'s protection; was he being reminded it could be withdrawn?

Dolvid could almost remember other times when he had

been trapped, then betrayed, by what he thought was friendship. Without that trust he would never have asked his question. Rather than a friend, he was a kind of pet dog, to be pampered or punished at whim.

But he had met the Patriarch, who knew who he was, who commended him, and there were surely things about *Menadhi* this Patriarch would never sanction, if He knew; the insults for Great Banak, or calling the realm Owan instead of Arbhal; *Menadhi* even used the forbidden term, *Lekh'Owan*. That Dolvid largely agreed with how *Menadhi* regarded the Others did not change anything; the Patriarch was against it. He imagined denouncing the man, being praised by Kamanasalladh, given a position beyond any assailing, the special ward of the Patriarch. *Menadhi*, reduced to a common *atarlai*, would have to plead with Dolvid to intercede for his reinstatement.

Trying to capture sleep, he turned in the bunk. His weals came throbbing back, and terror with them. What did it matter the Patriarch knew his name? he had no access there. A wave of *Menadhi*'s hand could banish him, and there was no appeal; *Menadhi* would simply tell the Patriarch 'the boy was not what we thought.' Thrown back into the depths of the *Mankh'*, Dolvid would have to serve three years, three years of menial tasks, set lessons and fierce punishments, unless he ran away to other narrow futures, as Faëdhal had laid out.

Hadn't it been Faëdhal too, an age ago, who had said *Menadhi*, while young to be the next Patriarch, might well be the one after? But if Kamanasalladh lived on for a dozen years or so, *Menadhi* might be just the right age, and could be Patriarch for a further twenty-five or thirty years, and then the *Atarlum* would be rededicated to the glories of Old Owan, the Old Tongue, the purity of Owani blood.

Suddenly, inexplicably, that seemed a catastrophe. He was proud of being Owani, and sure there was no other people half as good; why was he worried about *Menadhi*'s contempt for Banak-rai or Plakhsila *Kímukoi*, when the chief source of their fame was what they had done to advance the Other Races?

Kamanasalladh Himself did not coddle the Others; he was not going to let Deniants get away with not paying their *Atarlum* taxes. Yes, but not because He was Owani and they Mixed, but because it was right. Long ago He had also agreed with Banak-rai that it was wrong to use knowledge of the Owanilú to keep people (meaning the Others) out of magistracies and other posts, but *Menadhi* taught that was a mistake, because the language held the traditions needed for men of high rank. Yet Dolvid knew beyond any doubt *Menadhi* would find some other good reason for not appointing a Mixed who had become fluent in the Old Tongue; he was for Owan, fairly or not.

Unexpectedly, it was a wonder that anyone could believe, soberly believe the Others were unfit for leadership, at the same time doing everything to keep them from trying. If they were bound to fail, why worry about their aspirations? they would be gone before they could do too much harm, and then the Owanil could say `I told you so,' and the Others would stop trying to overreach themselves and go back to being good followers. But it was not fair to deny them rank because they had no learning, then call them stupid because they did not have rank.

One place that did not happen was in the Colony, with the Army of the West. Sebhal was there; *Menadhi* called him rash, but everyone else said he was a hero — just the sort of young hero Dolvid used to imagine being. Those dreams of success in battle had always come before sleep, and carefully arranging his body to outflank pain, it was pleasant to bring back his old vision of going to the West and winning glory, side by side with Sebhal. The thought of how that would annoy *Menadhi* only made it more soothing.

He woke stiff and sore, but sane. Brilliant changing shapes of light wriggled on Arnan; leaning, not sitting on his window-seat, Dolvid wondered if another summons would come from at-Dhanurai. He had food hidden here in the room, and rather than face the kitchens he munched his way through aging bread and eggs cooked hard. He was not consoled by the knowledge there were boys who were flogged almost daily, had turned their dozens, their hundreds of beatings into a sort of distinction, or kept up that pretence, proof against whispers, showing their world a face grinning with unconcern. But he could feel the loss there would be in surrender to that abject, *Who am I, then, to complain?* He was Dolvid, not anyone else, and he would cherish his sense of wrong, at least as long as he stayed swollen and tender. Perhaps long after.

Yet, as if it had come in his dreams, he could see the other part, his pride. *Pride, pride, pride*, at-Dhanurai had chanted, beating him, and he had been warned against pride in learning how to know, not-know. Most likely he would have been flogged in any event, if *Menadhi* had indeed left word for an occasion to be found, or manufactured. He could not accept pride was an evil if there was something to be proud of, and envy was baffling, but he must have carried privilege high-handedly to have made at-Dhanurai punish him with such unmasked relish, and the other boys witness it with the same delight. In an *Atarlum* book of moral tales written for the very young, unruly children were reformed by a single timely thrashing; that was false and stupid. The lesson taken to heart was to be more discreet with his superiority.

His sanity held; he went to his duties at the library as if nothing had happened, the next day was back with Silnath at the stables, knowing by now he still had his kitchen-privileges. The day after, he took Nuril and made for the city, though he had no real need, and riding was painful. The token *Menadhi* had given still took him past the Precinct gates and through the doors at the Bronze Residence. No new summons to menial tasks came from at-Dhanurai, and while in other circumstances that might have made the whole business more mysterious, to Dolvid it was only confirmation of his guesses. It had been an isolated warning, a rattle of weapons.

"Persistence, Dolvidh, is required." *Menadhi* had heard him in the Responses, and now the *ôdul* were unmasked, *raminat* ready. "Lambarr *Rabhsai* is always a polite listener." But would not act on what he heard, the implication was.

"*Menadhi*, is Laluvoi *Asayu* still at Kadon Dinul?"

A sharp look. "She is. But here we must deal with the *rabhsai* in person. There are many beggars in the realm, and Laluvoi's response is always the same, that of a generous woman, `give what he asks.' To anyone, I'm afraid, except one of her own Owanil."

Waving away frustration, he reached for the *raminat*-pot, asking, "And what about your studies?" Everything was the same as always, but nothing was; Dolvid had counter-strategies instead of trust.

"*Menadhi*, I want to study the tribes. Especially the Froghul." The need for boldness made him abrupt; he was testing *Menadhi*.

"The tribes! That is too big a subject. It might become your life's work, when you are *atarlai*. The Froghul — " He was weighing it. "A fascinating people, but with large differences among their various branches. A strange language, too, few words with many meanings, and they have kept to it very stubbornly. Yes, you could study the Froghul, at least the ones now east of Arnan. At-Oradhai can turn up a small volume on the language."

"He has already done so — " quite astonished at this quick consent.

"There is also a *ramidu* who speaks a few words of purer Froghulú. A *ramidu*, I recall, you have met more than once, at-Sepivadhi, who was with your father in his last sickness, and also tended you. He spent a few years in Lunu Tezh', and picked up a bit of the language. Other writings you can ferret out for yourself. Yes, we approve your choice, approve it warmly."

Dolvid was perhaps beginning to see the rules. He had been allowed to praise the Vrobanil, who, being long extinct, were no threat to Owani supremacy. Neither were the Froghul.

Among Other Races, those with Gabhani blood, whether calling themselves Gabhani or Mixed, actually outnumbered the pure Owanil. There were far fewer Froghul, and they seldom intermarried with other races, keeping to ways they had brought with them out of the Farther West. When the First Empire was falling apart, the band of salt marshes to the north of Arnan had evidently dried, and Froghul herders had come into the north of what were now the provinces of Dramal and Ân, not numerous but very hardy. Much later arrivals out of the West had settled in the Colony and Lunu Tezh' Protectorate to its south, while yet others were nomads on Landegh, like their ancestors a thousand years ago. The Froghul on this side of Arnan had never built roads or cities, but kept to their old ways, usually living in tents, herding goats or sheep. The rest of the realm knew them mostly for their wild dancing, which they sometimes brought to Kadon Dinul: Dolvid had seen them at the last Great Pledging, and would never forget their leaps and tumblings.

"In my absence, there has not been anything to interfere with your studies?"

"Nothing, *Menadhi*." He met the other eyes without a flinch.

"I ask only because instructions can easily be misunderstood. A person in authority has to deal as fairly as he can among differing needs. Within the discipline of the *Mankh'*, we would want those of special talent to be impeded in their work as little as possible."

"Yes, *Menadhi*." All vague rambling, unless he knew about and had commanded the beating, and wanted Dolvid to know, not-know he had, as well as why.

"Then you are content with how it has gone?"

"I thank you, *Menadhi*, yes."

Another long, half-smiling stare. "Good. Now, what about some smoked fish with your *raminat*?"

Ramidh am, let it be renewed. Not feasible; he had learnt cunning, and now, though only he knew it, they were adversaries.

The Great Pledging

The year was 2921 and there would be another Great Pledging at Kadon Dinul. In a year-and-a-half not much had changed. Complimented on a good piece of work, moved, as he intoned his Responses, by the strength and endurance of the *Mankh'*, the goodness of Aëlovoi Who brought the wonder of snow or of the spring, yearning to belong unconditionally, Dolvid came near forgetting, willing himself to forget *Menadhi* was not his friend. Obsequious pretense could easily become genuine devotion; and to keep apart and on guard was painful. No doubt, for the most part, he was treated with extraordinary kindness, and what might be in *Menadhi*'s heart did not seem to matter; the effects were real.

Still, the man could be outwitted. After all, he could not observe everything Dolvid was doing. Choosing set tasks as vague in outline as his study of the Froghul made it hard to keep a check on his exact doings, how every moment was spent, what volumes were consulted. He read on subjects that were, or he was certain would be, forbidden to him, and he started keeping private notebooks. In talk with *Menadhi* he made minor mistakes, knowing things he should not, but what did not pass unnoticed he was able to cover. Dolvid had identified a weakness; *Menadhi* was vain, vain about his powers, his acumen. He could be flattered, not with words, but by an attitude of awed admiration, into patches of real blindness. True, too, he had other concerns.

There must have been other years when Dolvid's blood mirrored how spring opened into early summer; he could recall a day two years ago when he had walked on the ridge, above the *Mankh'* wing where the *nôd'yanul* were. That was now his babyhood; here he was living the season, eyes, nose and ears alert for buddings, the chattering return of birds, the stir of ants and swinging patrol of bees as the hues of flowers brightened with the year.

In part this was because he had discovered the poet Bronal, not an *uzh'freladhai*, maker of epic, but *olúdhanai*, a lyric singer. Bronal came near the end of *Shud'rai baSibadhum*, the Blossoming Age of the First Empire, when there was more than a century of peace; arts and architecture, the crafts of weaving and dyeing, stonecraft and metalworking, as well as painting and poetry, music and dance, were all held to have reached their highest perfection. Bronal, above all the poet of love and desire made real as pain by his apprehension of beauty, was not a favorite at the *Mankh'*; he taught little that was useful. More honor was given to the epic poets who came before and after, even to jogging imitators who tried to make something of the dull, repetitious Island years. But Bronal for Dolvid seemed a magical eloquence of his own, while these poems gave him eyes to see this spring, trees and skies he had never really known for the lack of words to draw them in. Often he hardly dared breathe, for fear of disturbing that sharp glory.

"I have a task for you," *Menadhi* said, eight days before the start of the Pledging weeks. "An important task."

Also a curious one. There had been a number of disagreements, he reminded Dolvid, between a *rabhsai* and one of those governing the Colony west of Arnan, since its refounding in the reign of Kamsila. In the days of the House Gabh'Owan the *Atarlum* had most often sided with the *rabhsai*, and helped bring the Colony back to heel, usually by cutting off its supplies. This had been accomplished by closing the Strait, where the southwestern corner of the Island came nearest the eastern shore of Arnan. Now *Menadhi* wanted a list of all the occasions when that had been done, and the reasons for the blockade.

"When the Road was closed, also?" Although the way

across the Island was called the Forbidden Road, it had once been part of the normal route between Owan Sai and Kamsilat in the Colony.

"Not needed," and not altogether pleased by the question. "The earlier instances for the Strait would include the Road; there could be no case where the Strait was closed and the Road remained open."

"Will the Strait be closed again?" — supposing this had to do with the conflict over excess squadrons in the Army of the West, stilled but never resolved.

"Not very likely — " a confident forecast. "But Saidhan *Asai* will come to Kadon Dinul at last, for the Pledging, and when they meet, both *g'Asalladh'* and the *rabhsai* should have precedents for any sanctions they might threaten. Statecraft, Dolvidh, is often not what might be done, but what an adversary fears you might do."

"What if Saidhan lays down his command in the West?"

"No difference, unless he also disband the unlawful squadrons. We do not need ears in the Great House at Kamsilat to be certain Saidhan would only resign in favor of Sebhal. If the father stays *nim'* over the Colony, and the son as Captain of the West, what is changed?

"Remember," he cautioned, "this is for my use advising *g'Asalladh'* Himself for a meeting of the Council of Thirteen. You must use discretion, and work with all speed, but carefully."

Dolvid grew larger with pride. "*Menadhi*, I may have to spend more than one afternoon at the Bronze Residence, where the correspondence would be."

"Understood."

"It might be better if I stayed overnight, or till I am finished."

"Very good. Take bedding with you, and a change of clothes. Spend whatever time is needed, but do not waste it. I shall write you a warrant."

Silnath said, "Spending a night or two at Kadon Dinul, just like the *rabhsai*, if he still knows his way, say?" A standing joke; Lambarr had wintered in Thenimala, and after barely looking in at the Residence had gone down to Tan Lughsai till the weeks of the Pledging.

"Me, I'll be pleased when we're done with it. Then it'll be the Island for us. But you never saw such polishing and grooming. What would you give to see my boy's face if he could watch us take *g'Asalladh'* in at Harbor Gate and up the Avenue?" Well into his fifties, Silnath seemed rather old to have an only son of less than two. Perhaps that was why he could seldom go five minutes without mentioning the boy.

"I'm hoping to see Sebhal, and the Army of the West."

"Aha, you and a few others, they all want to see real fighting men. Well, you need to taste that young, like my uncle, eh? Battle, a cavalry charge, bruises and bloody swords, say?"

"What cavalry did your uncle ride with?"

"What? The *Adanum*. Always been *Adanum*, my kin."

This was puzzling. The *Adanum Plakh'* was a bodyguard, and surely had not fought any battles in living memory. "Then how could he have been in a cavalry charge?"

"I was no older than three, four, remember when he brought back the stump of his lance. Not that he was hurt."

Working the easy sum, Dolvid was perplexed; the *Adanum* had not played any recorded part in the War of the Widowed.

Silnath gave a huge wink for his frown. "A man rides under this banner or that, who's to say it's his. Gold, blue."

Sky blue was the color of Kargul. Dolvid's father had always maintained they had covert help in 2876 from the *Atarlum*. He meant, in trying to turn public support away from Great Banak, but if Silnath's recollection was not faulty, the then-Patriarch had gone so far as to lend troops to the side which eventually lost.

It required undistracted thought. Dolvid said, "You'll need all the mounts for the Pledging. Shall I walk?"

"Walk? No, you can take the piebald. Steady beast, but nothing for ceremonies and such. A fart in a flower-garden."

"I like Nuril's looks."

"Come, Dol — that great lump of a head? Willing as a week-wife, that I grant. Plenty of that to be had on the Avenue, next week." He gave his nudging chuckle. "You watch yourself, say? Some choice beginners'll be in Kadon for the Pledging. Not that I'm one for stringing a green bow — give me seasoned wood, sobe it's still supple, eh?"

"Yes. That is what I say, too." He had only a murky notion of what Silnath was talking about.

"Learn all about it, another year or two. You stay off town women, never be Patriarch once you begin that. You'll need a weapon, say?"

"Your pardon?"

"Pledging Weeks, you're not safe. Every thief in Six Provinces out lurking by a lonely bit of road. This shouting business doesn't help it — Gabhani justice, eh? Stabbed in the belly by the man you shouted for yesterday?" He was referring to amnesty by acclamation, a tradition of the Pledgings. Soldiers, along with shopkeepers, hated the practice, though Dolvid had heard from his father that vicious criminals were scarcely ever among those offered for the crowd to set free. Those released were men who had made drunken disturbances, small smugglers of monopoly goods, waterers of wine, and similar petty cheats. But Silnath was right about roads being unsafe for solitary riders.

"Better keep a sword at your hip."

Shaking his head, "Not permitted. Of the *Mankh'*, only the *Adanum* can have a long-weapon, outside the Precinct."

"Lose your head to keep the Treaty, say? Breast-scabbard here, and a darning-needle under your outshirt, what about that?" From a shelf he brought down the weapon in its sheath, a spike of a knife with no real cutting edge, a parry-weapon. With a firm wrist to hold it, the `darning-needle' could turn the most furious slash of a cavalry sword. In its sheath, haft near the hollow of the left shoulder, it was quickly drawn.   "There, young *jinza'dakradhai.*"

"I thank you, Silnath — " impatient to be where he could make notes about participation of the *Adanum Plakh'* in the War of the Widowed. In his secret notebooks Dolvid had a heading *Three Mysteries.* He would give half his lifetime to solve any of them. First was *Origins of the Jinzal,* a thicket of guess and legend, worn tales about *Lunu Jinzalladhiyu,* the impossible Valley of *Jinzai*-Fathering, somewhere in the lost West — so much airy speculation, he had never dared ask permission to study the question.   Second was *Plakhan's Bride-Quest,* forbidden as too obscure. Last came *The War of the Widowed,* especially its beginnings in the disaster of the Ní-Tilagh. With that, *Menadhi*'s wishes were plain enough; just for asking about the weather in 2876 Dolvid had been mercilessly flogged. One day he would be free to study what he wanted to.

In seven years the Pledging crowds had not lost their instinct for gathering where someone famous was about to appear. The afternoon was mild and sunny, and as Dolvid came jogging down to the Bronze Residence three sides of the wide Square were lined with the expectant, and there was a knot, mainly of children, clustered at the base of Yoëlladhu's Spear. More soon be seen waiting beside Harbor Way, where the shops and stalls, draped in festival colors, were not doing much business just now. Leading to the Harbor Gate itself, a half-squadron of Household formed a lane, lances grounded, twin files faced inward. Dolvid continued past the side-entrance to the Bronze Residence, then swung Nuril left to urge him up the grassy bank where, nearly three years ago, he had sat discussing his future with Faëdhal.

At once, down the slope of Harbor Way, he glimpsed the nodding heads of approaching *pefral,* flutter of lance-pennons, the bigger flap of a standard bordered in red, the colors of the Colony. Dust was rising, and voices beginning to sound. The *rabhsai*'s standard unfurled beside the other, and in interspersed half-files, more Household lancers and others that must be Army of the West came up, circling the Spear to ride in under the peaked arch of Harbor Gate, between rows of ordered lances. Though not as resplendent as the Household, who had their ceremonial saddle-cloths on, the men of the West were easier in the saddle, and Dolvid at once recognized the self-assurance of the battle-tried. Next, riding on a big roan between officers of both cavalries, a man wearing neither helm nor hat on his greying hair, raising a hand to acknowledge the shouts, "Saidhan! Saidhan!"

He was not as ancient as imagined. The feat that made Saidhan famous was over forty years past, but he had been not much beyond a youth then, and was now only in his mid-sixties, straight-backed and (as far as could be seen) content with his world. To Dolvid's sorrow there was no sign of his son, Sebhal.

As Saidhan went wheeling by the Spear, grounded lances were lifted in salute, and there were sharp trumpet blasts, followed by a flourish. Three riders emerged from the Gate, a tall man and two boys, one tall, the other short and square in the saddle. Surprise, then a thunder of approval, as Saidhan reined in and stretched to clasp the hand of Lambarr *Rabhsai*, then that of the Heir, Tholat. The younger boy Saidhan slapped across the shoulder; Banak-loi had not extended a hand, perhaps because his mount was twitching a little in the din.

When Saidhan gave the royal salute, Lambarr's response would have been apologetic for anyone except the *rabhsai*. Like his wife's father he was bareheaded, and looked very well, his face deeply tanned, as was the Heir's. Whose horse caught the mood of his small brother's, backing and dancing, Tholat not deft in checking him. A Household officer swiftly lent a hand, and even Banak-loi smiled at the little incident.

Followed by undiminishing applause, the four rode in at the gate, men of the West and lastly, with wonderful precision, the lancers of the Household, wheeling in at the rear. There was a rush of small girls and boys to the gate. On Harbor Way, wagons were grumbling up from Owan Sai.

Happy and a little dazed, Dolvid headed back for the side-entrance to the Bronze Residence. Pondering what the *rabhsai*'s cordial welcome might mean in terms of the quarrel with the Colony, he did not hear the shouted challenge, or called it part of the crowd's noise.

"Hoi, halt, I say — " voice at his ear. A dark, glossy *pefrai* was jostling his piebald, and the flat of a thrusting-blade came sliding in front of his chest. Irritated, he turned to see the sneering face of a junior Household officer, eyebrows raised, left wrist high with the reins, gloved right hand equally graceful behind the sword. The face, faintly moustached, might have been Owani but for the dark eyes. The forehead was broad, with near-black hair flattened back — the helm was hanging at saddle-bow.

"What is it?" Dolvid demanded.

"What? Rabbit of the *Mankh'*, you had better have some credentials to show me. These weeks you need special leave to go in."

With all the visitors at Kadon, a general increase in the watch might have been anticipated. Dolvid was wearing *Menadhi*'s token, and was well-known to the usual rather sleepy guards. At the last Great Pledging, he remembered, men from Nivu Din, after too much wine, had tried to steal the gilded wild boars from the New Residence steps, to take home with them.

The officer shook his head at the Patriarchal medallion. "No use to us. That might get you past them — " meaning the guards on the platform of the Bronze Residence proper. "I need to see a city magistrate's warrant, short of a token from the *rabhsai*."

"In the Bronze Residence, anyone there would speak for me." — deliberately omitting any term of respect. He was part of the *Atarlum*, and besides, this officer, moustache and all, was not much beyond twenty. The point at his chest, Dolvid felt stir that resentment of coercion by force inherited from his father.

"You think, Pledging Weeks, we can go running about looking for someone to say who you are? You must be mad. These mumblers of the *Mankh'* — they'll swear anyone in *Atarlum* livery is all right. Produce your own authority, rabbit."

"This is a token from the Head of my Order. My work is important to the Council of Thirteen." Late, he realized that should not have been said: *Menadhi* had told him to be discreet.

"Oh? And what new laws will you give us, *as'loi*? Come on, do you have a warrant or not?"

"I have a letter of *Menadhi*." Reaching in for the folded parchment, he touched the haft of his `darning needle.' He put that out of his mind, and handed over the document.

"Not good enough, no good to us." The officer had barely glanced at it, and Dolvid perceived he was no adept in written Owanilú, even in the ordinary letters. "Give me something to show who you are and your business, or I'll have you thrown in the sheepfolds with the other troublemakers."

"You do not have any authority over one from the *Atarlum*." Dressed in his one worn summer tunic over shabby breeches, he tried hard not to strike a note of pleading. To be detained, imprisoned, while *Menadhi* waited for his researches, was intolerable.

He began wondering whether Nuril, with a sharp kick and a wrench at the bit, could be made to rear. The *pefrai* seemed enormous. Dolvid did not go beyond his chance of wheeling away leftward and regaining the road. Under the outshirt where he had tucked the letter away, his hand stayed on the knife's hilt.

"My authority is here, rabbit." The officer made his sword-point circle a little. With a surreptitiously nudging right heel Dolvid was getting Nuril to drift into a very gentle movement that brought him nearer to facing the soldier. "I have this for my authority," the man repeated, congratulating himself on the phrase.

"And I, this — " drawing, at the same time making Nuril swing farther, the piebald actually butting the tall *pefrai*. Reaching out, he rapped down hard on the sword-blade, then quickly twisted his wrist. Almost worth whatever punishment would come to see that look of bewilderment, the officer gaping at an inexplicably empty sword-hand. Dolvid laughed out loud, disengaging his horse to race for the gateway.

"Wait — " came from behind, as three foot-soldiers ran in the way. Two had pikes, the third an arrow already nocked on his small bow.

"Hoi, no, wait — don't shoot him," the officer ordered. Just too distant to be sure of riding down the bowman, Dolvid pulled up, confronting the three. The officer came up leading his horse, having dismounted for his sword. He was laughing, not vindictively but in apparent enjoyment. Dolvid sheathed the `darning needle.'

"Caught me off guard. We hadn't heard the *Mankh'* was breeding fighting-rabbits — you're never from the *Adanum*, not on that mount. I'm Bolan — who are you, old warrior?"

"Dolvid Vidukhat." Too innocently the oficer stretched up a hand to be clasped. Dolvid gripped hard with his knees at Nuril's flanks, and the huge tug that came bent him low in the saddle but did not unseat him.

Bolan gave a loud laugh and let him recover. "Who's got a blade? — here, you, Varr, that's your name?" He was addressing the bowman. "Lend this lad your weapon, let's see what he can do without surprise on his side. Come on, get off. Varr will be glad to hold your — um — " He parodied bafflement. "Cow? No, no, I can guess. Sheepdog?"

Now Dolvid laughed, but dismounting was no more eager to take the sword than Varr to hand it over. This Bolan was surely not less than half mad, and in his restless enthusiasm had forgotten he had been trying to make an arrest. Fooling about with unbated swords and no protective clothing — the officer was in plain tunic, no breastplate — was no idea of sport. Given Bolan's temperament there could be blood shed before it was done, and wounding an officer of the Household might in the end be worse than to be wounded by him. He could not think of a way to avoid the bout.

After handing his reins to one of the pikemen, Bolan was pacing lightly over the grass inside the gateway, learning the ground. He would have more than the reach of Dolvid, who had not faced a real swordsman since he was eleven.

"Come on." Not willingly, Dolvid carried the plain sword down the slope. Another advantage for Bolan: he had much the lighter blade. If the bout (or was it a fight?) was a long one, a time would come when Dolvid could not hold up his point.

For his left hand the officer drew a slender dagger, made to match the sword. Dolvid redrew the parry-knife. They saluted.

"No one has informed us," circling, "the *Mankh'* has begun to make fighters of its clerks. We'll have to be polite when we dictate our letters."

Dolvid watched hands, watched feet, and said nothing. He could hear Kheval: *no chatter, no time for chatter, read your man.* Though Bolan's was a blade made for thrusting, the cock of a cavalry-officer's wrist showed a preference for the backhand slash. His feet were quick, and perhaps he would rather go left than right.

"How old would you be, rabbit of the *Mankh'*? Sixteen?" No break in tone as he stepped in between words, launching a downward backhand. Dolvid parried sword-to-sword, ignored the unguarded triangle of lower chest, and let Bolan step back. A shorter backhand chop, easily stopped, waist-high. The probing thrust that followed was turned aside.

"I see they've taught you to block a blow."

"Aye — " he could not desist. "And make a sword fly." Bolan scowled, and then came a set sequence, well done, flicking cut for the face, half-backhand thrust for the throat, short-arm downward chop to the head, jab for the abdomen, left hand square across to protect. Dolvid knew this as he did stanzas of verse, and held Bolan off, retreating over the dry grass. His confidence was growing, but he could see no way short of a wounding to end this bout.

"Good, good — " a little breathless. "No hacker from the *Adanum* taught you that defense." Casually, he made a feint left, then high right, then dancing back sent a whistling slash at the ribs. The parry-knife was there to guard, and as Dolvid's wrist felt the jar a small notch appeared in Bolan's fine blade.

"Curse it," he blurted. "What in Zhôl's name are you doing sharpening pens for the mumblers? You ought — " and he used height to launch a ferocious mixture of downward and backhand slashes, any of them killing strokes if unstopped. Dolvid gave ground in uneven jerks, had Bolan off-balance, crossed to his left to make him open, then slipped inside. He lunged to put his point to the man's throat, then flicking out backhand to keep the dagger from his forearm. The dagger fell, and Dolvid was back at the throat, holding his blade there long enough for Bolan to see how a real fight would have finished. A real fight, not a friendly crossing of blades, as this now clearly was.

Bolan saluted with his sword, retrieved and put away the dagger, then also resheathed his sword, after a gloomy look at the damaged edge. Dolvid handed back Varr's sword. All three auxiliaries were holding back grins.

"Truth, what's your age? I still don't see what you're doing in that get-up — you've learnt with Kheval, or I'm Odi Kukkuk. Tell me, go on, that cross-over, straight out of the Residence, not that I can get in there, curse it. Remember this, Dolvidh Vidukhat, not because you beat me, that parry-parry-flick style is very fine for swordplay on the lawn, but in a real fight two others'll make mincemeat of you while you're flirting with one."

"You've got a habit," judiciously, "of letting your eyes go to your next real target. You don't do it for a feint." He would rather not be thrown in the sheepfolds, but was not going to be condescended to by a man he had beaten.

He digested this. "You wouldn't have the chance for bouts, I suppose, a couple of times a week? I've banged about with some of Kheval's, but he's half-retired, and they're down in

Tan Lughsai all summer. All the princelings there are about,
Brodhai of Ân, Bradhinal of Ân, not to mention Lambarr's litter.
Birth's hard to beat for a good start, no room for talent. You
hungry?"

"There's food in my saddle-bag."

"Save it, let's share a pie." Leaving horses with the
guards, they started across the Square. The crowds had mostly
drained away.

"Men they give me," Bolan grumbled. "A cavalry-
officer, and they make me captain over a dozen levies — back
feeding pigs next week, and don't they look it! Well, if I get
permanent rank out of this... " On the right side of his tunic he
wore a file-leader's badge, but the permanent rank on the left side
was half-file.

"A long way from Captain-General," Bolan grinned.
"Oh, here, wear this." From a pocket he took out a small red
badge. "Keep you out of trouble for the Pledging. What's your
business there?"

Dolvid hoped Bolan had forgotten his earlier reference to
the Council. "I am trying to find the earliest account of the
mounted archers of the Froghul, and their tactics. They need not
be called Froghul in the account, so long as the weapons or the
tactics are identifiable."

"Those old fools at the *Mankh'* put you up to that?"

He shook his head. "This was my own idea. I may write
a book."

"About Froghul' horse-archers?"

"All about the Froghul. I want to find out all I can."

"What for?" the voice, with the eyebrows, went straight
up.

"To know."

"What for?"

"For nothing. For itself. For knowing."

The lower lip pushed forward. "Don't mind what I say.
All a mystery to me, the things men do. Wait here."
Acclamation must be hungry work; a good part of the crowd that

had cheered Saidhan and the *rabhsai* seemed to be packed into the pie-shop, loudly discussing details of ceremony and dress, or recalling past sights of one or both. Bolan said "Household," in a commanding voice, and kept saying it till he had shoved his way to the table by the ovens. In a very short while he emerged with hot meat pies and a flask of cold drink, made of barley water and fruit together with a root never named, sweetened with honey. Instead of crossing back to the Bronze Residence Bolan preferred to walk down Harbor Way past the end of the shops, and sit in shade on mossy rocks at the foot of the city walls.

"When you've found out whatever about the bandies," meaning the Froghul, who tended to be short and bowlegged, "that'll get you some kind of promotion?"

"There's no promotion at the *Mankh'*. We have only the apprentices, full *atarlal*, the four Heads of Order, and above them, *g'Asalladh'* — " making the thumb-sign.

"Oh, tell me the *Mankh'* isn't the same world I've lived in. There must be positions of influence, secretary to this one, advisor to that; the big men have their favorites there, as much as anywhere else. In more senses than one, so the tale goes." Meaningfully, Bolan raised his mobile eyebrows. "Well, some have to be scholars, I suppose. What I don't understand is the maggots — you see them all come crawling out at these holiday times. Loyalty's a fine thing, but I can't understand loyalty that makes a man a maggot for the Colony, let's say, when he could be a captain in Kargul. Remember this, and remember who told you: a lad's first and last loyalty is to a lad's best friend — " poking his own chest with two fingers.

"You said, baKir?"

"Bakir," with a grimace. "I'm from Kir and of Kir, but I don't have the nose to be baKir." He had said this often, tracing with the same two fingers the Owani hook that would have made the name possible. Though the nose he had was not thick, as with some Mixed. "Me, I'll be Captain of the Household, then Captain-General — you'll be putting my name in your histories one day. Or quit the *Atarlum* and come with me. I'll make you

my half-file, if you're sixteen, or soon as you turn sixteen, sobe
you can hold up a lance."

"That's more than a year."

"Come when you can, you can find me, you know where.
The Army's coming back into fashion. Has to. Strong *rabhsai*,
hang out at court, weak *rabhsai* — mind you, I'm nothing if not
rabhsayani, but you have a *rabhsai* who sooner than anything
would be swimming at Tan Lughsai, or doing the bounce-about
with his lady — well, sooner or later the Army's going to be
needed. Has to be."

"You may be right — " comparing this with *Menadhi*'s
eerily compatible views.

"May be, I must be. The old *jinzai*-chaser who rode by,
what was his age when Banak gave him his army? My age now.
Has the luck to catch Tobhsila baKargul tired from running, and
lives on the deed for forty years. Well, Banak — doesn't that
show where the army can take you when things go soft at the
center. The next few days, all the young Household officers will
be sniffing after Saidhan, trying for a chance to go to the West.
Not me — that'll be all Sebhal. I'm sick of hearing that name,
Sebhal, Sebhal, Sebhal, you'd think he was Larghai reborn to
hear them talk in the Household. But Sebhal's going to be the
West, unless he gets himself killed looking for feats. They say
there's new trouble on the Frontier, that's why he's not here, but
if there's all the trouble in the world there won't be enough glory
to go round, so long as Sebhal's there. Me, I'll wait for things to
happen this side of the water. Because it's coming, Dolvidh. I
can feel it."

"Have you heard anything about the dispute between
Saidhan and the *rabhsai*?"

"The extra troops? For all I know the old man could have
made up news about Frontier troubles as an excuse. He tried to
get extra *pefral*, Saidhan, offered to pay for them out of his own
pocket, so they say. Council said no."

"That was last year."

"Right. And he's beginning a new cavalry, putting them

on little horses — hill-horses, as they call them. Be nothing against *pefral* in the open field, but better than regulars, they say, for patrolling the — what is it?"

"Landegh."

"So it is. As far as I know, that's where it stands. Saidhan says the law is only about *péfrapravádal*, he wants to pay for these others out of his own pocket, that's his business. But they're afraid of him, the big families are. They think he's such a soldier, if he wanted to come and take Kadon Dinul, he could do it with his fighters mounted on geese."

"Why should he do that?"

"Who can tell? Make his son *rabhsai*, the way he did Banak."

"But his daughter is *rabhsayu* now." In fact, in the talk of a new cavalry that could be no threat to regulars, Dolvid could scent a compromise. His forthcoming report on blockades of the Colony was going to be a waste of effort.

"What about that, scholar," with a slyly knowing tone. "How it happened back in '76? That's what gives Saidhan his name — hand him his own command, and what's his first deed?"

"You mean, the Ní-Tilagh?" Dolvid felt his skin tingle; perhaps this man from a place not all that far from the northern edge of the Ní-Tilagh, Kir, where Saidhan took refuge in 2876, had a story or local tradition about those dark events, extinction of the House Gabh'Owan.

"He commands the escort, goes to the Ní-Tilagh, loses the reigning *rabhsaëyu* and the Heir, then saves Laluvoi to become his best friend's wife. And the friend becomes *rabhsai*, the son of a tanner — you could make more than one tale to explain all that, couldn't you? What do your books tell you?"

"I have not studied the matter - " frigid, offended by the insinuations. "But the tanner was Banak's grandfather, not father."

"Well, all a long time back. Are you going to come with us? You're a fool to stick to books, the way you can handle a sword. Besides, there's rumors Tovakh baKargul might get the

Household. You might go further than me, if names and faces like yours are coming back in fashion, you see what I mean."

"There is no Preference now."

"Oho. You try wearing my eyes for a while, you'll find out how dead Preference is."

Bolan's obsession was silly; anyone could see the Others were being pushed ahead, often enough (as *Menadhi* said) at the expense of an Owani with greater accomplishments. In any case, Bolan looked less of a Mixed than Arvus, who was in charge of the Treasury — for that matter, than the *rabhsai* himself.

"Not that it can go back to what it was, not so long as this Family has the Residence. But that's why I want to climb fast, I'll be too high for Preference to touch. But what about you? Can I look for you to join us, next year?"

"I don't believe so."

"You would rather shuffle about, spouting the wisdom of the Island? That's beyond me."

"Perhaps I am a maggot by choice. I thank you for the food."

"Thank the earth for food, remember my name." He brushed his hands together and stood. The words were a formula among country folk, who held it was bad luck to accept thanks for food, and those who did would come to hunger, odd to hear at Kadon Dinul, from an officer of the Household.

"Oh, I shall not forget your name. Bolan Bakir, to be Captain of the Household."

"Captain-General." As they turned back up Harbor Way, Dolvid realized this spot had been chosen for their meal so Bolan could not be seen by his men.

"I am pleased, Dolvidh, very pleased." The day, sixth before Midsummer, was very hot with mutters of far thunder, and *Menadhi* had taken him for a stroll along the edge of Arnan.

"You are growing, Dolvidhai," putting a friendly, unwelcome arm across Dolvid's shoulders. "There was a time, a very short time, when we thought we might have been mistaken in you, but now — " He halted, and turned Dolvid to regard him at arm's length. "We see you grow in many ways."

"*Menadhi* — " ashamed, feeling he had cheated for this approval. A year ago, he had become interested in the occasions when the Colony had been blockaded. Preparing *Menadhi*'s list he only had to refresh his memory about dates and reasons; much of the work was already done, and written in his secret books.

Removing a hand from Dolvid's shoulder, *Menadhi* shaded his eyes against brilliance to study the veiled metallic sky. "Yes. You have made yourself into a good scholar. Although I do not think we have seen all the fruits of your labors."

This with a sidelong smile. Dolvid tried to smile back, gripped with fear, return of the old certainty *Menadhi* watched everything he did, all he thought. They would have to kill him; his life would not be long enough for all the beatings.

"You have not yet shown me any of your work on the Froghul."

Hope flickered back. "Yes. I have been — there is much more to be studied. About language, the Froghulú Grammar of at-Rhubani is not very clear. I wondered if I should consult with the Master Faëdhal."

"With Faëdhal, Dolvidh?" They had resumed walking. "He is a peerless master of tongues, no one questions. Has at-Sepivadhi not been helpful?"

"Some words he has helped me to pronounce."

"I understand you. He is *ramidu*, not *manadu*. As a *ramidu*, also, he will soon be renewing his acquaintance with your Froghul. It is true. A clan of Froghul from Dramal have come down for the Pledging. They have a grievance, which also concerns the hunting-lands of our good friend Vinilat baDramal. They will get their hearing, everyone does; they have no chance of gaining their suit, which is an absurdity. Meanwhile, they are camped eastward of Kadon Dinul. Better than troubling Master Faëdhal, could you not learn from the Froghul at first hand? They are supposed to be hospitable, not so?"

"*Menadhi*, their oldest tribal law is not to turn away any stranger who comes in peace."

"Then you might stay overnight with them? Two nights, perhaps, or as many as three, if they will have you."

"Could I?"

"It is very warm for books and pens. I shall be in Kadon Dinul most of the week — yes, there is no reason why not, if the Froghul agree."

"I thank you, *Menadhi*." There was no strategy in this display of gratitude. "But they're poor people — "

"Yes, you must take them gifts. A little *raminat* for the head-man, and we'll see what food can be found. But you must remember you are an Owani, and of the *Atarlum*; not just Dolvidh but the *Atarlum* wants to learn their tales and customs. You can be trusted to earn their respect. You will have to carry a weapon, a short blade. Is that not a sign of worth with them?"

"It is. Their word for *wretch* means `no-knife-man.'" He felt excitement rise, with a tinge of fear in it. Great Banak had decreed the Froghul had full standing in the realm, but many people still thought of them as wild men.

"Also remember," *Menadhi* was saying, "the Midsummer others see as a chance for foolery is the start of our most solemn period, *Shuda'sai g'Asalladhi*. Don't fail to be back at the *Mankh'* for the first hour."

The encampment was on common ground beyond the stream, Shufloi Kadonu, that wound in a deep, densely-grown, bird-haunted crease, not far eastward of the city. Once again on the piebald, Dolvid rode beside at-Sepivadhi, more pot-bellied than ever, straddling a staid mare. Better, by orders of *g'Asalladh'* Himself, they had an escort, two men of the *Adanum Plakh'*. They held their *pefral* well in hand, lances slung and breastplates polished. Dolvid felt wreathed in glory.

He kept wishing someone could see him, and after running through a list of those he knew, came to the odd conclusion it was Radis he had in mind, a person completely forgotten till now, the young wife of whatever-his-name-was next door when Dolvid and his father came to Kadon. He had gone north to trade in fleeces. Darborr. But Radis had taken it on herself to wipe grime from the boy's face, or tidy his hair. If only she could see him escorted by men of the *Adanum*, she would know he could achieve things that had nothing to do with whether his face was once smudged, or his outshirt torn. Radis always smelt faintly of onions, nothing like the sweet freshness of his mother, yet he liked to remember, when she held him to scour the back of his neck, how his forehead had pushed the linen robe against her body, the slow rise and fall of her breathing.

The Froghuli camp was calmer than he had expected, made in a lower spot in high ground, a hollow in the embankment above the stream. Not the Kadonu, but a lesser tributary; they were just above where the two waters ran together. Where the the small stream was forded there had been an encounter with royal troops, General Cavalry, a half-file of lancers less resplendent than Household, nearly as tough-looking as the men of the *Adanum*. The men of the *Mankh'* had not enjoyed being halted, the leader of the others no happier about giving directions. Outside the Precinct there was not much love for the *Adanum Plakh'*.

From the summit where the narrow beaten path had led them, thcy looked down on tents and a central fire. Had he expected, then, to be welcomed with the somersaults and vaults of tribal dances? Gathering near the main fire, as the escort led down, were serious-faced men and women, their dark eyes watchful. The tents were made square with doubled poling, and were mainly of sewn goatskins. Not far away about a dozen goats were grazing, and others were tethered near the tents. A woman milking looked up at the newcomers without much interest. Some of the men had bows, held slackly or slung at their backs. There were fewer women in sight, most of them hanging back a little, grasping skirts or holding on to tent-flaps.

At one of the smaller fires a big iron pot was being tended by a slender girl, barefoot and nearly bare-shouldered. She gazed, caught Dolvid's eye, and turned away, just as he did.

At-Sepivadhi fussed to the ground, and Dolvid also dismounted. Drawn off a way the two *Adanum* men remained in the saddle, still and alert. From Nuril's broad back Dolvid unslung the pair of leather bags he had carried.

Three men were coming forward, all three wide-framed with thick, sinewy arms, though the tallest was only fingers above Dolvid in height. In his lame Froghulú, a dialect from the other side of time and the Arnan, at-Sepivadhi stammered, "We... from All-Father... greeting... have."

The eldest of the Froghul said forceful words to urge the one not as short as the others. Bowing, this man said in ordinary language, "Welcome. You honor us, *at'ai*. I am Ka-Nam of Tan Dramali. This is my father, Huro-Nam. Here is Inghi, our well-woman."

What had seemed the shortest and shaggiest of three men was indeed a woman, face powerfully lined, her arms not much less than the others. Like them she was in loose breeches, hitched with a tie above the knee. A well-woman! Dolvid felt a thrill, *asumun-vanu* as it was in the *Mankh'* chronicles. He had read that as wanderers on Landegh, that dry plateau, the Froghul gave high rank to those, women more often than men, with a talent for finding hidden water. Now, though they lived in moister parts, the title had survived, meaning something near *Bôdhrayu*, Chief Counsellor. He wondered whether Inghi, whose eyes were small and sharp with a hint of humor, had any gift for dowsing. At the Residence, one of the titles Rhunsilakh had accumulated was Judge of Lays, although he knew nothing about song, and there had not been a tournament of lays since Kamsila tried to revive them, centuries ago. In any case, Inghi would certainly be the tribe's Mocker, whatever that meant.

At-Sepivadhi was being dignified, although advancing to grasp Ka-Nam's hand he stumbled a little on uneven ground. Bestowing handclasps on the two Froghul, the *ramidu* managed to give the impression he was conferring a favor. Inghi made deep deference, fingertips touching her furrowed brow, and as she rose there was a feeling other than respect hinted in her eyes.

Now Dolvid stepped forward, holding his satchels, one with his writing materials and some bits of his clothing, the other with the gifts. After at-Sepivadhi had merely announced his name there was a new round of hand-claspings. Inghi said softly, "Not the healer's helper." Ka-Nam's speech had only the ordinary rhythms of the north, but hers was more heavily accented.

"This youth has come," at-Sepivadhi proclaimed, "sent by *Menadhi*, who is — " He fumbled for a way to convey *Menadhi*'s position to these people, then abandoned the attempt. "He is one of our highest ones. The *Atarlum* would wish to learn some of the tales of all the peoples who are... all our peoples."

After his lame ending, Ka-Nam, Huro-Nam and Inghi went on giving polite attention to the *ramidu*, and from the tail of his eye Dolvid could tell many of the other Froghul were amused by the awkward, frozen tableau. He made another step forward. Taking the pouch *Menadhi* had sent, containing *raminat*, something made him turn to the well-woman, and give it with a bow at-Sepivadhi did not approve.

Inghi, not exactly an old woman, sniffed at the dried leaves, and showed strong square teeth in a smile. "*Ram'nat.* Your highest ones are generous." She handed the pouch to the younger of the leaders, Ka-Nam, yet the ceremony with which it was passed and received made clear Dolvid had been right to begin with Inghi. The satchel containing various foods — apricots, raisins, crystallized honey, a quantity of wheat flour — he laid at the feet of old Huro-Nam. Then, from his writing satchel, he took two armbands of painted leather. These were Gabhani work, but a recent writer said they were "much esteemed" by the Froghul, at least those of the West. Dolvid had bought them himself, from a shop near Market Gate hostelry. The old man was shy accepting his, then met Dolvid's face with shrewd eyes, the color not nameable, neither black nor brown.

Ka-Nam took his gift with solemn courtesy. "Will you have drink with us?" At-Sepivadhi assented, confiding in the Owanilú to Dolvid, "We should have remembered this. These men will discuss no matters before hospitality has been offered and accepted." Dolvid, never having forgotten it, stared at the *ramidu*. Outside any tribal or racial custom, use of a language their hosts could not possibly understand struck him as a horrible breach of natural courtesy.

As they gathered near the smaller fire the awkwardness began to go away. Others of the camp came drifting in, and Dolvid, adequately separated from the *ramidu*, stopped feeling responsible for what the man might say or do. At-Sepivadhi had his own business with the Froghul, but Dolvid did not know much about it, the study of a rare, chronic disease found only among this people. Beyond the circle of the camp the men of the *Adanum* sat, statues cast in bronze, bringing back a recollection of the old awe, dulled in Dolvid by afternoons of shared swordplay and beer at the stables.

"What do they call you?" he asked the girl who had the task of ladling warm goats' milk with herbs into earthen cups. The bloom on her shoulders was disconcerting, and the moistness of the knowing eyes: her stature made her perhaps eleven or twelve, by Dolvid's guess.

"Tini-ra, please you Dal-vith, Tini-ra Gulas-daughter."

"Dolvidh." She had sharp hearing, or was a skilled lipreader. The girls, he recalled, took their mothers' names, so a brother and sister had different surnames.

Ka-Nam left his talk with the *ramidu*, and came round the fire to put his newly-banded left arm across Dolvid's shoulders, and give a firm hug. "Welcome, Dolvidh, not-the-healers-helper. What can we give you of ours?"

"I thank you, Ka-Nam, nothing except what is praised everywhere, the freedom of your hearthside for a while. I beg leave to stay with you for a few days — " He heard the girl gasp, and wondered at it. "I want to be able to write about your customs." He swung forward the satchel at his side, a gesture he immediately saw as foolish, as if that could illustrate the notion of writing.

Ka-Nam made his grave bow. "We are honored. What about the *ramidu* and his guard?"

"His task should be finished soon. They will go back to the *Mankh'* today." Dolvid would be here among foreigners alone, an adventure.

The girl had a filled cup for him. "We hope you'll be glad with Huro-Nam's people." She went back to her task, but looked up at Dolvid with each cup she filled.

He never wanted to ask why the Froghul took to him; on his side it was all admiration. Tini-ra's cousin Manto, his own age, showed him how to make a noose with a stop-knot, so it could be thrown over the head of a tough he-goat, and tighten securely with no risk of strangling the beast. Manto also gave him one of the back-sheaths the Froghul used for their long, slender knives. It buckled across the chest, and the knife was behind, haft at an angle between neck and shoulder, ready for drawing with either hand, or for a lightning throw. A few of the men gathered to show how they could send a knife whirling to thud and quiver in the stem of a small sapling from thirty paces, and Fru-Nam, the leader's younger brother, did his best to teach the proper whipping motion with wrist and forearm, but the knife would not behave as well for Dolvid.

When they put on bouts using staves Dolvid could show them a few tricks, though from the boys all the way up to old Huro-Nam the Froghul were more agile than he. Their short, graceless-looking legs had the spring of willow-wands.

Gula, Tini-ra's mother, after bewilderment and laughter at the request, showed him how to milk, and it was bliss when he finally caused a tiny foaming jet of thick warm milk to come from a goat who had butted him with no malice when he turned to reach for a bowl.

He watched the men play a gambling-game, casting short lengths of knotted cord into a circle scratched in the ground. He could not see any connection between the lie of the cords and winning or losing a cast, and was shy of interrupting the intense play to ask about the rules. Tini-ra, in a hushed voice, explained this was a game only for the men; women like Inghi used the cords a different way, casting them at the feet of one who had hard decisions to make, and then giving advice.

She, the girl, was never far away as he watched or joined any activity of the clan, or when he took up his task, questioning the Froghul, particularly the older ones, about their history. Whether or not he completely understood, he wrote down everything he was told, and Tini-ra watched him in silence. She made him self-conscious, but when she had her own work to do, and he glanced up to find her vanished, he felt disappointed, and missed her till she came back with her large, soft eyes. She might be only a child, but she knew, oh, surely she knew when he tried to show off for her. He saw her giggling with her friend Roti, the only other young girl there (not counting babies), and was sure they were making fun of his attempts to match her people in vaulting or throwing a knife. Happily, she was watching when he did not disgrace himself with the staves, and again when he sent the men into fits of amazed laughter by reading off almost flawlessly what had just been said to him in a language he barely knew.

One the clan's youngest might never speak. That was sad; the elders had decided ordinary language of Arbhal would be more useful for their children. Huro-Nam, the eldest, was comfortable speaking only the Froghulú, and when Dolvid was with him, his son Ka-Nam, fluent in both tongues, sat by to assist.

Huro-Nam was about seventy, judging by his memory of 'the *rabhsai* who drowned when I was a boy,' Dromladh, son of Plakhat III. But the Froghul' stories led backwards through time, and the strangest, most remote, were tales of 'before,' the age before herding was given to them, though they had never been 'men without camp-fire,' savages. In those days their head-man had deer's antlers and the hoof of a wild ox.

"He wore those?" — risking a question in his improving Froghulú, he won a faint smile.

Then Huro-Nam grew earnest. "Not wore. Antlers sat on his brow, and the hoof came to him in his years. His heart was eagle, and he was lion-handed, yet loving what must be slain."

Outmatched by the rush of animals, Dolvid asked Ka-Nam to translate this for him.

"This Lord *Nim'*," Huro-Nam, dourly, "he kills outside the love, bad-kills."

"Hush, father."

"No, say it to the boy. He's of their blood."

"Not of their heart, Inghi says." Ka-Nam half-shrugged, turning to Dolvid and changing back to ordinary language. "You must forgive us. Our own troubles become to us the whole realm. It can't be so, should not be so, for others."

"I have heard there is a dispute with *Nim'* Vinilat of Dramal." Dolvid had just worked out the Froghulú word for *lord* was 'eviscerator,' the one who draws game.

"The Lord Vinilat says, south of the road, for day-rides east and west, is all his hunting — " Ka-Nam glanced to be sure his father was following this. "And no one can cross its borders."

"Was this pasture for your goats?"

"No, no. Wild land, good for boars and birds, a few bears, it might be. We don't want the land, or anything not ours. But the Lord is putting his horse-soldiers on the road, to turn us back. In autumn we lost meat and milk driving the herds eastward for days. The snow caught us while we were still too far north, and that cost more animals. All we want is a narrow path through these hunting-lands. This spring we had to leave Dramaru too early, before we could be sure the snow was gone from the north. We spent more than a month on a ten-day journey, and lost many of the new kids."

"Why do you have to go north? Couldn't you stay at this

Dramaru year round?" As soon as he spoke the name he could answer himself; Dramaru, from *thramai rubha*, the Brown Heath.

"Not enough grass when the dry comes," Ka-Nam confirmed. "That's a life for the Froghul of Dramal, running away from the sun, then the snow, then the sun again. All we are asking is a path. Lord Vinilat says we frighten birds and beasts, and spoil his hunting in autumn, their matings and nestings in spring."

"Oh, aye, the thunder of a goat's hoof can frighten a boar two day-rides away." Inghi, eyes hot with sarcasm, had come to squat nearby. With her hand she mimicked the delicacy of foot Dolvid now could see in goats.

This was the suit *Menadhi* called an absurdity. "Lambarr *Rabhsai* may well say otherwise," Dolvid offered.

"That's why we came," Ka-Nam said. "If he will hear us. If not — well, we're a people who have come through other troubles. Too many, as have all who have been a long age in the world."

"We were driven off the Green Lands." His father turned back to his own language. "For that, we received herding in exchange. After, there came the tearers, which you call *jinzal*. But the goose-riders with their bright breasts drove us from the Green Lands."

"Is that plain?" Ka-Nam asked Dolvid, who asked for translation.

"They rode on geese?" he asked.

Huro-Nam gave an impatient little cough. "They were the goose-riders, and we say they were the ones who dried the Green Lands, and brought the tearers. After, there were no more antlered men. But Froghul can never forget these likings."

That night kid was roasted, and there was barley wine. As evening became night some of the men acted out one of the old dances, `blood-dance,' Inghi called it. Not a display such as they gave for Pledging crowds, this was for themselves, deeply serious, even about fun. To a sighing pipe and throbbing drums, eight of the men, perhaps, took part; hard to keep count as darkness grew and the flamelight left deep shadows. Once patterns were set they moved in pairs, hunter and prey, although with a change of drum-rhythm they could reverse their roles, a deer poised for flight becoming the ready bowman, a stalker with knife upraised shrinking into a partridge — here, old Huro-Nam was most lifelike, with a waddling walk and sliding motions of his head. When he panicked, Dolvid could hear the whirr of wings.

His son, the leader, did not change, but was always both hunter and hunted, lion and also lion-slayer, admired and feared. The other dancers would halt in mid-stride, then imitate his looping tread, moving with him, yet afraid. Behind the gliding figures, across the black gulf where the stream ran, the tawny walls of Kadon Dinul rose, pale shape of the Residence, and yellow lamplight and torchlight, cooler shine of *ôdul*, picked out commonplace details, horse with a slouching rider, the sway of washing on a line, only adding to the strangeness of what was near.

Dolvid's mind saw slantwise this was not alien at all; he could almost recognize it as something once had but forgotten. He was happy, and unbearably sad, close to weeping for what the Froghul lost in being driven from the Green Lands, the pact with death hunting people made, either as slain or slayer, each present in the other.

The pipe began to rise in sharper crests, mocking itself, the drum-rhythms starting to break and stumble. Head thrown right back, her hair dangling behind, Inghi came up from cross-legged sitting in a pool of darkness. She spread her arms as if announcing intent, then began to mimic the men, all the hares and stags, birds and wild oxen, all their earnest stalkers. A burst of excited laughter came when she caught and grotesquely parodied the menacing glide, the brandished forepaws of Ka-Nam. All others faded, and she and the head-man were face to face, making slow feints at each other, he doubly threatened with danger and danger of ridicule. After long clawing seconds Ka-Nam, laughing, made a slack gesture of defeat, two-handed, and sank down, legs crossing.

Inghi dropped her hands flat at her sides. One drum, played with fingertips, nails skittering, hushed to a ripple of sound, and the flickering firelight pointed the irony of Inghi's face, putting golden gleams in eyes that, opened wide, were not small now. Very rapidly she went through a sequence of mimicries, at first meaningless to Dolvid, though others clapped their hands in delight.

Then, given slowly, there came a small, pompous man, potbellied, dismounting clumsily, bestowing a greeting as if from the heights, tripping over a blade of grass without losing his stiff self-importance — at-Sepivadhi, exactly. The watchers' small noises anticipated more, as some of the Froghul had sidelong looks to see how Dolvid was taking this. There was no need to force his laugh. Visibly blushing for his older colleague, a youth stood next to the *ramidu*, and for a flash Inghi was Ka-Nam, overly courteous and cautious with the grown-up visitor, giving his heart to the boy, who moved his head as if pivoted, trying not to miss anything. Dolvid watched Dolvid presenting gifts, trying awkwardly to throw a knife as watchers ducked away or covered their heads, milking a ferocious goat, and triumphantly holding up a tiny cup, from which he tipped a dewdrop of milk. Then he was shaving at his pens, scrawling frantically as Huro-Nam told stories filled with tedious detail — all this Inghi conveyed unaided, and between episodes there was a repeated scene, a wide-eyed girl watching him with adoration, sighing and fluttering her lashes.

Once, long after, Dolvid would try to describe the uncanny performance, and was afraid it sounded cruel in the telling. At the moment, despite his blushes, his hope Tini-ra for now would not catch his eye, he was struck mainly by the craft and assurance that put any malice out of the question. And he knew what this was. Everything new was being danced and laughed into the clan, given its rhythms by this posturing enactment. What poetry did, Dolvid saw, then, losing the thread of thought, could not say what he had meant by that.

Inghi's Dolvid was losing his foreignness. He stopped gaping at the everyday things, smiled more, was becoming Froghuli. Dolvid, real Dolvid, got to his feet, breaking the rules for all he knew, and bowed low to the well-woman. This brought real enthusiasm, and as he sat again his back was pounded by everyone within reach. Ka-Nam filled his own cup and after tasting passed it two-handed to Dolvid, who drank with what he supposed was a hectic face.

The hubbub wound down, and Inghi was still, chin sunk to chest. Drums throbbed, and slowly she began her last performance, not for mirth. She was the sorrow of the Froghul. The pipe offered, again and again, a bare, falling figure that went nowhere. All life for all time was unconsoled memory of the lost Green Lands, gone, not to be reached for. The pace quickened, and here were new Froghul' griefs and grievances, loss of animals, death of old friends, a big-toothed lord with a drawn weapon, barring their way. Painfully, driving herds, they made their way about the proud lord, hobbling at last to where there was rest and soft grass. The season changed to cold, Inghi turned, and the way was barred again.

She stepped aside out of that scene, and was tall and cheerful, poking head forward as Lambarr did. Not abjectly, the Froghul put their case (here the watchers broke silence with suggestions and encouragement), and the tall figure stooped to listen. The earlier lord came strutting, brushing aside the Froghul as dead leaves, opening his palms blandly to the *rabhsai*. Inghi had seen Lambarr's pondering habit of resting his right elbow in his left hand, right knuckles to teeth. The drum died, and the pipe tailed into extinction. Inghi waited, still, a drawn bow.

Decisive, Lambarr gave the imperious wave of a *rabhsai*, and there was the lord, face shocked as he humbled himself. But the Froghul were free to pass, drums bounding to match their jaunty step, pipe carolling. To a loudening thunder of drums the watchers yelled their satisfaction. Inghi, sinking to her knees, covered her face with the backs of hands, then pointed like a shot arrow at the gleaming walls of the Residence, lips drawn back, face inspired.

She was finished. Everyone pounded fists and cups and wept, while a small, cool hand crept into Dolvid's. Tini-ra was crouched beside him at fireside, not looking into his face, her hair brushing his upper arm.

Before dawn when night itself was finally settling to sleep with a long sigh that stirred leaves and branches, Dolvid, on goatskins beneath his blanket, heard a low, fluid piping begin nearby. Incredibly, it was bird-song, trilling and warbling, easily disposing of any challenge remembered from the Froghuli music, loosing single notes, crystal water-drops. In darkness he held to himself the blood-dance, the hand of Tini-ra, all his happiness. The song outlasted his waking.

There was no doubt where he stood in the debate between his friends and Vinilat *Asai*. With others, including Inghi, Ka-Nam was going to ride into Kadon Dinul to enter their plea at the General Court of Grievances. Correcting their misunderstanding, Dolvid tried to explain this was procedure, not the hearing. The question, in which they spoke for all clans allied to this one, could only be heard by the *rabhsai* or someone else from the Council of Thirteen. The decree of Great Banak guaranteed them a hearing, but their plea still had to come in due form.

Ka-Nam unwound a carefully-wrapped parchment. "How is this, Dolvidh? We gave money to a man in Drin Dakani to make it."

He asked anxiously, "Not good?" Dolvid had not kept dismay out of his face. It was ridiculous. The scribe, who wrote with a good, clear hand, had not understood the case at all. The first impression was the Froghul were accusing the *nim'* of enclosing pasture. Later, poor phrasing made it sound as if they wanted the right to hunt on Vinilat's lands, and the last paragraph was complete muddle, where it seemed as if Vinilat's soldiers were being accused of killing Froghuli livestock. As in a way they had, but these easily-refuted charges could wreck any chance of a fair hearing on the real issue. If *Menadhi* somehow had heard of this document, his contempt for the case was easier to understand.

Dolvid tried to tell Ka-Nam what was wrong.

"You mean, what is written here can make our voices count for nothing, when Lambarr *De'* listens?"

Bewildered his clever new friends could be so stupid about law, Dolvid tried to be patient. "Lambarr will have dozens of cases to consider, and Vinilat has to have his chance to answer. It might be nothing except what is written here will be heard."

"But this is our grievance written here. Wrongly, you say, well, but surely the *rabhsai* can — " Seeing Dolvid's face, Ka-Nam broke off. "Well, it has to be written again. There is money for this; all the clans gave what they had. Kadon Dinul is filled with men who can write."

After thought, he said, "Time is short — would you come into the city with us, and see what is written is what our complaint is?"

Dolvid's heart started to thump. He was quite sure where *Menadhi* would stand, even after hearing the true facts. Vinilat was of Owan, of the Great Families, and he, Dolvid, had been told not to forget he was of Owan, of the *Mankh'*. Scribes from outside the *Atarlum* were always gossiping with *atarlal*, and if the Froghul won their case, and *Menadhi* came to hear Dolvid had assisted with their plea, the result was predictable. Withdrawal of protection, two years of menial tasks and many floggings, before he could be free — that, or escape into a murky future he was not ready for. Doing what Ka-Nam asked could condemn him to a whole life without the study of history, a sight of books, learned talk over spiced *raminat*. Without hope. He could not risk it.

All this went through his mind while he breathed once. Then he saw he could do more than was asked, and with less danger. "I'll write it for you." Just the same, the offer scared him.

Ka-Nam might be uncertain about written words, but he had a grasp of forces contending in the realm. "Dolvidh, I do not believe your *Atarlum* would speak against the *Nim'* Vinilat."

"No." Perhaps he could escape, after all.

"It is your tribe, the *Atarlum*."

"The realm is Arbhal," Dolvid rather surprised himself by saying. "There is one law, for me as well as you. Besides, it's not going against anyone to write what you want to say, just write it down."

"Ah, Dolvidh'... " Ka-Nam shook his head.

"Besides, if asked you could say a scribe did it."

"That we could say."

"Besides, I am one of Ka-Nam's clan. Inghi says so." In fact, she had said not a word about it, but there was no misunderstanding the dance.

In a low voice Ka-Nam said, "Tini-ra has tried to say so, too." Dolvid, with legal phrasing starting to run in his head, nodded vaguely. This morning the girl was absorbed in her tasks.

Taking parchment, he did the thing swiftly, in three short paragraphs. Though he could not recall exact years, he knew the laws and decrees about enclosures were of Plakhat I, Plakhsila, Thral-Sivu and Banak, which ought to be enough. After having to go through all the pleas and arguments in the case of the dowry-lands of Maso, wife and then widow of Kanavakh the Bloody, he was familiar with the style and phrasing. Since these pleas, by convention, were addressed to the *rabhsai* in person, he doubled normal use of `respectfully,' and ended with a formal prayer for the question to be heard under provisions of the one decree he could date exactly, that of 3 Banak (2880). Ka-Nam nodded earnestly as Dolvid read him what he had written.

"And this is how it is done?"

"Close to it. Why?"

"You do not say anything about — oh, about the bad heart of Vinilat. We left herdsmen short-handed so we could come and have the *rabhsai* see us for the men we are, with no bad intentions."

"Is that how the Froghul judge cases among themselves? In Owani law, which fathered the realm's law, we say only facts exist."

"Facts? How can law know what happened, unless the hearts are seen?"

"Well," struggling. "Let us say one man steals a thing from another man — "

"What man? What thing? What other?"

"Any man, any thing. A kid, then."

"No, Dolvidh. How am I to see, unless I know the man? Last year, Aud had a kid Kras-La said was his. Now, Aud's wife won't lie under him because she says he is unlucky, and Kras whispers in her ear, and he is a man who makes unloving bargains, being greedy for the largest tent. But Aud, though it's true he's got no luck to spend, would go out and look for another man's strayed goat, having the clan in his heart. Knowing all this, I could tell what happened."

"It is not the same here."

"So I see, but I don't see how that can be."

"Where there are so many people — in a city, a magistrate knows some but not others, and to be fair he has to keep to facts." This could not satisfy Ka-Nam, for whom events and their sources were not to be separated. Pressed, Dolvid would have had to admit it was a pious hope rather than what really was; in a battle with a Mixed, he, as an Owani, would certainly have a better chance with an Owani magistrate, which most of them were.

The parchment was dry. Ka-Nam accepted and carefully rolled it. "You know how law is at Kadon Dinul. We thank you, Dolvidh. I do not offer you payment." In the Froghulú he spoke what must be a proverb, and Dolvid had learnt enough to translate it as *To pay for friendship is to have no friend but money*.

Morning had steadily dulled, threatening later rain. While Ka-Nam with Inghi and others had gone to Kadon Dinul, Dolvid, with the aid of the younger son, had further speech with old Huro-Nam. Tini-ra was on the far side of the encampment, nearest the stream. She was busy sewing at vivid oddments of cloth.

Dolvid was beginning to see what a lot could be said by putting not many words into changing combinations. Order was very important; a phrase such as *then wild men came into our lands*, with a slight change of word-order, became *and so Froghul' forests were not burning*. In this the language was completely different from the Owanilú, where both poets and scholars revelled in the rich vocabulary and flexible word-order. Poetry must be practically impossible in Froghulú. That must be why they danced it.

As with the *Song of Tales*, the stories he heard, wandering in a landscape of no identifiable features, acknowledged no fixed boundary between legend and history, tale of marvels and sober fact. Perhaps they were right, these Others of other kinds, and there had once been a world where men changed into beasts or spoke with rocks. Perhaps somewhere, beyond any riding, that was now, and the god-who-has-no-name was still casting the cords with men, gambling to win back his beloved, fashioned from a wine-skin.

All smiles, those who had gone to the city were back after a few hours. Dolvid warned them they had not beaten Vinilat by having the petition accepted and entered on the list; the case might yet go against them. The hearing would be tomorrow morning, most likely, and nothing could disturb their conviction, shared if not brought about by Inghi, that their cause was as good as won.

With this much achieved, they all could go to Kadon Dinul and take part in the proclaiming and acclaimings. Then tonight they would celebrate Midsummer's Eve in the Avenue of Treaties. Small satchels were stuffed with cheese and bread, the *Menadhi*'s dried fruit, and also with festive scarves and sleeve-bands, caps and tassels in yellow, red and blue, to be worn for the dancing. These were the things Tini-ra had been helping to put into repair.

Dolvid would go with his friends. He could see no reason why he would be censured at the *Mankh'* for taking part in general celebration, so long as he was back there by midday tomorrow. If it had surely meant painful punishment, he still could not have refused.

Next morning was leavetaking; in only hours the sun would be overhead and time stand in equal halves; the solemn *Shuda'sai* at the *Mankh'*, while on the Avenue packed crowds would be greeting the year's summit with loud joy.

He could not complain. Yesterday he been there to shout with his friends. He had watched the Marionettes of Burantal in, after historical scenes, a piece coming perilously close to making jokes about a certain high lord who was never to be found at home. It ended with an extended procession of child-figures, boy, girl, boy, girl in ever-diminishing size, while the spectators rocked with laughter; last came a tiny, crawling baby, face made daringly to resemble Lambarr's, who said in a squeaky voice, "This, by grace of Hrafi, shall be my realm — " the words of Plakhat Gabh'Owan after concluding the Treaty of the Wind Caves. Loud cheering brought out the ageing Master of Marionettes, Nettumar, with his two sons. Dolvid hoped no one from the *Mankh'* had seen him here — although possibly *Menadhi* would approve satire at the expense of Banak's house.

As Inghi had promised, the rain held off. Much later, Dolvid watched his friends at their tumbling, leaping dances, which of course excited him, though he could hug tight the knowledge these were spectacles for outsiders; he had seen the blood-dancing. Later still, wineskins were passed, there were jokes and games, and when time came to light lanterns and lead their mounts back through night's cool Dolvid was blinking with fatigue, but happy and a little bit drunk, though not with the thin barley-wine.

Now, in a cool and misty morning, he would ride as far as Market Gate with those who were going to wait for their hearing. He was glad final farewells could be put off. He was collecting his things at the tent for unmarried men, where he had slept, when Ka-Nam came over, a long knife held between his fingers. He squatted with the ease of his people. "Dolvidh', I know my brother gave you a sheath. I would be made glad if you would rest this in it."

Dolvid's eyes opened wide. It was Ka-Nam's own knife, one of the slender-bladed, perfectly balanced hunter's weapons, a measure, as *Menadhi* had said, of Froghuli worth. He could not find a word.

"So you will always be, if you would want to be, a small part Froghuli," Ka-Nam almost pleaded. "Not to say you are not rightly proud of your own. But the Froghul of Tan Dramali will be proud to say you have been one of us, for a short while."

Dolvid accepted the knife. He tried again. "Ka-Nam, this is too much honor for me."

Ka-Nam patted his arm, and as they stood up together, two or three bystanders made an odd twisting motion of rubbing hands together, the sign of approval. Dolvid sniffed. Of all mornings this one had no bright sun to blame for his eyes.

As he untied Nuril and began to lead him up the rise, where those for Kadon were assembling, Tini-ra came running. Wordlessly, defiantly, she took his free hand, and stepped beside him, head bowed, eyes down. It struck him, with all the their time together, they had said very little to each other, bar her explanations, on the first day, of tribal ways.

"Are you glad you'll be going back to the North?"

"No."

After a few steps, she came close to looking at him, to say, "You did a lot of writing."

It did not sound a question. He shrugged at his satchel. "This isn't so much." He wanted not to go on, but the boast came. "At the *Mankh'*, I write much, much more. Pages and pages, many different learnings, do you understand?"

"Yes."

"It is only what I do, just like herding goats. Wise men at the *Mankh'* say — I do not say this about myself — they say I can write as well as — " He gave the same one-shoulder shrug. "As wise men do."

In a near-whisper, "And you learned the other language, our language."

"Not well. Some words."

"Why did you?"

They were coming up to the main group, and he was certain without being told Tini-ra was not coming to Kadon Dinul. Her last question stayed between them, and it meant, he could tell, much other than it asked, so he could not give the usual pat but truthful answer, 'so as to know.' He was growing hot with shame about how he had praised his own accomplishments, and there was a larger way he had made a fool of himself, nothing to do with milking or with throwing knives.

"We may meet again," turning to face her, turning her to face him. And perceiving, belatedly, that though small like all her people she was quite as old as he, perhaps a little older. Moreover, with her huge eyes, she was truly beautiful.

"No — " turning away any second chances. He opened his mouth and said nothing, and in her own language she murmured, "I wish you had liked me, Dol-vith."

Face burning, he said in the same tongue, "I do like you, Tini-ra," but he had the tense wrong, and the phrase could mean more and other than liking, so that bewilderment came into her face.

Which she dismissed, saying, "Good road, Dolvidh."

The night of the blood-dance, when excitement had quieted to embers of soft talk, they had left the fire together, hand in hand. She tugged towards the hillside, so slightly he could pretend he must be mistaken, though certain he was not. Drowsed, he turned for the tent where he was sleeping, forbidden ground for her. Outside, she turned up her face, and he had bent to kiss a cheek, with the dark bloom he could feel rather than see. There had been puzzlement in her parting, just as there was now.

"Farewell, Tini-ra." She had let go his hand, and now touched the back of it with light fingertips, wheeling away to run back to the camp. From the head of the rise he looked back, and saw her gazing after him. She used her right thumbnail to scratch a line down the inside of her left forearm, then turned to go where Gula, her mother, was pressing water out of a new-made cheese, eyes not leaving the slender girl.

Knowing

Barley-water, tepid and unflavored, captured the flatness of life after his days with the Froghul. Nothing else, not *raminat*, not milk or fruit drinks, was found at the *Mankh'* for the solemn time between start of *Shuda'sai* and the Patriarch's annual departure for the Summer Palace.

Having given him a cup of the soapy-tasting liquid, *Menadhi*, exasperated in every way by the Pledging, indulged for once in open criticism of the *rabhsai*'s policies.

"Understand, I do not deplore the reconciliation with Saidhan. But at what cost! Concessions, Dolvidh, everywhere concessions, even to the rebellious Deniants."

"But I heard they had submitted, and are to pay the Growers' tax."

"So they have, and shall. But now they are permitted to choose a new assessor from among themselves. Meanwhile Saidhan *Asai* can sail for Kamsilat, keeping his excess troops, and with the *rabhsai*'s undertaking make his own conditions for laying down his command."

That meant, Dolvid realized, name Sebhal as his successor. "If Lambarr *Deghi* did not want Saidhan as Captain of the West, could he not just dismiss him?"

"All Royal Captaincies are for life, except if there is treason, or some other grave charge the whole Council can agree to. With Saidhan, is that likely?"

"Because of Saëdhu *Rabhsayu*."

"Among many reasons. Saidhan remains *Nim'* in Kamsilat, and if Lambarr is serious about his projects at Tan Lughsai, he must have his long-timbers from the Colony." Sarcasm was unconcealed; Lambarr was erecting a new Great House at Tan Lughsai, and even the outside walls were going to be of wood, rarest of building materials here on the Mainland. The forests behind Kamsilat were the only ones where enough big oaks and ashes could be found, but who could seriously believe the *rabhsai* would base policy on that?

"And your hospitable friends have gained their precious suit; the *nim'* of a province is instructed to *allow these our subjects to pass freely along ways anciently theirs.* Laluvoi *Asayu* heard the case."

Dolvid sat tense, glad about the judgment, fearful his part in it would be seen or suspected. As in Inghi's dance, he could see the Froghul marching proudly along the trails Vinilat had tried to close, till they reached the summer pastures, and a hero's welcome from their kindred clans.

Menadhi was speaking. "I am told the pleas were framed so Vinilat had no answer, notwithstanding all the nonsense your friends had to say about good hearts and bad hearts. No Froghuli would have that skill; did you hear, while you were with them, any whispers about their consulting anyone, an Owani, perhaps, greedy for a fee?"

Here he could be adequately truthful. "Ka-Nam said they had paid a man at Drin Dakani to do some writing."

After considering, *Menadhi* nodded. "Gholat. He is at Drin Dakani. He began at the same *manai* as your friend Faëdhal. I would not have thought he knew so much law. More than ever with this Pledging we can see how quickly floodwaters can rise to sweep us away. Once again we must be the rock, the Island that does not founder." His face was rapt as he gestured westward, while Dolvid was deciding certain details would be left out of his book about the Froghul. No one at the *Mankh'* had seen Ka-Nam's knife.

"*Shuda'sai* again," shaking his head. "Time slides away, Dolvidh. In not much more than a year, you will take your Lesser Oaths, and after, make your journey to the Island, and be wholly ours. Do you remember when we first met?"

"Yes, *Menadhi*." He was seeing Tini-ra, pouring the welcome-cup.

"Do you, truly?"

"Yes, yes. In the Residence library." Hard to accept he would never be with Tini-ra again, not even to explain his ineptitude.

"You could not know what I saw then. How could anyone forecast what you would come to be?"

Dressed, as usual at the *Mankh'* for warm weather, in short summer tunic with no breeches, Dolvid was sharply aware of the muscling of his bare legs. He folded his arms. *Menadhi* leant back with a curious smile, then stood to begin pacing. After three turns, he faced Dolvid again. "The Pledging and its fruits mean I have to be absent on a long journey — long journeys, rather. Kamanta, with His Enlightenment, and then other distant parts. Inilun Barabhi in Kargul, for one. Tobhan is bitter, with good reason, that the *rabhsai* cannot find a captaincy for his son. I may not be back till past Halving-Day."

"Your presence will be missed, *Menadhi*." Except for the faint fear he might be thrown back with the ordinary pupils, Dolvid exulted at the prospect of three months or more without him.

"You have your little book to write, and you must learn the devotions for your Lesser Oaths, and the mysteries for your pilgrimage. Aside from that, instead of a set task, I'll give you a general charge: learn! I shall leave word you are to be admitted to lessons of the *Ramadilum*, to learn a little about the body, and a few simpler healings; also the garden-plots of the *Edhrodilum*, where you can observe and listen, and ask your questions. Not much planting this season, but you can still learn, as fruits ripen. You will not be idle or bored. Does this suit you?"

It did, and he would do these things. The *Ramidhai* was a tall, cold, rather forbidding man, but for a closer look at the bones and other relics glimpsed through an open door, Dolvid could brave that. Yet while he knew once again he was being given extraordinary privileges, gratitude, gratification, everything here was at the borders of his mind. He was preoccupied with the painful question of what Tini-ra must think of him, she and her clan, even Ka-Nam, who had watched. The Poet Bronal said, shame of a woman, taken by one she had not lain waking for, was not worse than shame of a man, not-taking a woman who lies waking for him. Dolvid understood that now, and for the hundredth time felt hot guilt rise to his face.

"What is it?" swooping for Dolvid, who hastily stood. They were eye-to-eye, and Dolvid would soon be the taller.

Menadhi was perplexed, perhaps anxious. He reached out to touch a cheek with his soft fingers, not a lot bigger than Tini-ra's. All at once he dropped that hand, and gave a laugh, startlingly hearty.

"I see, I see. Your pardon, Dolvidh, I am mocking myself. This dry old teacher tells you, learn the body, when it is your own body you need to discover. He talks about planting and breeding in garden-plots, when those of the *Nôdhilum* are where your mind is. Yes, yes, it is time, or soon will be." His renewed jocularity, nevertheless, sounded forced.

"I shall also leave word that after your birthday you be allowed a visit to the gardens of the *nôd'yanul*, for other instruction. A little early, my friend, but Aëlovoi's voice outbids the calendar. Does this suit you?"

"For everything, I thank you, *Menadhi*."

The name Bronal was Owanilú for 'Oaks,' and a short form for lyrics was called *brona'dodhi*, oak-leaf. Though often used by Bronal, it was not named after him, but for its pattern on the page, two short lines followed by three longer ones, two short again, and then once more, for fifteen lines in all. The rules for this were not as stiff as with some other forms; Island poets, scornful of its slightness, had never used it. Dolvid's earliest attempts at verse were *brona'dodhil*, correct enough for style, but with feelings borrowed rather than expressed, as he could always see when the immediate fever of composition cooled down.

But he did discover what Bronal meant, calling poetry *rhaël'olu*, 'loss-song.' He kept his feeling of guilt over Tini-ra, but began to hope she understood, or could remember it all till she was old enough to understand. If he had let her lead him to the hillside, he would not have known what to do.

Even her opinion of him was not the worst; worse was the loss. Not just of her; there was friendship, too, fellowship, the warm company of humans you could trust to say exactly what they felt, or to dance it if it could not be said. For a while his dream of vanishing from the *Mankh'* took a new ending, where he went north instead of west, and was greeted after a long journey by smiling Ka-Nam, Inghi knowing and ironic, a forgiving, yielding Tini-ra. Past this happy ending, sadly, was knowledge he could not live as a herdsman, waking and sleeping the rest of his life with nothing read, nothing written, nothing new to look forward to.

The *Mankh'* was home, or could be, if like the young officer, Bolan, in the Household, he could climb high enough to be beyond touching. That meant always and only fear of *Menadhi*, also the one most worth talking with, truly learned, quick to see and commend a new idea, genuine in his belief learning was important.

Could he continue as apparent disciple? With what mattered most to *Menadhi*, his older realms of unchallenged Owani privilege, it was becoming harder to agree, or to pretend agreement, because Dolvid was beginning to find untruth in the *Atarlum* writings that were its foundation. Froghul, his Froghul, could never have been the simple child-men of the accepted account, nor was the Owani race the only one with pride in its past, regret for lost glory.

At first quite idly he let himself ponder whether others of the Others might be as unfairly treated by their histories. The muddled *Song of Tales* was not the original Gabhani epic, but a compilation and retranslation made at the *Mankh'* from tales transcribed by the *Atarlum*. He would like to study the original versions in the Owanilú, to see what might have been altered. To get another stage behind those transcripts, he would have to study Old Gabhanilú, direct ancestor of the realm's everyday speech, although hardly anyone bothered with learning the difficult score-alphabet in which it was written. As *Menadhi* said, the effort was better spent learning the Old Owani Syllabary, which had far nobler things to record. But whether that was true was exactly what Dolvid would never find out unless he taught himself Old Gabhanilú. There really was no end to it.

Late at night he stood, in the passageway that served this wing, a little dazed, for a moment not sure which way to turn for his own quarters. Padding soft-footed on cool stone, one of the younger girls passed him, then turned back with a questioning glance, nearly a smile. Improbably, the widened eyes, though light, were somehow like Tini-ra.

One of Bronal's best-known poems was on the common idea that the remedy for hopeless longing was another woman's bed. Bronal did not accept it, and now neither did Dolvid.

He had been surprised at how readily he was admitted to the westward wing. Washed with more than usual care, dressed in his least-frayed smock, he had been greeted by a cheerful *atarlayu* of the *Nôdhilum* (least learned and most affable of Orders), like an amiable aunt, very possibly a former *nod'yanu* herself, to judge by the flowing grace of her walk, as she conducted him to a carpeted room. In muted light, he took in cushions and a low table, a flask of what might well be watered wine, a curtained bed.

Embhu, light-haired in a pale blue tunic rose and smiled gently as Dolvid was introduced. She was an Islander, from the village of Daëni Tâl, on Kamanta's eastern shore. Dolvidh, the *atarlayu* said, was a scholar of the *Manadilum*, who would, perhaps, enjoy hearing song. Then she was gone. The small feet of Embhu were bare, and the carpet had threadbare patches.

"Dolvidhai," in what he heard as a careful voice. "Will you wear a robe?" Out of an alcove she brought a loose-sleeved one of soft linen, and helped it on over his smock, with pats and pluckings of her fine hands. She was slender with a tiny waist and level hips; her neck was white and downed at the back. The eyes were set wide, forehead smooth and rounded, her mouth small, but with full lips which might be lightly colored. Her movements had a studied elegance, and she was a year older than he.

"Will you sit?"

When they were perched on cushions she poured a small cup from the flask, not giving herself any. It was wine, and it was watered.

"What should I do for you, Dolvidh?" When he did not have a reply, she said, "Should I sing?"

"If you like."

"What would you enjoy? Does poetry please you?" Under the table was a set of finger-drums. Taking them she accompanied herself in a section from one of the familiar longer lyrics of the Island period, marking pauses and stanzas with appropriate flourishes. Her Owanilú was very pure, with no Island accent, and though the style was one for whole gatherings rather than a single hearer, she did it quite well. At the end, she said, "The *Rok'olul b'Akhi* are among the most exquisite of our poems, are they not?"

"I have heard Banak-rai enjoyed them." He was imagining what that lout Yubhai would ever make of this performance.

"Small wonder. One of the consolations for the Long Night is that in their Island exile our poets found peace to perfect their craft; the *Rok'olul b'Akhi* were a light through darkness, and can never be extinguished."

He could have finished that for her, word for word from a *Mankh'* commentary he despised. He said, "To me, the lyrics of the Blossoming Age are better in every way. Even if you leave aside Bronal, poets then could write a song without fifty lines telling you they're going to write a song. All the best half-lines from the *Rok'olul b'Akhi* are borrowed, anyway, from earlier work."

He was going to cite examples, but Embhu nodded happily. "On matters of taste no magistrate sits."

"A wise heart is a humble heart," he replied. She nodded agreement. He said, "Do you really admire the Fire-Lyrics?"

This was novel. She blinked her wide eyes. "I am pleased by what pleases you. The bringer of joy has a happy heart."

"A minute's thought saves a day's error," he said, and Embhu simpered on. "Patience caught the cunning mouse," he continued wildly. "A still tongue speaks to wise — "

"Will you have a honey-cake?"

"I thank you, Embhu." She passed some. They were tiny.

After a crushing three-second silence she began again. "You're a scholar. What do you study?"

"Mainly history."

"History. That's very interesting. What parts of history are your particular interest?"

"At the moment, the Wars of Cleansing, Pir Kallikuk."

"Before the Return, is that?"

"Yes." He gulped down another little cake.

"The history of those years is very... " a loose wave.

"Interesting."

"Yes."

In this next halt Dolvid began to feel ashamed. Embhu was trying very hard. Not her fault she could not do the one thing that would please him, really talk about things she had been taught to talk about.

"Would you rather not have words? If you want, I can play softly on the *olútaloi* — " five-stringed on a curved frame, traditional instrument of love-song and lovemaking.

"And loudly?"

"Your pardon?"

"Can you also play loudly on the *olútaloi*?"

Embhu screwed her eyes up tight, her mouth twisting sideways, so he thought she might be at the brink of tears. She said, "Oh, Dolvidh," reproachfully, and together they began to giggle.

When that calmed down he asked her about Daëni Tâl, her home. On their close cushions they were leaning to each other.

She described what sounded a dreary place, a stone-built village, perched on Kamanta's impassable cliffs, facing a wide bay with the wishful name of Klam Nampai, `contentment.' Having come so far she put a hand over her mouth. "I shouldn't be telling about this."

"About the Island? I've studied it in my mapmaking."

"But we are supposed to confine ourselves to your interests."

"Well, this is what I'm interested in." When she laughed she was astonishingly pretty all over again, with one deep dimple on the right side. Her left. "Have you ever seen Lunu Midhi?"

"Oh, no!" She made a pious sign. "That's inland, beyond Drin b'Afon. The only ones who can go there — well, you'll go there, not so?"

"Why are you taught — " wrestling for a word. "Why do they give you such, oh, such formal things to say?"

"We are all part of the Memory of Owan. Men who travel — "

"Yes?"

"Are eager to hear old tales and new gossip. Only I don't have any new gossip."

Considering her classmates, that must be hugely untrue, but probably they were forbidden to discuss their various beddings, on pain of expulsion, or whatever punishments girls were given.

"Not everyone is a scholar like you, Dolvidh. Those who we'll meet at the *margú*, *Naëdhi* himself says, will want entertainment, with music and poetry."

"What about ones who do not understand the Owanilú?"

"We are not to let anyone feel lacking. If we desire, we can learn two or three tales from the *Song of Tales*."

"Or songs from the *Tale of Songs*." This was quite possible, but it made Embhu laugh again.

"Merchants, for example, ones of Mixed heritage, might not share in our Owani taste for song. Our task is pleasing. They might want to go direct to the couch." Eyes flicking to curtained bed then back to him, she made this the suggestion of a suggestion.

"Will that please you? The life of the *margú*, I mean," he hastily clarified.

Embhu was complacent. "We are lucky. Other girls of our birth will never possess land. At the end of her service, any *nôd'yanu* can — " Once more the hand went to her mouth. "I am not allowed to speak about that, either."

"Why not?"

"That is my craft, while a man is with me, to make him certain he is my only interest." Hands linked where the soft fabric of her tunic nestled between her upper legs, she frowned, recognizing an illusion that could not survive being talked-about.

"Also massage. A traveller of any kind might want stiffness from a day's riding to be smoothed away."

"Yes indeed." His crooked smirk came from boys in the general sleeping-quarters. Embhu reached up to remove the clasp holding her hair, which came tumbling prettily onto her shoulders. After contemplating the hands lying in her lap, she brought her eyes up to Dolvid's. "Are you ready for the couch?"

"There is no hurry."

She looked, and it was different, knowing. "You're funny," she said. While challenged, he felt his control of the exchange slipping away.

"What else do they teach you?"

"Many things. Things that please men." With a lithe movement she had left her cushion to crouch by his knees. The straight top of the blue tunic let him see the soft rise where her breasts began. The extreme tip of his tongue was nearly glued between his dried lips.

"Then this is your beginning. There is nothing to be anxious about. I'll show you."

Brooding all afternoon, he had been tautly primed for this encounter, tense and trembling. Now, with Embhu's hand on his covered thigh, he could not imagine he would be ready again, ever. He seemed to have withered away. The mingling of bodies was a ridiculous idea.

She rocked back and stood. Lidding eyes, she reached back to unfasten her tunic. After she brushed the loops from her shoulders it edged down with maddening slowness. When she leaned forward to take his hand, she was naked nearly to the waist.

In her fingers his hand was a clumsy club. He was on his feet, and thinking he was supposed to, started to lunge forward. With a sharp inbreath, she jumped back no more than a handspan. She held his eyes with hers, though he was conscious of the expanse of skin, tips of her small breasts.

"No, Dolvidh; before you touch me, tell me what you see."

This too must be a lesson learned, but he felt manhood stirring. Odd his body was easier to fool than his mind, but perhaps the body's needs were the simpler. He said, "In one glory, desire and fulfillment." That was from his favorite poet, but it pleased Embhu, and Dolvid himself found it apt. His rise in self-esteem was echoed by his blood. Embhu freed her waistband, and stepped delicately from puddled clothes.

A girl's entire body, with its neat keystone of hair so different from his own wire tangle, was wildly interesting. He had not realized how delicate it all would be, the polished rounds of her shoulders and long arch of thighs, ending at the top in delicious creases, were jewelry compared to the blacksmiths' work of his own joining. He could learn it all with his hands.

"Better now," Embhu, judging his state when he moved forward and now was allowed to grasp her. She started kissing in little sips, and he, clumsily but with mounting fierceness, kissed her till she was panting. One stride had taken him from indifference to impatience.

Behind the curtain once his clothes were gone she guided him adroitly, till no guidance was needed. It was good, but over at once.

"That is the first. When you are ready again, it will be longer."

"Will that please you more?"

"This is for your pleasure."

"But will it?"

"I am pleased by pleasing you."

It crossed his mind nothing could be better than knowing he had pleased Embhu, but that was the start of a childhood battle, well I will if you will, and so on eternally. He sank down beside her, and was silent.

She was right, longer, long enough for him to feel the interclasp of thought and feeling, till feeling broke loose and bolted with his mind. Embhu came back into his vision, also gasping. He wondered if she was going to sneeze, but with her strange whimper came a slewing of eyes. She hugged him down on her in plain gratitude, and after all he had not broken anything.

That was not the end: Embhu became ingenious, or wanted to show off skills she had acquired. He could amuse her, and she was marvellously capable. He did well, she said, though compliments, he did not forget, could also be taught. Once, when they had been laughing together, he was overcome with tenderness, wanting to share words about feelings never told to anyone, night-visions when thinking ran strong and smooth, magic steeds in a children's story. He got as far as saying his birth home, where his mother died, was in the South.

"In Ninkufu? Laluvoi *Asayu* also comes from there. Many who have been famous in our history came from the warm shores of the Southern Seas."

If he had said Kargul, the answer, he guessed, would have been much the same, only with Talbhan instead of Laluvoi, and ‘deep mountain-valleys of that renowned province' instead of the warm southern seas. The illusion of closeness ebbed away.

Outside in the corridor after goodnights, he was baffled so many satisfactions could leave him dissatisfied. He had found more than anticipated, yet something expected had not been there at all. That was stupid, and he was very sleepy.

The girl who had turned to help him had planed features of astonishing beauty, and an elusive, unreadable smile. Having remembered his way, he shook his head to say no, he did not need directions, and her smile deepened. A moment with no before or after, where he and she had a secret no one else could share; what it could be was beyond him. They turned away from each other.

Now strands were being woven, back and forth, to join him to the *Mankh'* forever, chantings, signs, prescribed observations, the ritual patterning of life so there would be no question without its echo-answer. Or a ship with announced destination, and he could watch Dolvid and all the other passengers coming daily closer to planned harborage; little Zhâlai, trying to ingratiate himself even in chanted pleas to Raëdh, Yubhai, big-boned and slow-thinking, rock-jawed in his determination not to be thrown overboard and picked up by the *Adanum Plakh'*. Dravadhi, as he came nearer the gravity of his future, more than ever resembled rulers of old, his face implacable yet filled with a merciful wisdom, as its owner was not. They and the others were nearing choice to end choice, and how much choosing could be left, after mornings and meals, beatings and kindnesses, a thousand recitations of the Responses, four times that many contemplations westward to the Island? After so many lessons, with all learnings drawn together by the strong, invisible Will of Raëdh, coming down to *g'Asalladh'* to give every action of His servants its inner meaning.

Seeing the art with which the threads were fastened did not make Dolvid free of their web. Most often, he did not want to be; he yearned for acceptance that would perfect faith, and bring him to the freedom of absolute bondage. On good days when his contemplations went well, not interrupted by distracting thoughts of manuscripts he ought to consult, he seemed to have achieved that, but then was sure he had not, because true belonging did not know but simply was.

Well, then, he was set apart by too much thinking, but that also gave him his privileged position, which, after all, might make life as an *atarlai* tolerable, half-guilty doubts intact. Through dying summer and into autumn he worked at his book on the Froghul, more exciting than he could have imagined. *Menadhi* at length returned, sunburnt from his travels, and they discussed the book, section by section and page by page. This was very serious business, and Dolvid was challenged at every turn, at times with what he took for deliberate cruelty. Grinding work, aware *Menadhi*'s unblinking eyes would spot every gap in knowledge he tried to disguise with a fascinating digression or ornate flourish of words. Here was a reminder of learning the weapons from Kheval, but *Menadhi*'s quiet vigilance could be painful like Kheval's remembered sarcasms or occasional abuse. Worse than the throb of an arm made to hold up a sword too long was the howl of body and brain together when he had to force himself back to his writing table and once more redo a passage from which many rephrasings had long ago expelled the joy there was in the first writing.

Amazingly, eventual reward was the same, passing beyond intolerable hurt to see it come right. All the temper and tedium culminated in a cold day at the *Mankh'* library, when Dolvid, his voice gradually ceasing to tremble with chill and fright, read aloud through his book, page by page, while five copyists (two of them full *atarlal*) scratched steadily with their pens, proofreading each other's finished sheets. *Customs and Lore of the Froghuli People* achieved an edition.

He wished his father could see it — that spoiled his mood of self-obliteration in the wholeness of the *Atarlum*, brought back the *Song of Tales*, and how his father used to rage about inaccuracies in the *Mankh'* version of the Gabhani epic, his resolve to teach himself how to read the score-alphabet.

But in fact he did not need that for the largest part; only a few of the stories had ever been written in that form, and the rest had been saved from oblivion by the *Atarlum*. So went the accepted account; after the Return, recorders of the *Mankh'* had been just in time to preserve a body of lore, accrued through ages, as the Gabhanil settled in cities and their customs changed, the old hard-drinking, tale-telling feasts themselves becoming history. Those parts had been written down using ordinary letters, and then translated into the Owanilú, so that when, during the long reign of Plakhval, the whole *Song* was retranslated into what was by then the ordinary speech of the realm, it was said the Gabhanil had been given back their own folk-history by the *Mankh'*.

Of admitted gaps in that edition, the usual explanation was that many of the tales had become hopelessly garbled in generations of retelling. In the published text as was were enough oddities: the Odi Kukkuk stories were acknowledged legend, and it did not matter if they were full of impossible wonders and magical feats. But Pir Perus, though his dates were hard to fix, was claimed by the Others as, anciently, a real, historical hero, a great war-captain, hard to reconcile with episodes where, for example, he was given a marvellous coat that changed color, or fought a bitter battle with the swallows.

Quite aside from the trap once set by *Menadhi*, Dolvid had often noticed how books and documents came tumbling into his hands, as if his preoccupation with a question had summoned them. He had not told anyone of his renewed curiosity about the *Song of Tales*, and yet while he was collecting materials for the book on the Froghul he kept turning up variant versions for parts of the Gabhani epic, both original transcripts in Old Gabhanilú, and episodes from the Owanilú redaction, suppressed in retranslation.

Suppressed, the word was forced on him. What at first seemed stupidity, and even his father had called the carelessness the *Atarlum* displayed with a history not their own, became more sinister. Consistently, the *Mankh'* edition had picked not the most but the least coherent accounts, and in virtually every sample he came across what was left out would have made better sense of what was included.

For nearly all the period called the Wars of Cleansing, before the Return, there were no Owanil chronicles for happenings here on the Mainland, and in the published *Song* the complicated Gabhani history came down to that of a simple, childlike but courageous people, achieving victory over many petty despots, and occupation of much of what had been the realm of Owan by preponderance of numbers, stubbornness, and reckless bravery, till the Owani aristocracy came back from the Island to bring them leadership and law.

If there was a truer tale, it would never be complete. Many hands had worked at collecting and editing, transcribing and translation; overlapping but patchwork portions in various stages were scattered through the *Mankh'* and Bronze Residence libraries, never properly catalogued.   But Dolvid's forays, breathless with fear of being spied on, taught him enough to be convinced the *Mankh'* version was a conscious fraud. He found a table showing slight local variants in laws held in common by all clans of the Gabhanil — not included in the published *Song*, where such things apparently depended on will or whim of local leaders. A colorful description of how the Gabhanil chose a High Captain of their confederacy, omitted from the book. With that, a speech or letter by one such leader, outlining strategy in the war — changed by the *Song*'s compilers into a simple exhortation to courage and steadfastness. No one reading the *Song of Tales* would ever guess, as he discovered, that the Gabhanil had graduated taxes and an organized messenger service, nor, certainly that the remnant Owanil on the Mainland at times served in the wars under Gabhani leadership.

Just after finishing the book on the Froghul Dolvid had come across another page not included in the *Song of Tales*, showing Kadon Dinul, under the Gabhanil, was already largely rebuilt and had become the seat of government by 2400 (Owani count), still about eighty years before the Return.

Painfully clear; but for the coming of the Great Plague, Konúrai, there would have been no Return, the realm would have become Gabhan with Gabhanil rulers, those of his people who wished to stay, the all-wise, masterly Owanil, humble subjects under Gabhani law.

Not long ago he would have struggled for a way to evade that conclusion, as a catastrophe too enormous to be contemplated. His few days with the Froghul had changed him, showing different ways were not necessarily inferior ways — though only faint hints remained in his book of the outrageous idea that child-men of an uncouth people might have valuable things to teach the cultured Owanil.

A history without the Return would have been unbearably sad, if it had truly meant the end of all the good and noble there had been in Old Owan. But there would still have been the Island for preservation, and Owanil of the Mainland could have put their learning and their skills to good use in the new realm, even without the devastations of Konúrai to put them back on top.

His father's charge, that the *Atarlum* deliberately withheld healing till the Gabhani leadership was decimated, became harder to resist. *Menadhi* called that 'an ancient calumny,' but Dolvid was becoming skeptical of everything from that source, everything that glorified Owan at the expense of the Others.

His one brief meeting with the Patriarch stopped him from calling *Menadhi*'s views those of the *Mankh'*; he was surer than ever there were factions in the *Atarlum*. He remembered *Menadhi*'s remark that the era had called for a conciliatory Patriarch, seeming to contain the idea that the faction *Menadhi* belonged to could advance a Patriarch like Kamanasalladh as a kindly mask to show the realm, while old schemes for restoring Owani privilege and ancient powers of the *Atarlum* went on in secret.

Dolvid did not believe it; it was the same as his preposterous hints wives of Owani race had in some way been foisted on Great Banak and his son; a *rabhsai* was not a puppet, and Patriarchs were not chosen by huddled conspirators. Besides, it would be carrying deception too far to pick a Patriarch who not only appeared to endorse a fairer division of power, but had joined with Great Banak to help foster it, introducing measures *Menadhi* deplored, and would undo if he could.

All these were blasphemous: the *Atarlum* worked the One Will of Raëdh, as interpreted by His Enlightenment. But as the peculiar young Household officer said, the *Mankh'* was part of the world, and Dolvid was certain the Patriarch, from the *Edhrodilum*, no scholar of history, was unaware the *Song of Tales* was a fraud, just as he was sure *Menadhi* knew, and approved of it. As of the usefulness of Konúrai in bringing about the Return.

That was a very old wrong, without a remedy. As for the *Song*, he could make himself half-crazy with desire to correct its untruths, but knew any attempt would doom him to horrible punishments; it would have to be a dream deferred, to be the Owani who found a way to give back the Gabhanil their real past.

There was still the future. If *Menadhi* in truth must eventually become the Patriarch, then Raëdh would change His Mind (the mere idea was appalling heresy), and lies would triumph. Was there anything to be done to prevent that? Dolvid had already seen that exposing him and his views to the Patriarch was an absurd fantasy, a boy denouncing a respected Head of Order.

But he would not always be a boy. Later, perhaps, when he had standing of his own —

Hardly realizing, he had been looking for a reason not to leave the *Mankh'*. He was happy here, so long as he was not being flogged, or worrying about withdrawal of *Menadhi*'s favor, happier than he could imagine being anywhere else. Besides, thought of *Menadhi*'s fury if he tried to decline his Oaths was enough to freeze him with terror. But *Menadhi* lied, and Dolvid could too; he could pretend to be his ally, and work, and wait for the chance to tell the truth. He really was *Menadhi*'s adversary. It might be his life's work.

When next he went to be heard in the Responses and to share *raminat*, a book bound in soft vellum was waiting for him on the little table. Opening it he found his own fair-copy of the book about the Froghul, sewn into a volume and given an elaborate title page by a craftsman of the *Mankh'*. It was his, to keep.

The small man sat smiling, eyes full of pride. Once again, Dolvid wished his father could have seen the book. He wished his father was *Menadhi*.

It shook him with its nonsensicality. Dimly behind it there was a recognition: with his father there would be no need for this jangle of contradictions, the gratitude and even love he felt for a man he planned to fool and betray. His tears for the gift were real.

Nuril was getting old. Well past his prime when Dolvid first rode him, his unhurried gait had not changed much, but the eyes were dulling, and for the last two winters he had developed a wheeze that persisted into the moist days of spring. For Nuril's sake Dolvid longed for warmer days, resting the piebald as much as he could. For rides in the Estates he was now allowed to borrow a *pefrai* of the *Adanum*, and after initial fear found the fiery animals could be mastered. For his journeys to Kadon Dinul, when weather was bad he tried to find a returning supply-wagon. More than once he walked both ways.

One day, cool and dry with a gusty wind off Arnan, he walked past the Bronze Residence, and crossed the Square to enter the city. In the house not far off the Avenue he was lucky to catch Faëdhal at home. The *rabhsai* with most of the Family had gone to Tan Lughsai for the first time this season.

"Ah, Dolvidh. Pleasure unlooked-for is joy indeed! It has been long, excessively so, since I have seen you. Nerumas — " waving at the lanky Mixed youth who had opened the door. "Warm *raminat* with honey, if you would. We shall be in my study."

He led the way to the book-lined room, delicately and expensively furnished; the chair he put Dolvid in must date from the early years of Plakhsila's reign, walnut wood, joined and carved with a skill now seldom seen. Ever since the Pledging, now eight months past, Dolvid seemed to have discovered time; all at once conscious of change, he could not see any in Faëdhal; the keen eye, the stoop, the leanness were all the same. Perhaps the bobbing protuberance in his throat was becoming more noticeable.

He had heard of Dolvid's book. "*Menadhi* spoke of it, as he generally does of you, when he deigns to visit us at the New Residence. He would seem, if one may say so, to hold you in high esteem."

Dolvid mumbled nothing that could be called words, and the attentive turn of Faëdhal's head was of an inquisitive bird.

"His admiration, may I venture, is not altogether reciprocated? No, forgive me, I do not mean to embarrass you."

The *raminat* was carried in, the cups fine earthenware, with a rich sheen to the deep blue glaze. Faëdhal gave Nerumas an affable nod, and he smiled in return.

"To be truthful," Faëdhal resumed when the youth had left again, "I see little of *Menadhi*. I am seldom at the library. Your father's post, as perhaps you have heard, has never been filled. Mere copyists nowadays keep up repairs and so forth."

"Has the new baby come to the Residence?" — choosing, a little clumsily, to change subjects.

"Not yet." He was never far from moist-eyed sentimentality when discussing the Family. "The *rabhsayu* is to remain in the South till warm weather comes. But said to be a fine strong boy, to be called Rodlakh, a fine name, if I may say so." This was Lambarr's fourth son — or fifth, if you counted the early, unnamed one who had lived less than a week — and seventh surviving child.

"Where do your studies take you," Faëdhal enquired, "after your triumph, if I may put it so, over the Froghul?"

"Many things, sir. For myself, the *Song of Tales*."

"The *Song!*" Bafflement struggled with distaste. "Surely the only readable text ever to come from that tangle is the *Mankh'* edition, which is most accurately translated from the Owanilú redaction."

"That's true enough for what is included. I am studying the original transcripts, many of which were not."

"Praise Hrafi, I do not wonder. For once, if you will pardon me, the *Atarlum* was of some service to the realm, in shortening the *Song*. Flying serpents and speaking bears, stories for children and chambermaids. I thought history was your preferred study."

"To my mind, Master, there is history to be unearthed in the *Song*."

"My dear Dolvidh! Odi Kukkuk and the Bull of Narn? Pir Perus and his wonderful outshirt? As what may be termed simple tales of magic, to my mind they are distinctly inferior to the best Owanil examples."

"The Other Races," nearly apologizing, "have been a special interest of mine."

"As we see from your book, yes. Then you have taught yourself the Old Gabhanilú?"

"Not yet the score-alphabet, Master, only somewhat, in transcription. Some pages I can't read at all."

"Not surprisingly." He stood. "As it happens I have a number of leaves in my possession, recopied from the originals." He went to one of the many shelves, and started searching through sheaves. "You say, pages you cannot read?"

"Many words I can find no meaning for."

"Aha." Faëdhal was pleased with himself. "The *Atarlum* scribes had enormous initial difficulty rendering Old Gabhanilú in the newer letters; there were sounds they found hard to capture. Some of the earliest to make transcriptions assigned completely arbitrary values to existent letters, with interlinear marks to show their departures. I have, as it happens, made a study of these practices, and think I may say I have solved most problems of their usage."

With manifest pride, he pulled out a rolled bundle of parchments. "That is why I am more familiar with parts of the *Song* than might otherwise be the case. This can only be a variant version of the last fight of Pir Perus — with swallows, was it not? In the margins, as you will see, I have noted departures from standard letter-values."

On the larger work-table they opened the roll of pages. Dolvid had spent hours wondering about the eccentric markings that sprinkled these manuscripts.

"It has long been my opinion," Faëdhal observed, "a translator of reputable rank should be willing to share, as it were, his schooling — where possible, for instance, appending the original words of a difficult passage, my own invariable practice, so others can make comparative readings. At the *Mankh'*, I fear, they have always been unconscionably high-handed, so any inaccuracy is called an improvement. Your *Menadhi* and I have often disputed the matter."

"He, I am certain, would forbid my study of the *Song*, if he knew about it." Dolvid was hardly aware of tactics in this.

"Ah," considering the decorated ceiling. "Then if I should encounter him, I shall not know, either. For all its improbable marvels, it may be the last word has not been said on the *Song*."

This was somewhere between an apology for his earlier strictures on the subject, and a sanctioning of Dolvid's studies. He insisted Dolvid keep the pages he needed. "These are facsimiles, and the originals are to be found in the Bronze Residence library, if I am not in error. The notes I made have served their purpose for me."

"This is very generous, sir."

"Ah, well. One must — that is to say, we serve the same

true master, in the end, do we not? Knowledge, that is, learning, as your much-missed father would say."

Dolvid, having evaded it once, guessed what was coming. Faëdhal, referring again to the unfilled position, Keeper of Books, observed it was generally held to be an honorable thing to follow one's father. Ardirr, father of Arvus, had been assistant at the Treasury where now the son was in charge, and Rhunsilakh had at last succeeded to his father's rank of Chief Counsellor, *Bôdhrai*. "Although," Faëdhal could not resist adding, "a mere Master of Languages is not ranked as *bôdh'loiki*, and one who can advise the *rabhsai* on earth closets for Tan Lughsai may obtain a readier hearing. But while the *rabhsai* has been understandably so preoccupied with his family, Laluvoi *Asayu* remains a pillar of strength at the Residence, or in the realm, one might say."

The implication was, Laluvoi would be the one Faëdhal might approach on Dolvid's behalf. He had seen her distantly at the Great Pledging, tiny and glad beside her old friend Saidhan on the Residence steps, and he remembered very well her potent blend of graciousness and steel. Very good, but was he going to win her favor so he could meekly succeed to his father's rank? He, with all his qualities, had never written any of the books he cared for. "I thank you, Master. But — "

"Not so, no, no. A suggestion, no more; no answer is needed, and neither are thanks for what has not yet been done. But I might also remind you there is — perhaps it is better put thus: the Oaths you will soon be asked to take are solemn ones, and they are for life. If occasion comes when a small sum might allow choices otherwise impossible to you, it should not be forgotten I am holding moneys rightfully yours, yours at a word. No fortune, to be sure, but enough, let us say, to permit you some freedom of action."

The day had changed for the return to the *Mankh'*; the low uplands to his left were dappled with shadows chasing sun, and soon there was a cold spatter of rain in his face. Using an elbow to keep the writing-satchel close to his side, he left the road to take the cross-country route that cut off its big bend. The mixture of weathers tried to recall a long-ago day with his father, but it stayed just out of reach. Soon, the rain closed in, and he was squelching through mud, outshirt sodden and face streaming.

All the same, he was happier for the morning's talk. Beforehand, he had convinced himself he was seeking out Faëdhal only to consult on the Old Gabhanilú, and there he had received more generous help than could have been hoped for. But it was not new learning that made him newly cheerful; it became obvious to him he had wanted to hear exactly the offer he had declined, to know his decision to stay and fight it out with *Menadhi* was not his irrevocable doom.

Days of sneezing, stiff joints and a throbbing head went by, and then by unexplained means he was in a bed that was not his, spinning into dark half-dreams that sidled into rancid waking. With the foolish droop of its lower lip the face of at-Sepivadhi came swelling to peer, and Dolvid was given a spoonful of brown, bad-tasting *ga-raminat*, just as his father was, by this same *ramidu*.

Red hair, ruddy face, a chin running blood, and a robed man was feeding bits of raw flesh into the sawtoothed mouth, till Kanavakh fell down and shrivelled like a salted slug. Wind as a vast cold-winged gull stooped to ruffle Arnan; rain rattled against the window, and his name echoed, his father calling him in from play, Dol-*vid*? A rising cadence he heard often in the squeak of an ungreased wheel, bird-calls, distant cries.

It was after a walk through cold rain that his father fell ill, but his father was no bloodthirsty despot, was not Kanavakh; why would the *Atarlum* poison him? Rising above that shadow, he skimmed wavetops with no fear, soared over guardian cliffs, circled the softly lighted mountain, Karg' Kamanta, with Lunu Midhi, the Valley of the Table, at its knees. The two blue drinking mugs were set out, but untouched. At the head of the table was a small, slight figure, face in shadow, Dolvid's father, a gentle man.

Dolvid drifted nearer, flamelight flared, and the face was *Menadhi*, and Tini-ra was lost forever.

"How do you feel, Dolvidh?" The red tint of *Menadhi*'s face came from a setting sun. Dolvid sighed, falling back into dreamless sleep, or perhaps a dream of dreamlessness, waking in cool, silvered morning, breath blessedly free in his nostrils. He could not remember whether the visit by *Menadhi* had been real. Certainly he was now in his own bunk.

His bladder demanded emptying. Sitting up, keeping a blanket over his shoulders, he used the night-jar for once. The connections in his knees were strangely loosened. At the window he could look down to see a boat newly docked, workers unloading bales and boxes moving without hurry. Arnan was blue-grey metal; often in clear morning air he almost believed he could see the tip of the Mountain. He did not turn thought to the Contemplation, but gazed out to where sea and sky shimmered together, recalling the muddle of dreams.

He was not as recovered as the exhilaration of waking clear-headed had deluded him; his shoulders ached, and his nose was closing again from within. Leaving the window he lay back on his bunk. Simpler if he died, as his father had, sidestepping all contradictions, decisions that made and unmade themselves. Anything he chose would have misery in it, and everything he refused, regret. He hid in sleep.

He wakened again with a small, cool hand on his forehead, *Menadhi*'s face close to his. Seeing who it was he involuntarily drew back, but instantly put on a smile, so his reactions could be read in reverse, recoil, then recognition.

The sunshine was very luxurious, flooding into the stable court. Silnath, grinning, said it would be a good day for Nuril. As they saddled the piebald, he tried, as always, to persuade Dolvid to bring his sword-arm to the *Adanum*.

"Not a world of time left," shading eyes to look where the sun stood. The words were almost Faëdhal's, though two more different men could hardly be found. "We'll be off to the Island.

When we come back, your turn, say? We only take one." He meant, oaths. The one the *Adanum* took was *Rakhi biKradha*, the Death Oath. "All done with this."

The afternoons of swordplay, good talk, beer-drinking, the fellowship of straightforward men whose feelings were real. Quiet panic came back to Dolvid's heart.

Silnath struck his forehead with the thumb end of his fist. "Minds me, there is this brooch." He fumbled in his outshirt pockets. "Broken, you see, and needs a new stone, here. You're right, though, a thing of not much value. A gift to my wife when the boy was born, I promised it would be mended before I came back. Time's short, but if I was to give you the money — ?"

"The shop in Harbor Way could do the work."

"See the stone matched, say, near as can be. Not overmuch trouble for you, I'll be obliged."

Nuril had been stubborner than ever in declining any pace above his habitual amble. Dolvid left him at the Bronze Residence stables. The top of Harbor Way was quiet, most of the stalls closed like sleeping birds with their wings folded about them. The shops by the city walls never lost their fascination, and he took minutes that he ought not to spare reaching the last, the master-jeweller, with its attached workshop.

The interior of the shop was dim, with small and precious things of rich metal and cut gems winking. Once or twice Dolvid had chatted with Vulakh, the master, but today the shop was being tended by a slender girl with bright hair, which, as he came in, she was coiling into the new fashion, using a burnished wall-plaque for mirror. She was yawning as she lifted bare arms.

"Isn't Master Vulakh here?"

"No, he's not." The way she stared Dolvid thought at first her eyes were bad, but then realized he must be hard to see properly, coming through the doorway with strong light behind.

"In the workshop?" He would have been glad of an excuse for going there, despite the heat from the furnace.

"My father's gone to Owan Sai for gold wire. My elder brother's in the workshop, and the men." This she added, he saw after, in case he was a robber.

"There is this brooch... " He pulled it out, wrapped in a piece of kidskin.

"Is this yours?"

"No," puzzled by the question. "I — "

"We only buy from the true and proven owner." Her voice had a curious wheedling, even complaining tone, obscurely challenging, though the girl's conceit was plain. "This," she judged airily, "would be worth very little, in any case."

"It is worth a great deal to the owner. I was not selling. I'll take the work elsewhere." He picked up the brooch from where she had disdainfully laid it down.

"Your pardon, *at'ai*, what was it you wanted done?"

In the doorway, turning. "I am not *atarlai*."

"You're from the *Mankh'*. You are going to be *atarlai*?"

He did not answer.

"What about the brooch, then?" She was placating. "You see, we have to be careful here. If it's a stolen piece, no one compensates us, not when my father's put out money in good faith." A second time unwrapped, she really looked at the brooch. "I'm sure my father could do this work, quite easily. For the price, you'll have to ask him. We don't have set prices; it all depends on the value of the new stone, and how hard the clasp is to mend."

"When will Vulakh be back?"

"Well — " She stifled a new yawn. "If he doesn't loiter to turn over everything the merchant has to sell, and if he keeps out of the quayside wineshops, and if he doesn't stay to hear all gossip from the seven ports of Arnan —   the indulgent expression, and this recital, must be borrowed from her mother — "He might be back mid-afternoon."

"I could come back. About the fourth hour?"

"You can leave the brooch, if you will, for him to see and decide."

"The clasp, you see — "

"I understand what's needed," interrupting highhandedly. "I'll tell him. What name, then?"

He told her. "And yours?"

"Valnoi, Dolvidh. Valnoi Vulakhilayu."

"Then I'll see you later, too?" Asking this, he was relishing the thought that if she had been Valnoi Dolvidhayu, she would have been beaten. Often.

The chin wobbled as she swallowed another yawn. "I was going to sew at the bodice of my new gown. I have to make it fit me just so — " She traced with two hands. "But I could be here, yes."

He had not meant to mean exactly that, but could not say he did not care whether she would be here or not. Things stampeded.

"Do you ever like to go walking," she was elaborately innocent, "in the Gardens of Kamzhinu?"

"In the — "

"They're just here, the other side of Harbor Gate."

"I know where the Gardens are. I haven't been there since I was a small child."

"They're peaceful, late in the afternoon. You can be there, and not meet anyone."

"I must go now. I may see you later, then?"

"I am going to wear my cloak of green metal-cloth."

As a strategy he had been careful to steal quarter and half hours when coming to Kadon Dinul, deliberately creating vagueness about exact times, so as he could manage things like his visit to Faëdhal, or this errand of Silnath's. Chance remarks and hints deliberately dropped made him aware *Menadhi* was kept informed; Dolvid could not dare whole hours, yet in some way seemed to have agreed to walk in the Gardens with Valnoi. This, he knew intuitively, meant putting himself at her disposal; he simply could not.

Besides, she was quite disagreeable, vain in assuming the invitation, so accustomed to thinking herself desirable she could not imagine a man would not want to be with her.

Certainly she was very pretty. Was she? Back with his studies at the Bronze Residence he tried to picture Valnoi's face, and managed only general descriptions; she was slender, not tall, had small, perfect ears — those he remembered from when the long hair lay across her upraised hand as she yawned in front of the makeshift mirror. The rest was wrapped in the magic haze she created by belief in her own beauty. He was not going to walk with her — yet it was unfair that vanity, plainly seen, could double back to offer a challenge of its own.

She was not there. He risked leaving half an hour before his usual time, ran down the main steps and across the Square, adopting an unhurried pace as he came to the shop. Vulakh got up from a chair to greet him by name, and Dolvid could not read his own feelings, whether relief or disappointment came uppermost. Vulakh's breath announced poor wine.

The business with the brooch did not take long; Vulakh's price was very fair, less than Silnath had said he would go to. As instructed, Dolvid handed over half-payment. Unless there was trouble matching the stone, the work was promised for this day a week.

Turning to leave, Dolvid said lightly, "I have met your daughter, Valnoi." He tried to imitate other people, his remembered father, when they made polite, casual conversation.

"She's out." Vulakh was still turning the brooch between thumb and finger. "Somewhere," he added. "You'd say she was beautiful, master?"

"She — I would — "

"Mother used to be the same. All comes from there. That's all, then, master?"

"I thank you, Master." He went out. Valnoi was not by Harbor Gate, not waiting at the entrance to the Gardens. Dolvid was not entirely sorry, except he had nerved himself to a test that had not come, and that left him feeling flat and useless. Perhaps, reading what he had into her reference to the green cloak, he had been the conceited one.

Endings

Valnoi: he discovered an amazing proportion of his days and nights could be spent brooding over her. To begin with, the subject offered an escape, itself guilty, from guilty thoughts of time draining away, from the duel with an unknowing opponent.

Over and again, *Menadhi*'s acumen failed with Dolvid. Evidently, as the pilgrimage to the Island came nearer, he ceased to regard him as separate in any questions of belief, seeing him only as a kind of mirror. When speaking about Lambarr's indecisiveness, Banak's partiality for the Others, he no longer troubled to disguise contempt, and blasphemy, criticism of the policies of their Patriarch, was never far away.

"Eastward of the Pass of Perus," he summarized at one of their afternoons, "formerly a prosperous corner of the realm, is wilderness, and a port of doubtful allegiance. In the West, Saidhan and his son stay defiant, and that encourages everyone to despise *rabhsayum* as pomp without substance. But how can there be awe for a post that becomes a prize for any adventurer to grab?"

That could only be heard as a reference to Great Banak. *Menadhi* was far from finished.

"The Descent is forgotten, and it is no longer taught lordship was Raëdh's Gift to Yoëlladhu Founder. Men die, Dolvidh, and are alone in knowing they must die. Unless they are taught to see their lives as ripples in the endless stream, flowing from and back to the One Source, they devote those small, separate lives to pleasure and greed. They become too arrogant for service, too selfish to care for others, they use up the earth and its riches with no notion of stewardship. That is why our *Manadilum* must be teacher to the realm — why the *manal* must come to flourish again."

Dolvid opened his mouth, and closed it. He could hear truth in what *Menadhi* said, but how could one who was all for Owani privilege keep a straight face while indicting greed? *Menadhi* had often expressed wonder the Patriarch, Himself of the Growing Order, showed little interest in *ga-Yalum*, the principle that only growing lands dedicated as part of the Blessed Gift should receive assistance from the *Edhrodilum*. But *ga-Yalum*, coming from a god the Others did not have, was only for the Owanil. Once, he would not have seen inconsistency, but since the law suit with his Froghul he had come to realize it was only Owanil who enclosed broad tracts of tillable land to grow wild for their hunting. Just about all important landowners of the Heartland, the magnates who controlled the corn trade, were of Owani descent, and the Craft Guilds, including the one Vulakh belonged to, never admitted anyone of Other Race.

Not long ago all this had been very fine to Dolvid, certainly nothing unnatural, but while he still doubted Others could ever match Owani accomplishment, he was suspicious about the Owani right to condemn, where excoriating greed meant Others were not to covet what they had; too easy for those who would never experience want to wave away a life of deprivation as a mere ripple in the stream.

Obviously, that was why men had to become Deniants, for people of Other Race to see everything about the *Atarlum*, Beginning, Descent, Gift of Aëlovoi, Lordship of Raëdh, as nothing but an elaborate fraud, providing justification for keeping them poor and subservient.

"You are to be part of that restoration." He reached a hand to rest it on edge, not-quite cupping Dolvid's neck. "Almost, I wish I could have my youth again, and live to see what you surely shall, ends and beginnings. Soon, very soon, I shall be able to talk to you more openly than I ever have. Not long, now... "

Having strayed into a rapt mood, he shook it off, and brought back the smile. "You are looking well again, I am glad to see."

Dolvid was in the summer tunic, wondering whether Valnoi, if she could see him, would notice the way-hardened muscling of his calves.

Work on the brooch was not quite finished. Vulakh emerged from the workshop flushed and blinking to promise it conditionally for that same afternoon.

While they were talking, Valnoi came in through the inside door that must lead to living-quarters above and behind the shop. Vulakh, explaining how a sweat-joint was made, lost Dolvid's undivided attention. The girl was in a light-colored gown of very clinging stuff, and there was a green and gleaming bundle under her arm. Dolvid gave her a faint nod, noting her beauty, on the whole, was much more in accord with accepted notions than he had recalled.

"Or, if you would want," Vulakh was saying, "I can try to find a nearer match for the stone. Would mean end of the week, soonest."

Valnoi was moving for the outer doorway. Dolvid said, "I have to come to Kadon again next week." There was nothing to say to the girl, but if he could once see her in full light he might be cured of the irritation of her elusiveness.

"No question I'll have it for you by then — all the better for not being rushed. Most people don't value what a business matching is, done right. This thing and that you have to look for, and you have to have an eye for it, to begin with. Where are you off to, then?" This for drifting Valnoi.

She turned against the light, and Dolvid would never forget the picture it made, swaying twist of that slender body, the hair, worn loose today, a luminous mist on brightness behind. "Market Square. They say there's early strawberries, from the south."

"Aye, priced for the Residence Quarter. And you — dressed in that. You! Some stranger'll take you for a week-wife, one of these days."

"Perhaps I'll let him, one of these days."

"Ffa!" a half-humorous noise of exasperation, as Vulakh

waved her to be gone.

"Is Dolvidh *Mankhati* leaving, then?"

Ignoring the taunt, he did. Outside, she swathed herself in the shiny cloak, green iridescence that of big, angry-sounding flies late in summer. The day was cool and white, with thin, high, featureless cloud.

In a deft two-handed movement Valnoi lifted her hair free of the cloak. Not achieving anything else to say, he told her he preferred it worn as she now had it, unbraided.

Small chin pressed to her shoulder, she grimaced sidelong. "So Ladhat was also pleased to say. All you men flatter yourselves we care about what you wish to see."

"Don't you?" — not intending any challenge, only wanting information.

The chin gave a little toss. "In what's worn, fashions in hair? I, for one, please myself. My new gown is blue, with a broidered band just up under the breast. Will you walk to Market with me, then? We can go through the Gardens." A slow, sly smile came. "Through the Gardens, as you promised. But you have forgotten that."

"I have not forgotten. Nor did I promise. You — "

She spun away a full step, cloak and hair following the movement with a slower grace. As she turned back the smile was radiant. "At the *Mankh'* — you don't have much to do with women?"

"Some *atarlal* have wives. And there are some *artarlayul*. And the *nôd'yanul*."

"*Nôd'yanul*! That's why to you everything women do is to please men."

"That is not what I think."

"Is it true, as I've heard, all reverence to *g'Asalladh'*, many of the *atarlal* have boys for their week-wives? Are you bed-friend to some withered old priest, then?"

"No."

"I have often heard that."

"I am only saying I am not."

"You must have been asked. Your skin is smooth enough for a *nôd'yanu*. I think you're very pretty. Can Dolvidh sew?" They were crossing outside Harbor Gate, and Valnoi threw a lidded glance at one of the guards. He stared back frankly, head set like a cat ready to fight. Under the swirling cloak her shoulders released a fluid shudder.

"I can mend."

"What?" She had lost her question.

"I have to mend my own clothes. Do you like poetry?" This bit of initiation was a blazing triumph for Dolvid.

"Does he think I'm going to round my back over smelly old books? Besides, reading clouds the eyes. My eyes are very clear, aren't they?"

He made himself not fear meeting them straight on. She was right, her eyes were light-filled, and had the troublesome clarity of unguessable depth.

Shaking free, he led the way to the wrought gate at the corner of the Gardens. From here steps curved down to what looked a natural gorge, planted with dwarf varieties of many bushes and trees. "This," he said, "was once the defensive ditch outside the old outwalls."

"I knew that."

"Kamzhinu was the first *rabhsaëyu* — the first woman who reigned in her own right. She was Plakhval's daughter."

"His sister."

"Not so, daughter."

"Sister. I remember, she came to Sword because her brother was drowned on Arnan, with the Heir, his son. Then —
"

"You have muddled two different people. Dromladh, certainly, drowned, and his elder sister succeeded him. But that was Thral-Sivu, and plenty of living people remember her. Kamzhinu is much farther back. She laid out the Gardens while her father, Plakhval, was still *rabhsai*. He deemed outwalls were not needed, the realm being at peace. In her reign, Kamzhinu made the Gardens open to all the people."

"His sister. His elder sister."

Exasperated, "I am a scholar of history. It is my craft. Plakhval lived to one hundred and four — how old would Kamzhinu be when she took Sword, if she was his elder sister? You — " he tried to keep down his wrath. "You are in error."

"I've been told she followed her brother. I don't care, what does it matter? You're so fierce. The Gardens are lovely."

"Because of his long life, Plakhval outlived his firstborn, a son. Kamzhinu was elder of two daughters — " he could have piled on facts, but faltered at Valnoi's look, which said he was being unduly, boringly persistent. It was true, he had forgotten how pleasant the Gardens were. Or rather, had never seen it, back when they were the terrain for vast wars, afternoon-long, which settled the fate of empires. A giant task, razing outwalls that had stood since the Age of the Shâls. Big blocks, removed intact, had been used in other building, and for repairs to the city walls proper. Fragments, still huge, had been rolled or pushed into this gully; weathered and lichened they were hard to tell from natural rocks.

Near the bottom of the former moat a brick pathway wound, using several bridges of carved limestone to cross and recross a wandering thread of a stream. From this central path others led off among rocks and bushes; in the lee of boulders there were little six-sided shade-houses of stone, and unexpected fountains and rock-carvings were to be happened on. Evenings in summer the Gardens were a favorite walk for lovers, but at this hour of a sunless day, as Valnoi had predicted, all-but deserted.

Instead of heading for the far entrance, where Burantal Road came up to Market Gate, Valnoi turned aside, leading the way up steps to a place Dolvid once knew well, a court paved with six-sided stones, a small garden-plot at the center. Slender river-birches and hazels were in fresh leaf, and a white lilac had already lost most of its densely-scented blossom. Behind was the bastion of rock, rear of the knoll where, long ago, he had stood in snow to watch the start of Fire Days. Down here, the rock, hollowed out in caves, was called the Grottoes.

"Don't you love this spot? You're no Island boy — why would you want to be *atarlai*?"

"Have I said I did?"

"Are you Craft family, then?"

"My father was at the Residence."

"The Bronze Residence, you mean."

"The New." Dolvid's advantage, but Valnoi parried.

"In service."

"He was Keeper of Books to the *rabhsai*. But he died, and I was made a ward of the *Atarlum*."

She was not sure whether to believe this. "Your father spoke to the *rabhsai*, and the Family?"

"He was treated as a friend by Laluvoi *Asayu*. I was taught weapons by Kheval." He realized this did not quite follow.

"You were not. Kheval teaches the Heir."

"Very well, I wasn't."

"Don't you think he is handsome, the Heir? He's very tall, for only fifteen."

"Fourteen. The height is inherited from his Gabhani great, great grandfather." This was always tricky for the Owanil, and Dolvid correctly predicted it would finish talk about the Family. But he kept one thrust in reserve, in case he ever needed it, to be spoken very offhandedly: *I used to cross blades with the Heir. He was no swordsman.*

They sat on the curving bench like a shelf or high step along the back wall of the large, shallow central cave, and the stone at their backs had soaked up the chill of winter, or of many winters. On hot days this cool could be a blessing, but now Dolvid shivered, palms held together between his legs.

Valnoi quietly opened her bodice. Leaning back against rock, head lolling, long throat smooth, she said, "Would you like to touch my breasts?"

As something for itself, no he would not; why could he not say that? He said, "If that would please you."

"As for pleasing me, lots of men want to do that. But how can you know what pleases you, without trying it?" Her head rolled back and forth on the stone, squeezing a wave of hair.

Dolvid extracted one hand and reached to touch her throat, then slide his fingers down to the fine collarbone.

"Your hand is very cold. No — " as he started to take it away. She captured the hand, and thrust it down beneath robe and undershift. Her breast was soft, trembling like a caught bird, and amazingly warm. Leaning so as to press his hand hard against her, she brushed her mouth slackly across his cheek, and kissed him softly on the lips. It was as if his mind had been immersed in a warm fog. He was shaken, not believing his whole body could be comprehended in a joining of mouths.

"Dolvidh... " a sigh. "Dolvidh, if you don't become *atarlai*, what are you going to do?"

"I — I know many things."

"So do I." Her hand replaced his between his thighs.

She was betrothed. This she told him in a bored way, a week after, on their second visit to the Gardens, where they found an out-of-the-way corner to pull off some clothes and achieve a rough sort of mating, her back pressed to a slope of bare earth between two bare rocks.

Ladhat was son of Khazubran, a master-enameller. It was a shock to realize Valnoi's future father-in-law was the man related to the *Bôdhrai* Rhunsilakh, to whom Dolvid, at twelve, had nearly become apprenticed. Son had followed the father's craft, and Ladhat with Valnoi would be a typical Craft Families marriage, no worse for bringing a closer alliance between the two fathers.

Vulakh, Valnoi said, had encouraged the match. But this was grotesque; Ladhat was nearly thirty, while Valnoi was less than two years older than Dolvid — somewhat more than a year, he preferred to put it, seeing her birthday was three weeks after his.

But although her question about what he would do if he left the *Mankh'* implied she was, woman-fashion, assessing him as a rival for Ladhat, he could not imagine her as his wife. He could not even say why he had to be with her; he did not like her any better, and their currency was mostly bickering. Yet, while he wanted to hold back time so it would never come to that terrifying moment where Lesser Oaths must be embraced or rejected, he wished away the days till *Shuda'sai* and *Menadhi's* departure for the Island, because that would give him more freedom for meetings with Valnoi.

Meanwhile, he went mad, retreating step by step into yearning. Sitting down to translate a passage he covered the page with Valnoi's name in every mode and style there was, trying it in both syllabaries, then transitional script and the Script of Shâl, all forms of the letters, the score-alphabet. He made scrollwork of the name, decorated it with leaf and flower forms, meditated its possible meanings, *vadh'oloi*, life-daughter, *van'odhoi*, flame-wife — though the obvious origin was *vaëlu-noi*, fortunate heiress or successor.

The songs he wrote to and for her were begging letters from a starved half-cousin, though he could not name what he could want from her that she had not given him. Perhaps for her not to be outside her own ecstasies: seconds after making nailpits in his back she could be telling him (though she might be talking to herself) about the new lacing being worn in the Residence Quarter.

There must be more to the girl than gossip and preening and the need to sting him with taunts; her eyes with their mysterious depths must hold unsaid wisdoms. But he could not make them look at him as Tini-ra's had. He could not alter anything about her.

A week short of Midsummer, *Menadhi*, after hearing his Responses, remarked this might be the last. "I have to leave before *Shuda'sai*. Messengers from the West will be coming to the Island."

Dolvid kept quiet. This was supposed to be a grave moment, but he could leap for joy that *Menadhi* was leaving so soon.

"How I wish I could take you with me! You have been taught about the Island, but no one can teach its beauty, for those who have chosen the Way. Well, when the harvest is ripening, and I come back, it will be to take you there."

He said nothing, head bowed.

"I am glad to see you have found some sun." The tone became less portentous. "After your illness your face was, as His Enlightenment often says of His kinsman at the library, the belly of a dead fish. Now — you are as handsome as I have seen you."

"I thank you." Warily attentive for what was to come.

"But there is something wrong. Is it true Yuvan Yuvakhati wanted to make war on the Aëni Confederation?"

Before the First Empire. The history of those remote ages, surely mainly guess and invention, always muddled him. "I don't know, *Menadhi*."

"That is what you wrote."

"Did I, *Menadhi*?"

"Is it not the truth that after his father's death Yuvan forbade Aëni to be mentioned in his presence, and it was his son, Hruval, who in the end forced his hand?"

"So it is written, *Menadhi*." Babyhood always came flooding back when he was caught in a silly error, and he found himself seeking impossible excuses.

Menadhi sprang to his feet. "For such a mistake, a second-year boy would be flogged. You, Dolvidh — are you spending too much of your thought with your crude tribes of the West? Lately, I have had to repeat myself to you too often, as if your wits have gone wandering with the Froghul. What is wrong with you?"

"I — "

"When I permitted you to visit the *nôd'yanu*, it was in hopes of getting rid of distractions, not making them. I am not displeased you have not often made use of the privilege; I never thought you would have much use for foolery. What is it, then?"

Dolvid had got up. "I cannot say, *Menadhi*."

As always, the man's censure had frightened him, but that was easier to bear than the sympathetic hug that came. "I know, I know," *Menadhi* murmured. "It is our sixteenth summer, and sitting still is a harder task than the taming of Hranakh."

He led Dolvid to the window. "While I am gone, you must go on studying what must be mastered. But you are released from your work at the library. I want you to ride, to swim, to enjoy swordplay with any of the *Adanum* who remain here. When I return, I want to find you bronzed and hale, a young lion such as the Island has not seen since the boyhood of Plakhat Gabh'Owan, when Kallikuk saw him at play, and knew he had found the destined ruler of the Second Realm of Owan. To use summer well, that is your only task, my friend."

"I'll try — " near tears, ashamed of lying. Disagreement and disapproval ought to bring dislike, and it would be more comfortable to hate this man.

Till now, meetings with Valnoi had maintained an element of chance. With *Menadhi* gone, as he began to make firmer plans, she became increasingly evasive. He should have made a stand on pride, but instead became angered with his obsequiousness. She failed to meet him as arranged for an afternoon outside the city, and he started again, never mentioning the broken promise. When she was actually waiting for him where they were to meet, he saw his surge of gratitude as yet more abject.

Besides, gratitude was sure to bore her. She was easily bored, and he was always anxiously aware of himself, his stiff attempts to amuse her, to hold her fluttering attention, to make her want to be with him. He was horrified by a willingness to be someone else, aping for a whole hour the crude jokes and stupid patter of an apprentice of the *Adanum*, a youth Dolvid despised, though envying his unseriousness. The worst of it was, Valnoi was nearer being pleased by the vulgar imposture than by any realler Dolvid.

It had become a dry summer, the hottest he remembered. Ultimate proof of his need for Valnoi was that more than once he recklessly borrowed Nuril for half a day, not even pretending to visit the Bronze Residence. These absences would surely be noted, and in due course reported to *Menadhi* — but by then, perhaps, provoking *Menadhi*'s wrath might be desirable, to free him from the attachment muddling his choices. Still, deferred dread gathered, a fist clenching at his belly.

She was no weight, and they could double-ride the horse, down to the water-meadows of the broad Paowan, or one of the shaded dells by Shufloi Kadonu. To be near running water was a necessity in this brazen summer. Relentless heat was wearying, and after frenzied coupling disturbingly often he dozed on Nuril's back, plodding for the *Mankh'* in uncooled evening.

Yet summer was passing with panic speed. Only time spent with Valnoi had any hold on his senses; three-and-a-half meetings (the half was a few desultory words as she listlessly tended shop) blurred into elapse of a few days, but were spaced over two whole weeks. The coming of Aëlovoi's Moon, which was also Zhôl's Day, midpoint between midsummer and Halving Day, shocked him. Paradoxically, hours crawled, filled with insatiate brooding on Valnoi. To recognize that his obsession had no effect on her was repeated shock: he would traverse a whole landscape of feelings, pass through scorn and rancor to forgiveness, tenderness and renewed desire, then meet with her again, and see she had never thought of him.

"Do you sport with Ladhat?"

"Oh, Dolvidh. You know you were not first." They were resting where Shufloi Kadonu was joined by its smaller cousin, not far below where the Froghul had camped. It was another warm day.

"I'm asking about now. Are there others?"

A small, high laugh. "I'm with you."

"Only that I want to know." The falsity of this jarred his own ear.

"To know, to know, to know." Valnoi, on her haunches, leaned to look for a button pulled off by his urgency. Her back was hatched with pink-edged patterning, one or two fragments of grass sticking to damp skin. The heat bore down, and there was no silence; insects mumbled and whined and pinged, while in the depths of the hawthorns birds chattered. Behind Dolvid the stream gurgled throatily, and under all there might be a dark rumble of far thunder. This summer had been filled with days when towering ramparts of clouds piled massively around the shimmering horizon. Nights sweated tensely, but no rain came.

"When he knows everything, what then?"

"When are you going to marry Ladhat?"

"Perhaps never." Careless, she did not know how his throat tightened. "You are all questions. I can't say what I'll do tomorrow — tonight. I bed where I choose, and I'll wed where I choose."

"What about your father?"

"What he might want is nothing to me. Though there is nothing prettier, is there, than fine gold and fine enamel together? My father chose the metal, and Ladhat is making a hair-clasp for my birthday, blue and red, with the gold. But I haven't got a robe to wear with it. I'll go naked, with just the clasp in my hair. It's too hot for sewing, too hot for clothes." Button found, she settled on the grass. "Too hot for this sport."

Everything hurt. In the *Mankh'* kitchens he had filled a leather bag with cold meats, fruit, cheese and bread. At his offer, she took a plum, bit away dull purple skin, and sucked at golden flesh. "No, I'm not going to see you again till the weather breaks. I hate being sweaty."

He reached for her; the skin at her waist was soft and damp, curiously cool. "We don't have to have sport. We can meet just to walk, or sit and talk. I can bring food, and there's Nuril... "

"Nuril — " a mocking sneeze. Everything hurt, but she turned derision elsewhere. "Sit and talk. You can't talk to a woman, you can only make discourse, the same as some mumbling *atarlai*. Why should I care who won some horrid battle in the Wars of Cleansing? I've got enough to think about, without filling my head with *Mankh'* learning."

That, he noted, was precisely untrue; Valnoi did not have enough to think about. "Haven't you read the poems I gave you?" This was not meant as an attack; he wanted her to see what his songs revealed, anything but the dry pedantry she charged him with.

She arched her neck. "You said poems are not meant for silent reading, but should be spoken aloud."

True. "I said, good poetry. Have you got my verses with you?" He was sure she had not, and did not want to read out loud the grovelling things he had written. That was why he wrote them down; they could not be spoken.

She spat the cleaned plum-stone into her palm, and just reached flowing water with an awkward round-arm toss. "Being read to is for children. Can't you remember your own songs?"

"No." Speech was abandoning him, and just when he wanted to distract her from deep growlings he was sure were thunder. Agony being with her, but she must not ask to be taken home, not yet. Not far downstream where the brook opened into a backwatered pool, a stray breeze sent arrowheads chasing each other across the mirror surface.

She brushed a bare arm. "Wasn't that a spot of rain? We should dress and make for shelter. My hair will be good for nothing."

"Look," he pointed. "Kingfisher." The pool was being patterned by a few slow rings from big raindrops, and where willows and a pair of gnarled field-maples fringed the water, the sudden stoop and brilliant flash of the bird came. Valnoi's gasp was nearly a moan. The bird spun, flicking the pool with a wingtip, whipped fierily about, and went dipping away downstream. The gleam of underfeathers flashed out once, twice more before lost to sight.

"Will it come back?" she whispered. She was leaning against him, and as awe at sight of the bird ebbed her excess caught him between gratification and embarrassment.

She said, "It's hard, writing songs. I made one once, about a horse." Before she could start to recite it he kissed her damp eye-socket, feeling her eyelash stir against his upper lip.

"Look at you," she reproached, as they swayed apart. "And we only just finished. And you say we could meet just to sit and talk. What a liar." But this was not left untouched by the tenderness the kingfisher had brought. Her clever hands had gone to greet him, and he nearly wept with pleasure and sentimental gratitude for all the felicities of her body. Beneath peremptory desire for coupling was an aching wish this Valnoi could survive: it was as though his gratitude invented her, making the Valnoi he wanted.

It appeared the main mass of thunderstorm was passing to the south. After those few gouts of rain, sun returned. From their low-lying spot they could see dark anvil-heads, but though thunder came louder, and pale lightning flickered from depths of purpling gorges, Valnoi said no more about a retreat, accepting his proposition they would be as likely to find as to avoid a heavy shower.

"I could never enter a Craft," Dolvid said. She was lying back, stroking her belly. "Your father's a good man, but that world is too narrow for me."

She agreed vehemently. "They only do anything with others from the Guilds. It's always the same. I hate it."

"Counting Old Gabhanilú, I'll have five languages, to write as well as read and understand. Four I speak well."

"Where is the good in following the latest fashion for dress, when I live among men who care about nothing but their work? They're so ignorant, Dolvidh."

"I once said I would be a soldier." His own words startled him.

"Of the Household? They're fine-looking men."

"Not the Household. I used to talk about going to Kamsilat. They say merit can get ahead, where Saidhan is captain."

Not easily, she raised her head to stare. "The Colony? Only Mixed get ahead there, and wild men out of the Farthest West. That's not for an Owani of good family."

"But Saidhan *Asai* — "

"But you'd never leave Kadon Dinul, would you?"

"Money is being held for me — a small sum. Another thing I could do is go to the North. There's money to be made there, trading fleeces." As not in years, he remembered Darborr, Radis's husband, who used to live next door.

Shuffling up, she used elbows for props. "But you would not leave Kadon Dinul? You're not going to go away?"

He gave the clumsy one-shoulder shrug he was trying to cure. "Well, if I want a chance to prosper... " Odd how easily he pretended, with her, that his leaving the *Mankh'* was certain.

"No, Dolvidh." Scissoring, she turned, reaching for him. Her cheek came against his lower chest, as he sat against his saddlebag, in turn against a rock. He had begun this with no intent to make plans, simply testing Valnoi's feelings. The result was beyond anything he could have imagined. "Don't leave Kadon Dinul, Dolvidh," she said very many times, rubbing her head against him as cats do. "Don't go away."

A loud, loudening hiss with a chatter in it, the sound not recognized before the wall of drenching rain came, turning all the world to white and grey and wet. Lightning came in a ripping flash, thunder battering behind it; eternally placid Nuril whinnied and shied, tossing his head and pulling at the halter that tied him to a sapling.

Water streamed from faces. Another clap of thunder came, so loud it was incredible nothing near was destroyed. The grass was a reedland, stream a frenzy. Valnoi clung to Dolvid screaming, but the screams were only laughter.

One day revelation struck that little Zhâlai was the perfect model for one sort of *atarlai*, unchanging into age. Encountered by the kitchens he was still child-faced yet swollen with self-importance.

"Dolvidh — you've heard the news?"

"Not now." He was hurrying, a meeting with Valnoi planned. There was ominous bustle about the *Mankh'*. Bedrooms and living-quarters were being aired out, and the stables of the *Adanum Plakh'* made ready; discipline was being tautened after the laxities of a hot summer. *G'Asalladh's* return from the Island was expected any day, and chances were *Menadhi* would be with Him.

"You can't ride for Kadon, it won't be allowed. Nobody can leave the inner Precinct."

Having made Dolvid halt, Zhâlai waited, smug, till the expected question came, "Why?"

"It's true. It's terrible. An *atarlai* has been killed, murdered, one of the *Edhrodilum*."

"Where? At Kadon Dinul?"

"Somewhere in Upper Nîv." That was days away. "He was attacked by farmers. They blame *edhradul* for the bad harvest. That's blasphemy, too, *the power to bring sun and rain in due season is no man's*."

For complacent quoting of a text when the world was knocked askew he could have hit Zhâlai. "What does a killing in Upper Nîv have to do with the Paowan, with the *Mankh'*?"

"Nothing, I suppose, but the gate is closed till word comes back from g'*Asalladh'*, by orders of at-Oradhai." As senior *atarlai* left behind, he was in nominal charge of the *Mankh'*.

All true, soon confirmed at the stables, and again at the gate, where a pretense his work at the Bronze Residence was too important to wait was firmly overruled.

As again, with gentle satire, by at-Oradhai, when Dolvid tried to obtain his exemption from self-imposed siege. The work that had been excuse for all the recent visits to Kadon Dinul was cataloguing books at the Bronze Residence not yet cross-indexed with the *Mankh'* library, and at-Oradhai suggested that task would be creeping forward when all of them were long dead.

This was a calamity. In the present Patriarchate the *Atarlum* was not unpopular, but the savage beating of the *edhradu*, who was rescued alive by provincial cavalry, but died next day, put old at-Oradhai in mind of times when, outside of purely Owani districts, no *atarlai* strayed far from armed assistance. At Kadon Dinul, a strong detachment of Household was guarding the Bronze Residence.

Back in his room alone, Dolvid wept with frustration. He could not see Valnoi, nor send word. No consolation she would be sure to hear about the closing of the *Mankh'*. Her sudden admission, before the storm, that he mattered to her, was a treasure he took out and looked at every hour, but in truth he was less afraid she would be annoyed at his absence than that she would not. She might not notice it.

In a clearer mood between despairs he decided essential supplies would still have to come from Kadon Dinul; wagons would be passing in and out. He kept watch on the gate all next day, but nothing arrived, while fragments of rumor circulated and recirculated. In the evening Zhâlai told him a mob had stoned the *margú* near Bathrâd, and Dolvid snapped back that a seagull must have brought the news, no horseman had. It turned out to be Zhâlai's revision of someone's misunderstanding of overheard talk about an event thirty years in the past.

Next day in late afternoon a wagon came with food. With empty shafts it stood near the kitchen entrance that night, and Dolvid made up his mind that at dawn or before he would creep in and hide among empty sacks and cases there would surely be. He had no plan beyond seeing Valnoi, though dimly he perceived this went beyond just a risky escapade.

Rising after short sleep he began to consider what he should take with him, and looking over his few belongings realized he could never come back here to face *Menadhi*, not after this. He had kept fending off final decision for all these months, and now, almost unthinkingly, it was done.

Or would be. Trying to gather together things he could not do without, he was all at once lethargic, as if his body was doing thinking his fogged mind refused. He wanted Valnoi, not clear what 'wanted' meant, but aware in a sane corner this might not be the choice he had waited to make, and surely was not how he ought to make it.

Sitting on his window-seat, the lid of the chest he had meant to go through for indispensables, he saw lanterns and *ôdul* down at quayside. Ships had docked, as rarely by night. The glint from helms and weapons could soon be seen, and horse-handlers landing *pefral*. Not less than one hundred of the *Adanum Plakh'* had arrived, no sign *g'Asalladh'* was with them.

Wondering how that affected his plan, he fell into a doze just at dawn. At some juncture he left nodding at the window to roll onto his bunk, but had no memory of that when wakened in early morning by Zhâlai, bringing the news. As well as troops, messages had come from *g'Asalladh'*. Confident the killing in Nîv was an isolated incident, assured from Tan Lughsai that royal forces would give protection, He had ordered the *Mankh'* to resume its normal life. Reprieved from his own recklessness, Dolvid had his breakfast, and went to the stables to saddle Nuril.

Vulakh came out of his shop into sunshine on Harbor Way, and said his daughter was out. He could not say where, nor when she would be back. He seemed amused by a private joke.

Dolvid went to the Bronze Residence and helped with the indexing. After a while he left, not bothering to make up an excuse, and returned to Vulakh's shop. Valnoi was not back. Dolvid overcame embarrassment twice more through a heavy afternoon, and got the same answer from her father. It was late, and the sun was dipping to edge an inky mountain of cloud with fire.

He went for Nuril, and swung up on his back. Out of the gateway Nuril turned westward with no need for guidance. The

Patriarch and the rest could not be far behind the bodyguard; they might already have come back to the *Mankh'*, and the unimaginable meeting with *Menadhi* might be this evening. Certainly no later than tomorrow.

No: he had to see Valnoi before. Nuril's ears twitched an astonished question, as Dolvid turned back.

Horse stabled again, he kept watch on Vulakh's shop from the grassy mound across the Way. The sun was gone, and sky blackened rapidly. Two half-masters who worked with Vulakh left for home, each looking up at the threatening clouds. Soon, with the help of his son, Vulakh put up iron shutters. They went inside, and lights soon shone from windows over and behind the shop, as from the city walls above. Wind came in gusts, and Dolvid, with only an outshirt, felt his skin crawl. A rider came hurrying up Harbor Way, cloak flapping, and went in through the city gate. The rain began.

It was icy, steady rather than torrential, although rivulets were soon running from the knoll where he stood, hunching his shoulders. His hands were dead white except for reddened knuckles; hair bowed to his forehead and dripped onto his nose. Remaining on watch in such weather made another kind of proof, he was not sure of what. The rain never paused, and at last he admitted wherever Valnoi was she was going to stay. He counted slowly to two hundred, and there was nothing moving but water in Harbor Way.

Among documents in his satchel there was still the note *Menadhi* had written long ago, authorizing an overnight stay at the Bronze Residence, meant for a particular occasion, but undated. A long last stare at Harbor Gate where, if anywhere, Valnoi should appear, and Dolvid retreated to where he could find dryness, towels, perhaps a warming drink.

In early morning he dressed, convinced he remembered every minute of the sleepless night, though he could not say when the rain stopped. Sodden clouds kept crowding in from the west; summer's back was broken overnight, and the day was cheerless. Picking a way through puddles, he was in time to encounter Vulakh unlocking the shop door.

He gave a long, hard look, as at one who had slept rough, but accepted a hand taking down the heavy shutters.

"Valnoi has not returned?"

"No, she hasn't. I thank you — " They lifted down the last shutter, and carried it inside. Vulakh started for the workshop, expecting him to follow. "Fire wants blowing up. Prentice work, but no use leaving it to helpers if you want good heat before noon. Valnoi, see, what with the rain, she must have slept at Master Khazubran's house. You'd know where that is, I suppose — " He paused before adding the usual — "master?"

"No, Master, I do not."

"Thatchers Lane, between the two Avenues, off Market Way going up the hill — can't miss it."

"I used to live near there."

"Well, then. Pardon, master, I can't say how welcome you'll be. Betrothed, they are, Ladhat Khazubranati and my Valnoi. Mine, her mother always swore, Ladhat's, never, except in law."

"Master?"

"Talk." He was starting to fuel the small but massive-built furnace. "Bad business, that *atarlai* of yours down in Nîv killed. When did Growers ever do anyone any harm? Got their rain, they have, too late, I don't doubt. Here's charcoal selling for twice what it should, and you get Residence Quarter folk dickering about the price of fine work. Ladhat's wanted the same wife ever since she could walk. Valnoi tells me it's so, and so it must be."

"Valnoi tells you?"

"Unless he changes his mind, which I'd never blame." Vulakh screwed one eye into perplexity. "Look here, Master Dolvidh, isn't it? wife or not, the girl enjoys men. She's not going to wear a sash. Oh, if she has a baby or two, that might change her, but now? Ladhat sees that, I suppose he must, so who does it hurt? Only if someone takes her for what she's not, am I right? She takes a fancy for running her own household, who's to stop her?"

"Then it wasn't you — " there was no acceptable way to finish the question.

Vulakh understood. "Mind you, I don't say I was ever against it — as a business thing." For the fourth time he bent to open the furnace door, and for the fourth time straightened again. "A fine Craft family, and we can do good work together. The father, between you and me, has connections at the Residence, and that does no harm. Good business makes good marriages — if it's sport you want, that doesn't need any vows, am I right? One like my Valnoi — well, you know her." He completed the circle of his speech. "What do you imagine I could force her to, if she hadn't already made up her mind, hah? What, on your way, then?"

"I must be back at the *Mankh'*." If Vulakh stooped to the furnace once more without adding fuel, Dolvid would shout with vexation.

"I'll tell Valnoi you were asking for her." The wry face that went with this came near convincing Dolvid his vigil in the rain had been observed.

Leaving off Nuril, he was obliged to be cheerful with Silnath, who had enjoyed his summer at Drin b'Afon. Listening to family news, Dolvid was keeping up a silent conversation with an invented Valnoi, telling her he had decided to leave Kadon Dinul, cross Arnan and either find work at Saidhan's Great House, or else join the Army of the West to become a renowned *jinzai*-fighter. In unheard report, *jinzal* were not quite as terrible as when the word was spoken out loud. Valnoi often begged his forgiveness (for what?), but sometimes simply vowed Dolvid was the only man she would ever want.

"Tall, he is, for his age," Silnath was saying. "You'll see. I'm senior file now, I'll have quarters here. Coming over, they are, she's a bride all over again — pleased as a tabby with the brooch, she was, my thanks to you. Hot here this summer, say?"

"Did *Menadhi* come back with *g'Asalladh's* following?

Is he here?"

"*Menadhi*? Oh, aye." He was measuring him. "Dark about the eyes, though. What, you found good summer sport?"

"I must see *Menadhi*. Let's have talk later." He patted Silnath's arm, but had offended him.

"Are you unwell, Dolvidh?"

Rolling his head back and forth he could not see who had spoken.

"Dolvidh, are you ill?" The voice was certainly *Menadhi*'s. Dolvid was in his own bunk. Swinging his legs over the edge, he woke fully, and stood to make deference.

"*Menadhi*, pardon. I am glad to see you again. No, I was not, I am not ill. I was very tired."

"Sit, sit." With small, neat steps he went to the doorway and stopped a pair of passing boys, telling them to go to the kitchens and say *Menadhi* wanted refreshment brought here. The boys, first-year pupils, looked terrified, and vanished at once.

Instead of sitting, Dolvid had used the chance to splash his stiff face with cold water, and run fingers through matted hair.

Menadhi was in no hurry to say why he was there. He glanced out at Arnan, at what books were out on the table, then pulled out the chair to sit, waving Dolvid back to the bunk. His face, as often, was hard to read, not forbidding. "How have you passed summer, Dolvidh?"

"It has been very hot."

"So too at Drin b'Afon, its celebrated breezes notwithstanding. You seem tired — you have lost flesh, not so?"

"A little, perhaps."

"It shows in your face." He reached to touch a cheekbone with his fingertips, and trace the sooty channel under the eye. "I am told you have spent days at Kadon Dinul." To Dolvid's relief he took the hand away. "Too much study? When you have read everything, what then?"

The echo of Valnoi was almost comical. Tears started behind Dolvid's eyes. "*Menadhi*, I have not done much studying this summer." The page on his table at the man's elbow was covered with renditions of Valnoi's name.

"And you have not done much swimming, or spent much time working in the library, nor with *nôd'yanul*. Not spying, Dolvidh; we try to keep watch over those we are concerned with."

The refreshments arrived. The bakers must have come back with *g'Asalladh'*; there was fresh wheat bread, together with butter, cheese, cold *raminat* and a bowl of ripe plums. Dolvid's thirst was fierce, and he had to force himself not to gulp when the drink was poured.

"These are Island," the plums. "On the western side, there was a little more rain. But the *Edhrodilum* can cope with drought — you can see the same on the Mainland, east of Talbronu, but those canals and ditches are not as elaborate as on Kamanta — the Garden of Owan, as you will see, quite soon. But the rain will be welcome there, too."

"It is very late, *Menadhi*. Many crops are past helping."

"Well, last year was an abundant harvest; there will be little shortage, though much fear of shortage." His small fist clenched, resting on the table. "How could there be a better opportunity for bringing Saidhan back to heel? In the Colony, drought has been worse, and at the best of times they cannot feed themselves except by obtaining Heartland grain. Not Saidhan's hothead son himself could resist for long a demand the extra squadrons be disbanded, if the *rabhsai*, on pretext of shortage, stopped all corn sales to the Colony."

He studied Dolvid's expression. "You find that harsh, my friend? You have not seen the agony civil war can bring. Let this chance go, and in the end the suffering may be worse. Do you understand me?"

"*Menadhi*, I do." And admired nothing about it. The man's obsession with Saidhan's forces, however, was beyond grasping: he could not seriously maintain there was any threat there to *rabhsayum*.

"So I trust. I would be unworthy of my position if I had

failed to notice those doubts of yours, certain reservations, to be seen in what you leave out of your writings, as much as what you have written. Your testing is very near, and I would wish to see your questions beginning to resolve."

Dolvid's heart started thumping, as he saw the crisis had all-but arrived.

"There is room for doubters, even here at the *Mankh'*. Some might nonetheless have healing skill, or be able to give good advice to a farmer, or keep a welcoming *margú*. Not for the *Manadilum*; we are the North Star of Owan, and unless we keep the One Way, no one can find his true direction."

"This you have taught me, *Menadhi*."

"On that very day when we met I had been thinking about a disciple, to share my journey, to sit beside me — and, Dolvidh'! one day I may come to the highest Seat of all."

This, to aspire to Patriarchy, was a huge blasphemy, and *Menadhi* was aware Dolvid knew that. He was revealing himself without reservation, and Dolvid, sensing unbearable embarrassment to come, wished he would stop.

"You, of anyone who has ever been here at the *Mankh'*, have been closest to my mind, with the keenest wits to understand me. Ever since I was raised to be Head of this order, I had hoped to find a young follower and friend. We men of learning, Dolvidh, as we grow older, it is not that judgment fails. But there is a loss — I am boring you with this."

"Not so." No complaint, so long as he kept to these generalities.

"Yes. Youth is always bored with talk about not being young, which youth itself prevents them from imagining — this can never have anything to do with you." He laughed with a gentle melancholy not seen before.

"There, then, is the loss; I have grown up enough to be able to envisage age. I need one beside me who has not yet glimpsed wearing and decay — oh, for others, perhaps, never for himself. For one in the middle of life, youth is a looking-glass, with the flattering tint of undamaged hope." He got up, and sat beside Dolvid on the bunk.

There was an unthinkable mistake. Once, riding south of the *Mankh'*, Dolvid had seen in the distance a monstrous five-legged animal, crouching in wait. He had watched it with gaping fascination, till in a blink angles changed, and he was staring at a pattern of slender tree-stems and shadows. That same shift came now; what there had always been between *Menadhi* and him could be seen for what it was, and how it could ever have been mistaken was ridiculous. Valnoi, with nothing to go on, had been there before Dolvid.

Menadhi put a hand on his bare leg. The face was very near, long vertical scorings, the penetrating eyes. "Both son and companion, to share my vision. One with beauty as well as intellect, whom I respect and trust, as well as love." Tiny hand gripped tight, and he kissed Dolvid, not with simple affection, but passionately, near the base of his throat.

Coldly, he broke free to stand up, and the other stood too. Watery sun was coming in at the window; came the disconnected thought it was afternoon, not still morning; ample light to see the flaccid wattling of the neck, gathering muscles at the mouth, where the skin was thin and taut. The ripe moistness of Valnoi was plain in Dolvid's mind; repellent to hear breath laboring in *Menadhi*'s nostrils, as it had then in his.

"Dolvidh — "

"I am no Changer." He saw the term used by the Others, or his flat tone, had irritated *Menadhi*, who put clenched hands together, thumbs aligned, and closed his eyes, silently speaking a word. This was one of the Exercises. Dolvid now would never learn it.

Quickly calm, *Menadhi* said, "Haven't you understood? I had intended to wait for your Island visit, but always believed you knew. Your Lesser Oaths are to be, equally, your declaration to me."

A yet more staggering blasphemy; with `equally' he put himself beside Raëdh, the Father of All. "Not so," Dolvid said.

"I have been very patient, Dolvidh — so patient. When

you came here on the death of your father, I carried you to my bed — my own bed. Not a night since then I have not seen you there, strong and loving, my own Dolvidh. I would not force an unready child, but you are a child no longer, but a young man, and a lovely one."

Those were words. With his brain, Dolvid supposed they must belong to feelings. He could draw the parallel with his yearning to possess Valnoi, but it was like hearing a man blind from birth tell him what seeing was, outside his imaginings.

The eyes had not left him, watching how his words were received. He shifted, and was more recognizable. "I need not say what I am offering is far beyond anything you could hope for, otherwise. You have seen what it is to be an ordinary pupil here, and can guess the life of an ordinary *atarlai*. As my companion, no one can challenge you, short of *g'Asalladh'* Himself — and *g'Asalladhum* is going to be mine, Dolvidh. You will have power."

"I don't want power."

"Oh, but you do. It is everything, my friend, anything you want; work, leisure, study, command, to witness events or cause them — it is freedom, the only freedom there is. You want power, because you want choice. Not this minute, perhaps, or today, but very soon your choice will be between the power you can enjoy with me, and the life of, let us say, an at-Dhanurai."

He was reaching forward, but Dolvid stepped back, folding his arms. "Or to leave the *Mankh'*." It was said.

"You cannot leave. You will not leave." Again, odd echoes of Valnoi.

"I do not want this life." Because this was so much easier to say than he had imagined, it became truer in speaking; how could he ever have fooled with visions of opposing *Menadhi* from within the ranks of the *Atarlum*, year after year?

Conviction became a near-tipsiness, and this, too, had to do with Valnoi. "I don't want to reach for what's gone. This is Eighteen Lambarr, not the Blossoming Age. Owan restored is in the past, in dreams of old men." Eloquence faltering, he said again, "I am no Changer."

Perhaps for `old men,' *Menadhi's* cold anger was instantaneous. "And you have spent whole days away from the *Mankh'*, not at the Bronze Residence. You have been wasting your substance with some stupid town-whore. Last night, you did not return. I gave you access to the *nôd'yanul* to save you from worse, and thought you had brains to learn the emptiness of that fooling. It would be otherwise with us, a part of shared dreams. How could you not know my plans for you?" A firm step forward.

"If I had it wouldn't have meant any difference, except to make my mind up sooner. I cannot serve the *Mankh'*."

"Outside, you will starve."

"I would sooner starve than follow a Way that is not mine."

Now fury came hot. "You dare? A boy, a blasphemer, a nothing, daring to judge the majesty of *Atarlum*? You imagine you have been beaten before? I'll see you flogged by troopers of the *Adanum* till you are screaming for someone to kill you and end the agony."

Here was a clear sight of cowardice. He could ask for pardon, even if it meant letting *Menadhi* slobber on him. There might be a chance to kill him, later on.

"You read a dozen pages of the *Kezhul*, and you have acquired undying wisdom. Without my guidance you are barely fit to clean out a stable, and you have the gratitude of a jackal."

In the move from threats to complaints could be heard faint hope. Yes, *Menadhi* fell silent, and the eyes were cooling.

"It seems I have frightened you." The voice at once was the ordinary controlled and controlling one. "I have, having always tried to give you a model for equanimity. Understand, Dolvidh, my shock. All my summer was thoughts of you, and I imagined you were prepared for me."

"Never," a simple statement. No need for this to be full of hate.

"You have been startled, too," ruefully. "Let us try to forget the wounding words that have been spoken. Maëdhi *Maëdhu* gives us wisdom to seek good, if we are wise enough to accept it."

He smiled slowly, shyly, if that was possible. "Apart from g'*Asalladh'*, there is no one else alive whose pardon I would ask." Now with affection, he reached out his hand. Dolvid stayed with arms folded.

"Come. Quarrels are ugly, but we have been good friends, and now you have seen me as a man, with both the love and anger of a man." The last part spoiled it for Dolvid, who perceived he was to feel flattered.

"You want time," *Menadhi* suggested. Did that mean he would leave him alone? What did `time' mean? Five minutes, a few hours, a day or two to decide between offer and threat?

"You must believe, don't you, I could never see you harmed — have I not always shown you my favor?" He evidently recalled some of the same exceptions as Dolvid, saying, "All I have done has been for your good — " which was not quite the same thing.

A tapping at the door. One of the boys who had brought the food had come to collect dishes and remains. He was hungry, Dolvid saw, remembering his own early days here, and hopeful.

"Yes, yes," waving. "Take them. Leave the plums. You may want to finish them," to Dolvid. The boy, dishes carefully balanced, went out again.

"Yes," to nothing in particular. "A space for earnest reflection. What I have to offer would be worth considering if you were of high rank in the realm. Will you give it your thought?"

"I shall, *Menadhi*." All he wanted was for the man to leave. The indecision was easily read; he was weighing whether a present renewal of the offensive was worth risking against a calmer future. Dolvid was giving no ground. The new wave broke and receded.

"No more talk of leaving the *Mankh'*, then."

"No." True; there was no more to be said.

"Your place is with us. If you were to consider a life outside the *Mankh'*, we should speak about it as friend to friend, so I could help you determine your future; I have influence in the wider realm. But we have both said unmeant things, not so? We shall speak again, when you are rested. Tomorrow."

"Yes, *Menadhi*." Again he had gathered to leave. It was more maddening than watching Vulakh not-quite add fuel to his furnace, again and again.

Not yet; he laid his hand on a forearm. "I am inviting to you be a part of the future. Love brings much beyond what bodies can apprehend. Sharing a bed is good, but often means nothing; you have already discovered this, of course, with women. But two sharing so much... You do not need to fear what is new; I can guide you to your nature — "

"*Menadhi* — "

"And if you should still need the soft clasp of a woman from time to time, that, too, can be provided — "

"*Menadhi* — "

"No more now. Tomorrow, Dolvidh." He rocked back, but simply stood, gazing into Dolvid's face.

"Tomorrow, then." Quickly, *Menadhi* brought his lips to Dolvid's cheek, turned away, and was gone, quiet-footed. Truly gone. Absently Dolvid bit into a ripe plum. Valnoi.

Even as adversary his strength was a pillar of Dolvid's world, and the biggest shock of all was seeing *Menadhi* shrunk to a supplicant. The parallel with his own feelings for Valnoi was there to be recognized, though to imagine a man with that same hunger for him was too strange.

And frightening; declaring affection, the man could not speak except with the lances of the *Adanum Plakh'* behind him, the deep foundations of the *Mankh'* under his feet.

But the affection must be real, realler perhaps than his own. If he had the power to threaten her with deadly floggings unless she gave up Ladhat and swore there would never be any others, Dolvid would not have desisted: he would gladly enslave Valnoi, and had been saved because *Menadhi* wanted willing, not forced submission. His concession at the end, the offer of occasional women, was a bid, not a threat.

So far. It could not be trusted. Dolvid had seen murderousness, quickly masked, and it was still there. Another refusal could make it blaze up out of control, and inside these walls *Menadhi* was all-but his own law.

Long before dawn he was working by dim lantern-light, separating out books that were his own, his secret, ciphered notebooks, other belongings he could carry. As sky began to pale, he put on his outshirt, picked up the bundles, and crept through empty halls, hearing the kitchens start to stir, expecting a challenge at any step. His only hope was the vanity of *Menadhi*'s that had kept him from seeing how deep Dolvid's disagreements went. In the same way, perhaps, he could not quite believe Dolvid would really leave the *Mankh'*.

The man on watch at the stables was nearly a friend, a new trooper of the *Adanum*. Dolvid had met him as an apprentice, and shown him a few of Kheval's sequences and parries; he did not question the tale about carrying books urgently needed at the Bronze Residence. Nuril, making himself for once hard to saddle, had an instinct this was no normal ride, or perhaps he was only affronted at being called so early. Day was growing lighter, clouded but so far dry, as Dolvid came to the gate, and guards there passed him through with yawns and a familiar wave.

He pressed Nuril as much as he dared. There was every chance *Menadhi* might come to his room early (affably, bringing *raminat*, perhaps), and the swift *pefral* of the *Adanum* could easily overtake him. He would not feel safe until he was inside the walls of Kadon Dinul. If then: he could, as Faëdhal urged, throw himself on the *rabhsai*'s protection, but was not sure what powers *Menadhi* could bring. The Treaty of the Wind Caves could be read either way; if he was shown to have committed crimes against the *Atarlum*, the *rabhsai* was bound to surrender him back to the *Mankh'*.

This was no time for remembering other feelings, regretting the end of the satisfactions and even joys there had been, and from the crest of the rise Dolvid did not glance back at the crouching *Mankh'*. He was looking ahead, to Valnoi.

There had to be a misunderstanding. Possibly she had not heard why he could not come to her, and had spent that night with Ladhat believing he, Dolvid, had changed his mind about her. Of course she'd had many nights with Ladhat, but that was before; it must mean something that she had asked him (not Ladhat, Dolvid), practically begged him, not to go away from Kadon Dinul.

If he gave up any idea of going to the West, and accepted Faëdhal's offer to speak for him at the Residence, he would not have to be apart from her. She despised the Craft families, and would enjoy visiting the Residence, which would gratify her love of fashion.

Did this mean he wanted Valnoi for his *wife*? He was too young to be married yet, and marriages and wives in fact had nothing to do with his feelings. But the world was as it was, and Ladhat could not be disposed of, Ladhat and all others he stood for, without a counterbid. According to her father, Valnoi prized the idea of wedlock more than she did her intended husband, and would surely be pleased if she could look forward to marrying (in a couple of years, perhaps) the one she had implored not to go away.

Nothing overtook him on the road. He passed Harbor Gate, and rode straight to Faëdhal's house, catching him just as he was leaving for the Residence. The Master of Tongues was quite calm, and when Dolvid gasped out the news he had fled from the *Mankh'*, not saying anything about the final cause, Faëdhal, with a species of sculpted coolness, commented, "Not an hour too soon, if I may say so." Over food, he was airily dismissive about *Menadhi*'s chances of bringing Dolvid back.

"You are, let it be remembered, a subject of Lambarr *Rabhsai*, not a chattel of the *Atarlum*. Once the *Bôdhrai* Rhunsilakh hears how matters stand, you will be under the *rabhsai*'s protection. You had better accompany me to the Residence, and this can be settled in an hour."

This Dolvid refused to do, saying he had errands. The return of the horse, for one, so no one could say he was a thief.

Faëdhal's glance was not dull, and Dolvid knew it sounded thin. "Surely, for a small payment one might find a man or boy to take your animal to the Bronze Residence? You do not mean to venture there, I trust, yourself?"

He promised to take Nuril no farther than Harbor Gate. Still puzzled and disapproving, Faëdhal told him to be careful. "In the meantime, I shall speak with Rhunsilakh at once. No doubt I shall see you later?"

Only late morning, after so much event. The clouds over the Avenue might be a little higher, but it was very cool, no longer a break in summer, but distinctly autumn.

Halfway between the Disc and Harbor Gate, he caught side of Valnoi just ahead, going in the same direction. As many people did here, she walked on the smooth reddish stone of the Avenue proper. The flagged walk, half-screened by trees, in front of the big houses, was uneven to walk on, and often congested with porters and pedlars.

The man whose arm she held was of average height. As Dolvid came up he saw an ordinary Owani face with the arched nose. The man's clothes were muted, of plain cloth, his build was moderate, and to Dolvid he seemed nearer Vulakh's age than Valnoi's.

Dolvid called her name and she looked up, startled. Then she smiled, catching at the stirrup-leather by his leg. Her hair was worn loose, and after so much debate about her he was nearly shocked by how pretty the actual Valnoi was.

"My father told me he saw you." The voice, not attractive for itself, brought back all appetites. "This weather! After such a summer as we had." Meant, the sly allusion to their times together.

A breeze came to lift a corner of Valnoi's cloak, and stir her hair. "Three nights ago, the night of all that rain, I had new shoes ruined. My hair is not fit to be seen even now. If I take a chill, can you be my *ramidu*?"

"I have quit the *Atarlum*."

"Left your *Mankh*?" If there had been no other reason, it would have been worth doing, just for that moment of wide-eyed wonder. "What are you going to do?"

They had arrived at Harbor Gate. Valnoi's companion swerved right to pass through the side-archway for those on foot, while she kept her hand at Dolvid's stirrup as they took the main way. In the wide opening to the Square, she glanced over a shoulder, and the man came up as Dolvid was dismounting.

"Ladhat Khazubranati, here is Dolvidh Vidukhat."

The handclasp was firm and friendly, as was the face. His voice was assured. "You would desire speech with Dolvidh — your father is waiting for me. *Naëmpo*, Dolvidh'."

"*Ke'naëmpo*, Ladhati," nodding back. Ladhat went off purposefully, after kissing Valnoi's forehead.

"Would I truly desire speech with Dolvidh?"

"A moment." There were always boys and workless men near the gate, ready to run errands for a small payment, and Dolvid quickly found a boy to take Nuril across to the Bronze Residence stables. All at once this was a farewell. He patted the blunt nose of the steadfast Nuril, mumbled foolish thanks for faithful service, and quickly turned away.

He could not see Valnoi. Perhaps, after all, she had gone on to the shop. No, she was under the arch, talking to a dismounted traveller. Laughing, she put a hand to the man's cheek, and walked over.

"Who was that?" Without a word they had agreed to go to the Gardens.

"Ladhat?"

"That."

"Oh, no one I know. Only, he asked was I waiting for someone."

Down the stone stair they descended into a heavy smell of wet foliage and sodden earth. Leaves, many still green, had been beaten down by the rains, and frequent puddles were littered with twigs. The rill at the bottom was a bubbling stream. At the Grottoes, pools stood on the paving, but the wide cave was dry enough.

Sitting, Valnoi shrugged back her cloak. She was in soft white stuff that traced her body. Her head was set so her lips were offered, and Dolvid, with misgivings, kissed her, still able to lose his bearings.

He disengaged from the improbably soft mouth, gathering her hands to put them on her lap. "Your father says Ladhat is your own choice." This was not how he meant to begin.

"The note you left — I don't understand. You were forbidden to leave the *Mankh'*. How did you bring the note? And now you say you've left the *Mankh'*."

To have forgotten about the *atarlai* killed in Upper Nîv, or not to have listened when told about it, was exactly Valnoi. "You told me your father wanted you to marry Ladhat."

"So he does."

"But he says Ladhat has always been your desire."

"So he has. What's that to you?"

"You asked me not to leave Kadon Dinul."

"Not — " She gave a small giggle. "I have always told you, I do what pleases me. I don't care what pleases my father."

True, she had said so, but he could not simply have made up her dissatisfaction with Ladhat. "You have often said you hated the Craft Guilds. You — " he could not say *begged* — "asked me not to go away."

"He's always so fierce." Reproach clouded her eyes. "Of course I don't want you to leave Kadon Dinul. You please me. You please me more than anyone, when we're having sport."

"What about Ladhat?"   Once seen, unremarkably real Ladhat did not evaporate as easily as when only a name.

"It has always been understood we would marry. I should marry someone.   If all goes well, we'll have a house in the Residence Quarter one day."

"What about me?"

"Well... you can take me riding. I'll have use of a saddle-horse, and you'll have your *pefrai* when you join the Household. Didn't we have plenty of good sport this summer?"

The Household! That was not worth his attention. "Did you — was it so you could be Ladhat's wife and have me to go riding with that you told me not to leave Kadon Dinul?"

"Why else?" Her astonishment at his sour tone seemed genuine. "Ladhat knows I'm not taking sash. He hasn't asked me to.   You sound like a wife-beater of the Other Races — a Gabhani of the *Mankh'*, who ever heard of such a thing?"

"I never said you should wear sash. Do what pleases you." If not solely his, she could be Ladhat's, alone or with a hundred others. Dolvid would not be one of them.

As on the day he first touched her, she rolled her head to and fro against the rock wall. "I've told you what pleases me. You do, Dolvidh."

"No I don't," in a rush of bitterness. "You never listen to anything I say." All the same, this was unreasonable. More than by his poems, or by poems much better than his, she would be pleased by a yard of velvet ribbon, and why not? If all he loved was boring for her, why should she pretend? Because her eyes had made him insane?

"What you do pleases me."   She gave her spine-long shiver. "And you don't flag, as — as others do."

"And that's why you said, don't leave?" Again, why not? She was not responsible for his pride.

"I say what it comes into my head to say, you know that."

"But not — " He gave it up. She had said it, not once in passing, but many impassioned times.

He demanded, "What's wrong with me?" He had nearly asked the real question, why was he not enough for her? It was stupid in either words.

"Nothing, truly. I've told you how you please me. You please me above anyone else."

"I need you." It felt true, and here there was no distinction, despite logic, between seeming and being.

"Well, I've told you — " She stopped, her mouth open wide. "Does he mean, to marry?"

Not if it meant no more than replacing the amiable Ladhat. He desired an absolute, impossible kind of possession that included marriage, or could omit it as superfluous. To kill Valnoi, and then himself might be the only real way to attain it. This was not the dream of anything that might happen, but Dolvid at last saw what his feeling for Valnoi was. He had been misled by words. There was no word for it in ordinary language, and many people who knew the Owanilú quite well thought it was only with poets, long ago; *zhin'paghai*, a kind of illness, nothing to do with love, much less liking. Poets feared and did not welcome it, except for the fierce sense of being alive it brought. Bronal, in a wry mood, had written the price in pain was too high; it cost less to get sick on wine, and that was over sooner.

She gave her high laugh. "What would be the advantage if we married? You don't have property, or position. You don't have a craft."

"I am going to be at — " he began, then despised himself for entering the bidding. "Property, position! You Craft people — you would buy and sell the mercy of Aëlovoi, if there was a profit in it."

"The *Mankh'* would try to make mysteries out of food and a roof over your head. Why talk about marriage, if property doesn't come into it?"

"I didn't. You did."

"Yes, but you — "

"Don't tell me what I said. When you asked me, over and

again, not to go away — "

"If you misunderstood me, I ask pardon."

"I did."

"That's not my fault."

"No."

"Your feelings are — your own feelings. I never made them, I didn't ask for them. I have never belonged to anyone." She was becoming aggrieved, and Dolvid, who'd had to endure *Menadhi*'s unasked endearments, felt a crippling flash of sympathy for her. With another shift, he could begin to feel sorry for *Menadhi*.

"Valnoi — " wearily, he tried to bring back a passion, to summon up a word to cancel Ladhat, his rancor, her narrow vision, the feeling everything was spoiled. No use; he was not cured, but she was his illness. "This is the last time we'll meet." Stupid; it could only affect her if she cared, and then it would not be needed.

"You don't want to see me any more? I don't believe you. You just said you needed me. Why can't we be good bed-friends? Haven't I pleased you? I can please you better."

How that tugged at his loins angered him. He could be turned into her pet creature, part of her fondled property.

"Dolvidh?"

"No." He immediately wanted it unsaid. This actual second he wanted her. All summer, knowing and not-knowing, he had accepted less than all of her, and surely that was better than losing her altogether. This was senseless. She knew.

"I wish you well, Valnoi," standing, moving away. Senseless but necessary, a lie he had to hang on to.

Bewildered by abruptness, she followed to where the shallow steps led down. "You'll change your mind. Later you'll want to see me. Dolvidh, I'll let you, if I'm free. I'll always want to see you."

"I shan't be at Kadon Dinul." Anywhere would be better.

"You were going to be at the Residence."

"And you said — never mind." A very fine rain had begun, and she turned her face up, enjoying the tickle.

"Don't you want to kiss me?" The cloak was open, her body a slim shaft of white. He took her shoulders, and kissed the mouth with its downturned corners. His being the one to say farewell reversed all magic; as never before in all their minglings he was the one in charge, submitting no sort of plea. Her body did not fail to feel the difference, and reach out, interested. The deceptive moment of control ebbed away, and he could have laughed, or sobbed.

"Dolvidh, it's mad. You have made me happy, and I have you, or so I thought."

"I am leaving Kadon Dinul." Words had more substance than feelings, which could change before a sound died. A life could not go fluttering like a pennon as the breeze shifted. That was why words were needed, with their comforting, false persistence, their binding strength.

"Where will you go? How are you going to live?"

"What — " does it matter, he nearly said. Then, "Why should you care?"

"Very well, I don't care. Plenty of men left who think I'm good enough for their beds. I'm not going to do without sport."

"I'm sure of that."

"What, then? You're too conceited to enjoy what pleases you, and so I should give up everything I enjoy? That's not my way."

"I wish you well." He did not, but wished he could.

He left her standing on the top step of the court by the Grottoes. His revenge would be simple. Not revenge on Valnoi, exactly, but on the mean obsessions of the Craft Families. He was not going to the Residence, nor to the Colony. He would make money. He had far more than enough brains; fools often acquired wealth; Zhival, the big landowner, was one.

Land was for those already rich; dealing in goods was what made money grow. Not here in the Heartland, where the important food crops were controlled by the magnates, and most other goods either in the hands of guilds or else subject of monopoly grants, which were bought and sold for large sums. In the outer provinces there were chances for small dealers in hides, fleeces, furs, animal feeds, and lesser foods such as oats and cheeses, dried fish, honey. Dolvid had neither knowledge nor money to set up on his own. He would start by buying a share with an established dealer, and later, when he had some experience, become his own man.

He had never felt greater scorn for money, or those who prized it, but *Menadhi* said he was unfit to be a stable-boy, and a house in the Residence Quarter, use of a saddle horse, were more to Valnoi than all the poems ever written. He would come back to Kadon Dinul a wealthy man. The idea of being respected for what he despised was very satisfying.

When he revealed this plan, Faëdhal doubly objected, saying the Residence was where he belonged; only there would he be entirely safe. This was doubly awkward; he needed the money Faëdhal had kept for him, but beyond that sharply wanted to have the scholar's approval.

"I shall be a long way from here. *Menadhi* will be angry I left, but he has more to do than scour the realm for one obscure runaway." Sufficiently true, surely: after initial fury the man's vanity would not let him treat Dolvid's disappearance as anything important to him.

Theep frown gave way. "When I was first, ah, cast adrift, as it were, at the closing of the *manal*," he reminisced, "I saw myself betrayed by learning itself, and vowed I would have nothing more to do with hard languages. A young man, we see, can make poor guesses about his future. If you must go, you will come back to us."

They could part now on good terms. Faëdhal embraced Dolvid, asking to be kept informed by letter, and promising to reply. The sum he handed over was more than expected, or than seemed possible as Vidukh's final salary, but there was no courteous way to ask, and so might never know how much of it was Faëdhal's own money.

Nevertheless, he meant to come back: Kadon Dinul had all the people to give his triumph any meaning. He was heading north, to Dramal or Nearer Ân. That was remote enough from the *Mankh'*. Hovering, also, was the half-thought he might somehow meet up again with the Froghul, Ka-Nam's people. With Tini-ra.

End of the First Book

Dolvid

II

(2928)

Irbat

From south the road looped into Irbat by a long causeway on stone piles set in broad tidal mudflats. A dreary place, scored by lethargic creeks, no hedge or stand of trees to protect against the wind, which in winter persisted sourly off Shemufegh Rai, the endless waste of salt-marshes to the north and west.

A dismal scene, but these flats were good for mussels, small clams, an occasional crayfish, and Dolvid was there with basket and digging-stick, though there were thin, crackling patches of opaque ice, islands of skin left behind by peeling sunburn.

He shivered, frowning at inapposite comparison. After a fourth winter Dolvid was unreconciled to the nagging wind, the late springs here, even if its position on Arnan saved Irbat from the worst of the snows. They fell instead on the uplands of Dramal, away south and eastward.

Wearily, he stirred at dark, slimy mud with his stick. The basket was more than a third full, but his haul would shrink drastically when he used the creek to wash away mud. Besides, mussels, like lords, enjoyed roomy dwellings, and the amount of actual food here was small. This was the leanest season of the year, and it took many hours of digging to make much difference to the late-winter diet of bread and *Irvati*, a soft, salty ewe-cheese made locally. Travellers who came here thought *Irvati* a treat not to be missed, but they had not had to live on it; Dolvid used to think it tasty, though not to be compared with the milder goat-cheeses of the Froghul. Now he did not exactly hate it, but just wished he would never have to eat it again. When he earned a little money he would almost run to one of the small, smoke-filled cookshops at wharfside, buy a reeking chunk of mutton, dripping with fat, and choke it down gluttonously, with fresh, fragrant bread to soak up the grease. That was always a reminder of his feast with the Froghul of Tan Dramali, the seared and searing chunks of spit-roast kid.

Seven years when summer came (if summer ever came); there would be a Great Pledging at Kadon Dinul, but that was long rides into the south and the past, nothing to do with him, except as a measure of age. Slackly, he wondered how many children Tini-ra had borne by now.

For food it would be better when shearing came, and he could find paying work. He was good at making out bills of lading and cargo manifests, adding accounts; he was one of few who could readily translate the peculiar fleece-measures of the sheepmen into standard weights. Or if no one wanted help with written work he would again be a dockside porter, lifting tight-packed bales of fleece on the start of their journey to the weavers and dyers of the Heartland. For that work, competition was keener; the prosperity of Irbat had long been in decline, and many strong arms were idle much of the year. More than once he had begun a resolve to leave this unfruitful port, turn south again for Dônshei, the softer towns of the Paowan. Always, lassitude stopped him; there was nowhere he wanted to go.

Straightening to ease his back, he waved to another mussel-digger sixty paces away, down towards the huddle of the port, a woman swathed in dark, lean and curiously sinister as she planted her feet on a slight rise, no-color sky behind her, where there would soon be a sparse crown of tough grass. As she raised a hand in reply he saw it was Rhonis, who lived not far from him, in the southeastward quarter, below the Mounds. She made her living selling driftwood for fuel, and doing small repairs to clothes of people hardly less poor than she.

Over to the right where the causeway went curving was the ancient stone watchtower guarding approaches to the town, home for an under-strength file of General Cavalry. In provincial towns, most men could handle a bow or pike if called as auxiliaries, but it had been years since either regulars or the Irbat watch had needed more force than it took to quell a mariners' brawl.

All the more startling, then, to see a red warning-flag go flapping to the end of the yard-arm which projected sideways from the tower, a signal, with the accompanying cry of trumpets, for the town guard to stand to arms. Simultaneously, a message-rider started in the direction of Irbat, going at a good canter.

By clambering a bank and leaping to the mossed shoulder of a piling Dolvid was able to intercept the rider near the mile marker.

"Horsemen — cavalry, two squadrons at the least," in answer to a shouted question. He barely slackened pace, and Dolvid jogged beside the horse for a few steps. "What cavalry?"

"Royal, or their banner is; just came in sight over Klamuru Gap. Can't be too careful, these days." He kicked up his mount, and Dolvid slowed to a walk, reflecting the last was just a habit of speaking; these in fact were particularly eventless times. True, he was cut off from (and indifferent to) affairs of the wide realm, but news overheard in the street was not of disturbance or war: the Family had gone on growing; Dolvid was uncertain whether Lambarr had six or seven living children, though he had heard the eldest, Laloi, was betrothed. At Tan Lughsai the fabled Wooden Residence remained unfinished. Colony vessels docked at Irbat, and news out of Kamsilat was that Sebhal, son of Saidhan, Captain of the West in all but official title, had caused a stir, and earned open censure of the *Atarlum*, by stealing away and marrying a *nôd'yanu* from the *margú* near Banakit. She was Aëlu, very beautiful, and people in general were in favor of her becoming wife to the most famous of younger warriors. What annoyed the *Mankh'*, that Sebhal had stolen his bride with years of her indenture to run, only added to popular approval.

As for the rest of the realm, poor harvests in 21 Lambarr had caused some rioting, even at Kadon Dinul, but there had been two bountiful years since then. Outlaws were making it risky to travel unescorted in lonely country, but outlaws did not ride in squadrons under the *rabhsai's* colors, and while the gates of Irbat might be closed, he had no fear of being caught outside by hostile forces. He walked back and sat on the mile-marker to see what was going to happen. Why as many as one hundred cavalry should come here was beyond him.

Not long, and a new trumpet call sounded from the tower, answered from out of sight. Over the mudflats a pair of curlews went with their dipping flight; Rhonis with her basket was trudging back to town.

Above the watchtower, provincial colors, deep blue with a white ram depicted, were dipped in salute; the bronze-bordered royal banner appeared over the brow of the curving rise, then lance-tips, heads of horsemen. The banner showed the Sword, and the soldiers' tunics were plain; these were General Cavalry, their breastplates and shoulder-guards making a brave show on this cheerless day. But their commander, beside the standard-bearer, wore under a billowing cloak the color of beetroots (but lined in white) a tunic with Household facings.

Behind him, as the message-rider had said, came two full squadrons, but after them came a pack-train escorted by additional lances. As the foremost of yet more troops following the baggage rode into sight, the leaders were nearly up to the mile-marker. The smaller pennon under the royal colors had double squares to proclaim a full captain.

The commander, moustached, leaned to speak to the officer at his right, big and broad-shouldered, with a remarkably ugly face. Abruptly, the captain wheeled his grey *pefrai* aside. The big horse's nostrils were practically in Dolvid's face, and he hoped there was not going to be some nonsense about failing to stand when a royal captain rode by.

Also he was nominally subject to levy in time of war. He stood, the Froghuli knife, always worn when he was out alone, ready in its back-sheath. Battle with a couple of hundred regular lancers should make his death worthy of at least a comic song.

The big *pefrai* sidestepped, as the officer, gloss-booted, swung out of the saddle, his lead squadron riding on. "As I thought — the *Mankh'* rabbit, or has he a brother? Dolvidh, Dolvidh Vidukhat."

"Dolvid." The Owani aspirate had gone for good. Bolan Bakir had thicked out a little, waist and thigh, in seven years, and a broader stripe of moustache aided the newly resolute look. The neck, also, was sturdier, but the quick eyes were the same under mobile brows. Amazingly, he had made a good start on his ambition; his acting rank (insigne worn on the right) was full captain; the left side, for permanent rank, empty. He tugged off a white gauntlet to tuck it under his arm, and reached out to grasp Dolvid's muddy hand. "Knew I knew you. I wouldn't believe it at first, but who ever forgets one he battered blades with, hah? What in the name of Hranakh are you doing in this *rabhsai-*forgotten corner?"

"Not quite forgotten, it seems. I might ask you the same."

"You could, you could, and get an answer. You ride? Of course you do. Hoi — !" The last rank of the rear squadron was leading a few spare mounts. In a moment a roan less massive than some *pefral*, with a lively arch to its neck, was led beside Dolvid, who decided he would leave his basket of what looked like mud-lumps next to the marker. Bolan's eyebrows had already made comment on his threadbare outshirt, stained breeches and worn, clotted boots.

He fit his foot into the wide military stirrup and got up, instantly feeling return of a mounted man's mysterious authority. Bolan was up beside him, and they fell in ahead of the pack-train.

"So you've quit the *Atarlum*?"

"Nearly six years ago."

"Didn't I say that was no life for you?" His eye again swept emblems of poverty. "Neither is this, whatever it is you're doing. Irbat, in the name of Larghai?"

"It doesn't matter. What about you?"

"Big doings." He stood in his stirrups. The lead troops were coming to the tough-cobbled space in front of Irbat's main south-facing gate. "Look, there'll be balderdash here about tendering the *rabhsai*'s warrant and so forth." He examined his right hand, muddied by grasping Dolvid's, and brushed it against the flank of his horse. "Who's this Iriban Baëtufi?"

"Warden of the port and chief magistrate."

"That much I have. What's he about? Old local family, by the name."

"No one ever forgets that. No one had better."

A nod. "That sort. Can he be trusted when it comes to quartering my people?"

"No — " a little annoyed with himself at being flattered by these questions. "I'm sure you'll have to wave your warrant about. Don't let him give you the old sheep-pens; besides the stink, they were used for grain the year before last, and there are rats. Good-sized houses are standing empty, north end of the Mounds. The hostelries can take your officers, there is not much business now. Plenty of room for the rest, and the animals, in the shearing-sheds — Iriban will not like that, but they are not going to be needed for five weeks or more — you'll be gone by then?"

"I had better be," grimly. "Shearing-shed, not the old sheep-pens, north end of the Mounds. Dolvid, good. Meet me for dinner later — what hostelry is best? Iriban is going to have to dine without my table-talk."

"To stay, they say the *Golden Shears*. For a meal, it used to be the *Praf'Rabhsai*, on the harbor."

"An hour after sunset, then, the *Praf'Rabhsai*. Bring the roan."

"No — have your man lead it. I shall be taken as a thief."

Bolan caught at the halter, nodding, as Dolvid dismounted. "My thanks. Now for the rites." A good horseman, he shook his grey into a trot, overtook the rear of his squadrons, handed off the spare horse, and went loping to the head of his little army.

Ahead by the city a handful of provincial cavalry had appeared to flank the gate with its lumpy stone arch, pikemen of the watch at the center. Behind, mounted soldiers were still coming onto the causeway, but only file-leaders and above had the appearance of regular cavalry. The rest, with their uneven ranks, lances at many angles, riding styles varying between the forward lean of a mounted herdsman and a farm-boy's easy slump, had to be auxiliaries at best. The ones with neither helms or breastplates must be new levies.

Down at the gate, Iriban with his under-warden had obviously been taken by surprise. His traditional hat was on crooked with the tassel hanging over one eye.

When he stepped across the threshold of the hostelry under the supposed likeness of Dromladh, for whom it was named, a serving-man tried to bar his way, muttering about `troubling good folks when they're at their food.' Not sure whether he was being taken for pedlar or beggar, he maintained the demand the cavalry-captain be sent for. At length the man, making `Wait here' sound a threat, withdrew. Very soon he reappeared in obsequies of apology, closely followed by Bolan.

Who grumbled, as the serving-man went away, "I thought you would at least put on other boots and breeches. Or are those your only boots and breeches?"

"My only boots, my best breeches."

"Save us from the everyday ones. Come on — appetite?"

He led the way to a private room, where wine and cold foods were waiting on a side-table. On the main board, candles were cheerful, and seated there was the ugly young officer seen earlier. Like Bolan he had a Household tunic, and he too had insigne for only temporary rank.   "Dolvidh, no, *Dolvid* Vidukhat," Bolan said, "Acting Under-Captain Shumat Shurris-son."

"Shumat," Dolvid said. The man was frowning, but there was no mistake; the face was changed, but low forehead, flat nose and crooked, broad-lipped mouth must be the same. Dolvid said, "We used to conquer empires together, in the Gardens of Kamzhinu. You went back to the Angle, twelve years ago, when your uncle's business failed."

"Your father — " frowning, "was at the Residence? Books?"

"We would make rules for all the others."

"Would we? You, I remember, had a bow — or was that some other boy?"

"No, I had the bow. You were the best of us at staves."

"I learnt from my uncle — whose business never failed, though it came close. Well met again, Dolvid." Lopsided as ever, the remembered smile flashed out, and Shumat put out a thick, strong hand to grasp his. "So," to Bolan, busy filling glasses. "I've known your Kheval of the *Mankh'* since I was ten."

"Eight. We are the same age. You came back to Kadon Dinul, then?"

"Six years ago," Shumat agreed. "After my father was made assessor in the country east of Kred Bakali, I was able to be apprenticed to the Household."

"Where he has risen quicker than any man since Saidhan." Bolan held out filled glasses. "Look, tales of yore will have to wait, we've got plans to discuss. One toast to reunion, then — " They raised glasses, and Bolan added, "And to Lambarr *Rabhsai*. He's footing the bill."

He waved at the sideboard. "Have some of this, whatever it may be."

There were tarts and cheeses, smoked salt fish and a kind of custard made with lamb's blood and marrow, and better than it sounded. "Will the lamb be good?   That's what they recommended."

"It ought to be." Dolvid was ravenous. He took robust helpings of several of the cold foods, and sat down, glass refilled. All unreal; Irbat had always been strange, Irbat with Bolan was hard to accept, but adding Shumat made it far less possible than many dreams. His hands were clumsy as he broke pastry, and wondered if he could be drunk on two mouthfuls; he seldom had wine nowadays.

Having opened his mouth, Bolan seemed deliberately to make another choice of subjects. "How is it you're in Irbat, then? Your *Mankh'* learning rusting away, along with your swordsmanship."

"I came here," with careful precision, "on behalf of a man called Darborr. I had bought into the fleece business he had in Dônshei, sorting, grading, reselling them to weavers. Darborr was son of a housekeeper we had when I was a child, or rather, husband of her daughter. After I left the *Mankh'*, I was making my way north, and ran into Darborr at Dônshei Bridge. He was looking for fresh capital and someone to keep his accounts; I had a little money to invest, and needed something to do. Later on I began coming to Irbat at shearing, to buy fleeces." An adequate account, with a lot of unneeded muddle and pain left out.

"But that's not what you're doing now?" The glance again took in Dolvid's shabbiness.

"We quarreled. Darborr started speculating in grain, and bought half the oats of Ân. That was for Twenty-two Lambarr."

"Then he was a made man," Shumat said. The year — otherwise, 2925 — was famous for its harvests.

"It ruined him. He contracted to buy oats at a price based on scarcity, which turned out to be twice what they would fetch on the open market."

Bolan frowned. "I don't understand these things. A man can lose money, then, even on plenty."

"Darborr could. He had to sell up the fleece business, and I was left stranded here."

"But you said you quarreled," Bolan said. "Now you say he lost all his money."

"And mine," finding it harder to stay away from the bitter parts. "He was drunk the evening he agreed to buy the oats, and I said from the start the price was too high. But I was eighteen, and he was a proud man." There was much more, and Darborr's wife, Radis, came into it, but not for this telling.

Bolan said, "Why have you stayed here? Just the same as when we first met. If I had half your brains, or you had half my ambition, one of us would be Captain-General by now, or *Bôdhrai*. You could walk to El'tuf and keep accounts at the Great House — you could work passage on a ship to Kamsilat, and get a post with old Saidhan. Boast about being Kheval's pupil, and you could be a teacher of arms, or someone's master of tongues, with your *Mankh'* learning. Hrafi's elbow, men less learned than you keep themselves in comfort by droning on about books at dinner, and you've got the blood for it. Here you are with one pair of leaky boots, and you look as if your last good meal was in the Night of Owan — go on, tell me this is your choice for a life."

"Did it go well with Iriban Baëtufi?"

The attempt to deflect him failed. He thumped the table with his fist. "That's exactly what I mean!" The serving-man, just then kneeing open the door, staggering under a wide tray, said, "Yes, sirs, coming, just coming." Two assistants followed him, and set out a roast of lamb flanked by carrots and parsnips, little bowls of pickled apricot with stewed onion, a monumental round loaf with a crackling crust, and several other good things. "Hardships of the soldier's life," Shumat commented.

Once their plates were heaped, and the servers had withdrawn, Bolan resumed. "You were exactly right about Iriban. He did his best to bed us down with the rats, and told me, otherwise there wouldn't be room for all of us. I said, `What about the houses empty at the north end of the Mounds?' and we had him. Same with the shearing-pens, he tried to make out they'd be in use — these local lordlings! We need someone like you, who can shame them."

Here he exchanged a look with Shumat, who was eating steadily. "To be exact," Bolan said, "we need you. Speaking of oats, how much feed can we get in Irbat? You know the dealers? Are there wagons to be had?"

Dolvid told what he could, but rather warily. He was puzzled by the question; whatever this cavalry had been brought together for, Bolan must have a royal warrant, giving him very wide powers, including, as last resort, seizure of goods or animals. Well short of that, as he reminded him, farmers and dealers must let him have what he demanded, at a fair rate of compensation.

"Would you act for us?"

Cutting meat, Dolvid paused. "Would I?"

"The prices will double as soon as they think they see a good thing. I'm no good at haggling, and we've been given a short purse. We have to find a way to feed regiments, out of subsistence for companies."

"Regiments?" All he had seen was about five squadrons, not all of them regulars.

A loose gesture. "I left another *kimuko* of cavalry at Dônshei. I couldn't wait any longer. They'll be moving up to El'tuf in the next few days, with whatever levies they've found horses for. I've got authority to make up two to four squadrons from the eastward garrisons, and borrow two at Yuvakh Din."

"Then you're going to Narn." The only answer; after ten years the *rabhsai* was doing something about the far Northeast.

Grudgingly, as Bolan explained it. Lambarr had been put in a position where no *rabhsai* could afford not to act. Over the past few years rule of law in that quarter had broken down, and unrest had spread to the eastward borders of the realm proper, so that the cavalry commander in Yuvakh Din had become strident about his need for additional troops. Still the question had been shelved, but then from the port of Narn had come a petition to the *rabhsai*, from men calling themselves the Loyal Elders, and signed by many leading citizens. It prayed for relief from the oppression of outlaws and adventurers, who all-but controlled the port by force. Bolan had not actually seen this document, but knew copies had also been sent both to Sebira and El'tuf last year, while the original came to Kadon Dinul overland.

"Shrewd, hah?" Bolan grinned. "Under pretext of ensuring their message reached the *rabhsai*, they made certain it would be seen by at least two of the *nimul*, Vinilat here and who's it, in Ân — "

"Daënakh," Dolvid said.

"So it's been chewed over by all the lordly cousins, and every Great House in Six Provinces is waiting to see what Kadon Dinul does. How can any *rabhsai* calling himself *rabhsai* be seen ignoring such an appeal?"

"We can't say he wouldn't have acted anyway," Shumat said.

"No, no, no one knows that. But as Merovas says, he's cautious son of a bold father, and much taken up with family matters... "

Dolvid pushed his plate away: disappointingly, his capacity for food had been shrunk by privation. "I see why there is an expedition. When the Narn garrison first mutinied, when I was a boy at the *Mankh'*, the *Atarlum* tried to urge action."

No way to finish; Bolan could not fail to hear the unsaid *but*. "No senior commander wanted it. Then there was a rumor Tobhan baKargul was offering to contribute twelve squadrons of provincial cavalry, on condition his son Tovakh commanded any expedition. Well, who in the Heartland would put up with that, the army Banak beat putting the realm back together for Banak's son?"

After long absence from Dolvid's thoughts, the Great Families, with their compound connections of blood and marriage, began to fall into tidy order again. "Kargul? he said. "If the troubles have reached Yuvakh Din, I would expect Daënakh of Ân to be the one ready with troops. He has sons, too. Isn't the elder going to be Lambarr's son-in-law?"

"Brodhai," nodding. "He's at Kadon Dinul. He would have gone, and I volunteered to be under him, never mind his

Household rank is only squadron leader. But Brodhai's cockles went cold when he heard the piddling forces the *rabhsai* could spare. Kizhunai's senior to me in the Household, but he's another cautious one, and old Merovas supported me for the job — more out of fear they'd take up Tobhan baKargul on his offer, I think, than any love for Bolan Bakir. Well, when will there be another opening half as good? Only a once-in-a-lifetime stroke of luck I got my squadron, and another chance that made me *kímukan*; I could stay *kímukan* for twenty years, unless I can get into a fight."

"Is that your permanent rank?" A nice point which called for double wonder, that Bolan had attained that level so quickly in the placid Household, or having done so had been entrusted with this command. A small army, but a great deal more than the two paired squadrons a *kímukan* led.

"A gamble," Bolan went on. "It's all a gamble. If we don't all starve in the wilderness, and I'm not killed by a rebel arrow, most likely we don't have the forces to succeed in this jaunt. Well, I'm a gambler — life's all a gamble. This can be the making of us all."

This had the sound of one trying to convince himself above his listeners. "How will you proceed?"

Apparently, orders could not be vaguer; Bolan was to reach Narn, and renew its allegiance (he sardonically quoted the language of the Elders' petition; `Let the justice and wisdom of the realm rise again with the sun over this royal port'), then do his best to ensure it would remain loyal, using local revenues for training and upkeep of local forces. Clearly the *rabhsai* was not prepared to expend treasure maintaining a port of no practical importance to his domains, and was, as Bolan said, trying to avoid embarrassment as cheaply as possible.

"I'll have ten real squadrons, at most, and we'll be lucky to cobble together that many levies — I can't force anybody, this is not called a real war. All levies get is the two-thirds pay, as if they were manning the walls of their own towns, and going home for their meals and a wallow with their wives, this to come riding with me off the edge of the maps. The enemy is rabble, there'll be nothing in the way of ransoms, and if the Northeast is what I hear, there won't be much booty, either."

Dolvid said, "I heard plunder had been forbidden, since the reign of Plakhsila."

Shumat, with a wry look, put in, "We are supposed to be giving back to the loyal what's rightfully theirs."

Bolan stared hard at his second-in-command, then at Dolvid. "Well," at last. "For what we offer, the brave youth of Dramal is not flocking to the colors. All you get is boys out for adventure, farm-lads tired of breaking their backs, scarecrows with no other work — off-scourings of the province. Well, we've got good file-leaders in the General Cavalry, it may begin to look an army by the time we get to Yuvakh Din. What we need — we were talking about this on the ride, Shumat here and I — is a man who knows buying, who can work out what is needed for the numbers and distances, a head for all that."

"Thinking can only go so far. You could not be starting at a worse season. All the lofts are at their emptiest, and up north, beyond El'tuf, there won't be a new blade of grass for six weeks or more. Even this side of Drin Dakani, you may still find roads blocked by snow. Why now?"

"You understand this, that's exactly why you have to ride with us. Look — " Bolan refilled his glass decisively. "The *rabhsai* is not going to spend money on a campaign lasting two summers. If we're going to be at Narn in strength this summer we have to start early. I ask for good men, and they give me Shumat — " This was a friendly insult, and they grinned at each other. "No, he's the only fighter this side of Arnan with some spirit to him, but he'll be needed up front. You will be our quartermaster, with the same acting rank as his, under-captain, same pay, same share of any — " his mouth made *booty*, but he changed it to " — any lawful prize-money."

Beginning to be interested, Dolvid would not be swept up by Bolan's flattery. "How do you expect to finish this quickly? Are all these rebels and outlaws going to line up in companies so you can beat them in one big battle? Why would they not take to open country, or to their ships, those that came by water. You push through to Narn, raise the colors — "

"And our objective is accomplished," Bolan said. "If it can be done with little or no fighting, none of us will be heroes, but we can return without any disgrace. What's your point?"

"You turn your head, and the rebels come back. Narn would be out of the realm again before you reached Sebira on the way home."

Shumat said, "Not if we can leave Narn with an effective garrison of its own."

"I am a Household officer," defending against a suggestion never made. "My right place is Kadon Dinul. I am not authorized to garrison Narn with my own men. Besides, the road there has never been entirely closed. Even the year before last, when these Loyal Elders were as good as prisoners, there were goods from Narn coming to Yuvakh Din."

"Even thieves need stuff to steal," Dolvid said. "*Where can Narn sell its goods, if not to this realm?* — the Patriarch said that, ages ago. Though I believe he was quoting Laluvoi."

"She is a marvel," Bolan said. "She sat at all the meetings, and spoke more sense than anyone. You'd never take her for — what? She must be seventy-five."

"She married the Gabh'Owan Heir," working it out, "thirty-four, sixty-two years ago. She is eighty, eighty this spring."

"May she live forever," Shumat, quietly fervent.

"I doubt there would be any expedition, but for her," Bolan said. "The *rabhsai*, mostly, was off sailing toy boats at Tan Lughsai, or sucking peaches with Saëdhu in the south. Ten years ago, she said, this rebellion could have been put down with an effective blockade, but she sees this cursed Petition leaves no time for that."

"A blow has to be struck," Shumat agreed. "For the good name of the realm."

He seemed sincere, but Dolvid was not sure about Bolan,

whose outline was faintly dishonest, as if he was aiming to achieve something with enough semblance of victory to advance his reputation, not caring what happened to Narn next year, or in five years. To be fair, however, Lambarr *Rabhsai* was evidently in the same conspiracy.

"You want to know how we'll proceed. Come with us, and help decide. I told Merovas, and he agrees, we are soldiers. How Narn is to be kept loyal is policy; our job is to defeat the enemy in the field. The enemy in the field," he repeated, as if that might persuade them to meet him in open battle.

Dolvid took a tooth-twig from the sideboard, charred it in the candle-flame, and pushing plates and dishes aside began sketching a map on the table-linen. "Some here in Irbat," he began, hearing his voice take on the tone of a teacher at the *Mankh'*, "predicted loss of Narn would be to their benefit. Ships coming across the Eastern Ocean, rather than being subjected to extortion landing goods in Narn, would round North Cape; larger ships would have to dock at El'tuf, but vessels of shallower draft could use Dromladh's Canal, and make port here. That's nonsense; once a ship passes into Arnan, why not continue down to Owan Sai, or to Zelkova in Kargul, where they have goods and foodstuffs to exchange for what is brought in?"

The growing map fascinated Bolan, and Shumat nodded confirmation to his glance; there was going to be increased pressure on Dolvid to join the venture.

"Narn, you say, can be bypassed altogether?" Bolan prompted.

"Except midwinter, when no one wants to risk the storms and floating ice at North Cape. But it it is not a real question: who can name anything that comes to us across the Eastern Ocean we can't do without?"

"Spices?" Bolan ventured, "Pepper and such."

"Once," Dolvid conceded. "Now Hrin traders bring those to Thenimala in Ninkufu. Back before the Night, so I was taught, before we had learnt how to make the hardest steel, we shipped dyed goods eastward in exchange for weapons, but our own steelmakers of Upper Dakbân have surpassed anything we could import. Narn — " he put a cross at the extreme right of his map — "has a small hinterland to feed its own, and has to do some trading, but the empty country behind it is wider than the entire Heartland, before you come to our borders."

"Empty," Bolan said, "and fit for nothing but jackals, so they tell me — and the human jackals who live by waylaying along the road."

"In Larghai's age, it was the Province of Naëni, fertile and prosperous. Bring that back, and Narn can flourish again."

"What you're saying is what is hinted at Kadon Dinul," Bolan said. "The realm doesn't need Narn."

"Its people are asking for the *rabhsai*'s protection." Shumat was vehement. "You can't measure that by whether it can be made to pay. It must be attempted, at least."

"So we shall — attempt it, that is. If we can force some sort of battle, half a dozen good squadrons of *péfrapravádal* can chew up ten times their numbers of armed rabble. At worst, we'll bring back trophies, and a mob of prisoners to salt eels for *g'Asalladh'*, and that's more than anyone in the Household expects, of that I'm sure. If only the cursed *jinzal* will stand and fight!"

Shumat's head went to one side. "There aren't any *jinzal* in the Northeast, are there?"

Dolvid matched his innocence. "Not that I've heard, since the Wars of Cleansing."

"A manner of speaking." Bolan was gruff, suspecting he was being made fun of. "Look, enough scholars' talk. So you're coming with us?"

"Not as a soldier." This was implied admission there was something he would go as, and sketching his map he had surely felt the stir of feelings he had been living without, the craving for new scenes, adventure. Bolan's cynical view of the expedition was less repellent out in the open: any soldier, given an impossible job, had to seek ways to come out of it with as much credit as he could. But it would be an improbable fulfillment of childhood dreams, to ride alongside Shumat — east, not west — on the business of empire.

"What, then? This is an army I'm leading, there's no room for a song-maker. Though it's true," turning brightly to Shumat, "we could use a trained pen in the company, to make our dispatches sound better."

"I might come as an agent attached to your staff. Farmers and factors would deal more reasonably, not seeing a soldier's tunic." Considering he might starve before shearing, this was setting his terms high, but he had to have more freedom than as Bolan's direct subordinate, bound by military disciplines.

"So you can pick and choose which orders you obey, is that it?"

"I am not looking for glory, or advancement in the Household."

Bolan tried to squint beneath his motives. "And you'll want to be in charge of the treasury, naturally. Then if you save anything on prices, you can discreetly share the difference with the *rabhsai*."

"You can disburse all payments in person. I shall render written accounts, signed by each supplier. Every bag of oats reweighed when we receive it, and a signed record of everything given out."

"Oh, but look. Any army staff makes a bit on supplies — Saidhan himself, I wouldn't wonder. It's the expected thing."

"Then alter the figures after I submit them. If I come, my accounts will be correct to a half-tobhai. You say you're on a short purse — there's no room for the expected thing, is there?"

He knew this was pompous, but being in business with Darborr had left him with small tolerance for self-defeating cleverness. Bolan, meanwhile, after starting to take offense, looked actually relieved, as if rescued from the burden of dishonesty. "All right, rabbit — done. You'll be paid as an under-captain, but with no share of any prize-money. And you'll give a hand with dispatches?"

Dolvid nodded acceptance, feeling his heart quicken,

with fear as well as anticipation; after years of letting himself be ruled by circumstances he was not nerved for newness. Yet ever since morning, when, for a few minutes, a *pefrai* had been moving under him again, he had been yearning for the reality of that sensation, the power *Menadhi* once spoke of, perhaps, to bring about change. Vaguely he foresaw he would influence the course of this expedition. Bolan was refilling glasses for a toast. It was very strange, life.

"Who'll pay for this table-linen?" Bolan complained.

X

Eastward

Still some mystery shadowed Bolan's plans, things left out of his expositions. Or perhaps only Bolan was mysterious, viewing himself as open and straightforward, but filled with unexplained contradictions. Dolvid rode beside him from Irbat to El'tuf, heard contempt for pampered Residence Quarter families mixed with admiration for Khelagh, perhaps wealthiest of them all, jokes about the *rabhsai* and avowals of loyalty, muddle over whether his personal ambition was only that or a desire to do good. After a day's listening he did not know any more about what really moved the man.

Shumat was left behind a few days, to add new recruits to those he was drilling, the real purpose for their coming through Irbat. The way north and mainly east was a dull one, for miles following the course of Dromladh's Canal, with its towpaths, steady march of planted poplars and alders. Across the strip of water, a long, low ridge was crowned with bushes and stunted, wind-crazed trees; beyond that was Shemufegh Rai, a treeless desolation of salt-marshes. At the pace of pack-animals and wagons, a full day in the saddle, but less than a half-dayride for a horseman alone; Bolan was astonished Dolvid had never seen El'tuf.

"Some day you'll give me the true reason — one with your, um, talents, rotting away in lovely Irbat." During his days there he had taken a thorough dislike to the Arnan-port.

Dolvid's *pefrai* did a little dancing sidestep past one of many small trenches where neglected ruts had widened. Two days ago he had pitched his old boots into the mud-hemmed bay, yesterday said farewell to his few acquaintances; he had never left any place with fewer regrets. Now he told Bolan this had once been among the busiest roads of the realm, with wagons and animals carrying goods in both directions between Irbat and El'tuf, till completion of the canal, linking Arnan to the River Tufa, and so, by El'tuf, to open sea, had made Irbat unneeded for a transfer point.

"Aye, our coming there is the only thing in a hundred years to wake them up. Well, they got fair prices for their goods, and that gets a bit of money going about. Half-a-dozen weekwives are down from El'tuf, I hear. What'll you give for Shumat's maidenhead?"

The running joke about Shumat's lack of experience was ignored. "It did better. Malvan, who is about the biggest of fleece-dealers, is afraid he's not going to find men when shearing comes. He's hiring half-pay help a month early, so they won't sign on with us."

"Malvan — he must be the one I heard grousing over his wine at the *Shears*, saying the *rabhsai* was bidding up the price of a strong pair of shoulders."

"That's a price needs bidding up in these parts. Mostly, there's three idle for every man needed. Malvan and his tribe could name any pittance for a day's work."

Bolan shook his head. "But it's no joke getting a good day's work out of men lacking sense to move on when a town goes to the bad."

An inward wince; tact was not Bolan's best strength. More wonder he had risen so fast in the Household, with all the ceremony, the daily encounters with the Family.

Bolan was moving along the same path. "Look, it's long miles east. A royal captain's going to have dinners to face — big landowners, Great Houses, I don't doubt. You'll have to stay close and make table-talk for me. You'll be darling of the Great Families, now you look less of a beggar who lost the knack." Dolvid was dressed in plain breeches, and an officer's outshirt with signs of rank removed.

"The *nim'* at Sebira, who's he?"

"Daënakh," supplied for the second time.

"Daënakh — well, when we get there — don't they say

he's a scholar of history and so forth? If we're asked to dine with him — " and Bolan plainly decided not to say any more. "Well, there's plenty to think of before Sebira. Getting there with full packs and full bellies. Not all adventure, is it?"

"This far, none of it has been adventure for me." At once he recognized this as a double lie, double in implying adventure was not his desire. His whole body was waking up to thought of the long road ahead and the storied things he would see, Drin Dakani, Luskran Bay, Sebira and the Pass of Perus, the broad waste of ancient Naëni, and in the end, fabled Narn on the Eastern Ocean. Right now it was all excitement, practising swords with Bolan or Shumat, feeling old muscles and old teaching come back to life. Visiting farms to dicker with farmers for food, feed and animals, wrestling with the task of supplying a campaign in the leanest part of the year — after fallow years pleasures of purposeful activity were fierce and intoxicating.

"We may find our tents at El'tuf. Other than that, horses will be the worst problem."

"The *rabhsai* won't spare any more *pefral*, and no one else can have them to spare — that's Plakhsila's Law, isn't it?"

"Sebira's a bay that breeds good horses."

"For little ladies to trot in the Residence grounds."

Patiently, Dolvid pointed out saddle-horses could be used to free *pefral* for battle. Most new recruits, being farm-lads, could at least ride, whatever their clumsiness with weapons. Mounted on lesser horses, they could be used as message riders, escorts for the supply-train, and for scouting and foraging.

Bolan was dubious. He had planned to create new squadrons using a dozen regulars to give spine to three times as many recruits. He wanted at least fifteen squadrons to put into the field. "Still," he wavered, "most of the regular squadrons have been together years, and it may be a mistake to break them up."

"This is your profession, but the historian of the *Mankh'* wrote each soldier of Larghai was worth six men, with trust in the comrade at his side."

"Historians of the *Mankh'* didn't have to run a campaign with one-sixth the men the job needed."

He frowned over the question for whole minutes. "It's true," he allowed, "you're not going to turn a farm-lad into a lancer in a month, hard as Shumat is pushing them. Escort duty, that's mostly the look of the thing. An escort that appears strong enough should never have to fight. How many saddle-horses, would you say?"

"One hundred would help. As many more as we could hope to get."

"You must be mad. Where are we going to get cash for a hundred horses worth slapping a saddle on, not to say the saddles?"

Dolvid, watching the shrinking treasury, had already thought this out. "Daënakh of Ân would not ask for gold in advance; he would accept the *rabhsai*'s draft."

"No, no, no. We can't go begging to Daënakh, he'll want too much in return — too many promises."

The mystery again. Before he could be asked what this meant, Bolan had a new thought. "Wait. You could approach Daënakh *Asai*; you have no power to make commitments. You could use my name with him — *Akaëkhi-kindhri*, I mean." The tone demanded Dolvid ask for an explanation.

"*Akaëkhai-kindhri*?" he duly asked and gently corrected. Properly formed, it meant `Market-Victor.'

Bolan, with a transparent preface about the habit of thinking what was famous at Kadon Dinul was so everywhere, told his tale. This was the stroke of luck responsible for his rapid promotion.

Three years ago, after the second bad harvest, there had been unrest. That winter the Household had been strengthened with levies, and units on loan from the General Cavalry. There were rumors, probably true, that big factors were holding back stocks of food, to force up prices. Among the hungry, tempers were short.

"I loathe a street-mob. Hunger's bad, but these were

mostly scum looking for things to break, and Laluvoi *Asayu* telling us, over and over, curb our force. Easy to counsel calm when you don't have to be where stones are flying. Though Laluvoi, I'll give her that, rode out with an escort of four when things were at their worst. She, you'd guess, came to no harm, and spoke with some of the rioters. Laluvoi." The admiration was unwilling.

Tempers were shortening for the soldiers, too, and one day in Market Place it came to a head. Some farmers, having sold what little they had, were hitching teams and starting for the gate when men began bawling they were taking their goods where they could get a bigger price.

"That pulled the stopper out." He took off a gauntlet to push a hand back through his dark hair. "Neither I nor anyone else could tell you all that happened. In three minutes a dozen men of the guard were pinned against the gate, and the wagons were rocking back and forth in the middle of this howling mob. I thought the farmers were going to be torn apart. So did the farmers. If my squadron had been scattered all over the square, I couldn't have done anything, but I always kept a file together and in the saddle where the covered steps come down — next to the troughs, you know."

By some means he had taken these troops through the press, rescuing first the farmers and then the men by the gates. Just then, by luck, wagons arrived from the Burantal country, with flour to sell. Bolan bellowed out unless order was restored he would lock the gates and send the wagons away.

"It was an enchanter's spell. Sheep could not have been so docile, filing past the wagons, but a fool could see it would all begin again unless the flour went around, so I took it on myself to see no one could buy more than a single measure. As it turned out there was a measure for everyone there, and they all went home happy, except the ones with bruises to count."

"Nothing worse than bruises?"

"How could there be? That's what I say, for that duty Laluvoi took away our weapons. All we had was staves. If there had been any blades in the mob, we would've been a prize flock of geese to carry the Banner. All luck — *Akaëkhi-kindhri*, they still call it after me in the street."

That action made Bolan's squadron rank permanent, but his squadron was paired with one led by Brodhai of Ân, which seemed to cripple chances for further advancement. "Then he went south with the escort, winter before last, when the *rabhsayu* went to Thenimala. Laloi was in the party, and anybody could see the cow-eyes she had for Brodhai. So he was ironing out the *rabhsai*'s daughter by the Southern Sea when old *Kímukan* Arodinal died, and they made me acting-*kímukan*. Then Brodhai was betrothed and didn't do much riding with the Household, so the rank was mine to keep. Talent's not much good without a portion of luck."

Was there a link here to his fear of appealing to Brodhai's father, Daënakh? Yet Bolan had said before that Brodhai had turned down command of the expedition.

"One thing. If your men had carried lances that day, would you have used them?"

"Would we not! Hrafi's earlobe, if you'd been there — ! Besides, I am a soldier. Using weapons against lawbreakers is what I'm paid for."

"But bread can sometimes be the best weapon."

"Aye, and a good man can be killed for lack of a blade in his hand. Do you believe they're all his?"

"What?" Bolan's baffling question was asked as he stood in the stirrups, surveying the column-of-march.

"Lambarr *Deghi*. He makes up his mind by such slivers, you'd never think his weapon was worth much. Yet Lady Saëdhu never glances at any other thigh. She keeps a journal, they say, and every day since they married she's been writing down the wise deeds and witty sayings of the *rabhsai*." Bolan held up his hand, thumb and forefinger barely parted, then ruled against the sally.

"The Heir, let me tell you, also wanted to command this Narn jaunt. Shâl's balls, Tholat! The hands on him — they flap like a rook's wings. Try to tell anyone I said that, you'll be salting eels before you can say Kamanta."

"I used to cross blades with Tholat. He was no swordsman. How was he kept out of the expedition?"

"Oh, year of the Great Pledging, Prince of the Paowan, the Heartland must not be deprived of his inspiring presence... Laluvoi, after Merovas had a word with her. Superb, but I wouldn't want to be out of favor with her. Well, Brodhai can have Laloi. The next girl, Sai-Nivu, is more to my taste — not thirteen, but she has the eye. She's all dimples when I have the escort. Going to be hot sport for someone there."

This must be typical talk among Household officers. Half-teasing, Dolvid said, "Return to Kadon Dinul as *Narnai-Kindhri*, and the *rabhsai*'s daughter might not be out of your reach."

"That I know," completely in earnest.

Limestone here weathered to a deeper shade, but with turf-roofed houses at its outskirts El'tuf resembled a bigger, busier Irbat. Yet first sight, first smell, conveyed a difference beyond mere size; purpose, a future. This was a living port, a sprawled place that had outgrown the walled city now its upper, northwestern end.

Klam Dramali, a wide inlet of the Northern Sea, was calm most days, with the cold, veiled gleam of seldom-used pewter. On its shore Bolan's forces gathered and drilled. By direct road from Dônshei came about eighty regular cavalry and nearly a hundred recruits, led by Onebhal, a tall, lean Owani with a dry, effective manner, and a complete contempt for the countryside he had passed through, as for anywhere that was not the landscape of his birth, the soft green downs west of Bathrâd. Dolvid, besides his work with supplies, was helping teach rudiments of swordsmanship to recruits, and became friendly with Onebhal, a man of level temper and good sense, a painstaking teacher with lances, strong for discipline, but popular with the men, who saw him as fatherly. He had been General Cavalry since he was nineteen, and was looking forward to farming in his own country. His permanent rank was squadron-leader, but with the expedition he was acting-*kímukan*, and third in command.

Shumat, who soon came up from Irbat, recruits weeded out to the ninety most promising, was popular in different way, admired for his skill and flair, liked for his readiness to swap jokes with the men, his loud enjoyment. At swords he was a plain, muscular fighter with more to learn than Bolan, but when he picked up a lance everyone stopped what he was doing to watch that gifted handling of both the long-weapon and a *pefrai* at the charge. His ugliness was still attractive to women, who waved and often called out to him when he led troops clattering through cobbled streets — not just brainless fillies, Bolan said in fascination, but some a prettier man could spend fortunes on, and never see their heels in the air. A waste, he complained, when all Shumat did was smile crooked and wave his hand, but at least it kept his energy for soldiering.

Both Onebhal and Shumat were on Dolvid's side in the opening controversy with Bolan. It began when he noted enough ships were lying idle or could be assembled to carry the expedition to Sebira, saving the long march, avoiding chance of being delayed by snow. The coastal waters were generally calm at this season, and even with all roads open the journey overland, at the pace of wagons and pack-animals, would take days longer.

Bolan was completely opposed, more stubbornly so than could be explained by the argument he gave: the extra men he was authorized to borrow from garrisons eastward had to be collected in person. If he sent written orders from Sebira the various commanders would invent excuses for dragging their feet, or sending fewer men than demanded. Besides, added recruits might be signed up on the long march.

It seemed unlikely the empty spaces of the North would supply many men, and Onebhal agreed, saying they would probably lose as many or more to desertion, after a few days of digging through drifts, or nights of sleeping in snow. Then Shumat, reminding Bolan that roads open to men on *pefral* might be impassable for wagons, suggested supplies and baggage, spare mounts and most of the recruits could go by sea, leaving enough of the faster-riding regulars for Bolan to impress garrison-commanders eastward with the importance of his command.

While Bolan resisted, Dolvid on his own told the Warden of the Port to pass word to ships' masters that if they kept their vessels ready unexpected business might come their way. Bolan's hesitation contradicted his own favorite speech, about the need to take the field as early as possible.

One afternoon, returning from his fourth unsuccessful attempt to find a farmer with stored apples to sell, Dolvid was intercepted by a file-leader, saying the Captain wanted to see him at once.

At the inn where Bolan and his senior staff were quartered, in a low-ceilinged, whitewashed room, with a window looking out only on another wall with a window, Bolan was sitting behind the rough table he used for a desk. The seal of the *rabhsai* was on dispatches open in front of him. Dolvid's cheerful greeting was answered by a troubled, almost stern look. By the window Shumat was slumped in a chair, legs stretched out, feet twined so both rested on one heel of his riding boots. He rolled his eyes upward, broad lower lip jutting. Something had gone wrong.

"Why was it you quit the *Mankh'*?" Bolan, without preamble.

"What?" — mind going slowly to a period so remote from present concerns. "You said yourself I was never meant to be *atarlai*. Many reasons — I discovered fraud, deliberate falsifications, in the *Mankh'* edition of the *Song of Tales*."

Bolan's turn to be bewildered. "You left because of errors in a book of wonders?"

"It's more than a book of wonders," Shumat said. "Grown men can't believe one word in twenty, but I'd rather hear tales from the *Song* than the long-winded chants you make so much of." His `you' meant Dolvid, or his race in general.

"So, shocked by this fraud," Bolan came back, before Dolvid could begin a defense of Owani literature, "you stole away from the *Mankh'* at dead of night, without a word to anyone?"

"Come," Shumat appealed across Dolvid's bafflement. "You have to tell why you're asking him all this."

Bolan heaved his shoulders. He picked up a parchment, and cast it down again with no pretence of reading. "Myself, I don't care if you stole the Golden Seat."

"Who says I stole anything?" Clearly the implication.

"As you recall, Kadon Dinul was informed of your name and your post with the expedition."

"I was the one who penned the dispatch."

"Now, learning of your whereabouts, the *Mankh'* wants you returned to face a charge of theft. The *Bôdhrai* Rhunsilakh — " Bolan began shuffling pages in earnest. "Here, `the charge was made in the *rabhsai*'s presence, by one high in the *Atarlum*.'"

"*Menadhi*." An eerie sensation, after all these years, to sound the name and call back the person.

"He's the little one with the lined face? Always hanging about the Residence. Why Lambarr permits it, next Patriarch or not — You know him? Are there reasons he would make this charge?" The stiff, official manner was moderating.

"I was his personal pupil, he wanted a disciple. He would never have let me just decline the oaths, as others sometimes did. That's why I had to leave as I did — at daybreak, not dead of night."

Shumat said, "So this would be his revenge, then."

Bolan kept reading. "According to the *Bôdhrai*, the *Mankh'* says your guilt is proved by your flight from Kadon Dinul, and your complete disappearance."

"I lived openly, under my own name, at Dônshei and then Irbat. What did I steal — Treaty Stone?" — angrier with Rhunsilakh and Bolan than with *Menadhi*.

"What did you take with you from the *Mankh'*?"

"Belongings of my own. My clothes, all well-worn. My books — "

"Books." Bolan was on this at once.

"My writings — I suppose you could say the parchment belonged to the *Mankh'*. Otherwise, I was very careful to take only my own books."

"You're sure? Oh, well, but books are in the charge, see, `a number of rare and irreplaceable volumes.' What could those be?"

"If the writings of a sixteen-year-old... well — " he was suddenly amused. "They are certainly irreplaceable for the *Mankh'*, since I am not going back there."

Such an accusation might never be entirely expunged. His mind was back in that confused and terrifying time, and all at once he thought of Faëdhal, an island of calm when all other firm ground was failing. After things had begun to go wrong with Darborr, Dolvid had never written to Faëdhal, and often blamed himself, but quite aside from feelings of shame, he had not wanted to make further claims on the man's generosity, or risk seeming to.

"According to Rhunsilakh," Bolan resumed. "The law is, never having formally declined your oaths, you might still be subject to judgment under *Atarlum* law, not the *rabhsai*'s. That would have to be determined, at Kadon Dinul."

"When I return there."

"Or are returned there."

He feared what *Menadhi* might be able to do, but was sure he would never face judgment by the *Atarlum*. "Once there, I would invoke the *rabhsai*'s protection; I was never apprenticed to the *Mankh'* by a guardian, and never consented for myself." He did not want to leave the expedition. He discovered he cared, not only about his own tasks, but about the campaign. Setting out this morning he had seen two squadrons drilling, one of regulars, the other of the best recruits, beginning to shape like real soldiers. Unexpectedly, he felt pride; he was part of this venture, and would share its fortunes.

Shumat was eying Bolan. "We're not sending Dolvid back to Kadon."

Bolan started shuffling sheets again. "The Captain Merovas must have been in on all this. He's written separately, in his own hand, here it is. `The law is the law, but I never heard the *Mankh'* could decide who is to be part of a royal expedition — '"

"Old Merovas was upset," Shumat, grinning.

"` — nor do I believe Banak, when no higher than an under-captain, would have answered, much less submitted to such a demand.'  Rhunsilakh, he says, has to follow procedure, but agrees military needs should be given priority, and commanders in the field must have, here `the widest discretionary powers.'"

"As much as to say, ignore this," Shumat interpreted.

"As much as to say the *rabhsai* is, as usual. let's say, steering a careful course."

Seeing how this was going Dolvid could afford to smile, not forgetting Bolan, too, had hedged his bets, beginning with the accusation in its baldest form.

"There's another hint here I don't understand, about *Nim'* Vinilat being a good friend to the *Mankh'*."

"So he is." Vinilat was away from the Great House, visiting his cousins in Kargul. Till now Dolvid had rather regretted his absence; it would have given him wry pleasure to be face to face with the man he had helped defeat in the dispute with the Froghul.

"If he comes back today, what's he going to do? Send provincial cavalry to arrest a man of mine in the middle of a royal army?" This sounded defiant, and as usual Bolan soon found a way to dilute his resolve. "On the other hand, I don't want trouble with anyone who sits in the Council of Thirteen."

"Merovas is saying, don't stay too long in Dramal," Shumat said.

He met Dolvid's eye, and they both knew the quarrel over ships had been settled by this unexpected intervention. "By road, with the wagons," Shumat observed, "even if there's no snow to hold us up, the quickest we could be across the provincial border is four, five days."

"We're not ready to ride," Bolan said.

"Dolvid, together with most of what we'll need, could be out of Vinilat's reach by noon tomorrow."

If Shumat knew any more of what was in Bolan's mind he did not tell it, although he and Dolvid shared an unspoken understanding their commander occasionally needed prodding into the right choices. Weather staying calm, they spent most of the day on deck of the largest vessel in their flotilla, sometimes practising with weapons, often just talking together, while the whitened uplands of Dramal crept by on their right. By night they could watch the bobbing cluster of ships' lights; many of the soldiers, not used to sea-journeys and willing to endure cold sooner than the closed-in darkness filled with strange creakings below, brought sleeping-bags on deck, huddling together till morning came and they could stamp and kick stiffness from their muscles.

The horses were not so lucky. Huddled in the afterwell, forty of them, with no chance of exercise before Sebira, stood and trembled, their eyes glazed over. It would have been worse without a soldier called Norlum aboard. Coarse, a rough-tongued veteran of eleven years' service, he had a gift with horses, and when there was a worse patch of water would soothe great *pefral* with the voice a mother uses to a frightened child, swinging down into the hold to pat noses, and lift hoofs over a tangle in the hobbles. Otherwise listless, the animals would twitch their ears whenever Norlum's voice was heard.

"I should be with Bolan — " Shumat, gazing across a half-mile of cold water to where hills rose almost to the height of mountains. With four squadrons carrying their own supplies, Bolan had started for Drin Dakani by road.

"He will not have those hills to cross. Our course has turned northward, that's Tan Dramali we're coasting." Tan Dramali! but Ka-Nam and his Froghul would be far to the south, at their winter home in Dramaru.

When he spoke about those few summer days seven years ago, Shumat said, "I have never talked with many Froghul; my people say they are uncouth. Their dances I've seen, and they make good fighters — there's a good bit of Froghuli blood in the new cavalry Sebhal's got in the West, on little hill-horses. They say they would follow him if he rode into Arnan — there's nothing they won't do for a leader they admire." His eyes were glowing excitement. "What Bolan would give to have that sort behind him; a man could do anything. But my father says they're dirty in their ways, though they honor their women as we do. They would kill them, or sell them outright, sooner than see them go as weekwives. Could it be this little Tini-ra of yours thought the rich young Owani might buy her?"

Dolvid, stunned by what Shumat, without any irony, called honoring a woman, and could not take offense. "Ka-Nam's people might not have mastered Kadon Dinul ways, but they could not take me for a rich young anything — they knew what the *Mankh'* was. Besides, they gave me presents and did not expect anything back. You have seen this — " reaching back for the long knife, worn constantly since he joined the campaign.

Shumat admired the weapon. "Your love for the Froghul must have made you popular at the *Mankh'*."

"Oh, they don't mind praise for Others if they keep to their place, as the Froghul do, or they are all long dead, like the Vrobanil."

"And you left them over the *Song of Tales*? There wasn't a woman in that, too?"

He tried to explain how falsifications in the *Song* were not just quibbling-points for scholars, how the Night of Owan might well have been the Gabhani noon, contrary to the picture drawn by the *Mankh'* edition, where the accomplishments of the Gabhanil had been deliberately, systematically distorted and obscured.

"Is this news? We all know what the *Atarlum* thinks of any history except Owan's."

"But this, if you'll pardon me, comes down to how Others think of themselves. Great Banak with his Gabhani strain admired the *Song of Tales*, so do you. We are going to be in the country of Pir Perus. He was not a fantastic fable, but a real war-captain of the Gabhanil, who had long wars against the Empire of Owan."

Shumat was pleased by the notion, but, "That magical outshirt he wore? What about his battle with the swallows?"

"The armies of Owan, in the Age of the Shâls." Dolvid explained how he had gradually come to believe this, nudged by the Froghuli story about `bright-breasted goose-riders.' In the years when the First Empire was expanding, campaign season in the south and west had been autumn and winter, and in the north and east, just as for Bolan, spring into summer. Those struggling against the might of Owan must have come to link the annual return of their enemy with migrating birds, swallows in spring for the Gabhanil of the Northeast, geese in winter for the Froghul of the Farther West. For centuries the armies of the Shâls had fought in wedge-formation, giving the Froghul another reminder of geese. "But the Froghul must have lost their fight long before Pir Perus was beaten by treachery in his last battle with the swallow-riders. I have seen an earlier version of that tale, and it has an ugly ending." That was the sheaf of pages Faëdhal had given him to help with the language, but that purpose had been overshadowed by fascinated horror at how the story went on past the published version, to describe the victors lopping a right hand or foot from every surviving man and boy in dead Pir's following, so they would never have to be fought again. Revulsion had turned to shame when he recognized `swallows' could only be the armies of Owan, perhaps those of the immortal Larghai.

As one who called himself Gabhani, Shumat's tepid response to the mutilation, either of his people or their history, was a disappointment for Dolvid, who wanted the same outrage he felt. In the end Shumat said it was interesting, and repeated his conjecture, more annoying for being true, that a woman must surely have had a part in the breach with the *Mankh'*.

Dolvid, assessing part of Shumat's seeming shrewdness was only the curiosity of his inexperience, told about Valnoi, less than everything. Not much feeling was left for the telling; it had worn itself out, and there had been too many other miseries since then.

"I could never be like that for a woman," Shumat declared. "Yearning's not my way. Make your offer, if she refuses, bid for another. But this trothplight of your Valnoi's — Ladhat? What a fish he was, accepting the little tart on those terms! And then, meekly walking away while you went off with his woman for who-knows-what — !"

"Or else very wise. He had made up his mind who he wanted, and made peace with her nature."

"Hmm!" To Dolvid's delight Shumat squeezed up his mouth, making, deep in his throat, exactly the same growling noise of perplexity he had as a child. "Your Owani cleverness is too twisty for us. But at Kadon our women are getting their virtue from the Residence Quarter, too; stale goods is all you can find. Some of that in this falling-out with your partner, too, no?"

"Perhaps." He was not going to talk about it, especially now. He had been a fool to let himself be bed-befriended by a Mixed woman, a sash-wearer, married to a drinker, a violent man — and his partner. He did not see how it could have been avoided.

"And you lost money of your own on that with the oats? Your luck was about due for a change, when we trotted into Irbat. Well. Bolan has luck for any ten others. You realize, don't you, when he's against offending anyone in the Council of Thirteen, he's thinking ahead. Either for Captain of Household or Captain-General, he'll have to be confirmed in Council."

"Let's have a bout with knives." Rehearsing past agonies had made Dolvid restless.

"Swords," Shumat overruled. He wanted to keep learning, and with knives — or their wooden simulations — was usually the winner.

Alliances

Sebira Bay opened in the sudden rounding of a headland, town itself startlingly close, a ring of hills broken at the center to divide Sebira in two halves, white and brown houses on the slopes, their roofs glazed tile, while through the middle the wide avenue of open courts mounted, slender trees leafless now, eye drawn up to where, in the saddle, the curve of the celebrated Terrace Houses could be discerned. Leftward was a mound nearer the water, crossed and recrossed by wide courses of broad, shallow steps, crowned by the Great House of Daënakh, a low and graceful building with a pillared portico. Approached from seaward on a crystal-bright day, it was by far the loveliest town Dolvid could remember.

Shumat had waited to tell about Daënakh's two sons, both of whom Dolvid had known as boys in Kheval's sword-classes. About the time the elder, Brodhai, was betrothed, there had been a falling-out, and the younger, Bradhinal, left the Household, after less than a year. He had shown promise as a soldier, according to Shumat, and now led a squadron of his father's provincial cavalry.

"Crop-wardens. Bolan wishes he could lay hands on their *pefral.*"

Shaking his head. "By Plakhsila's Law, he couldn't take them beyond the borders of Ân. If he wants help with escorts within the province, Daënakh, surely, would lend him troops, mounts and all." He began to expand. "In fact, they would very possibly take over duties from the royal garrison at Yuvakh Din, releasing men for — "

"At least three Provincial squadrons," Shumat interrupted, "are already attached to the Yuvakh Din garrison."

"Doing what?" This was most unusual.

"Bolan!" under lowered brows. "How he expects you to

tackle the *nim'* about horses — I'll tell you after."

He had broken off because they were about to be greeted; a small, nimble craft, showing the colors of Ân, red-brown banner with white Bear depicted, had tacked within hailing distance.

There was a brief, improvised ritual at quayside; representing *Nim'* Daënakh, the Warden of the Port, a tall, dry, nervous man, welcomed the *rabhsai's* men to Sebira. Though their arrival by water was unexpected, advance notification of the expedition had come from Kadon Dinul; a site was prepared for their encampment, and the Province of Ân, the Warden said, wished to offer all possible assistance.

With unnecessary pomposity, this speech was delivered in very formal Owanilú, and Shumat was soon struggling. For him, Dolvid declared they would attend at the Great House to present the *rabhsai's* warrant, as soon as disembarkation had been overseen.

As the ceremony ended, Dolvid, having explained it to Shumat, was making for the second ship to dock when out of the small gathering of spectators a man accosted him, short and ill-fed, with a limp, one shoulder held higher. "I am Stanni, I was stableman to Ott."

No doubt the man could not help his hollow-cheeked face, which was both sly and stupid; his small black eyes apparently incapable of a straight look.

"We don't need a stableman."

"I served Ott, Ott of Ottsvale. I can tell you his secrets. Where he hides."

"What is Ottsvale?"

Stanni decided this was a joke. "Ott," he said. "Beyond Yuvakh. I was his man, I am in his mind."

Probably mad. "See me tomorrow, after we're settled. We might need more helpers."

"All I ask for is my keep. I hate Ott."

"Tomorrow." Up ahead he could see men about to start

piling flour-sacks in the only wet patch on the entire quay. When he had the chance to think of it again, Stanni had disappeared.

Before they went to the Great House Shumat wanted to walk up to see the Terrace Houses, and the shrine to Zhôl they enclosed, but as they walked and he showed little interest in sights, it became clear his real desire was for talk.

"Surely the royal warrant could be delivered by a messenger," unhappily.

"We'll speak ordinary language there. *Nim'* Daënakh is not a petty official who needs to show off his command of the Old Tongue."

Not Shumat's worry. "Bolan doesn't — we shouldn't go there before he arrives."

"Let me hear how you would have declined the invitation," Dolvid challenged him. "Sebira in winter is a backwater deader than Irbat; our arrival is a big event. Unless —" he halted to face him. "Unless you have other reasons why Daënakh is so eager to see us."

"Have you read the *rabhsai*'s warrant?"

"Just the top sheet with the General Charge. General, it's certainly that. Go and settle what's wrong in the Northeast." The actual language was far more high-flown, but his version was not unfair.

"According to Bolan, all it refers to is relief of Narn."

"Well?" This was mystifying. "Isn't that where the cry for help came from?"

"Not the only cry, nor the first one. There's an under-captain of General Cavalry, Antrovai, at Yuvakh Din, who has been howling for relief for three years."

"Bolan mentioned unrest had spread that far."

"Unrest!" They had reached the graceful curving sweep of the Terrace Houses, and stood leaning on a parapet above the Shrine of Zhôl with its big stone bowl for the midwinter fire, shaped like the cup of an acorn. Face barred in late sun by shadows from bare rowans, Shumat looked up at snow-streaked hills, and with bleak reluctance told all the story. Eastward from the town and fortress of Yuvakh Din all the way to the frontier was a country in open revolt against the authority of Daënakh (not to say the *rabhsai*); taxes unpaid, roads haunted by robbers, cavalry patrols waylaid. Farms actually within sight of the fortress had been raided, and landowners loyal to the realm murdered or taken for ransom.

"Bolan wanted this kept from you till we'd left Sebira, so you wouldn't have to discuss our plans with Daënakh."

It came clear, and many evasions were explained. To avoid being trapped in a long campaign there, Bolan meant to bypass an insurrection inside the realm, so he could take on what might be the simpler and must be the shorter task at distant Narn.

"To be fair," Shumat amended, without much conviction, "He maintains the strength we'll show on the road from Yuvakh Din may give rebels there something to think about. Also a victory at Narn would be bound to help pacify the entire region."

Dolvid was going grimly on. "And I am going to ask *Nim'* Daënakh to supply us with horses. He, naturally, is sure we're here to restore the eastern marches of his province, and if I was not privy to Bolan's plans, I wouldn't be able to tell him, oh no, we're just going to ride through and give the rebels an opportunity for thought."

"I told him it wasn't fair." He genuinely deplored the deception of Dolvid so as to deceive Daënakh, but was more deeply troubled, as at last he admitted, by the notion a captain of the *rabhsayum* could pick which rebellions to deal with, ignoring ones that looked too hard. Shumat's interpretation of the vague instructions in the General Charge was exactly opposite to Bolan's; they had been sent to do what could be done about any troubles they encountered, not to ask which might bring them greater and quicker fame.

They had returned to the mushrooming encampment, to collect their horses and an escort for the ride to the Great House. Shumat was wondering whether he had gone too far in criticizing Bolan. "You can see his worry. It might take sixty squadrons five years to put the Yuvakh country in order."

"How many squadrons in garrison there?" — doing sums.

"Twelve, fifteen at most, but a lot would be under-strength; Antrovai has complained of not getting enough replacements. He'd have auxiliaries, too, bows, and men to man the walls."

"Under the law, Daënakh can have twenty-four squadrons in his provincial cavalry. Why are only three or four on loan where there is an uprising against his authority?"

"I don't know. Bad blood, it might be, between the provincials and the *rabhsai*'s troops. That often happens when they try to pull in harness. I haven't heard anyone compare Under-Captain Antrovai to Sebhal Saidhans-son. A Heartlander, they say, but he's been out here years."

"If Bolan did decide to tackle the Yuvakh Din rebellion, his warrant would give him authority over both Antrovai and whoever commands the provincials."

A hard glance. "Don't. I had the same idea. If you made a commitment in Bolan's name, he'd just sack you and say you were not authorized to promise anything."

The Hall of State in the Great House was high-vaulted, made of many arches, where much carved wood had been used. It was written there were once vast forests here in the north, but that was an age ago, and this house was not that old, or anything near.

Daënakh received them standing in front of a highbacked chair of state, with his wife Leghayu. She was also his first cousin, a tall woman with a hint of copper in her elaborately braided hair. Taking an ornate cup of worked metal from a servant, she sipped, and passed it two-handed to a Shumat doing his best not to appear nervous.

"A custom," Leghayu, smiling, "we have adopted from our G — " For the first time she took in Shumat's face, so obviously not Owani. " — Gabhanil friends," she finished in a voice from which condescension had been banished. Shumat accepted the cup and drank, masklike.

Dolvid did not announce that the Gabhanil in turn had
borrowed the welcoming ritual from the Froghul. When it came
to him, this cup had a light, inoffensive wine. He drank, and
passed it to Daënakh, Owani lord of a province where not one in
a hundred was unmixed Owani.

In Dolvid's lifetime the *Nim'* of Ân had always been
Daënakh, and it was a little surprising he was no older, clear-
eyed, with a face neither unkind nor stupid, of middle height with
wide shoulders but a youthful build, no close resemblance either
to the firm-chinned cousin beside him nor to another near
relative, Laluvoi.

"Shumat," he mused, setting cup aside. "Are you by
chance connected with Shumuvan baNivu, of Dromladh's
treasury?"

"*Asai*, I don't believe so."

"A worthy family, good stock," Daënakh murmured.

"*Asai*," Dolvid bowed slightly. "If I may presume, in
years to come it will be asked whether one is connected with
Shumat Shurris-son."

Leghayu peered; she must have poor eyesight.
"Vidukhat?"

"Of the South, *Asayu*, though I grew up at Kadon Dinul.
On my mother's side, we claim relationship to Saidhan's lady,
Doleni." In fact, he seldom had claimed it, but then he had not
often been where bloodlines were so much discussed.

"Then, welcome, kinsman," Leghayu, tilting her head.

"*Asayu*, far nearer kin could not ask for a more hospitable
welcome than ours in Sebira." Dolvid felt he could keep this up
for hours if needed.

"You have ridden with our sons?" Leghayu asked
Shumat.

"*Asayu*, Brodhai's squadron was — has always been
among the finest."

Daënakh took up the thread. "I must say I had hoped he
would be given more than mere ceremonial command, especially

when his own province is concerned in your business."

Shumat cleared his throat. "My understanding, *Asai*, is, Brodhai declined this command — "

"But surely, if the *rabhsai* had been more insistent — "

With Shumat struggling, Dolvid leapt in. "I was told, *Asai*, the *rabhsai* knew the whole realm would be hoping to see your son beside his daughter, when they gather for the Great Pledging." This was pure invention, but seemed to give satisfaction all round.

"Of your Bolan," Leghayu resumed, "I have heard nothing, except he helped put down a bread-riot."

"My dear," Daënakh remonstrated, not an instant too soon; Leghayu must be aware her remark, to Bolan's subordinates, was grossly improper.

After that short opening bout, a draw with no mortal hits, they all withdrew to a smaller room Leghayu was evidently proud of, hung with weave of rich purple and deep blue with darts of crimson and brilliant green, Heartland work with no equal.

"Our northern winters," Leghayu said, "weave for the walls is no luxury." Windows here faced south and east to white hills desolate under light fading to grey evening. Nearer, where snow was only a pocket here and there in shadowed hollows, yellow lantern light gleamed from windows.

"We would winter in Kadon Dinul," Daënakh, with an audible nudge and wink. "But it would be wrong to take space at the Residence from the growing needs of the Family."

Having smiled dutifully at the everlasting joke, Dolvid said, "The tide is surely on the turn, *Asai*. The children of Lambarr *Deghi*, and children of those children, will soon be filling the Great Houses of the provinces."

Leghayu was preoccupied. "Besides, the situation here has demanded the *nim's* continued presence."

Daënakh took it up smoothly. "I am eager for Bolan's arrival, so we can concert our plans. So far I am a little unhappy with the numbers the *rabhsai* has sent. I am told you have three hundreds or so, but of those only three squadrons seem to be regular cavalry."

"Others are riding with Bolan," Shumat assured them. He was uncomfortable with this subject, though the flicker of a glance told Dolvid he found satisfaction Daënakh's observer had mistaken some of the recruits they had trained for real soldiers; only two squadrons of regulars were with them. Part of the little army had gone on foot; not all the levies could yet be trusted with *pefral*, and if every saddle had been filled there would not have been enough horses for all the men.

"Bolan was to leave Drin Dakani," Daënakh, blandly, "let's see, it would be yesterday, with six or seven squadrons. Ten squadrons at most of *péfrapravádal*! I do not pretend to be a war-master, but are such numbers adequate for the task?"

"Other garrisons, *Asai*, can be drawn on." Shumat was not giving away anything, though he'd had no news of Bolan till now.

"He must realize the Provincial Cavalry is a limited force to keep order for all of Ân. But we might find him two squadrons in addition to those already at Yuvakh Din, making five in all."

"*Asai*, that must be discussed with Bolan when he comes." Shumat sidled past the trap, where to accept the offer would commit them to the Yuvakh campaign.

However, a slight advantage to Daënakh for the second bout. All four of them had drawn nearer the fireplace. Fire-stone, a local commodity and cheaper here, was burning quietly. Above the mantel war-trophies were hung, including a shapeless piece of battered and corroded metal, which Daënakh called a family heirloom, reputedly one of Yuvakh Martyr's greaves.

Dolvid said, "I hope to visit his burial-place while in this part of the realm."

"Ah, history interests you?" Daënakh's face showed animation. "We had a find here, not long ago, hard to fathom. Sea-stone, as is well-known, is dug on the north side of the bay. The vein seems to go deep, but will never be found, probably, far from salt water. Resistance to cold and wet, I conceive, stores up fire in the stone."

Dolvid, taught not to indulge this sort of barren theorizing, only tilted his head a little.

"Digging there, men came across an immense nest of ancient bones — well, what were once bones; they are yellowed chalk, and careless handling turns them to dust. But this was no former burial ground, not as we understand it. There were very many of these bones, but they were all of only two kinds — "

"Right hands and feet — " afraid he would be taken for mad, but unable to stop his violent trembling.

An odd, searching look. "Hands and feet, certainly. Whether all right ones I can't say. I had no idea news of this discovery had reached Kadon Dinul."

"It has not. That is to say, *Asai*, I had not heard about it before." Trying to be calm, he told Daënakh about the grisly aftermath of Pir Perus's last battle, prudently omitting his conviction victors and mutilators had been the Armies of Owan.

"This, then, would be the war with the swallows," and Daënakh won Dolvid's respect by adding, "I have often thought *swallows* must stand for something else — a banner, perhaps. I am convinced more than one piece of nonsense in the *Song of Tales* might have a real story behind it."

Servants brought light food, miniature loaves of oat bread, wafers of sun-dried beef, and a heaped dish of tiny Sebira Bay crabs, a rare delicacy at Kadon Dinul, where half a dozen cost about the same as a haunch of mutton. In Leghayu's talk of guests soon to arrive it became clear Shumat and Dolvid were to stay for dinner.

Somewhat hesitantly, Bradhinal of Ân came in. Leghayu, as she remarked he was, as always, not far behind the food, lost so much of her stiffly forbidding air, it was plain this must be her favorite of the two sons. Hardly more than a boy, not particularly tall, he was big-framed and massive in the arms, tunic of the provincial cavalry taut across his chest. He moved with the slight awkwardness of strength not yet fully harnessed, adding to the impression of shyness, as did the uncertain glance. Dolvid had last seen him as a boy of eight or so, but recognized him before Leghayu spoke the name.

Bradhinal obviously did not remember him, but greeted Shumat warmly. "I watched you come ashore, your men looked splendid. I saw you were carrying steel-tips. You won't be fighting men in body-armor, you know."

"They make a better show," grinning. "We have long lances with us, too."

"I did not mean to offer advice unasked," the young man mumbled, shy all over again.

"We'll need all we can find, from anyone familiar with the North." Shumat was at his ease as not since entering the Great House. "You've put on a little muscle, not so?"

"And you some rank. This is where the work is to be done; I would give a lot to be beside you. My mother wants me to go with the Pledging escort, as if one toy soldier in the family was not enough."

Leghayu uttered a sharp reproof for this characterization of his soon-to-be near-royal brother. While Daënakh, plainly embarrassed after making so much of the important duties of his cavalry, dug into the bowl of crabs, and gave his son Dolvid's interpretation of the find of bones on Sebira Bay, snapping off little claws and sucking at them as he told the tale.

Bradhinal listened perfunctorily, and was soon questioning Shumat about men they both knew in the Household. Daënakh, annexing Dolvid as a fellow-scholar, began on a quite unrelated conjecture about the origins of *jinzal* as a race of men cursed because of their cannibalism to lose the power of speech and become hideous and homeless outcasts. This theory offered no explanation why there seemed to be no *jinzayul*, females, and how, despite that, *jinzal* did not become extinct. In fact, it all came from a plodding poem of the Island years (possibly written by one of the obscurer Patriarchs), and Dolvid, while following Daënakh's retelling, could give most of his attention sidelong to Bradhinal and Shumat.

Shumat related Bolan's view that not only time but lives, often, were wasted in trying to conciliate rebels, and a single swift, hard blow to bring rebellion to its knees was, in the end, most merciful. He omitted mentioning where Bolan intended striking that blow, but Bradhinal commented that in the Yuvakh country revolt had no real center, where a decisive battle could be provoked. Hitherto, he said, there had not been enough fast-moving soldiery to strike here and there without leaving other places unguarded. Here, veiled criticism of Under-Captain Antrovai could be heard in Bradhinal's insistence on the need for spirited leadership at Yuvakh Din; with that and good cavalry, he said, the job could be done.

"Levies are no use," becoming excited. "*Péfrapravádal*. If I could have a company of *péfrapravádal* at Yuvakh Din — " He turned to his father. "You would have let my brother command troops, and anyone can tell you I'm twice the soldier he is."

This evidently continuing debate was not allowed to go farther; Leghayu sent her son to the great hall to greet any early guests. Not pleased, Bradhinal left.

"Horses, *Asai*," Dolvid told Daënakh, "are going to be a large need." He had never expected to discuss this face-to-face with the *nim'*, but so far had not met the *bôdhrai* Daënakh must have to advise him.

"We have, as law limits us, no *pefral* to spare."

"Understood, *Asai*. But there is more to a campaign than cavalry charges, and the excellent saddle-horses of Ân could free our *pefral* for actual fighting."

"How many horses?"

"Two hundred would fill foreseeable needs," as off-handedly as he could manage.

Leghayu demanded, "The *rabhsai* wants to buy two hundred horses?"

"The *rabhsai* would pay for their upkeep during the campaign, and a fair price for any losses or injuries, the remainder to be returned to your possession."

"Otherwise said," Daënakh clarified. "You are asking to borrow two hundred horses."

"To have use of them, *Asai*, to accomplish things to the general benefit." This drew a glance from Shumat, both quizzical and warning, but Dolvid knew what he was doing.

After reflection, Daënakh nodded. "We have the horses."

They went on to negotiate over supplies the expedition would need. Evidently Daënakh must have started laying in stocks as soon as he heard about the expedition; whenever Dolvid mentioned a specific need, not forgetting apples, the *nim'* was confident it could be met. He even discussed cost; feeling he had made a concession with the horses, he insisted feed and foodstuffs would be charged at local prices, about one-fifth higher than Kadon Dinul. "I presume you don't expect to borrow your food, too."

"The *rabhsai* wants fair prices paid."

"In gold?" Leghayu asked. "The *rabhsai*'s bond is good, of course, but next harvest will be in and forgotten before Kadon Dinul redeems its drafts."

An awkward point: there was no excess of money, and Bolan had to be sure he could pay his troops. "We shall pay one-fourth in gold," Dolvid proposed. "The rest in drafts, which you may redeem against your remittance of taxes to the Treasury." This completely unauthorized plan, invented at that moment, shocked Shumat, but was quickly approved by Daënakh, who added that since pacification of the Yuvakh Din country would bring in many long uncollected taxes, the *rabhsai* certainly would not be loser.

"Daënakh and his Leghayu haggle like a couple of Old Town housewives over a bag of peat," Shumat said when left alone with Dolvid. They were waiting for warmed water to be brought so they could clean hands after their battle with the crabs. The lord and lady had also gone for repairs before greeting their dinner guests, and Shumat, uncertain of who might be listening somewhere, made his voice forceful but low. "Taxes! Not a word about those who long for the realm's law, *rabhsai*'s justice, safety from robbers and rebels. At least the Loyal Elders of Narn didn't write a petition about profits."

"Because they had none to offer. The honor of the *rabhsai* is all very well, but in the end what will decide whether Narn stays in the realm is whether it can be made to pay. Daënakh knows what he's doing."

Shumat made a face, but did not debate that. "You weren't going to have any part of fooling him."

"I am not."

"What about the horses? He thinks they're for Yuvakh Din."

"Bolan," simply, "kept me, and wanted you to keep me in the dark. All right, I'm doing just what I would if you had never told me anything. It's not my fault, what *Nim'* Daënakh assumes. Let Bolan tell him there is not going to be a Yuvakh Din campaign."

"He'll kill you."

"I don't see how he can blame me, unless you tell him you disobeyed, and let me in on his secret. If he is brave enough to disappoint Daënakh, he can negotiate for our supplies, too. The horses he will never get."

"You're really upset about this," he perceived, then, "Oh, but how can any officer of the *rabhsai* keep his manhood, carrying the Banner through the heart of a country in revolt and doing nothing?"

The voice he used had grown with his conviction, and belated fear he might have been overheard caused embarrassed silence, as towels and hot water arrived with servants, and behind them, almost surreptitiously, young Bradhinal returned.

There were jokes, references to men, women, and events at Kadon Dinul Dolvid knew nothing about, but Bradhinal's real purpose, never quite expressed, was to have Shumat have Bolan intervene with his father, so he could be part of the Yuvakh Din campaign.

"What will the strategy be?" he asked. "A fresh mind is needed."

"He can't make any firm strategy," unhappily, "till he can see the country and the situation first-hand."

"Antrovai has been there too long to see anything but failure. The man must be forty-five, nearer fifty, it might be. He hasn't even been able to capture — well, you don't want my ideas."

Shyness again ascendant, he had to be persuaded, and told how his father was especially bitter about one of the rebellious chieftains who had made himself strong enough to defy Antrovai, and sent an insolent offer to negotiate with *Nim'* Daënakh direct. "As my father says, we need an example. I would begin by capturing this Ott, and give him a slow death all the others could hear about."

"Ott?" sharply, having heard the name earlier today. "Of Ottsvale?"

Bradhinal was surprised the man had become so famous, and Shumat, conversant with old-fashioned Gabhanil ways, said the man must have been a leading farmer and clan-chieftain, probably a horse-healer, too, though his district might well be called after a grandfather, or earlier forebear of the same name. But Dolvid was trying to remember another name, of the weaselly little man who had accosted him at dockside, saying he had been Ott's stableman.

While they made use of warm water and towels, Bradhinal mentioned the Warden of the Port was among guests for dinner. "You'd never credit it to look at him, but he has three choice daughters, all unmarried. Sholu, the youngest, can see herself as my mother's other daughter-in-law. We may all do well."

As they gathered themselves, Dolvid still trying to dredge out a name, Bradhinal asked with monumental offhandedness, "Are you riding at lances tomorrow? Could I bring my squadron and drill with you?"

"Very good," Shumat, without joy.

"Others of the squadrons may also want to come."

Resignedly, knowing Bolan would not approve it, Shumat agreed.

"If it's not too early," Bradhinal amended. "You would take little Sholu for a beginner, but she could wear out half a squadron."

This was all bravado; obviously he would be there if Shumat called the cavalry-drill for dawn.

"I must find a man called Stanni," Dolvid said. The name had just come back to him.

"You must be mad." Bolan stripped off his white gauntlets and threw them down on the table. "Didn't I say, keep a distance?"

They were in the unused warehouse Daënakh had lent as headquarters. Bolan had just arrived, at the head of eight squadrons. Shumat, having word of his approach, had paraded all the lances, and under a pale sun Bradhinal, for his father, had welcomed him. Their captain only just waited to be alone with Dolvid and Shumat before he let annoyance show.

"Telling the overgrown cub of Ân they could line up four provincial squadrons with ours, as if they were part of the army. We're never going to be — " Recollecting Dolvid was not supposed to know, he tailed away into a complaint about parade-ground puppets having no place in a force preparing for war.

Onebhal, coming in, overheard. After greeting Bolan he said innocently, "Beg pardon, Captain, the Ân squadrons are good enough soldiers from what I've seen. Hold their formation in massed movements, and they've done well in mock-battle, too."

"They have been drilling with us?"

"Every day," Onebhal agreed.

"Shâl's elbow."

Dolvid was well-prepared. "It was suggested when Daënakh agreed to let us have spare horses."

Bolan wheeled on Shumat, but he too was ready. "What

could I say? Dolvid is aware of your concerns, about having Daënakh try and make our battle-plans for us."

"But Daënakh agrees," Dolvid said, "the Cavalry of Ân is to be part of your overall command. He'll find a fifth squadron here; with three already at Yuvakh Din that adds eight to your strength of *péfrapravádal*, and nothing to our expenses."

"What is the use of doubling our strength," Bolan demanded of Shumat, abandoning any attempt to keep Dolvid half-informed, "if we take on ten times the task? We could spend five years, ten in the Yuvakh country — you want to spend half your life freezing your pleaser off in this empty cursed country?"

Shumat had taken a liking to the North. "If this is the weather, a week before Halving, the winters have been slandered."

This increased Bolan's annoyance. The sheltered bowl of Sebira was noted for its mildness, but just over the circling hills winter still lingered, and Bolan's road had been a snow-walled corridor from central Dramal to beyond Luskran Bay. Too often, his men had been obliged to dig their way through new falls, and once, unable to reach inhabited parts by dark, had been forced to make cold camp in the wilds. With half his mind visibly trying to find ways to be rid of both Daënakh and the Yuvakh campaign, he recounted these trials as if created just to add to his miseries. "Sebhal may boast about tweaking *jinzal* noses, but he never had those hills to cross in knee-deep snow. You were right about sending supplies by water, at least. With a pack-train we'd have been a month, with wagons, a lifetime."

"Other things Sebhal has never done," Dolvid said. "The disaffected lands here are wider than all the Colony."

Bolan made an impatient noise. "What have you promised Daënakh about his rebellion?"

"I've promised nothing at all. Dolvid can tell you, he's given us all we've asked for, and more."

After leading Shumat aside and carrying on a low-voiced discussion needing many gestures, Bolan announced he must see

Daënakh. He would in any case be expected to do so, in courtesy.

That decision made, he debated changing his clothes, spent minutes settling the proper number for an escort, and wondered whether he needed the Royal Warrant, Shumat having already presented a copy. Ready to leave, he stood, slapping his gloves against the side of his leg. "You've put me in these tongs," to his subordinates in general.

Plain what he meant; Bolan wanted to bypass the rebellion he called Daënakh's, but what he had planned by evasion would now need a plain declaration. The words a captain might use to the *nim'* of a province in such a case could hardly be imagined.

"Will you come with me, Dolvid? I need someone with Great House phrases."

"What was Shumat dreaming of?" he muttered savagely, as they started up the hill with a file for escort. "He could have found a way to warn you. This is just the trap I was afraid of. What can any of us gain in a campaign this side of the mountains?"

"Without it," shocking him, "I don't see what you can hope for on the other side. How can you bring a hand back to life with the arm cut off at the shoulder?"

"Policy. This is policy. To free the road, yes. But this Daënakh is a cunning one. He's trying to embarrass me, as the Loyal Elders did the *rabhsai*."

"He sits in the Council of Thirteen, next to Vinilat of Dramal."

"If I don't help him, you mean, he might turn on me."

"His brother Laënakh is *Nim'* of Nîv." That would make two votes against Bolan's dream Captain-Generalcy.

"It's in Council his business should be proposed," Bolan complained. "I am a soldier, and they sent me to relieve Narn."

Dolvid lost patience. "You'll never get there, if you don't do something about the nearer question. From Yuvakh Din to the Pass of Perus is a full dayride. Beyond, there is the wilderness of Naëni, days across, where there is hardly a blade of grass, so I'm told. Every mouthful for men or horses would have to be carried through a countryside in revolt. Without Provincial soldiers, you'll use most of your troops guarding the road. You won't have three squadrons for any fighting at Narn."

"No, I must have twelve squadrons there. Twenty would be better."

"That is if you have any supplies to escort," sourly. "Take away Daënakh's stocks, you'll be foraging in ten days."

"We shall," Bolan corrected. Taken off guard by Dolvid's outburst, he could still be seen trying to invent a stratagem to give him Daënakh's troops without fighting Daënakh's campaign.

"You," Dolvid insisted. He had made up his mind to leave the expedition if Bolan ignored this child's lesson in strategy, not to fight on the far side of hostile country.

"Well, look, we might be able to do enough at Yuvakh Din to satisfy Daënakh. Nothing says every rebel has to be dead or disarmed before it's safe to ride on. Then leave his provincials to fight there and keep the road open, while ours make for Narn. If we can give them a sharp rap or two, hah?"

He was talking as if he would fight this side of the mountains just to please Dolvid, who had found what would please Daënakh. However, though it might be for bad reasons, he had abandoned a suicidal plan. Dolvid, who had been curiously caught between sadness and annoyance, saw with relief he did not have to leave a job he loved.

If they had ridden by moonlight, Onebhal would probably have noted its inferiority to the moon in his own country; he continued to find fault with the North, even when on the second day they descended from bleak, snowstreaked uplands into sheltered valleys with usable pasture, pockets of orchard, as yet with not a blossom or leaf. Onebhal was in charge of the strong escort for the supply-train, first to leave Sebira, expecting to be caught by the rest of the cavalry before reaching Yuvakh Din. Despite grumblings of the lean-faced *kímukan*, Dolvid was in an exalted state, as they moved, however slowly, towards mountains, edge of the realm, lands he had never expected to see.

He could not be depressed for long, even by the company of Stanni, former stableman to Ott, found again at Sebira and hired for the expedition. He was a man made rancid with resentment, cheated, he said, by Ott, after years of service with nothing to show for it but a misshapen shoulder and an injured foot that would never completely heal; Dolvid had seen the man washing and was sure the shoulder at least had been so from birth. That did not begin but added to doubt about how much to believe Stanni's tales that made Ott of Ottsvale into a nightmare, a man of huge size, past middle life but still with strength to wrestle down bulls, having equal appetite for power, possessions and cruelty. He maimed men for nearly nothing, enjoyed inflicting pain, and was unchallenged leader of a like-minded clan.

Whether or not much of this was true, Dolvid began to get a clearer picture both of the uprising, and the site, a wet country, which bad roads and difficult terrain made hard to control. Revolt had apparently begun with refusal to pay taxes, and gone on to the murder of tax-gatherers, assessors, magistrates, then killing of soldiers sent to protect those functionaries. It had worsened with arrival of what Stanni called out-men, landless and lawless people who came from beyond the Pass of Perus (that being wilderness, most of them must have come, before that, from Narn). They waylaid the road, and fought both to dispossess the rebellious farmers, and against the soldiery. These out-men usually made up more numerous bands than the original rebels, with the exception of Ott, who could command, according to Stanni, several hundred, including many deadly bows.

"He's made strong, secret hides in the hills around Ottsvale, and stocked them with food," Stanni said.

"You know where they are?"

Stanni spat. "What is the difference? Horsemen can't take them. No one can, without losing hundreds. You have to lure Ott out, and cut him off from his hideaways."

The implication was that Stanni knew a way to do so, but if so he did not offer his plan.

From this direction the approach to Yuvakh Din kept near the brow of a tapering mound thrust out into the valley, and at the two-mile stone nothing could be seen of the town, only walls and tower of the fortress against space and the farther background of dark hills, behind those the main mass of mountains; in this final stretch Onebhal's command was at last overtaken by the squadrons of cavalry. Leaving their troops to attach to the end of the supply-train, more than half a mile back, Shumat and Bradhinal came loping up, both boisterously happy.

"Great Zhôl, this is a country with some breadth," Shumat called out. "Mountains! Let's take charge of the rebels, and make this our own realm." He half-turned to aim a playful punch at Bradhinal, who jounced in the saddle, and threw back his head to bawl out a fragment of song, "Father, oh father, I'll come home no more," actually about a girl's elopement. Both men bent over in what, in anything but two brawny cavalrymen, would have been called giggles.

Onebhal, judging by his sour face, believed officers should set better examples, and Dolvid abruptly suspected Bolan had made up reasons to stay a while at Sebira, leaving another awkward meeting to his subordinates; he could not imagine this pair frolicking so with their commander watching. Trying not to make the question too pointed, he asked where Bolan was. Shumat used a thumb to indicate, back with the main body of cavalry.

"We are probably being observed from the fortress," Dolvid remarked. They were in easy sight of a stone gateway, and for instant confirmation a small detachment emerged there, under General Cavalry colors, and stood to greet them.

The commander had sent his deputy, also an Owani, the *Kímukan* Indhil, sharp-nosed, severe about the mouth, and unbelievably neat for an officer in the field. How Under-Captain Antrovai would take to having his command usurped by a man who, in the year he reached his present rank, was guarding the

Bronze Residence with a rag-tag of levies, had been a subject for speculation.   Bolan   had   instructed   everyone   to   avoid provocation, and kept swearing he would consult the older man in all important decisions.   If this greeting was any sign, however, Antrovai had already settled on petty obstruction; Indhil began by reminding Bradhinal the Provincial Cavalry must formally request special permission to enter the precincts of a royal garrison.

Though correct in the letter of law, this was filled with absurdities; squadrons of Ân Cavalry were already serving at Yuvakh Din, and the five waiting to enter were under Bolan's command, on loan to royal forces. Seeing Bradhinal's reddening face Dolvid quickly murmured in his ear that this officer was a fool, but it did no harm to make the request.

The unmistakable son of *Nim'* Daënakh coldly asked leave, which Indhil precisely granted. All the sillier considering Bradhinal, though in charge of paired squadrons, was not even senior officer with his father's troops.

Bolan came up, a copy of the Royal Warrant ready in his hand, but Indhil's few men had already drawn aside from the open gate. Past the archway was a wide, paved space next to the fortress, and a first real sight of the city. The oldest parts were to the front, sloping down to city walls so thick four men could have gone abreast on the battlements. Leftward the ground fell away steeply with masses of brown rock bulging up among houses which clung to the slope. A number of streams went coursing down to feed a long lake below, walls sweeping wide to incorporate it in the city. Between the mound surmounted by walls and the edge of the water the narrow and often muddy strip was crowded with a mean makeshift village of shabby tents and shacks, most looking as if a stiff breeze would level them. There were also shelters hollowed out in the face of the mound. Ragged children were playing in the mire, a few short lines of washing hung drearily between leaning stakes, and where the water was bordered by rocks, ten or a dozen men, some aged, sat with their bodies slouched into dejected purposelessness, talking together or doing nothing.

These, Indhil answered Shumat, were farming families the uprising had driven from the land. All they could do was till fields, and there was no work in Yuvakh Din, no houses for them. Their presence, Indhil added, had been an uninvited burden, considering how there was barely food for the town's useful inhabitants. Shumat, keeping in mind Bolan's warnings, bit back an angry answer, but while his face was grim, his eyes were glistening with unexpected tears.

Though the Gabhani element showed in his features far more than in Bolan's, he was much less conscious of race, seldom mentioning the subject. Yet Shumat, listening to this disdainful Owani officer, obviously thought of the dispossessed beside the lake as his people, and at that moment found a new resolve.

His earnest mood, bordering ill-tempered, did not abate. When the Under-Captain Antrovai said he could accommodate only officers and a couple of squadrons of men at the fortress, Bolan, saying the air there reeked of defeat, declined hospitality and actually stayed under canvas with all his forces. Their encampment was outside the city walls on that north side, readily defended, since the stream running out at the foot of the lake joined another not far to the north, making a natural moat. But Shumat, usually leader in ordering a camp, had not much to do with this one. Quickly finding local guides other than the timid ones in Antrovai's pay, he took a pair of squadrons out on a patrol his second day at Yuvakh Din, and soon made longer excursions, exploring difficult country away from the road, and spending a night away from Yuvakh Din to climb to near the foot of the Pass. In a skirmish two of his men and one mount were wounded by arrows, and Shumat found it hard to pursue the ambushers. These were strange lands, where stony hills, dense thorn-brakes and dreary marshes interwove with patches of pasture rich as anything the Heartland could show, and seemingly endless and impassable thickets of close-set, weedy white alder and hazel abruptly gave way to fertile and well-kept growing-lands. Some farmers had to make half-day rides around bogs and reedlands to visit neighbors within easy sight, and it was always risky to predict the eventual destination of the many winding paths and trails. As Under-Captain Antrovai said at their first meeting, a land to swallow up armies, but Shumat was not ready to concede to the hopelessness they met with here; keeping the fresh forces on the move was best way to miss catching that infection.

Bolan approved, though worried by the casualties of that little initial fight. He would obviously be satisfied with a token victory here, so he could make the dash for Narn, forces intact, and of all unpromising facts learnt from Antrovai, the worst for Bolan was that the Pass of Perus was undoubtedly still blocked by snow, and expected to be so for several weeks.

He spoke about digging a way through, and Antrovai warned of huge drifts, pointing out that floundering soldiers would be very vulnerable to attack by bands of out-men with bows, to whom the foothills and higher crags gave excellent cover. At the head of the Pass of Perus there was a *drin'loi*, a small fort or blockhouse, for at least a year ungarrisoned, Antrovai admitted, because of casualties suffered keeping the road open.

That withdrawal was vexatious to Bolan, but staggered Dolvid; the *drin'loi* stood at the actual border of Ân, indeed of the realm, and on his own authority Antrovai had in effect moved the frontier back to Yuvakh Din. Yet it was hard to echo Bolan's contempt or Shumat's anger for the commander, who had tried, with thirteen often under-strength squadrons and a fluctuating number of auxiliaries, not always reliable, to campaign against what might be seen as two separate enemies, rebellion and invasion. Far to the west, in the Colony, Sebhal had become famous holding another frontier, but with three times Antrovai's numbers, and the best cavalry in existence. Collapse of the empire in the West had doomed Old Owan, and out of the West *jinzal* came, as well as inexhaustible numbers of potential tribal invaders; history had made this job at the other end of the realm an obscure and thankless one.

Especially next to the immaculate *Kimukan* Indhil, Antrovai was rather rumpled and worn-looking, tall with rounded shoulders. His acceptance of Bolan's authority under the *rabhsai*'s warrant was suspiciously bland, but any irony was as lifeless as the pale grey eyes. Most of his speech was a style Dolvid recognized from his studies but had never expected to hear spoken, the remote and stilted language of military reports.

On the sixth day Antrovai came down to a general council called by Bolan, and observed there were now enough troops available to carry out a policy he had advocated more than two years ago, when formally requesting the established strength of the garrison be increased to not less than twenty and as many as twenty-four squadrons. He called the strategy *depriving rebellion of its sustenance*; he meant, starving it. Farms would be seized one by one, crops destroyed, livestock driven in near Yuvakh Din, or slaughtered for current needs. For any supplies to come in from east of the mountains was unimaginable — the out-men, rather, made their way to this country in search of food — but when the Pass was open again, it could be seized and held in force, leaving enough men to make patrols and to guard stored foodstuffs, not forgetting Yuvakh Din, where raids might indeed be attempted as outlaws became increasingly desperate.

Bolan tightened his lips. "This would need all our men from now till next harvest."

"Longer, perhaps," Shumat said. "Some of the rebels have large stocks of their own."

"Well, we came to put down revolt, using the time it takes," Pranuvi said. He was nominal commander of the Provincial squadrons, a pleasant, easy-going man, round-faced for an Owani. Dolvid did not envy his position, responsibility without real authority: Bolan could commit his provincials to battle, while in questions of policy Bradhinal, obviously, carried the weight of his father's exalted rank.

He spoke now, though probably not in words Daënakh would have endorsed. "We came to claim new allegiance. You might use hunger to make men submit, but who is going to give his heart to a *rabhsai*, or to a *nim'*, whose men burn food? An affront to Aëlovoi *Yoëlu* — " and he made the proper sign, all four fingers folding down to the base of his palm.

Bolan used a lofty tone to disguise his determination not to be stuck in the mires of Yuvakh Din. "I have to consider the region as a whole. Narn's need is desperate, and can't be put off till next year, as this starving-out of rebels would mean. New allegiance, yes, but our constant object must be to punish wrongdoers."

"A firm policy, steadily pursued," Antrovai agreed, incidentally rebuking Bradhinal, "is all these people understand."

Shumat urged that now, while the Pass of Perus was closed, might well give the best chance to strike against the raiders. Farm-folk he talked to said out-men had often escaped that way, since abandoning of the *drin'loi*.

The *Kímukan* Indhil was scornful. He probably judged Shumat's permanent rank, and almost certainly believed his race, inferior to his own. "If you go for news to that scarecrow village — " gesturing at the city wall, beyond which was the lakeside encampment of the dispossessed, "you'll hear soldiery blamed for everything."

His glum commander said, "Up in the mountains are hiding-places for ten thousand rebels; holding the head of the Pass is putting a stopper in a smashed bottle."

"For myself, Under-Captain," Shumat, lightly but with a dangerous edge, "I'd let go everything short of the city walls before giving up the *drin'loi* without a fight."

"For yourself, Under-Captain," Antrovai shot back, "you have not had those choices." A first real sign of life, and there was no mistaking the astringent emphasis on Shumat's acting rank.

"If we didn't keep watch on the hills about Yuvakh Din," he went on, "nothing would prevent Ott and his following from marauding in central Ân. He's had a taste of power, and there is no limit to his ambition. And he is only one among many."

"He's the one who is hero to all others," Shumat said.

"The one," Bolan said, "who must be killed or captured. I'm going to make that the first and only job for up to ten squadrons." Exactly the quick and recognizable victory he needed before riding for Narn.

Antrovai saw difficulties, speaking about Ott's elusiveness, and the accuracy and power of the bows he commanded, Gabhanil longbows that could penetrate body-armor at close range. He estimated there were upwards of one hundred, far short of the figure heard from Stanni, but quite enough to be deadly from cover against ordered cavalry. But Bolan meant to force the ground for a battle, by sending forces to camp on Ott's farmland, to set fire to the buildings there, and homes of his followers. For his prestige as a leader, Ott, surely, would have to fight.

Grudgingly Antrovai allowed it might work. For him, such offensive operations had always been hampered by insufficient overall strength, and need for maintaining defenses elsewhere. "But you'll suffer losses," he warned.

"Wars are not won without loss," Bradhinal said, while Bolan worriedly counted his forces again.

"It might be done," Shumat, not waiting to be asked. "My question is, should it? Will the Yuvakh country, or Yuvakh Din itself, be safer for the death or defeat of Ott?"

This was new to everyone there except Dolvid. After his first long patrol Shumat had begun speculating on the proper war to fight. Going for guides to the lakeside encampment, conversing with ordinary people in both city and countryside, he had discovered that except for regular soldiers and moneyed men (to which could be added the former stableman, Stanni) no one seemed to hate Ott, and everyone loathed the out-men. Further, all of them, people still loyal and law-abiding, even men levied to help defend the walls, resented how the soldiery (and, as they naturally assumed, both *nim'* and *rabhsai*) lumped together as enemies those out-men, marauding invaders, and rebellious farmers, native here. who to begin with (so it was said) had understandable grievances against the methods of apportioning and collecting taxes.

Shumat's conclusion, that these rebels, under arms and already fighting against the out-men, were natural allies rather than inevitable enemies, had been more sympathetically heard by Dolvid than it now was by the captains. Antrovai was sour about those who, in a few days, became expert in subjects to which others have given years, and was supported by discreet sarcasms from his senior *kimukan*. Shumat's proposal, however, might bring about instead an equally improbable alliance, Antrovai with Bradhinal, who expressed what might be his father's feelings against leniency towards the disloyal.

"We must capture and hang men such as Ott, at the main gate, for everyone to see," Antrovai insisted, forgetting he'd had no plan for doing so.

Bolan, having settled on Ott as a beatable enemy, was perplexed by Shumat's novel attitude, equally set against anything that might be seen as weakness. Then, noticing Dolvid's only contribution had been to suggest they all listen to what Shumat had to say, he asked him aside from the others, "What do you say about this?"

"Well," reluctant to speak when he knew nothing first-hand. "The current policy is no quarter for anyone who has rebelled. But except for the narrow strip by Yuvakh Din, and the homeless who have come here, that's everyone. Hanging Ott is not going to awe men into surrender when surrender means death, and I think they may kill a lot of us before they're all killed."

Bolan stayed glumly thoughtful, as Antrovai went on enumerating the crimes of the rebels; not only out-men, he said, waylaid the road and stole from wagons, or claimed territory not their own. Ignoring him, Shumat told Bolan, "I haven't seen many fields for a cavalry charge in this hole-and-corner country. What we need against the out-men is what we're shortest of, good bows."

"Most ordinary men here can shoot," the *Kímukan* Indhil said. "We've levied bows in the past, but they are not reliable in a fight."

"Ott already commands a battle-hardened force of first-rate bows," Shumat said.

"Leaving justice aside," Antrovai said, "what makes you imagine Ott is ready to be our ally? I suppose you have put the proposition to him?"

"Yes," Shumat said.

This was completely new even to Dolvid, and for the others Shumat must either be joking or speaking in an emblematic way of sending out a message to the rebel leader. Not so; he had spoken face to face with Ott just yesterday.

Quite easily, he said. Guessing Ott must have friends in the city, observing he had many not his enemies, Shumat had let it be known in drink-shops and at the lakeside encampment that he would meet the man in any place and with any sureties for safety Ott wanted to name. The offer had been taken up far more readily than he could have predicted.

("Aye," Antrovai, harshly. "That's why we have not used as many levies as we might. Spies are everywhere, and Ott had timely warning of all our moves against him.")

The night before last a woman had approached Shumat, and said if he would walk with her alone, out of call of the camp and not carrying a weapon, she might have some news. When he followed those instructions she met him, not only wearing a knife, but with two companions nearby in the dusk. For a moment Shumat thought he had come ambling into a trap, but after some ritual menacing the woman had given him careful instructions for the next day — yesterday.

In the morning he had taken a patrol out, but, as stipulated, left his squadrons on the far side of the small hamlet on the road for the Pass, and ridden on alone, following a cart-track. As the track wound in rougher country he glimpsed bowmen lurking in thorn-brakes, but gave no sign he had noticed them. He had a strong feeling of being shadowed by mounted men, but did not try for sight of them, riding on steadily.

He came to a rutted spot he had been told to look for, and a site where farm buildings had been burnt to the ground. From the shelter of charred and broken walls, men with bows ready called on Shumat to dismount and lay down his weapons.

"Did you?" Bolan demanded. Only the self-evident fact Shumat had survived his adventure was keeping him rational.

"I told them I didn't have any weapons. That tickled them, but they had me dismount anyway, and one of them led my *pefrai* away."

"You weren't afraid?" Bradhinal asked.

"They could have held you hostage," Bolan fretted.

"No they could not," with a flash of pride. "I would make them kill me. But, if you want to know, I nearly pissed myself."

Remounted on a small hill-horse led by a man on another, he had been taken an hour through tortuous country. The way included much doubling back, changes of direction in the middle of thickets. Since making sure he was the officer expected, his companions had scarcely spoken. When in sight of a low, stony ridge, they blindfolded him, and again by a winding path they mounted slowly till, when they let him see again, they had reached what must be one of the strongholds Stanni had described. More bowmen were posted among rocks, at the edge of a broad, bare shelf, with caves in the rock-face behind. A stream flowed at one end of the encampment, and as well as ample supplies Shumat saw livestock; several goats, a flock of chickens. All men were heavily armed, and the women seemed about equally formidable. Inside one of the caves a baby was crying.

"And you met with Ott?" Bolan asked.

"We spoke for an hour, over beer, and later food."

"How could you be sure it was Ott?" Indhil asked.

"Why should he lie? He was in charge there, a knotty oak of a man. But he had the scar I had heard about — " tracing a line across his right cheek.

"The scar he got from me," Indhil said, "four years ago, when he threatened the tax-gatherer."

Shumat gave him a long look. "According to his story, he drew to protect himself, only after being assailed. He had refused to pay his portion until he was assured of some protection against raiders, who were stealing corn and cattle from his people."

"He was first to draw his weapon," the *kimukan*, coldly.

Hard to imagine Indhil using a sword at all, but his bland statements were stranger still. Though it must have capped years of resentment on one side, mounting exasperation on the other, this was the very incident with which open revolt began.

"The old story," Antrovai said. "How many ways are there to blame the soldiery for all misfortunes? Since then, Ott has killed men of the cavalry, and carried out raids for corn and cattle."

Shumat nodded acceptance. "He started out with threats. Then his wife brought the welcome-cup, and after that I was sure he would not harm me, unless he believed there was a trap. I was afraid some of my own men would disobey orders, and try to follow me." This was for the watchful Onebhal.

Letting signs of irritation show, Bolan asked, "Well, what did you talk about? I hope you informed him you were there on your own, with absolutely no authority to negotiate?"

"I told him that before anything else. Everything I told him was true. I suggested his life would be harder, now new strength had come to Yuvakh Din. He shrugged, and said 'a thousand men, not all of them soldiers.' I said, yes, but led by Captain Bolan, the famous *Akhekhai-Kindhri*."

"*Akaëkhai-Kindhri*," Dolvid automatically corrected.

Bolan objected, "Ott, in any case, wouldn't know about that."

"Would he not! He told me Ottsvale was no market-place, and his followers not just townsfolk upset about prices. He is a rough man, but not stupid."

Shumat's main thesis with Ott had been, there was an enemy they shared, the out-men. Ott said if so, he was doing more than his share of the fighting; out-men would have been at the gates of Yuvakh Din long ago, but for his bows. Challenged, he conceded the protecting of Yuvakh was not why he continued to fight, though he would wish to see the city brought back to its health, so people could bring their goods to market there, and buy what they needed or desired.

"Like a child," Antrovai commented, "crying over the toy he broke with his own tantrums."

"I told him that while our new forces were surely enough to defeat or scatter his, to my mind it was foolish to destroy a fighting force that, as our allies, could help drive away out-men, and let everyone go back to their proper lands. He laughed at that, and then asked his wife to tell me about Ottsvale in the old days, how pleasant it was when there was peace."

"Was anything said about how Ottsvale men would murder neighbors, rape their women?"

"He did speak about long feuds. He said, any wise man would rather trust to law than his own vengeance, if there was a law to be trusted. One of those raped women is mother of Ott's grandchildren, his eldest son's wife, so it hasn't all been loss. Two other sons and a daughter sat down with us when we had our food. His wife is a strong woman, no fool."

"What was the food?" Dolvid asked.

"Meat, bread, fresh fruit, goats' milk. There wasn't any shortage; it would take an age to starve them out. I could see big stocks back farther in the cave."

Antrovai regretted the care taken by Ott's men to confuse the way to this fastness. Otherwise it might have been surrounded, and the food stocks, if not Ott himself, captured. Shumat, justifiably proud of his head for terrain and distances, answered that though led back by a different way, no less twisting, he could easily find the hideaway again. But to capture it would cost too many lives, so long as even a small number of defenders had arrows to shoot.

With a contemptuous gesture certain to irritate, Antrovai said it hardly mattered. "Thanks to your courteous warning, Ott can make even better places to hide his supplies." But Shumat refused to be baited. "As you can see by his count of the reinforcements, Ott did not need much informing by me. Maybe I've helped him a little to be prepared for war. It seemed worth taking the risk, for the chance of finding an ally."

"Well?" Bolan demanded. "Obviously he didn't lay down his arms on the spot."

"With proper guarantees for a truce, Ott would agree to meet with the *rabhsai*'s new captain — not where we met. In Ottsvale. I told him it might be done."

"You must be mad," Bolan said.

Morning had been misty, and there was shimmer and doubt at the edge of vision as they rode to the crest of a low ridge. Their guide, Stanni, pointed. The other side of a gradual downslope of salt wasteland a shallow saucer of rough pasture began; a half mile or so away there was a hornbeam with many stems, standing on a slight rise, the chalky streaks on its dark-grey bark easy to see. Ott had chosen this place well against any traps; no other trees were near.

Shumat said, "This is as far as troops can go." Five squadrons including Bradhinal's pair of Provincials continued to deploy along the ridge. Less than a dozen men would be directly concerned in the meeting.

Bolan still did not trust the business of exchanging hostages, and Shumat told him again he would see the need for it if he were Ott. Dolvid's mind went to a former parley, not less than fifteen centuries ago, when Pir Perus had trusted to the word and honor of the realm.

"If he meant to take me prisoner," maintained Shumat, who was to be hostage from their side, "he could have done it quite easily when I met him alone."

"Minds change," Bolan said. "How can we be sure it's his son he sends us?"

"I met him before," Shumat said.

Dolvid added, "Stanni can identify him."

"Yes, I know Ardi Otts-son," Stanni darkly agreed. He did not grow more lovable, though he tried to ingratiate himself with his new employers. According to Norlum, Stanni could never have been much use as a stableman — but then Norlum had contempt for how most men treated horses.

Bolan said again they must be mad. After lengthy debate he had agreed to this meeting only on the understanding that to talk meant nothing, and he wanted it kept in mind he had been dragged here against his better judgment. It worried him that Antrovai (with the *Kímukan* Indhil) had withdrawn early from discussion, and since informed Bolan that in his personal dispatches for Kadon Dinul he would disassociate himself from any concessions to the rebels. Technically, having assumed command here, Bolan could forbid the Under-Captain to send dispatches of his own: in private he threatened to do so, but Shumat convinced him it would be bound to come out, and suppression would look worse than anything Antrovai could write. Then Shumat and Dolvid together half-persuaded Bolan the best way of demolishing Antrovai was with successful negotiations, or by defeating Ott in the field if negotiations failed. They also had to convince Bradhinal, first that there was no loss of dignity in attempting to return subjects to their allegiance, and then that no matter what happened with Ott there would be plenty of what he had come for, fighting. He had moved to a wary tolerance of these proceedings, having heard nothing from his father.

Yet Dolvid himself had waverings as, with only a file of lances for escort, they started forward, Shumat a little ahead, followed by Bolan, Bradhinal, Stanni and Dolvid. Seeing the main force of cavalry Ott would know he would have to pay for treachery, but it must at least cross his mind here was a chance to kill or seize not only captain and his second-in-command, but the son of Daënakh. As a captive, Bradhinal alone ought to fetch a good price; Dolvid, worth nothing as a live prisoner, lifted his elbows to get rid of the crawling between his shoulderblades.

Somewhat nearer, Ott's choice of spots was doubly good from his standpoint; not far beyond the solitary tree there was a bank of brush that could hide a host. Figures could be discerned there; Shumat turned and said quietly, "Wait. Here I go forward alone."

The others reined in to watch him ride on slowly down the faint slope. Everyone jumped at a sudden dark flight of birds. Bolan was muttering, "Onebhal had better be alert." Twisting in the saddle to view the long line of bright helms along the ridge, Dolvid's eye was held briefly by a nearby bush, with tufts of vivid yellow blossom among thin, looping branches, as yet with no leaves.

From the distance a man strode out towards the royal lines, crossing with Shumat and exchanging a perfunctory salute. As he came close he was about Shumat's age, with a leanness that reduced the characteristic Gabhani breadth of feature, though the thick nose was unmistakable. Half a dozen paces short of Bolan's small group the man halted, and swung a clenched fist across his chest in the military royal salute. Shumat was dismounting by the shock of tree-stems, met by a few drably dressed men, one very big and stooped. Soon Shumat passed out of sight beyond the tree.

Bolan asked, "Ardi Otts-son?"

"Captain Bolan Bakir," Ardi acknowledged, then turned to Bradhinal with a correct half-deference. *"Nim'loiki."*

When two lancers dismounted to search the hostage, one found a small knife sheathed in Ardi's belt at mid-back. Ardi smiled. "My gutting knife, for small game, Captain. When your Under-Captain came to us by himself, he had a little dagger he thought we didn't see, hidden in his boot."

"Search him carefully," Stanni urged. "He's Ott's son."

Ardi had his feet planted well apart. "You've got fine soldiers, Captain, but your guides are ditch-filth. Don't let him stray near me."

"He is very brave at a parley," Stanni taunted.

"As you are, sheltering among lances, horse-thief. Be sure to keep count of your *pefral*, Captain — and your gold."

Dolvid said to Bolan, "Our guide could return to the main force."

"Good," and he told Stanni to report to Onebhal. The former stableman had a last loathing look as he wheeled his horse, and Ardi Otts-son spat. "I'd rather have a vulture in my house," an intended reference to Stanni's hunched shoulder.

Bolan abruptly dismounted and stood eye-to-eye with Ardi. "I don't have much hope for this parley. But if there is an agreement, you won't be living as a young bush-rat outside any law, but as a subject of Lambarr *Rabhsai*. Get used to that." Bradhinal's face approved of Bolan's speech.

Dismounted, he and Dolvid went forward with Bolan, eight horsed lancers a few paces behind, while four remained to guard the hostage. They went in silence across scrubby pasture, except sounds Bradhinal made, between lip and upper teeth, more hiss than whistle, just recognizable as a traditional marching song.

Halting about twenty paces short of the hornbeam, Bolan motioned the lances to stay back, then laid his sword down on unwakened turf. Bradhinal did the same, and a knot of four figures emerged from behind the cluster of tree-stems. Two grounded bows, while the biggest with a quick bend stuck a long knife into the earth.

Size and the angry scar were the first things about Ott to be noticed. Dolvid, uncertain guessing the age of a Gabhani, put Ott at no less than sixty, a giant, with forearms like the calves of a dockside porter, neck sheathed in hard ropes of muscle. Despite dominating scar, the broad face was frank and expected frankness in return.

The fourth in the group had no weapon to lay down, and in fact was not a man. At the *Mankh'* Dolvid had been taught, often with amused wonder, that among old-fashioned Gabhanil in remote parts practically the only possible cause for divorce was that either husband or wife was a Changer, and mere appearance could be enough to end a marriage: a man's shirt too full in the sleeve, or shoes to give him a mincing step. Women, it was said, often worked in breeches, but these must not open at the front, and their shirts were not permitted a man's collar. And here was a Gabhaniyu woman all in man's clothes, shirt to boots: either *Mankh'* stories were false, or this was evidence of how much lives here had been changed by hardship and danger. She was Mandellis, Ott's wife, with a lined and brooding face, eyes kept mainly on her husband.

"We're glad to see you here, Captain and *Nim'loiki*," Ott said. "Perhaps in a while we can drink a welcome-cup." His voice was strong but kept surprisingly soft, as if apricots were picked from oaks. No comparison between Bradhinal and Ott; as the introductions and namings were accomplished the young man's muscling was all at once puppy-fat next to Ott's weathered gnarling.

For all that was formidable about him, he spread an air of cordiality, so that except for Mandellis everyone was smiling. Though Dolvid had small doubt this man would sacrifice his own son to achieve a worthwhile objective, he lost the last fears of a trap. Sixty or seventy paces the other side of the tree Shumat could be noticed with a group of bowmen, quite at ease, drawing in air what might be an explanation of squadron tactics for cavalry. Just outside that circle was the slim figure of a dark-haired girl, and Dolvid had to rescue himself from the tug of distraction with the reminder he was alone in what had been the shared job of making Bolan better than he wanted to be.

Bolan was brisk in coming to the point. "Master Ott," he began. "In talk with Under-Captain Shumat you are said to have laid claim to certain lands. Before anything else, tell us their extent." The sardonic forecast of Antrovai was that Ott would ask for half the Yuvakh country, everything southward of the road, from the Pass of Perus to the gates of the city. Even the wide territory over which Ott and his allies ranged, far less than that, was much more than could be granted. To happen at all, these talks had to begin with a substantial concession from the rebel leader.

Ott said, "There is no one on your side, Captain, who knows the country well enough, or the lands my fathers had."

Bolan, testy too soon, retorted, "I'm not asking which bush and what brook. I am under the banner of Lambarr *Deghi*, and Bradhinal *Asai* can speak for Lord Daënakh. All ownership descends from *rabhsai* to *nim'*, and so to subject, and that title can't be — "

"Revoked by unlawful acts," Dolvid supplied, glanced to for rescue. Bolan's land-law was suspect, but adequate for this occasion. "Seizing lands, Master, does not make them yours."

"If we are not to tell about which bush or stream... " Ott gave a massive shrug.

Seeing Bolan, for all the coaching he had been given, was not going to trust himself here, Dolvid became spokesman, briefly outlining legal conditions binding both lord and subject. Strictly interpreted they would keep Ott from adding a herb-garden or a berry-bush to the lands held when the uprising began.

The language might puzzle him, but Ott had no trouble grasping the general meaning. He bent while his wife spoke in his ear, nodded, and replied, "You are saying, go back to the farm I had before, and then perhaps we can talk, if out-men don't murder me first?"

"Well, what would you propose?" Dolvid asked, violating, inside five minutes, Bolan's fixed position on this point. No one interrupted.

Again Ott complained they could not speak about his lands, or those of his followers. Summoning all his temerity, Dolvid said, "I do know leaders have to reward their followers, or they won't have any."

Still Bolan said nothing. "Tell us," Dolvid urged. "We'll try to understand."

"Tell him," Mandellis said. Her quick look in his face overwhelmingly put Dolvid in mind of another meeting, another woman, seven years ago. Not that Mandellis resembled the well-woman Inghi in any way (except that as there, he had first taken her for a man), but here again a respected woman was telling a leader she judged this one could be trusted. This would be a useful gift, if only he knew what he did to create the impression.

Ott waved an arm like a tree-limb. "This is Ottsvale. My lands, my fathers' lands, have always been here. Others had farms, not always the best farms, although some were on good lands, you understand me?"

"I think so. Ott, and those allied to Ott's house, were good farmers." Old feuds underlay Ott's words, and Dolvid's answer was as bland as he could make it.

Ott's face told him he was half-way there; feuds, yes, but they were not the reason for revolt. Dolvid ventured, "But the less-good farmers perhaps might be better friends with the tax-assessor."

Ott's nod was just like *Menadhi* encouraging him to go on. Bolan had a dour face, but Dolvid dared, "The *rabhsai* wants taxation to be fair everywhere in his realm." Ott waited for something else. The nature of the country, where a farm might have to take in marshes and other useless land, suggested what it must be; this had been an issue before, in other regions of patchwork fertility. "If one farmer is allowed to choose between assessment by yield or by acreage, then everyone must have the same right. That can be a written guarantee."

Ott nodded at him as a clever lad, but Bolan's scowl was deepening. All that prevented an outburst, probably, was his desire not to be embarrassed on a subject he knew nothing about. Yet he easily had power to make this rash-sounding promise, and to see it kept: fairly apportioned taxes authentically were a policy of this *rabhsayum*.

"But now — " Dolvid prodded Ott.

"Now, the others are all gone. Some of them are dead, some ran away from the out-men — different things have happened. If we could have peace again, I would want to settle Ottsvale with men of Ott — not only my close kin, but others who look to me. My farm always needed a strip of pasture by the river, and a patch of woodland. Let me divide up Ottsvale, and it will be done fairly."

Dolvid had been carrying a roll of documents under his arm, the largest a rough map of Ottsvale and its surrounds, prepared with the help of Stanni and others who knew the country. Gathering six stones for use as weights, he spread the map on the ground. Ott watched intently.

"Can you read this?" Dolvid asked.

Bolan spoke at last. "We're not at a land-giving. This is the Province of Ân, not new empire."

"But if peace comes," Ott said, "there'll be a stampede to grab up empty farmlands, unless settlements can be made beforehand. Not all former owners can be found. The *Nim'* gave land above Sebira to ones who fled, and not many would ever come back. Is there going to be no land for those who stayed here and fought?"

As the man bent over the map Dolvid murmured, "That might depend on who they were fighting."

Ott smiled bleakly, but straightened again to say, "With enemies on all sides, there's no chance for *we might be friends if only such-and-such*. We did not shoot your Shumat, and we've done more warring against out-men, this past two years, than the soldiers have."

"Show us the extent of Ottsvale — " taking a piece of charcoal from his pocket, and marked in a small X. "Here we are. This is the ridge. This is where the river runs."

"Then this is the road for the city. The Pass is this way. A good map. This — this would be the hill with shape of an Owani nose? Where the road makes a loop? Good." Using these landmarks Ott could outline the boundaries of his empire, an amazingly modest one, less land than Vinilat of Dramal left wild as his private hunting-lands.

"This is very much what we discussed," Dolvid told Bolan, putting him into a state between relief and new apprehension. He had approved boundaries no one thought Ott would ever accept.

By mid-afternoon, with Bolan still insisting he had made no promises, Dolvid, steadily accumulating items for a draft agreement, found it hard to believe there would not be amnesty and a treaty. The day had grown unseasonably warm; Bradhinal, losing interest in detailed haggling, and with it the stiff-necked awareness of representing his father, was swapping jokes with three of Ott's bowmen. At some juncture Ardi Otts-son had been allowed to join the discussions, and Shumat, only casually watched by his guards, strolled over to offer his comments.

With him came the slender, dark-haired girl he had been keeping near him. Strong-limbed but light on her feet, she was dressed properly by her people's standards in a woman's breeches and a square-necked shirt; no beauty, she had the prettiness of her youth and quick changes of expression. She was Ott's one daughter, Manda, with no resemblance to her father, although her chin had the same sometimes-stubborn set as her mother's. Mandellis kept a close eye on the pair, once heading them off when (perhaps) they were about to wander into the brush; Shumat accepted the interference with a smile. Just as well; Shumat was no Owani, or city-bred Mixed, who could plead ignorance of old-fashioned Gabhanil ways; a few minutes of pleasure-taking by him and Manda could have wrecked any hope for an agreement.

Ott had a ponderous kind of ironic humor, and pride in how well he was informed. Bolan having showed sign of thawing, he told him, "Captain, while a third of all your men sit up there on the ridge, and you have nearly as many again lurking over here to westward in case you decide on battle, part of my bowmen with my eldest son are keeping watch on an encampment of out-men. They are getting hungry, and with nothing on the road to steal, they'll be looking this way again."

Bolan did not argue about his concealed squadrons. "How many out-men are there in all?"

"The camp we are watching is about one hundred, but that's with their women. All told? Hard to say. They are not fighting for justice, or their rights. They bicker among themselves, and only need makes them band together. Away from Ottsvale, north and east of Yuvakh Din, out-men are sitting on farms not two hours from the city. Are they allies to these nearer ones? Could they be allies, if things went bad for them? Let me say this: they promise to protect the very men they've robbed, and there'll be men to listen to them and join them, so long as — " He broke off with one of his heavy shrugs.

"So long as the *rabhsai* gives nothing to hope for but death," Mandellis spat out.

"Talk!" Shumat, with inexplicable violence. "When can we finish with this chit-chatting, and do some man's work?" He slapped at the sword now back at his hip. They were coming to the last swooping bend in the road before it climbed to the gates of Yuvakh Din. Against evening sky the citadel was a bleak shadow.

True, the ride back had been filled with controversy, not yet done with, but possibly the long, inconsummate day spent with Manda Otts-daughter had more to do with Shumat's loud impatience. Yet it had been hiss bold seeking out of Ott that began all the talk. History at first hand had elusive themes much subtler than the large, inevitable movements of history read; if Bolan had found any other for his lieutenant there would have been no parley, and the *rabhsai*'s forces would be committed to a long war of attrition — Bolan would never have dared carry out his threat of leaving Antrovai to his failures, pressing on to cheaper glory at Narn.

He, Bolan, agreement with Ott hovering, had maintained he must submit the whole question to Kadon Dinul. But that, as both Dolvid and Shumat protested, meant a delay of not less than two weeks, much longer if the *rabhsai* was in no mood for making decisions, or was playing down at Tan Lughsai, or both. It was precisely because such delay could be dangerous that Bolan had been given wide discretionary powers, and Dolvid, who by now had read every word of the Royal Warrant, assured their commander he did indeed have the authority, on his own, of granting everything discussed for the treaty, even including an amnesty, not confined to the Ottsvale rebels, but to be offered generally.

"How can we pardon all the crimes?" Bolan complained. "And there'll be new murders and new robberies. Antrovai may be worn small by too much responsibility, but he's no fool. He'll say this agreement makes his garrison work impossible, and it'll all be in my lap — resettlement, boundaries, arbitrating disputes — this is the trap I've always feared. I should have ordered a general attack on Ott and his whole household, while we had them there. He bragged about knowing we had squadrons on his flank, but he didn't have any strength to counter them."

"Oh, that would have made Antrovai lord of the dungpile," Shumat said. "We three would all have been killed, and Bradhinal. The battle might have been won in the end, if there was anyone left to tell the cavalry they had to dismount — Ott had about fifty bowmen in the brush, where riders couldn't come at them."

"A time limit," Dolvid said, to prevent fresh argument. The plan grew as he explained it: Bolan should proclaim there was to be amnesty for and a treaty with the Ottsvale men in, say, a week, and anyone else could have the same terms if they agreed to the same, the end of occupying lands not their own, reacceptance of lawful authority, liability to levy for war against the out-men. Names of all those claiming ownership of lands held by others could be entered on a roll of cases, to be adjudicated later, after the region was pacified. Bolan could ask Daënakh to set up a court, and an expert in law could be sent from Kadon Dinul to represent the *rabhsai* — a special magistrate, like the one appointed to settle such affairs when the War of the Widowed came to an end.

"See what it is to read history?" admiringly, delighted to hear he could avoid getting bogged down in civil affairs. "You think this might work?" The question was for Shumat.

"If we play fair with Ott. At first there'll be plenty to say it's a trap, and Ott must be getting old and stupid to fall for it. The period for amnesty will have to extend beyond the treaty with Ott, so others can see we're living up to it."

Shumat was getting cleverer; in this innocent recital there was a masked warning to Bolan not to dream of treachery.

That done, Shumat went on to say, Ott's name would be enough to sway many rebels, especially when it could be used as a threat as well. In fact the offer of amnesty should make clear all those who refused it would have to take their chances against new strength of royal and provincial forces, *together with their allies*. Everyone would guess that meant Ott's bowmen, and fear it, men who knew every wrinkle of this mazed country, all the hiding-places and sites for ambush.

"Everyone," Bolan said. "In this country, how can *everyone* hear about this proclamation, all in a few days?"

"They can," confidently.

Nervous about both weather and the chance for pilfering, Dolvid moved the larger part of the supplies into what had been the busiest and was certainly the largest mill at Yuvakh Din. The owner had left, perhaps for good, when revolt disrupted harvests; relief supplies sent from Sebira had included milled flour, not grain.

Unlike the encampment, it was within the city walls, perched on the northward slope, where one of the main torrents feeding the lake below had turned the giant mill-wheel, now disengaged and silent. The building itself was stone-built and sound, with a courtyard where wagons could come, useful hoists, and plenty of dry and airy storage space. Guards and workmen had quarters off the courtyard, and there was living-space above, where Dolvid had installed his work-table, a couple of chairs and a bunk.

He sat up into the night working at documents requested by Bolan on his way to what might be a stormy dinner with Antrovai; the treaty with Ott, proclamation of limited amnesty, dispatches, one for the *rabhsai*'s own eyes (that really meant, direct to Rhunsilakh). Yes, but Bolan, and not by oversight, had not actually assented to anything. Nevertheless, he had told Dolvid to dwell on the lives that could be saved by the reconciliation, the restored revenues, the advantages for the forthcoming Narn expedition — as so often, a man convincing himself.

By lamplight Dolvid made up details for the amnesty. It could not include crimes against the *rabhsai* or his goods — by law, that meant any traveller and any goods carried on the main road, and the distinction might help separate those involved in the many private wars from mere raiders.

The Ottsvale men, with an established leader, were a special case, and for most others laying down of arms would signal acceptance of amnesty. Many who did so, unable to return to farms and villages controlled or threatened by out-men, would be somewhere between prisoners and a numerous addition to the squalid lakeside encampment. They would need food — but that would be true without the amnesty. A further condition must be surrender of all hidden stocks of foodstuffs, so they could be shared out, and that meant someone to oversee the sharing. There were dealers in Yuvakh Din, but none to be trusted not to look for ways to make a profit from seized supplies. Curiously, the city had no government of its own,; if there had ever been an hereditary local ruler, as at Dônshei or Irbat, or a council of elders such as many cities had, no one said what had become of them; no law was left except the military commander's, the last real magistrate having been murdered a year ago.

The city had been abandoned, also, by the *Atarlum*. Dolvid made a note for the general dispatch, to mention there was work here for as many *ramidul* as could come, sick children and adults, many unhealed wounds. The *Mankh'*, of course was aware how little Owani blood was here, and he did not expect much result, unless they could by some means be shamed into it, or unless — and he decided this request would be, rather, for the *rabhsai*'s dispatch, appending the phrase, *this might be brought to the attention of* g'Asalladh' *Himself.*

He yawned, wishing for *raminat*, and also for a few *ôdul* lanterns, so he would not have to keep trimming the wick of his one smelly lamp. Watchfires were yellow below, reflected in the lake and also in the camp beyond the walls; their loneliness in the black brought him a penetrating sense of an unknown world; roads, message-riders, dispatches were fragile threads with no holding strength, giving only an illusion of control.

A guard at the courtyard entrance barked out a challenge. Rattle of hoofs, bang of the outer door, booted feet thumping on stairs. Dolvid opened his door just as Bolan came from the other side into the little vestibule which, when the mill was working, would have kept clouds of flour from billowing into the living-quarters.

Bolan had drunk wine. He was a little wild-eyed, his normally smoothed hair sticking up in spikes. "She's a lovely lady," he said, coming through and throwing his gauntlets on a chair. "The wife of Antrovai. She was born in the Heartland, but wouldn't live at Kadon Dinul again if you gave her a Residence Quarter house. Hah."

Dolvid had briefly met her, a pale-faced woman who was wrapped in what seemed aloofness, but might only be the sour boredom of her life here. There were no children.

"How was her dinner?" deliberately setting calm against the obscure danger of Bolan's mood.

"Mutton. We care only for plain food, now, and fashion means nothing to us." Having reversed a chair and seated himself astride, he gazed at space, chin resting on hands resting on the chair-back.

"Antrovai is sure I'm mad. Is the *rabhsai*'s dispatch done?"

"Hardly started. We have to settle the — "

"I must have it tomorrow. We'll make sure it goes by

water from Sebira, unless you can find out if the roads are clear by now — fast-messengers would be better then. I have a special seal for urgent dispatches. We must have Lambarr's ratification as soon as can be."

"All you can do is get Rhunsilakh to bring it to his attention."

"Aye. It would be good if I had Laluvoi's ear. I might send word to Khelagh, but..."

He broke off. That was twice he had mentioned the prominent landowner, Khelagh, but though influential among the Families, what he could do to speed approval of a treaty escaped Dolvid.

"It's going to be my head or Antrovai's," Bolan resumed. "I have no desire to break him, but he is forcing this; he'll go behind my back. Do you trust Shumat?"

Dolvid almost began a laugh, then seeing this was serious, said quite flatly, "Of course."

"I know where I am with you. I can't see what you want for yourself, but it's nothing that's mine. If Ott betrays us, I'm finished, that's flat. Antrovai says he is sure to. I must be mad, letting myself be caught in promises; I could have killed him today. A few warm days and the Pass will be open — we could have ridden for Narn, and left Antrovai to steep in his own sour pressings. What if Daënakh sides with Antrovai? This is all Shumat's doing."

Hard to connect the dinner with Antrovai to this torrent of doubts. "You have other news?"

Bolan blinked at him. "Paired squadrons are overdue, one of ours, and Provincials with Daënakh's man, Pranuvi. Because of the parley we only had five squadrons in the field. Pranuvi was engaged by bows, north of the hamlet. He chased the ambushers, lost touch with the paired squadron, one of the cobbled-up ones, half of it Household under Kennar, who's General Cavalry. Last word from him, he was going after Pranuvi's lot."

"They may only have ridden too far and been caught by nightfall."

"We can't lose a hundred men in a day's campaigning. It will come out I had more than ten squadrons tied down for the parley with Ott — Pranuvi was the only senior officer in the field. A provincial, Zhôl have mercy."

Dolvid wished Shumat was here to help calm Bolan. "Today, as far as I can tell, was the only good day's business for these parts in years. It's not as if your ten squadrons were wasting time in foolish games."

"There's going to be a full muster at dawn, and I'll take out six, eight squadrons in person. I'll crush these ambushers. Should we hold up the amnesty for Ott?"

"Why?"

"He bragged about having bowmen in the field. What if talks were just a ruse to keep most of us occupied, while he waylaid our squadrons? He knows too much about what we're doing."

No convincing a man who wanted to be tormented with doubt. "You have seen the man's face." That, and the force of Ott's personality, far beyond the tactics of Shumat and Dolvid, were what had carried Bolan along, till he was left with the unexpected treaty. Not recognizing this, Bolan, once away from Ott's compelling presence, was bewildered by what he had agreed to.

"Treachery — there's nothing worse. A man has to have allies he can trust. Banak was right to stand alone."

"He trusted Saidhan."

"And I have Shumat, you mean?"

He had meant no such thing; he would not have dreamt of comparing Bolan to Banak-rai. Not noticing his astonishment, Bolan continued, "What about Shumat with the prime filly of Ott's. Can that do anything for us?"

"Keeping in mind the risks, but he's aware of that. Ott's people can be touchy when it comes to violation of a maidenhead or a married sash."

"What do you know about it, out of the *Mankh*?"

"Quite enough — " not ready to explain further.

"Have you found a woman here?"

"On the north side of the market square, the inn there." He assumed Bolan was asking a different question. "But half your army will hear about it next day."

"What does that matter? No, you're right, it's no good for a commander to have the whole camp gossiping about which way he prefers it. You haven't brought a woman here? Is that the only bed?"

"There is another set of rooms across the stair. I could have a bunk put in there."

"You have wine?"

"That could be brought, too. Or do you mean, now? There's nettle-milk. I could warm it on the lamp."

"Don't bother." He fell silent, chin on hands.

A problem had been troubling Dolvid. "We'll have to keep Ott and the *Kimukan* Indhil apart. The bad blood there could wreck the treaty."

Bolan grunted, not attentive. Then, "Dolvid, you're such a — *sage*. Weren't you ever young? Don't you ever dream?"

"I told you seven years ago what I wanted."

"To know? Always the same? I never forgot that. Great dong of Raëdh," Bolan blasphemed, standing, knocking the chair over with a bang. "You're such a grave-opener, all shuttered up with parchment and lamp-oil. Don't you wonder what it feels like to ride at the head of five hundred lances? What about haggling with that old rogue Ott, and getting more than you asked for? Haven't you ever been worked at by a woman till you could not prop on an elbow?"

"You are mustering at daybreak?" pointedly.

"What? Yes — " struggling against a new fit of anxiety about the overdue squadrons. "We may have to be days afield — you'll have that dispatch for me to look over? You could ride with us part way, and take any alterations I want — is that possible?"

"Possible, yes, but I can't explain a treaty that is not yet fully drafted." Dolvid rattled pens and rustled pages on his work-table. "I have work to do."

"I'll leave you then. Don't mind what I say — a man has to follow his nature." Bolan bent to pick up the chair. Seated again, he gave no sign of leaving. "It would be a good thing if you could devise a way of bringing supplies forward, so we can make long sorties away from the road — there'll be need for this after the Pass of Perus."

"I have given thought to it — " and had suggested it to Bolan.

Now, brooding, Bolan chewed over the army, naming every squadron-leader in his command. The shortage of senior officers troubled him; there were only five *kímukan*, instead of the eight to ten there should be, but to advance any of the young squadron-leaders over others before they had a chance to prove themselves in battle would only provoke jealousies.

"Antrovai. He just won't — he has some experienced squadron officers, but how am I to tell which way their loyalty lies? Besides, he's got them all filled with his despair. Antrovai! You'd think he would welcome our coming, or have the brains to keep quiet, claim a share in our success, or else crow if we make a mess of it. But men who fail too often come to need the pain of it. I wonder why his lovely wife has stayed?"

No new subjects could be found. "Well, you want to be at your scrawling." He stood.

"Goodnight, Bolan. Till daybreak." It was not so far away.

After struggle, he spoke again. "I have a dream, once in a while. I am commanding in battle, and when I ride forward my men won't follow me. This is not anything I fear when I am awake."

He could not manage any answer. "Tell the *rabhsai* — " he began. "Well, you'll think of what to say. You are a good fellow, Dolvid."

"I must — " gesturing with the pen.

"Without a couple of hours' sleep, I'll be fit for nothing."

"Goodnight, Bolan."

"Write plain. I may have to read in the saddle."

Dolvid bent to his work. Opening the inner door, Bolan stood without moving. His audible breathing made Dolvid uneasy.

"You might say good night."

"Your pardon. Goodnight, then."

"The dream I told you about — there's no need to repeat that to anyone. To Shumat."

"Of course."

"You're a good fellow, Dolvid. Goodnight."

"Goodnight, Bolan." He was gone.

In grey morning while Bolan was readying his relief force, two men of the Provincial Cavalry brought word of both strayed squadrons. Their own, though suffering one killed and some wounded, including Pranuvi himself, was in good order, watching dense woodland where the raiders, thought to be more than one hundred strong, had taken refuge. They were in touch with the other squadron, a couple of miles away in open country, camped on the enemy's most probable westward line of retreat; they were expected to prefer breaking out southward, where they could go from cover to cover, provided they could recross the road where the provincial cavalry was spread thin.

That would take them to the fringes of Ott's country, and Shumat, saying this was a chance for Ott to show good faith, set out at once for Ottsvale with his own squadron, leading twenty-five of the saddle-horses lent by Daënakh. A little later Bolan, after telling Dolvid impatiently his cursed scribbling would have to wait its turn, led out the main force, and not till evening did Dolvid hear the full story from tired and elated men.

When Bolan met the Provincials on the road, the enemy had already slipped across. Meanwhile, Shumat, coming up from Ottsvale having lent mounts to a company of picked bows, including Ott and two of his sons, found the raiders, and used his squadron to protect the bows against a sudden rush. Ott's archers, he said, outshot the enemy by thirty paces, and were able to flush them from hiding. Evading Shumat's lances, they fled straight into the path of Bolan's slower advance from northward.

A tough remnant of enemy tried to make a stand on a low, bushy ridge, and Bradhinal of Ân, not waiting to be supported, led the charge that broke and scattered them. "Idiocy," Shumat insisted. "The sheer nonsense of it is what beat them — imagine, charging uphill on broken ground, squadron all out of formation — horrible. Luckily their bows had about a dozen arrows left among the lot of them, and those they shot wild in their disbelief."

Of twenty-eight prisoners, only a few belonged in the Yuvakh Din country, but nearly half were women. Like alliance with Ott, granting of quarter had come in advance of the offer of amnesty.

On the day of the signing Ott rode in to Yuvakh Din, a slouched giant in the saddle, and got a big welcome. Not only from the encampment beside the lake, or the recently-amnestied; ordinary townspeople gathered by the gate and in the market-place to cheer him as if a victor. Bolan had squadrons standing to arms, and the colors were dipped for Ott at the head of eighty bowmen, auxiliary soldiers of the realm. Shumat's squadron was riding escort, and in the midst of Bolan's camp there were handclasps, followed by speeches filled with hope.

Most lasting memory of the day was Antrovai. Still refusing to have anything to do with the treaty, he put two squadrons in the forecourt above, as if Ott was going to change his mind and storm the fortress. In the midst of all the clamor for Ott's arrival, Dolvid's eye went up to the distant, rigid figure of the mounted Antrovai, watching. Here, he had spent years and lives with the wrong war, fighting for law, yes, but law turned into oppression by corrupt tax-gatherers. What was going on behind that pale face was hard to imagine, but Dolvid felt pity for a devotion to duty that made an honest soldier into a faithful, failed defender of injustice.

The Pass of Perus

The hasty plan of Shumat's that won their bigger fight quickly became normal tactics for war against the out-men. When a raiding-party was sighted, bowmen provided with mounts would be escorted to where they could advance on foot as skirmishers, cavalry hovering behind and at the flanks, ready to charge when the enemy tried closing with the bows, or to pursue any retreat. Participation had cost Ott some men, including a nephew, but his clan remained leaders of the bows, even when joined by many men not from Ottsvale. As amnesty made added levies available, infantry carrying long pikes gave close support to the archers, helping to reduce losses. The enemy fought mainly with knives and short swords, and once driven into the open had no chance of standing up to *péfrapravádal*, having few horses, those mostly ill-fed.

Spring thaw was under way, and every stream was swollen, marshes full, spreading over lower-lying farmlands. Between Yuvakh Din and the foothills, farmhouses and the ways joining them kept to higher ground, and as wide stretches of lowland became uninhabitable the policy of garrisoning larger farms and keeping them linked with strong patrols became increasingly effective; the out-men had no choice but to move into narrower uplands, or retreat into the foodless hills. It was rumored large bands were beginning to gather eastward towards the Pass, whether for a withdrawal out of this inhospitable country or a trial of strength with the soldiery remained to be seen. Closer, weary and half-starved men and women often waited at roadside to give up without fight; others kept trying to ambush soldiers or supplies. There were quick attacks on farmhouses, where half-files of soldiery supported by bowmen defended themselves till their signal-trumpets could bring cavalry to their relief. The line of secured farmsteads crept eastward, and behind it Shumat and Ott hunted down lessening enemy bands.

Most of this Dolvid heard of and wrote about rather than saw. Bolan was dispatching daily, even half-daily reports to Kadon Dinul, and every day Dolvid tried to convince him over-use of superlatives created an effect opposite to the one intended. In Bolan's versions, mainly reworked from Shumat's descriptions, not a day, barely an hour went by without accomplishments that were glorious or unprecedented; the behavior of his forces superb or incomparable, results magnificent.   Even after heavy pruning, these accounts of skirmishing over a few miles of ground made overripe reading, and were sure to create skeptics at Kadon Dinul.

He was busy with many other jobs; as soon as reasonably safe he established a forward camp, just to the near side of the hamlet, a third or more of the distance from Yuvakh Din to the Pass. The road there swerved past a hill, steep-sided with outcroppings of bare rock, though sloping less abruptly behind, on the north to northwest side. The narrow tracks which came down to the road just by the hamlet were the real starting-line for many patrols, and his supply-camp on the hill was only just staked out when Bolan saw it and wanted it enlarged to accommodate added cavalry.

Cattle-owners of this country used lightweight, densely woven willow hurdles for movable fences, secured by lashing to stout trestles, which in turn were pegged into the ground. Enough were collected to enclose the whole camp in a single line of hurdles, even at the head of slopes almost sheer, but where an attack was most likely there was a triple line.

For this work no soldiers were taken from regular duties. Men just amnestied, mostly gaunt and bright-eyed from living wild, were glad to be rewarded with their meals and safe sleeping-space, and a little later when a few prisoners from the terrible out-men were added, it was hard to tell much difference. One of those men suggested a defensive ditch, broad and straight-sided, between the first and second fences on the more gently sloping side of the hill; tangles of thorn were cut and pushed into this outwork. Where the slope was longest a road of sorts was made, filling low-spots with packed earth and bundles of brush. In the event of an attack, the gateway gap could be closed with hurdles. Wagons were rolling down under escort from Yuvakh Din with sacks and barrels, lumpy swathed shapes of salt meat; long wicker platforms kept supplies off the ground, and for bad weather there were tarred canvases. Dolvid risked unpopularity insisting the scoured barrels within the camp be kept filled with fresh water, though a stream wandered down from the hills not fifty paces outside. No one seriously expected a camp so often busy with the coming and going of heavily-armed soldiers to be besieged, but so much food must tempt the starving, and desperate men might try anything.

Any question not directly concerned with fighting soon became Dolvid's; map-making, timely baking of bread, keeping the roll of land-disputes pending, and a list of skills among the amnestied that could be drawn on: smithing, harness-making, sewing, bootmaking, carpentry. He was not idle, and had chosen his part, but could feel wistful watching the day's squadrons riding out in misty morning, and coming back late with their tales of battle.

Shumat punched at his shoulder. "Put a sword on, and I'll show you tactics. Ott calls me Pir Perus — well, but where would we be if I hadn't brought him in on our side? This flanking move we made — " The point of his account was, very few leaders could have brought cavalry already engaged into column swiftly enough to round both enemy bows and a patch of bog. This action had resulted in a haul of eight prisoners, and Dolvid questioned privately how hot the fight could have been, but wondered more at this new self-praising Shumat. In some way it linked to Manda Otts-daughter, or to his unbedded yearnings. "She obeys her mother, always," he once said irritably, but when Dolvid remarked what a pleasant and pretty girl she was, Shumat was brusque. "Here at realm's edge, perhaps. At Kadon Dinul, who would give her a second glance?"

From the summit of the hill where standards of Ân and the realm flew side by side, the mountains seemed nearer each day, as deep color crept up their white flanks.

"That cursed country is all traps," Onebhal said at one of the captains' meetings. "I lost a man yesterday, an arrow from among rocks, and couldn't leave the road to give chase."

"How many enemy are up there?" Shumat demanded.

"My men say out-men are making a big camp, overlooking the road." Ott waved a massy hand. "Up near the last climb for the Pass."

"Here we're straining the dregs," Shumat said. "Only twenty captured yesterday, fourteen in one haul, where the fir-woods are, over north, most of those women and children. I hear the women were too famished to give much sport." He nudged Ott.

"I won't have any rape in this army," Bolan, sharply.

"Then fight the war with eunuchs. Easy, Bolan, they were Household men. The women were willing enough, for the chance of a half-loaf."

Dolvid fought off revulsion: the women would live now, and reach a place when they could choose; quite a few of the widowed and never-married among the amnestied were serving the needs of the army for their keep. Sad all the same to ask what had become of the Shumat whose eyes misted over when he first saw the squalor of the lakeside camp. Ott, too: here was a father who by Gabhanil rules would try to kill his friend Shumat if he took Manda, with Manda's consent, even at her urging. How could he grin about women bought with camp-bread?

Dolvid said, "We should not cling too long to our line of farms."

"Too long!" Shumat, with the near-bored manner he had adopted for any comment on strategy from the non-soldier. "It's only now starting to succeed. We're beginning to take some foodstuffs prisoner — even you must call that a victory."

"I do," ignoring sarcasm. "But enough hunger is bound to make the enemy strike westward again."

"Let them come,"

Dolvid reminded him of what he must know: there was not the strength to hold the long line of garrisoned farms, nor cavalry to reinforce them all, especially if attacks came at two or more points simultaneously. "Once they can break back into the country we call safe, raiding begins again."

"No, no," Bolan said. "This campaign is going to be fought only once. We should be thinking of Narn."

"They might yet strike at Yuvakh Din," Dolvid said.

"Oh, just let them," Shumat, fervently. "A rabble against the city — even Antrovai would bestir himself. If only we could tempt them to try it! That battle could settle everything west of the Pass."

At this, Bolan's eyes gleamed, but clearly, while such an attack would certainly fail, that probably would not be till after the enemy broke into the city. Here, all at once, he was supported by Bradhinal, normally shy and awkward at these conferences. After the fight decided by his charge, and the earlier wounding of Pranuvi (now recuperating and helping to train recruits at Yuvakh Din) he had become, with no formal declaration, field leader of the Provincials, usually content to be Bolan's or Shumat's subordinate, part of their plans. Now he found his voice. "A soldier is paid to protect lawkeeping citizenry, not use them as bait for a battle."

"But if the enemy, taking the bait, destroys himself — " Bolan said.

"Antrovai," sure this would win the debate, "could say, when things were worst, he at least kept Yuvakh Din free from assault."

Shumat made a face, but Bolan was warily waiting for word from Kadon Dinul to ratify his treaties. "What we need, then is a way to force a decisive fight, without putting the city at risk."

That wish for the one big battle harked back to their first conference, the three of them, at Irbat. They had all changed since then, not all for the worse, but he wished Shumat could have a naked hour with Manda, and lose that hunter's eye.

Gradually, with no orders to that effect, without ever saying he would, Dolvid found himself making sure no one starved, not prisoners, nor the recently-amnestied, nor, in the end, those living in the swollen encampment at Yuvakh Din. The early days after the treaties there had been a mood of sharing, but that soon vanished; many whispered the troops would ride away and lawlessness return. Stored foodstuff was being withheld, and he had to ask for troops, recruits and new levies with a scattering of regulars for officers, so as to enforce seizure. Next, men unsuitable for fighting were drafted to assist with distribution; Dolvid paid for what was taken, and obtained payment in money or work for what was given out, but prices he helped fix made him unpopular with the meat and grain dealers at Yuvakh, who had hoped for large profits out of shortage.

His days were shared between the forward camp and the city. It was in his quarters above the mill he was next together with all the main leaders. Both Ott and Shumat had slight wounds to be attended to, and Bolan had come to draft dispatches.

He was worried over the most recent fight. "How many others were hurt?" he asked Shumat.

"Most, one way or another. We had four killed; blade-to-blade at the finish — difficult ground, but we had them caught. I killed their leader myself." He exchanged smiles with Ott.

"I was hoping to form two new squadrons," Bolan complained. "If all the best-trained have to be used as replacements — "

"You can't fight without losses. Theirs were much higher."

"If you had them trapped, couldn't you have waited for reinforcements? Why fight on equal terms?"

"You want to go back to Antrovai's way, waiting for help? We've got the upper hand now."

"We've got Narn to think of."

Shumat became rigid. "Are you saying, I was wrong to fight? Give my job to one who doesn't mind being called coward, if you're dissatisfied with how I'm conducting war in the field."

"I didn't say that — be easy. It was a brave fight. Dolvid can tell you how I've praised you; Kadon Dinul must be sick of your name."

Shumat stayed stiff-necked. "You can have my command whenever you want. I would not want to spoil better tactics."

"I'll keep it in mind," drily. "A fat fool I'd look at the Residence, relieving an officer I've sung to the skies."

Ott, perhaps designedly, dispersed tensions with a report from his scouts. Out-men were gathering again near the foot of the Pass; hundreds were in the stronghold there, but very short of food, to judge by the stench of roasting horse-meat.

"What about the *drin'loi*?" Dolvid asked. The blockhouse at the head of the Pass kept coming to mind.

"Don't doubt the horse-eaters have it," Ott said. "I haven't had a man up that far, but the road is clear, or nearly." Of snow, he meant.

Bolan had news, too. A large farm in the north, Allistead, had been raided yesterday by a strong party, a well-planned attack, winning some supplies, the raiders vanishing before cavalry could come up.

Ott, glumly, "Yes, Alli — an important man in that country."

"That's in the sandhills?" Shumat asked. "Well, we can't be everywhere at once." But he was restless to be back in the saddle. This was what fear had predicted; Allistead was supposed to be secure behind the line of defended farms.

He stayed reluctantly to hear a plan already discussed with Bolan, to force the big battle they wanted. It was quite simple: rumors would be put out that they meant to establish a camp farther forward, beyond the Pass of Perus, both to open his campaign for Narn, and to cut off retreat by out-men. A train of wagons would be used to bait an attack, with the mass of cavalry kept back till the enemy appeared.

After asking for more details, Ott gave his near-royal approval. "A good plan, if the horse-eaters bite."

"Aye," Shumat said. "We can't rely on this enemy. Fighting them in the field, they don't always do what we ask."

"At worst," Bolan said, "we can seize the *drin'loi* and hold it."

When the other two had gone, Ott with his arm over Shumat's shoulders, Bolan turned as if to apologize for his second-in-command. "He's not last month's Shumat, but he knows how to lead in a fight. If he was at Kadon, with his victories, he could have any woman he wanted for the price of a grin. Hero of the hour, and the only thighs he wants to spread belong to little Manda."

"He can't have that, unless he makes certain avowals."

Bolan moaned. "What would she do that's any different?"

In light without color before dawn on a damp, chill day, wagons rolled slowly down the hill, double-teamed for the long climb. Behind came a dozen loaded packhorses, then the second squadron of escort; Onebhal had one already assembled on the road, and Dolvid was with them. He grimaced wryly when a wagon got its rear wheel momentarily into the ditch, and was worked with little difficulty up onto the road. Any watcher would guess the wagon was empty, too late for a spy to bring that news to the enemy. He was certain the out-men must have agents near the camp or in it. His helpers had loaded the wagons with foodstuffs and other supplies yesterday, but picked men had unloaded them again well past midnight.

Column formed, the cavalry moved out at a walk, big *pefral* shaking their heads, wishing for a better pace. Orders, for no particular reason, were being conveyed in undertones. They passed through the sleeping hamlet, and a mile beyond, where the road climbed on a curve between dark swellings, a halt was made. Dolvid dismounted to peer into the brush. A soft call came, and with little noise the looming form of Ott appeared, bow slung, a sheaf of arrows hanging at his chest. Behind came two of his sons, Ardi, and the married one, Ottar. From cover other bowmen were appearing, immediately to vanish again under wagon-covers, twelve to fifteen men to each wagon. Back near the hamlet a cock crew.

The column moved slowly, the way always uphill, the big draft-horses with some burden. Going was firm, but Onebhal said they would strike mud where the road levelled and then dipped a little before the true assault on the mountains. "That might be the place for an ambush," he suggested.

"Farther up, I would say. They would expect a fight for the wagons, and they know we have signal trumpets."

"I hope the Under-Captain stays near enough to hear ours, if we have to sound them."

"They can't be too close. We want to draw enemy to us, not frighten them off. Shumat will not let them savage us, unless — " and Dolvid fell into the soldier's way of speaking his worst fears — "unless they miss their way, or find a task that interests them more."

Onebhal grunted. Phrases written so often about the courage of these men were coming to life; there was scarcely a step safe from bows that might be concealed in dark brush, among broken rocks, but this man had brought patrols this way a dozen times. Mounted bows went with the lead squadron, to discourage anything less than the full-scale assault the column hoped to attract, but the reins in Dolvid's hands felt a little slimy.

"They'll try it with the least shooting," Onebhal said. "They need animals."

To carry away what was supposed to be in the wagons. The *pefral*, too, were hugely valuable in themselves.

Climbing steadily, the column emerged on a long spur, foothills to either side, drear and barren except for clumps of matted thorn or shocks of dry growth like bundled spears, slivers of pale green pushing up from below. Dull clouds were overhead, and as a bright rim of sun edged into a narrow gap between cloud and hill, they looked rightward to the south-facing slope of a sheltered valley, where new grass was splotched with color, white, yellow and purple flowers, a glimpse into spring. Nothing was said then, but after a mile of steady progress Onebhal remarked, "Trees would be out in the Heartland."

"Well out, if spring came early. Plum, cherry-blossom. Crocus."

"Four years, I'll have my own land. Green hills."

The road swung south, soon between banks once more, no longer climbing. This was Onebhal's muddy stretch. Ahead and left the mountains were coming very near; impossible to perceive any sort of gap where the Pass must be.

"What I want to do — " Onebhal began, and without a break went on, "A scout, man with a short bow, behind that stand of growth over right. Ducked away, went up the hill, by the big rock with the yellowy streak."

"*Kímukan* —" a file-leader softly called.

"All right, all right, I've seen him. Don't — no, don't point!" As if troubled by a twisted stirrup-leather Onebhal bent over, letting the lead lancers come up to him. "You, drop back and alert Ott's men, and pass the word to Kennar's squadron. No fussing about."

As the file-leader — it was Norlum — edged out of line and let others pass him, Onebhal kicked the flanks of his horse, and came back up to Dolvid. "Will you go to one of the wagons?"

"Not yet, I want to see. This was my plan."

"No reason for getting in the way of an arrow. You're not dressed, so to speak — " knuckling at his breastplate. Body-armor had saved many lives in the campaign, and not dressed was just how he felt, also without a helm. But Shumat's remarks, near enough to taunts, stayed with him, and he would not cower in a wagon.

For half an hour nothing happened. The road, here in very poor repair, made a long swing left, climbing more steeply, draft-horses plodding. On either side the embankments fell back, mounted, merged with refolding hills, juts of rock, spurts of brush. Then a sharp turn back right, and the towering walls miraculously parted, right-hand wedge drifting rightward as they climbed. A slash of cloud-covered sky plunged deep; they were looking up into the Pass of Perus. Cool eddies of wind came with a prickle of fine rain. Mouth tight, Onebhal glanced at Dolvid.

"We'll go on."

At the rear a man said he had heard the drum of hoofs. Onebhal called a halt, lead squadron keeping watch to the front, rearward lances faced about. A single rider came round the last sharp bend, going hard. A cavalryman, an officer, lanceless, Shumat.

"We've got them," he panted out, as Dolvid and Onebhal walked down to greet him. He and his horse were plastered with mud. "The valley about six miles back — we saw the tail of a large column of men on the far rim, headed westward. They must have thought it safe to move after you'd gone past. We could count about sixty, but that's only the part we saw; they have their women with them. It's just luck we saw them."

"This might be a ruse," Dolvid said, "to draw you away. When have they ever shown large numbers so openly?"

Shumat's hunting blood was up. "I told you when you made your plan, what this enemy might do need not be what you expect. You have to change to meet circumstances. I wish we hadn't given you so many of the best bows. Where's Ott?"

"Here." He had slipped out at the tail of his wagon and was nearby.

"If only we had horses for your men — "

"No. We'll be needed at the little fort."

He accepted that. "If it's defended at all, it won't be in any strength." He spoke to Onebhal. "We may need bowmen; I'll get word to you. They could double-ride with *péfrapravádal* if they had to. If the enemy retreats this way, you can hold them with your forces. I'll send word before the day's out."

Dolvid tried again. "Would you not consider keeping to the plan with a part of your force, four squadrons, three?"

"Bradhinal has already taken three cross-country to head off the enemy; I can't spare more. This is our best chance of smashing them. Look, Dol — " in a soothing tone which increased irritation. "If it is a trick, we'll find out soon enough, and follow you, no harm done. Just wait up at the Pass."

"Aye," Onebhal said. "Good hunting."

Shumat caused his *pefrai* to rear as he wheeled. They watched him out of sight round the bend.

"We're missing the real fight after all, then."

"I hope that's true." For this he got an odd grunt. Onebhal probably shared Shumat's view of his proper talents. That did not annoy him as much as how Shumat, where no one could do better than guess, was letting experience persuade him he could not be wrong. But it did not take any knowledge of war to see that the enemy, if they had sent out a strong raiding-party, would all the more want to hold on to the *drin'loi* and a possible way of escape.

The doubts must have shown in Dolvid's face; Onebhal said, "They're strange fighters, these."

At the end of the long, straight climb they came to the true foot of the Pass. Beside the patchy road there was the weathered stump of a broken column, reverting to natural stone except for traces of an inscription, once deeply incised, blurred into silence. Many centuries ago this had been a boundary between two provinces, but when the easternmost, Naëni, fell to wilderness, its neighbor, Aëni (now Ân) grabbed the top of the Pass for a defensible frontier, where it had remained till tacitly ceded by Antrovai.

Going was very slow as the road wound across the face of a steep escarpment, sharp turns hard for the wagons, especially where rocks had rolled down onto a way already pitted and with crumbled edges. Some of the cavalry dismounted to help shove wagons over difficult places, grumbling half-joke insults at the archers invisible inside. One spot, where the road looped about a giant boulder, wheels had to be skidded sideways to clear the rock; hard to imagine how a fully loaded cart or wagon, with six times the weight of a dozen bowmen, could ever manage this. But after that there was another steady climb, fairly straight.

Half way, they could look back to the country they had crossed, south and west. Rains hung like clouds of smoke, and the straight stretch where Shumat had caught them was almost at their feet.

Onebhal called, but Dolvid saw for himself. The road, on both sides, an anthill with many entrances, was alive; bowmen, men armed with swords and with pikes, some with axes, were swarming onto the road. Heads and weapons of others could be seen among folded ground.

One group were shoving and pulling at a big rock, and as they scattered it rolled down into the roadway. From higher another boulder was handled down to fit next to the first, and many lesser rocks were being rolled and dragged to complete the barrier.

A well-chosen site, the road a clear field for archers, the ground on either flank too broken for horses. Bowmen were taking up position on the back side of their wall, others among rocks nearby.

This was only a rearguard, facing back along the road, dividing the men with the wagons from any reinforcement. The main band of out-men, not disciplined but eddying into a rough sort of order, had turned eastward, treading in the tracks of the wagons. Obviously a settled plan.

"Four hundred," Onebhal estimated, meaning those on the move.

"More," They were still coming onto the road.

"They're not in much of a hurry."

"That means they have the *drin'loi* garrisoned. They're sure we are trapped." With good reason, Dolvid did not add.

"That rabble, against Household, General Cavalry? We'll mince them, then go down and scatter their rearguard."

"No," seeing cavalry torn apart by bows they could not get at.

"No," the big, soft voice of Ott agreed. He had emerged from his wagon to make his own assessment. "They know this country better." On the hillsides faint trails could be half-discerned, and Ott gestured to where enemy bowmen separated from the main body and crossed rough ground beside the road to make straight for the steeps. Next moment they were out of sight beneath the watchers' feet.

The column would have to find cover. "How far to the head of the Pass?" Dolvid asked.

"Not far now," Ott said. "You see where the notch comes down."

"We have to have the *drin'loi*. They do not know we have bows."

The man nodded agreement, and told Onebhal, "There is a wide level where cavalry could be used, so long as enemy is cleared from the little fort above."

Onebhal, who had lost men on patrol to solitary concealed bowmen, was glad of a plan, however sketchy, to get the *péfrapravádal* to where they could be more than targets. Reluctant even now to give up surprise, he saw speed had become most important, and the archers dismounted from the wagons, each one going to the edge for a look at the enemy, pressing on in a dense mass, filled with a palpable confidence.

As the column moved forward at a better pace Dolvid wished out loud there was a way of getting word to Shumat. As often, Ott shrugged. "If he could be found, and isn't halfway back to Yuvakh Din." Still, he went and spoke earnestly to the youngest of all the archers, who might be fifteen. He kept nodding he understood, and Ott gave him a slap on the back. The boy handed over his bow, and without any fuss went to and over the edge of the road, quickly disappearing among rocks.

"My wife's cousin's boy," Ott told Dolvid. "A born lurker. When apples are missing, his father thrashes him, whether or not anyone saw him in the orchard."

Now the head of the column turned the swell of hillside, and the southern side of the pass rose to greet them, dark tiers mounting far above. On the left they could see the squared shape of the *drin'loi*, slotted into a shelf of the mountainside. The air was colder here, and abruptly they were marching on thin snow, with drizzle changed to the sting of small ice-pellets. A short, somewhat slippery climb led to a level stretch where the wind out of the east was a slap in the face, road scoured clean of all but long arrowheads of snow, like sandbanks in quick, shallow water. Ahead was a gradual rise to what ought to be world's end, a notch between cliffs opening on nothing.

Ott with a sharp whistle recalled his rearmost archers, who had been crouching at the last turn, watching for followers. If they waited for a shot the line-of-march would be too extended.

Up ahead on the right side the cliffs drew back to make a sweeping bay, while the left-hand wall, tapering down, prevented any view of the *drin'loi*. Onebhal was bringing the lead squadron up in fours as if for a headlong charge, and Dolvid warned him, "The road is sure to be blocked here, too. Bows, probably, up on the left."

He thought it through, and told the lead squadron to dismount, keeping the other mounted in case of surprise attack from behind. Leading *pefral*, the vanguard went up the final slope. Ott said there was a narrow, curving way for horses on the far side, leading up to the gate of the *drin'loi*; the slope in front was steep but not unscalable, up to a breast-high wall.

"We can rush them with swords, if — " Onebhal began,

and dropped to his knees, an arrow in above the breastplate. It had come from above and leftward.

Half-supporting Onebhal Dolvid made for the shelter of the left-hand escarpment. Arrows were still sailing, but the over-eager bowman who had shot Onebhal might have saved them all from annihilation. Fifty paces more, and the entire column would have been exposed. Here, backs against the rock wall, they were inaccessible to the bows, but the numbers of wasted arrows suggested a dismaying array. One of the horses shrilled, hit in the rump.

Dolvid's hands were trembling, but he was agreeably surprised to feel excitement rather than fear, and his mind was magically clear. Onebhal was out of battle, probably dying, and the leader for the other squadron was Kennar, a good young officer of no imagination. When he came up, staying close to the rock-face, and joined with Ott in asking for a plan, it was nothing strange, and he was ready.

A cavalry charge was useless; the men would be visible to the archers as soon as they mounted their *pefral*, and Ott said the front slope to the *drin'loi* was too steep for horses. A pause came in the shooting, though probably the pack-animals in mid-road, certainly the wagons, could be seen from above. Arrows were buried to the flight in the hoods, and one had reslain a side of salt beef, to the complete unconcern of the packhorse carrying it. Obviously the enemy were hesitating to kill usable animals; they must expect easy victory and perhaps costless capitulation when the main force came up from behind.

That approach made everything urgent. With Ott Dolvid made his way along the bank till they could peer out to where the road widened, a natural oddity, a broad, flat oval, plain as a paved courtyard among broken cliffs and jagged peaks. At the far end where the sides closed in again an archway used to stand, its top long broken, and the space between two half-pillars carved from living stone had, as anticipated, been blocked with piled rocks and rubble. To the immediate left was the sharp, rocky slope up to the low front parapet of the *drin'loi's* forecourt, startlingly close, heads and weapons of perhaps two dozen bowmen to be seen.

Antrovai had said something about 'bowmen above' when explaining how the *drin'loi* had become too costly to hold. Thoughts crowded so fast Dolvid babbled, and had to begin again.

"If we take out the teams and push wagons up from behind they'll give us enough cover." Kennar was at his elbow. "Face your squadron downslope, but where you can't be shot at from the *drin'loi*. We have to discourage the ones following us."

"We can't charge that many — between walls?"

"No, but they have to think you might. Ott will give you — a dozen bows?"

He nodded.

"Have them shoot as soon as they can reach any enemy — we want to slow them, you understand. But you will be needed here."

Ott went to pick his dozen. It seemed an hour since Onebhal was wounded, and might perhaps be four minutes. A file-leader was trying to make the *kímukan* comfortable; his face was drained of blood, lips the dead color of cheese. Dolvid told the half-squadron leader, "Get your men together, secure mounts — we'll push wagons out in front of the *drin'loi*."

"We'll all be killed storming those bows."

"They won't be there. Ott — " The hulking man was back from posting his men. "The *drin'loi* couldn't be held, once there was enemy west of the Pass because the forecourt can be commanded by bows from there — " indicating the opposing heights. "They can be scaled from this side. While the enemy is shooting at wagons, can you take men across the road and up, where the big boulder is?"

"Yes." He saw at once what was wanted. High up, spars of rock made a kind of ledge, and bowmen there would be looking down across the road into the forecourt.

"When your men are in place, give me a shout."

Again with minimal excitement, Ott went to tell his men.

The half-squadron was collecting his, unhappy about fighting on foot.

In a scuttling rush Dolvid rounded the leading wagon, whose horses had plodded on a few steps after the arrows had begun. Crouched by the wheel he found a soldier. "Help me take out the horses." He was not sentimental about the draft-animals, but if any were killed in the traces it would be impossible to move the wagons forward.

"No, not there," the man shouted, as Dolvid went crouching towards the front of the long shafts, an arrow whining near his head.

"We have to."

"No, knock out the shaft-pins." To show what he meant, the soldier used his sword-hilt to bang at the metal pin holding shaft in its bracket. A second rap and the pin came free, shaft dropping out held only by the traces. Ducking under the man attacked the center shaft, and other less exposed men were doing the same to the following wagons. As he turned again the man between the shafts was hit twice by arrows. Dolvid ducked lower, not ashamed to use the body hung over the shafts for shield. The man must be dead, with the tip of an arrow showing at the back of his neck. Retrieving the dropped sword he sent the third pin flying, and the shafts drooped, linked by cross-beams, reins slithering from the driver's seat. Another arrow whirred loudly past his ear.

Himself clear on the side nearest safety, he dragged the man's body out, laid it down, then whacked with the flat of the sword at the rump of the closest horse. At once, in a sedate walk, horses dragged empty shafts across the wide open space, leaving Dolvid with a wagon, and a crumpled body at his feet. When he started to pull the body under the lee of the bank, he was helped by Norlum, whose face was filled with excitement and genuine anger, that perhaps at the prospect horses might be hurt.

Once teams were out, the pushing up of the wagons was absurdly safe except for the chance of the main enemy coming up behind. From sixty feet above, though some kept shooting, the archers had no target, as many cavalrymen on the blind side guided the wagons to make a crosswise line in the widening space.

Now Ott came jogging at the head of about twenty men. They had cut diagonally across the road before the enemy above could tell what was happening, but at the big boulder as they scrambled to begin the climb there was a delay, and one man went down with a shaft in his upper leg. The rest were out of sight as soon as the climb began, and Dolvid craned, trying to tell how long they would take to reach the ledges above.

Crouching along the bank, a man from the rearguard came near enough to bawl out, "Enemy in sight — " jabbing a thumb back down the road. The Ottsvale archers there were shooting, but if there was any answer it fell short. Dolvid shouted, "Bows to fall back as soon as we charge. Then horse. Understand?" The man — a boy, really — waved, and went running ape-fashion back down the slope.

A bloodcurdling bellow from above, and a dense cloud of arrows sailed from the crags. Cries of pain, rage and fear came from the *drin'loi*, and shafts from Ott's side were so many it was hard to believe there could be so few bowmen there. A few desultory and half-hearted arrows attempted to reply. Ott's huge battle-voice roared again, nothing intelligible.

It was now. Faces were turned to him for a word, and Dolvid with a yell, "We go," rounded the front of the lead wagon. The slope was steep but not difficult, and he was halfway before he realized he had not brought a sword. He reached back for the Froghuli knife by his shoulder, and was crazed enough to have stormed the *drin'loi* alone hardly knowing it. But many others were with him, and they went over the low parapet, a spring storm over a sea-wall.

Men felled by the Ottsvale archery were everywhere, and others crouching to shelter from bows were quickly hacked down. The *drin'loi* was a square-built stone structure with a stubby watchtower, and Dolvid found himself near the entrance.

A crude two-handed swordsman made a swipe easy to avoid, and he closed to send his knife in over the heart. Pulling the knife free he stabbed overhand at another man going past, piercing the shoulder and tearing open muscle with the man's own momentum. Dying was going on all about, helmed cavalry, angry about the trap and having to leave their horses, killing with ferocious joy. With help of auxiliaries, a few Household men assailed defenders just inside the forecourt gate, and soon overwhelmed them. Someone bawled to Kennar's squadron down below, and they came up the circling path, leading the mounts of the other squadron, crowding in at the gate to join the fight, some pausing to let bowmen slide from their saddles behind them.

Now madness ebbed. For a month he had been seeing men ride in with shirts and breeches blood-blackened from the day's work, hearing them tell their brave tales. Now he was soaked to the elbow with red, and he did not much care for battle.

This one was nearly over. Odd and distasteful how fighters among the beaten side came near inviting death; three by the wall of the fort, pressed back by better fighters, better-armed, and Dolvid saw sword-arms go limp without discarding weapons; men surrendering to death instead of to adversaries. Nearer, a short, tattered man made a feeble mow with a short-sword, and cringed, shutting his eyes, as Dolvid parried and could have struck back. Only proper to kill such weak creatures, murderous rage said — and as brown eyes came open again Dolvid held back his blade, putting a knee instead into the man's belly, and disarming him with a chop of fist to forearm.

Young Kennar, new to the fight, grim, had dismounted and was boring in, wanting someone to kill. Dolvid stepped over a hedgehog-quilled corpse, and clutched at Kennar's arm, feeling the strong, deadly purpose there. Empty eyes came on him.

"What? I could have — " Fury rose, then drained away, as Kennar looked down at his sword, then back into Dolvid's face. "What?"

"Defense. We have to defend this — " with gestures to the front parapet. Noise was all about, grunts, clatters, screams.

Kennar's eyes came alive with intelligent purpose. Single killings were going on all over the forecourt. Dolvid turned again to the doorway, center for the main remaining fight.

"Drop your weapons, surrender," he shouted at the enemy.

"They're beaten, lads," Kennar roared, and called men back by name, like stopping a sea-storm, but most here were trained cavalry with habits of discipline, and there was an ebbing, at first wary.

"Throw down your weapons," Dolvid shouted again at the last doomed knot of resistance. Astonishingly, one, then some others, did, and in moments half a dozen soldiers could shepherd sullen and frightened losers through the breadth of the *drin'loi* into a small enclosed court behind. The rest of the *rabhsai*'s forces, a hundred-odd, not all unwounded, were facing the other way, going back to the parapet among the fallen, puddles of blood.

Below, the road was very quiet; the three wagons stood there, and up by the stopped archway four horses were standing still. Back where the embankment blocked full view, the second team of draft-horses could be seen, and the heads of pack-animals.

"Onebhal?" Dolvid abruptly asked.

"What could we do?" Kennar said. "He is left at roadside."

The giant Ott was glimpsed up and across on the ledge. "We... stay... here," he bellowed, half a question, and Dolvid waved assent. Unless that height could be held, nothing prevented this assault from being duplicated by larger enemy forces to come. With the bulge of cliff below them, however, Ott's bows could not find any targets before they started up the slope to the *drin'loi*.

If they ever did. There were lunatic calculations about how many arrows could be shot by about fifty bowmen in the unknown time it would take for the slope to be scaled, and how many would hit their marks; however done it came to the conclusion, if the enemy had will and discipline for it, a sustained attack by three hundred of them could not be held off. But unless they had hoards of treasure or big stocks of food here, why would they try it? They would be disappointed to find they had captured empty wagons, but the pack-train was real, and they would surely want to get away before fresh royal forces came, which their roadblock would not prevent for long.

But Shumat might be half a day away, and he could not let judgment be biased by his ardent wish for no further fighting. Ottar, Ott's eldest son, was standing near, his cheek scratched. Dolvid said, "Save arrows for when an attack comes." Ottar, calm as his father, nodded, and moved off to tell the bowmen. Arrows were not unlimited, though many had been captured, others recovered here.

Part of the main enemy came in sight, moving cautiously, not sure of what had happened. Some sort of leader walked on the near side of the wagons, and shouted up, "Ho, there!" Ottar put an arrow in the man's heart, then ducked below the breastwork after a cool wave for his men to do the same. Confused shouting and a ragged shower of arrows came, harming no one.

That began a tense half-hour. When a small crowd of out-men came out from cover to secure the wagon nearest them, Kennar was itching to remount his men for a charge, but glumly accepted Dolvid's assessment; not worth the losses there would be; the one path down was a narrow one and the cavalry could not deploy without exposure to many bows. A longer pause, during which the enemy, having discovered the wagon was empty, were presumably debating what to do next.

Assault won the discussion. The quick bob of many heads could be seen as they gathered by the rearmost wagon. All at once a pack of bowmen went darting across the road, just as the Ottsvale men had. Here it was no surprise, and their numbers were halved before they reached the base of the big rock; three lost heart and returned before getting there.

The frontal rush was over practically before it began. Lacking discipline to extend to their right, enemy came jostling round both sides of the wagon, and went forward in the face of accurate archery only as long as men were pressing on from behind. But concerted resolve soon failed, and the attackers receded, leaving a dozen dead or disabled on the slope. Ottar spat, and Kennar was again glancing to his *pefral*.

"Wait," Dolvid said. "If they retreat, you might shadow them, at least to see where they leave the road. Then you could look for Shumat." Kennar appeared happier.

Evidently withdrawal was the plan below; the heads of horses were faced downhill. Two brave or greedy men made the dash across the gap to be sure the lead wagon was as empty as the others; they reached it safely, but when they attempted the much longer run to try capturing its team of horses a volley of arrows from the *drin'loi* brought them down, one spinning and rolling almost to the feet of the horses.

There was an unexpected hesitation in the retreat. Horses still in view halted, and some were turned. A small group of men reappeared, running to shelter behind the remaining wagon, some diving beneath it. Their glances were back over their shoulders rather than up at the parapet. A larger cluster came in sight, undecided whether to stand or to attempt the *drin'loi*, where bows were at work again.

Kennar said raptly, "Shumat!" Many men were running, and more; the wide space was becoming a confusion. Men discarded shapeless bundles, spoils from the pack-train, men were dropped by arrows, stood frozen, looking everywhere for an escape. A few got as far as the crude barrier across the road and tried to clamber it, but Ott's bows could reach them there, and Dolvid did not see any get across to safety.

Out of sight down the road there was an indescribable yelling, terror and agony Dolvid never wanted to hear again. A roar of hoofbeats, clang and batter of weapons, sight of helms, breastplates, a banner, and into the clear space Shumat burst with his men, swords and lance-tips red, lances splintered, great *pefral* snorting. Like the rush of water in a basin the cavalry swirled, enemy cowering, running in every direction, trapped in corners, trampled, skewered as they ran. A wagon crashed over, men along the parapet were yelling, and Dolvid heard himself shouting, too, wordlessly. Shumat, sword high, gathered up men to spur back down the road, where fighting could still be heard. A small band of men crouched till now against the near embankment broke cover and made at the run for the road barrier, end of the realm. They made twenty, thirty yards, and no one watching above thought of shooting. Then again there was an irruption of cavalry, this under the Bear of Ân, Bradhinal out ahead with his sword at full stretch. They flashed into the opening space, gaining on the fugitives. Well short of the barrier the out-men turned to face thunder, and horses were upon, among and trampling over them. Dolvid left the parapet, having seen enough battle.

The lower level of the plain-built *drin'loi*, with mere holes for windows, smelt strongly of human waste. A litter of bedding and packs, and the victors appeared already to have rummaged for any valuables. On a platform at one end there was an aging stock of flour and a few other eatables. Up a steep ladder and through a hatchway was a smaller upper level, with cracked windows as well as a few slits for bowmen. It was all dank and chilly; blankets rumpled on the stone floor, and here again packs had soon been rifled. Odd bits of food and clothing were scattered, and Dolvid stooped to pick up an object booty-hunters had missed, a woman's hair-comb of bone, with a strip of silver along its spine, probably stolen in a raid on some farmhouse.

Above again, the hollow tower. He went carefully up narrow steps with no handrail set on the inside of the walls, and after three turns reached another hatchway. Wind whooshed hoarsely through embrasures; wincing with raw cold he faced to the east. Under layers of cloud and squall, he had his first sight of Naëni, a serried wilderness of lessening peaks, blurring greyly to the edge of vision.

Down below battle was won and over. Squadrons were reassembling, and among bloody ruins of so many enemy it was surprising to see numbers of prisoners being herded together.

Going down the steps he was met by the foul stench; their prisoners were going to be given work they might have done when free, for their own sakes. Light came from the opening to the rear court, and from that direction, a roar of laughter, then again.

Coming out into the open, he needed a long count of seconds to decipher what was going on. To his left, seven or eight of the men who had stormed the *drin'loi* were in a rough half-circle, while captives were against the wall to the right. But one, legs trailing on the ground, upper part of his body propped on one hand, was straight in front of where Dolvid stood. Bent over, proffering a water-bottle, was a cavalryman, Norlum, the man kind to horses. Making a choked moan that might be attempted speech, the prisoner lunged for the flask, and Norlum jerked it away. The man fell forward on his face, not before Dolvid saw mouth and chin had a terrible sword-gash, bleeding freely. Then he observed the man's right leg was nearly severed above the knee, and he had left a scarlet track in his crawl over wet-patched flagstones. With agonized effort he raised his body again, making his wretched, disgusting noise, slowly extending a hand. Grinning, Norlum kept the flask just out of reach.

Dolvid was revolted by the scarcely-human creature, not able to stand or to speak. It came clear to him the cruelty of the captors began in the same horror, even as he blazed into wrath against Norlum. All feelings occurred and were examined while he took two strides, and snatched the water-bottle with his left hand, shoving Norlum in the chest with his right. Stepping across the wounded man's body, he helped him painfully and bloodily to drink.   Dark eyes did not change expression, bewildered and fearful. Dolvid fumbled out a kerchief, and pressed it against the gashed mouth. His anger going away, he wondered whether the soldiers would attack him.

Some had turned away, and had clearly never had anything to do with tormenting the captive. No one wanted to meet Dolvid's eye. Norlum's face was as if masked, but he reached back to fumble a strip of cloth from his pack. He nearly spoke, then came, also avoiding eyes, and did what he could to bind the deep leg wound.

Another soldier came to take over, pressing kerchief to the mouth. "Not much that can be done, sir." He was right, the man was certainly dying.

Dolvid stood, and there in the doorway was Shumat, his face a riddle. "My friend," he said, as they met, "I'll never see anything braver than that. Are you wounded, too?" — seeing blood on shirt and breeches.

"I have been fighting." They walked together through the breadth of the *drin'loi*. "As for bravery, you — "

"All right," he broke in, before Dolvid could begin to list the risks he had taken. "But a lot of men I know would be much gladder to face death than be, well — "

"Than let themselves be seen as softhearted blubberers."

A nod to say that was adequate. "I'm glad you're safe. It was a trick. Partly. These heroes here had refused food for anyone who couldn't fight, and driven off women and children, the old and sick. They sent them westward to decoy us, meaning, I suppose, to round up those who were left, after we had been destroyed. Bradhinal overtook them, but by the time he got back to me with the story, there was a barrier across the road."

"We watched them making it. There was nothing we could do."

"Ott sent his young kinsman to warn us, that was a help. We had eleven killed there, but it would have been worse if we hadn't been warned about the bows. Bradhinal and six of his crawled half a mile in mud at roadside to roll the largest stone aside; we were already coming at the gallop when the breach opened. The out-men lost their nerve and scattered, but I didn't trouble hunting them down; I made certain we would be too late. If they had held the *drin'loi*... How was it taken?"

"Ott and his bows were the key." They had come into the forecourt, and Dolvid indicated the opposing heights. "If you fortified those crags and kept bows there, you could hold this against hundreds."

Shumat wanted all the story, but left it for now, giving details of his ride. Onebhal had been found at roadside, alive and cursing every place north of the Paowan River.

"After this, you'll wear a sword."

"After this, I shall write dispatches and count bags of flour."

One more of the sidelong looks Shumat had been indulging in. "The glory comes back. After that first fight, when Ott's men joined us, I knew I could never face battle again. Not much glory for me here. If I had followed the plan, good men would be alive this minute. How many did we lose here?"

"A dozen, not more. The defenders began shooting too soon, as Onebhal can tell you."

"I was sure there would be a massacre. I've never been so mad."

"Angry enough to charge uphill on a narrow front, without waiting to assure formation — " shaking his head solemnly, but regretted it when Shumat grimaced, and began to speak again about good men killed. Dolvid stopped him. No one foresaw everything, and this was an important, almost certainly a decisive victory. The word tasted sour in his mouth. "They made mistakes, too. I am beginning to think wars are never won, only lost."

Shumat went on frowning. "A miracle this stronghold could be taken with so little loss. Who led the storming, with Onebhal down?"

Dolvid explained instead about the wagons, and then Kennar came up, brisk and unwounded. "Will we garrison the *drin'loi*?"

Shumat, about to answer, stopped. Kennar could not have failed to see him, but had plainly addressed Dolvid.

Who answered, "Yes, till we can find how many enemy remain at large. The wagons can be dragged up for extra sleeping space. Unwounded prisoners can scrub this place out. Is that all right?" — belatedly consulting Shumat.

"It seems so."

"Very well, sir." Kennar hesitated, then carefully saluted the small gap between the two men.

"Your report for this action," Shumat said as the officer left them, "should be worth reading." From somewhere out of botched plans and a snatched victory, comradeship had come back.

A little later, when someone had managed to brew warm drinks, Shumat talked about Manda. She had ridden alone with him, but would not agree to try his bed. "She wants it, she wants it as much, more. But they're at least a century out of date here, and anyway I can't spoil her for the husband-market, can I?"

"Wouldn't just riding alone with her be — "

"Ott thinks we're as good as trothplights," painfully. "My friend, but Bolan says if I give him the truth I might as well go home; we need our allies. I tell Ott if I have not asked for Manda, it's only because each day I might be killed, then she might not find herself a husband — but that's gnat-shit, they would all come running. All the Ottsvale bachelors want me dead; catch me riding out ahead of their bows in a fight!"

"But you are not going to marry her."

"That's the whole story. I want to have her, yes. But when I've done that, once or twice?" Desperation was in his face, and lack of sleep. "I'm not Bolan, but I'm entitled to my aims. If I live, I'm a made man at Kadon; they have to give me my *kimukanum*."

"After today? Your full captaincy; this was undoubtedly the biggest battle in the realm for fifty years."

"Well, but can you see Manda at Kadon Dinul — at the long-table in the Residence, say? Banak-rai made changes in this realm, but I still have to marry well — he did, didn't he?" tugging fiercely at an eyebrow. "I am not saying she's not a fine girl, for Ottsvale, and I could bang bodies with her till she cried for joy. I wish at times I could get myself killed."

"No you don't."

He laughed. "No," he agreed. "Well, this is one for your history, the biggest thing since the War of the Widowed; Battle of the Pass of Perus."

Dolvid tasted that. With a name, less bitter. "Wait till Bolan hears our news. He'll be overjoyed. And envious," he added.

"That, too," Shumat agreed.

Narn

A clear morning, a keen breeze from the northeast; Dolvid sat in the saddle and wished ceremonies of farewell and departure were done with. Only Bolan's anxious insistence over dispatches had stopped him from riding with the supply-train, this one genuine, that had gone plodding ahead with a strong escort two days ago.

He amused himself with the cryptic arithmetic of victory; their forces grew by diminution. Plakhsila's Law took away the battle-tested provincial cavalry once he crossed the borders of Ân, but six of those eight squadrons were to remain here under the recovered Pranuvi, enough, now they were blooded, to mop up the remaining patches of resistance here, and that let Bolan borrow four of General Cavalry from Antrovai's garrison. Enough of the earliest recruits now rode as lancers so losses could be replaced and two new squadrons formed, leaving men for escort, foraging and other duties, so Bolan had sixteen fighting squadrons for the Narn venture, of which twelve, divided into three companies, would press on ahead as far as supplies would take them. Shumat would command that force overall and lead one company; Onebhal, lucky to be alive, was lost as a leader, but not Bradhinal of Ân. He had sidestepped Plakhsila's Law by reenlisting in the Household, and would lead another of the companies, with field rank of *kímukan*.

Besides, while Ott was going home to oversee the agreed resettling of his region, two of his sons would be with Shumat, at the head of one hundred bows, about half of them Ottsvale men. Mounted on Sebira horses, they had assembled with the regular troops, and Shumat was delaying mounting while he said farewell to Ott. To Manda as well, who smiled with a tear-wet face as he spoke earnest things to her. Bolan nearby, every bit as restless as Dolvid, coughed.

They were waiting for the squadrons from the Yuvakh Din garrison, yet to ride down. In dazzling sun Bolan squinted up at the fortress. "He wouldn't dare keep them back. There is no argument with success."

True; not Bolan himself could challenge it. In eight days since the Pass of Perus news of the battle and the newly invincible royal armies had spread by magic, and whole clans of out-men asked to lay down arms. Yuvakh Din had revived overnight, and there had been the first market day in two years, not showing much to buy or sell, but a brave emblem of restoration. Not even indecision from Kadon Dinul could make Bolan question victory. When a message came from Rhunsilakh saying ratification of amnesty had been put off for the meeting of the Council of Thirteen at midsummer, he only snorted at what a short while ago would have crippled him with doubts. They could unpardon all the rebels, he said, and send them out to begin the war again; *Nim'* Daënakh would be no end pleased.

"Have you seen his letter?" he asked. "He plans new building at Sebira when the weather turns, and asks politely if he can borrow some of our left-over prisoners, as many as a hundred. They would remain the *rabhsai*'s prize."

This seemed to be a question; mysteriously Dolvid was in charge of keeping prisoners as well, though the distinction between them and the amnestied quickly became absurd; he had found good and honest workers and some idlers and thieves amongst both groups. "I've recruited as many as I can use. Daënakh can have the rest, all of them, if he will feed them."

Bolan held his answer, as they saw the flash of breastplates and helms on the way down from the fortress.

Antrovai was at the head of four slightly understrength squadrons. Proper for him to take part in the ceremonies, but curiously his officer's outshirt showed no insigne of rank.

That was soon explained. Formally delivering the troops to Bolan's command, Antrovai named himself as their leader in the field.

No doubt he meant it; his face was set with a stubborn determination. Bolan said, "That's preposterous. You command the garrison here."

Spurring nearer so as to speak confidentially, Antrovai said, "I would guess, wouldn't you, that my command is, or soon will be, finished. Do you want me to end my career with ignominy?"

"Your rank — " Bolan said. "It is out of the question."

"With the Heir in Ân, I'll take field rank of *kímukan*. You command this expedition, and I'll follow Shumat's directions."

Discussion went on in low, tense voices. Bolan clearly did not want so senior an officer, one he had been in conflict with, in his command, and Antrovai, just as plainly, was determined to come, if it meant riding as a common lancer. He recalled his early days as a file-leader with the Drin Dakani garrison, when he was acknowledged the best lance there. But by the time he found a war, he was an under-captain, sending other men to do the work he was trained for. Now, with nothing to show for it except failure, he did not want rank, or a voice in overall strategies, only to take part in the last big fight he had any chance of seeing.

Antrovai's talk of last things was chilling, as if he was looking at the end of more than a career. Yet Dolvid would have said yes, and could not see how Bolan could refuse; that would be to throw a painful confession, an openhanded apology back in the man's face.

Bolan tried. "There may be no big fight," with the testiness of a man in a corner. "We might be riding to a parley, a renewal of allegiances. In any case, Under-Captain, a soldier has to take the duties he is given."

"Well then, Captain, you will have to arrest me, or have me restrained by force."

Bolan flapped his white gauntlets, held in one hand, with a gesture of unconscious impotence. "There can be only one commander."

Skirmishes came where the road, dropping steeply from the Pass, wound down amongst brown foothills, but these fights with small bands of lean and desperate men were postscript to the old campaign rather than start of a new one; captives taken knew Yuvakh Din, and nothing about Narn. These men waylaying the road, as well as signs of recent larger encampments, did, however, modify Shumat's plans. At a good but not killing pace, taking a few packhorses for supplies, especially water, he could have been at the gates of Narn in six days, sticking to the reasonably good road. Now he thought it wise to take longer, scouting to both sides of the road to be sure there was no enemy strong enough to close on his rear, or to overwhelm the smaller forces with the following supply-column.

Not that there was any hope, not in a year or with ten times the men, of quartering the length and breadth of this mainly trackless, often waterless country. West of the mountains the road led into a narrowing strait that was the Pass of Perus, but here was a small stream spilling into the ocean. After foothills there were bare lands with no discernible end. Barren ridges, line after line, brown with sudden outcrops of white rock, measured off flatlands without memorable feature, shallow bowls with scrawny trees or wiry scrub, entire plains of pebbles and small boulders so evenly spaced they looked as if they had been placed by design, wind-carved rocks like anvils, pedestals, crouched forms of unknown animals. Twisted watercourses carved into the earth were often empty, seldom more than moist, and when there was a living stream they did not miss the chance of filling barrels carried on wagons, though the long delays caused grumbling.

This, incredibly, had once been forestland. An age ago when the Gabhanil first came over the ocean they had been hunters and trappers, as confirmed even by the name, not their own, but accepted when given, from the Owanilú *gaëbhu*, a hide or pelt. Then, after swathes of forest had been cleared, there was grazing, enough to support sheep and fewer cows, probably never as rich as the Heartland or the deep-grassed valleys of Kargul.

Dolvid's view had long been that disintegration of the First Empire in the Farther West had been accompanied, in part caused, by a gradual change in weathers. Not a year or a five-year spell of drought, which would have been chronicled as such, but a slow drying over decades, enough to change the vast western plateau, Landegh, from good growing-land to a barren waste. It was certainly recorded that in those years the great salt marsh, Shemufegh Rai, had shrunk so it became possible to pass dryshod north of Arnan, and at that same time, Shemugrân, the freshwater marshlands of the Mainland, dwindled too.

But if there had been such a period of scant rainfall, it had long passed, and the marshlands had filled again; why was it Landegh in the west or these empty eastern lands did not restore themselves? The Valley of the Heartland might be more fertile than before the Night of Owan; Dolvid had lived through a dry year there, and seen how, when rain returned, thirsty fields closed their crevices, and fresh green came almost while he watched; here the cracks only seemed to gape wider, hurrying away what water there was.

The *Edhrodilum* had no answers to those questions, either, and apparently were not much interested. In the Heartland the farmers had advice, just as the sick had healing, but not a single *edhradu* or *ramidu* had been seen since leaving Sebira, where one of each had been at Daënakh's dinner. At the *Mankh'* they might say both wastelands, eastern and western, were proof of what became of the earth when left in care of those not taught about the One Way, and whose fields had never been consecrated as *ga-Yalil*.

When camp was made near a stream there were sure to be signs others had done so before them, but Dolvid's company did not encounter any strangers, friendly or hostile. Though they would soon have to be uprooted again, he took the same care with supply-depots as before; he had brought wicker hurdles for barricades from the Yuvakh country, and sites were chosen for possible defence as well as shelter from the wind. Soon empty wagons were trundling back westward, but Shumat borrowed two for decoys as at the Pass of Perus. In this country, as not west of the mountains, he could send flanking squadrons wide on each side of the road, ready to close in when trumpets sounded. Twice minor bands of raiders took the bait, giving the cavalry easy victories. Another day, Antrovai, leading his company on the northern flank, came unexpectedly on an encampment of well-armed men, who gave fight; Shumat arrived to help hunt down the remnant, after Antrovai had accomplished a successful charge.

Dolvid saw him next day when he brought back wounded men, and those needing lances to replace those broken in the fight. Antrovai seemed content, and the vast breadth of wilderness, which made many of the soldiers gloomy, only challenged him. "He has taken off years — he's a colt just out of weapons-class," Shumat said. Dolvid could not quite agree; young soldiers, Shumat for one, found their joys in unconsidered ways quite different from Antrovai's deliberate savouring of freedom regained. But Shumat took back all his contempt for the man, and gave him ungrudging if astonished praise: he entirely accepted his part as leader of a company carrying out tactics determined by others, and kept to a plan rather better than Bradhinal. In the field he had talents wasted as a garrison-commander, and his personal courage, Shumat said, was almost excessive; Antrovai apparently enjoyed testing wills with bowmen by riding unswervingly at them when arrows were already at the string.

Shumat himself was driving hard, covering big, rough distances, hunting for people who left signs of their eating and sleeping, their wastes, but were themselves elusive. In that week-and-a-half Dolvid saw more of Bolan, who with a couple of squadrons held to the road, riding forward to keep contact with the foremost troops, back to be sure of the supply-column, and to bring news for the daily dispatch. Bradhinal's company, on a sweep well north of the road, vanished for three days, and returned with food and water nearly gone, having ridden almost to the feet of new mountains, and come in sight of what seemed to be a ruined and deserted city set on rust-coloured cliffs. Their description fit in with ancient tales of a minor realm called Y'ath, which again might be the Hlaod or Ekhladhi of even older rumour, where a woman ruled, and each woman who married took two husbands at the same wedding. Not (as the *Mankh'* chronicler primly explained) because of their appetites, or that there were twice as many men as women; women who never married made up an actual guild, and followed the crafts. Since a woman with any number of mates could bear no more children than with one, their custom was evidently a way of keeping numbers down, where land for growing and grazing was limited. The people were believed to be an offshoot of the Vrobanil, and their tiny realm, never conquered, had remained when the First Empire was lost. Dolvid wished a week and an escort could be spared for him to go and see the ruins for himself, find if anyone living there had memories of those unique laws and customs.

And yet, as he told Bolan, for patrols to be going so far was absurd. The road for Narn was all that mattered.

The face was perplexed. "This is opposite of what you said when I was planning to make straight for Narn."

He meant, at Sebira, before the Yuvakh Din campaign. "I said, you could not bypass a country in revolt. If we had done that, the Pass of Perus would be closed behind us, and reaching Narn would mean nothing." He explained the distinction; all Naëni could not be reconquered with their thousand men, and would add nothing to the realm except expense if it could. Though the road might never be entirely safe for unprotected travellers; if anything of value had an escort and raiding became too costly, wanderers here might find other ways of living.

"Not if we can't put Narn to rights." Bolan was comically gratified to find that was exactly Dolvid's point. Not waiting to look over the newest dispatches for Kadon Dinul, he rode forward with his two squadrons to renew Shumat's orders: narrow his efforts and press ahead for Narn, get news of the Loyal Elders whose petition to Lambarr had begun all this. Dolvid in turn was told to keep supplies moving east. This meant dismantling of another camp just fortified, which was tiresome, but there were not enough troops to man a chain of outposts, and any camp left standing could then be occupied and held against its makers.

For the next few days he was effective commander of his own small army of levies, men recuperating from lesser wounds, workers recruited at Yuvakh Din, a handful of regular cavalry, crawling with the wagons and pack-animals across wrinkled emptiness. Proper scouring of barrels, making sure a sack of flour filled with weevils had not contaminated others, sending out scouting-parties for water, these were his realm, and everything else was becoming unreal; Narn was an eastward dream that came no nearer. On the third day, having had news from one of Antrovai's squadron-leaders that Bolan was not far away, he began to make a new camp, on a low, regular hill circled by a sluggish but usable stream. Late next day they were overtaken by fresh messages from Kadon Dinul, congratulatory but cautious, pleased by the Pass of Perus but warning against added expenditures.

He was able to read them that evening in Dolvid's tent, and threw the pages aside with an impatient bark. By lamplight his face had much of the same wild look he'd had above the mill at Yuvakh Din when he had dined with Antrovai. The night his squadrons were overdue.

As then, if there was bad news he was going to circle all round it. "The *rabhsai* would see us ride off the edge of the world before giving us another tobhai to spend."

"I am not sure we haven't done so."

"You need a woman," he judged. "How long since you went to bed with anything more exciting than a grocery-list?"

"Last night I had sand fleas in my bed."

Bolan scratched his forearm. "Aye, I've found things that

bite. Antrovai had a man bitten by a snake. He may not live. You could ride back for Yuvakh Din, if you wished. For a night's sport, you needn't go that far. They say the garrison at the *drin'loi*, at the Pass you know, has help with its sewing. You could be back in a few days."

This was grotesque. "Who will see to supplies? And we'll need another camp built, farther east."

"You have scarcely built this one."

"That's why we brought wicker hurdles."

Bolan came at last to his real news. There was a small fertile valley, Odis Combe, less than a dayride short of Narn. Shumat had been ambushed and defeated there.

"Defeated? Is he all right?"

"Seemingly. He rode back for fresh troops, and the bows." For the sake of speed Shumat had left the bows on their slower mounts with two squadrons of his company, riding ahead with the other two. At Odis Combe he had been surprised by unknown numbers of an unknown enemy, evidently prepared for his arrival. Checked by well-hidden bows, he drew back after failing to break them while suffering serious losses.

"I have nothing but secondhand stories. He borrowed a squadron from Bradhinal's company to make good his losses — an entire squadron? Word from Shumat, through Bradhinal, is that he could have beaten this enemy, but bows would let him do so at less cost. Also his supplies were running low."

That last was puzzling. "There must be water in this Combe place."

"He is trying to lessen failure," despondently. "Does he think I'm a child? If we fail here, and have to retreat, no one is going to remember the Pass of Perus."

As before, considering the worst that could happen gave Bolan new resolve, and at once he decided to go forward in the morning with all speed taking every man he could collect. Guard

for supplies would be stripped to the minimum, and all escort,
patrol and foraging duties halted. By now Shumat must have
made his second attempt at Odis Combe, but no matter how that
had ended, Bolan would reach Narn, or use his last lancer trying.

Late, with nothing further to be done tonight, he sat up to
reflect aloud. "If this outing had ended after the Pass, Shumat
and I would both be made men. I would be the darling of the
Household. Kadon Dinul needs someone, you see, as
counterbalance to Sebhal. They fear him."

"Who does? Not his brother-in-law." Lambarr.

"All that extra cavalry he has no right to," rather vaguely.
"People among the Families think Sebhal is a threat. You know
Khelagh?"

That was third mention of him. "I know his big house,
fronting on the Avenue."

"He has been a good friend. He's the one who holds they
need a reputation to set against Sebhal's."

"I am not up on ins and outs at Kadon, but for choice, if
I were an army man, I would rather have Sebhal for an ally."

"That can't be. We're bound to be rivals, that's the nature
of the world. If I can come out of this with a whole reputation."

This was very puzzling. Sebhal as a threat to anything
but *jinzal* was a strange idea, but Khelagh had not become
Bolan's friend without hope of profit, somewhere. It was all
worlds away from this.

Dolvid said, "Doesn't Shumat always ride to the front of
his lead squadron in battle?"

"Even against bows, which is foolhardy. And?"

"He was alive when he borrowed men from Bradhinal.
He could not have lost a whole squadron."

"We can't lose Shumat," frowning. "The dispatch for
Kadon Dinul; we must make the best of what we have —
Bradhinal said something about a man named, ah, Norlum, who
helped rout bows on the flank. No need to say he was making
for Narn — a patrol in strength, hah?"

Dolvid was very familiar with a style, which so often had tried to make transient setbacks out of gigantic historical disasters. "*Suffered losses,*" he recited sardonically, "*meeting larger enemy forces, but carried out a successful withdrawal, having accomplished its purpose of assessing enemy strength.*"

"That's it."   With Bolan words could change what happened. "It's true enough I told him not to attempt Narn with a few men if there was too much danger. I'll sign a page and you can write this up." He was crestfallen when reminded that with every available man going forward with him, there would be no means of sending any dispatch.

What would be in any event last camp could not be far short of Odis Combe. The country was somewhat moister, and from the look of the sky behind the line of high hills ten miles south, that must be the coastal range; from its crest would be a clear view to the sea, the Eastern Ocean. From that direction came an occasional prickle of faint rain.

The camp enclosed a gushing spring within its boundaries, and was protected north and east by a sheer fall to the brush-choked gully where the stream vanished. Feeling naked with nothing for guard but the most unapt of the levies and men recuperating from wounds, suspecting there were enemies not far away, perhaps watching from the surrounding hills, They worked hard to make defences stronger, and before the ring of hurdles and ditches was complete they had to deal with a night raid, evidently an attempt to steal horses. Four ill-armed raiders were killed, an unknown number escaped, leaving the defenders with only superficial wounds, but the incident was the end of complacency. Men who had grumbled sceptically as they erected barriers only to dismantle them, never tested across the breadth of the wilderness, now remembered they were a feeble few making tiny islands in a vast hostile sea, and none of the many ideas for improving defences was rejected, or even criticised as excessive.

No question, Bolan was right to put all his forces into the attack, on the theory that if he won Narn he would have supplies, and if he lost they would not be needed. Still, capture of this camp would probably make a retreat the way they had come impossible, and Dolvid, for his own sake, wanted to go on living as long as he could, even if Bolan failed. On the other hand, an enemy with strength to defeat Bolan would not take long to overwhelm this place.

The wait for news was a long one. On the march Dolvid had briefly seen Shumat, who had missed Bolan, and come back with the same purpose of bringing up all the extra men. He was grim-faced but not dismayed; his losses at Odis Combe had been fourteen killed and twelve seriously wounded, but since then Antrovai had worked his squadrons along ridge-tops past the Combe, and Shumat, with the bows, had combined with him to rout that enemy. Then Shumat with three squadrons and added bows rode on to the gates of Narn. After a wary exchange of greetings he was admitted into the city.

Though the Elders had met him with smiles and weeping, loyalties there were otherwise uncertain and shifting. At the time of the petition to Lambarr the Elders had raised enough force to expel a despotic and erratic ruling body made up of local adventurers, together with pirates and raiders from over the seas. Those had made their own settlements along the coast before harrying, plundering and at last seizing the port, but constant quarrels amongst themselves weakened them.

Since their expulsion, however, a strong chieftain had emerged for them, a man whose name was something close to *Grenaspaluk*, by his description as huge as Ott and cruel as Kanavakh. He had established his camp, a second, rougher city, on the south shore of the deep inlet of Narn, and his ships, made for fighting, completely controlled access to the port, seizing vessels, but more often imposing what he called a tax, consisting of half any incoming cargo. With his large (though uncounted) numbers of fierce fighters, he could also cut off the city from its hinterland, and it had been a detachment of Grenaspaluk's men Shumat had fought at Odis Combe. The outlaw chieftain had failed in one attempt to take the walled city by force, but many merchants and ordinary citizens in Narn were ready to support Grenaspaluk, or capitulate to him, as the only way of ending their miseries. Shumat suspected the Loyal Elders had quietly hedged their bets by negotiating with him, and had probably paid tribute. Foodstuffs were short there, and prices staggeringly high.

Complete defeat of Grenaspaluk, Shumat believed, was the only way to bring Narn back to allegiance, and it had to be done now; by late summer it would be too late, and if Bolan failed, the next expedition would find a city ruled by foreigners, capable of withstanding a siege.

Wherever he came from, Grenaspaluk was no ignorant savage, but a careful strategist, who had fortified the landward side of his settlement, and used bows cleverly at Odis Combe. He would be difficult to beat, Shumat warned, with all their forces. Aware of facing a new threat, he might make another attempt to seize the city before the storm broke, and if that succeeded Shumat said, the expedition would fail. "We're cavalrymen. Siege war is a lost art, even if we had equipment for it. We might as well ride home and tell the *rabhsai* Narn is lost."

Then he was gone, wanting to confer with Bolan, who had veered north to join up with Bradhinal, but should now be at Odi's Combe, wondering where Shumat was.

After that were five days without news. Dolvid made his camp, and the day after the night attack received, briefly, an unexpected reinforcement; wagons from Yuvakh Din with feed for the horses caught up, having an escort of about two dozen men recovered from their wounds, led by Onebhal. He had a stiff left arm and a nasty-looking pit in his chest, but was too anxious about the campaign to wait for better health. Onebhal had it fixed in his mind Dolvid had saved his life at the Pass of Perus, and kept thanking him, despite all disclaimers.

He gave the little news of Yuvakh Din, where *Kímukan* Indhil, nominally acting commander of the garrison, never left the fortress, convinced if he did he would be murdered in revenge for wounding Ott. Onebhal also took the opportunity for various disparaging additions to previous sour assessments of the climate, terrain and general usefulness of the Northeast, before deciding to ride on with his cobbled half-squadron, to see if they were needed.

After the last of them had gone into the uncertainty of early half-light, Dolvid felt isolation close in on the camp. Contrary to the terms of the treaty he armed not only the ones who had taken advantage of amnesty, but also those still designated prisoners. Rather pointlessly he discussed their defence with the highest-ranking soldier left, a file-leader with a bad leg, and they agreed if the camp was overrun, especially by night, the best of poor chances for survival would be to break out in small groups, and try to find a way back across the wilderness of Naëni, living off the lean country. The enemy leader, Grenaspaluk, had a reputation for cruelty, and surrender would merely provide him with fresh sport.

All day nothing happened. To keep men busy, the newly-arrived wagons were unloaded and stores rearranged so the oldest feed would be used soonest. Working, everyone kept watch, and the tension was so much, a veteran of a dozen fights could flinch at the scuttle of a lizard. Night came with slow fading of a scarlet and purple sunset, and Dolvid did not try for sleep, pacing the innermost ring of hurdles and joining in low-voiced talk about Kadon Dinul and the women at Yuvakh Din, drink, and the *rabhsai*'s policies. The cheerlessness of the long hour before dawn was matched by the grim thought that if attack came, he and the rest could die here without knowing whether Bolan had succeeded or failed.

Sun came, pale gold with the breeze stirring. Shivering with fatigue Dolvid munched bread and dried beef, and watched the southward hills waken from dulled blue to sharp-scored browns and pale green. Suddenly he felt happy, not for any reason. He had not attained hope, but that seemed not to matter. He was alive in the moment, noticing everything, a spray of tiny blue flowers by the corner of his tent, how rising mist sketched a veil across long ripples of high cloud where the ocean must be.

Soon, yawning, he told the file-leader, his relief, he was

to be called at the smallest incident, and lay down in his tent. He was wakened by shouts. Middle day, or a little past, and men were dragging the gate-hurdles aside to admit a solitary rider on a hard-ridden *pefrai*, the purplish-brown mount Shumat rode most often.

He looked exhausted, but the wild fear he must be only survivor of a catastrophic battle was immediately banished by the blithe, lopsided grin. "We've won," he called in a big voice, as men came to hold the horse. "They're beaten, annihilated. Bolan killed Grenaspaluk."

With the Gates of Narn Dolvid became certain no battle in history, no action bigger or more complex than head-on clash of two dozen men, had ever been accurately recorded. Soon after the fight while recollections were fresh he could ride over the battlefield, speak with captains, with ordinary soldiers, citizens of Narn who had been spectators, enemy prisoners. What he assembled went into by far the longest of all his dispatches, but twice as much had to be left out, and not only to keep the length within reason. If *this* was true, a contradictory *that* could not be, and he had to weigh probability, the credibility of his informants, and how could he tell what he wrote was not partly determined by his own opinion of how battles ought to be? By far the best general account, accommodating without strain the most detail, was the first he heard, from Shumat, who had an uncanny eye and memory for space and the features of a landscape.

Even more than with the Pass of Perus this battle evolved out of a plan gone astray. Bolan's intent was to sweep up odd bands of enemy roving near the city and its immediate hinterland: if he could clear Odis Combe and keep a road open from the camp to Narn itself, he might conduct a campaign much like the early days at Yuvakh Din. Bradhinal's company he dispatched to stiffen the resolve of the city, with orders to join with the most reliable of the foot-soldiers controlled by the Loyal Elders, and intercept any enemy retreating from Bolan's advance, before they could take refuge in their fortified settlement.

Shumat arrived in time to lead. The purpose of his company was to draw out the enemy, but not encountering any they arrived with a suddenness that surprised them on the tree-sown rim of the Bowl of Narn, hillocky and fertile, with brakes of rough growth, but also open stretches of coarse turf to make it good cavalry country. The enemy they were looking for had gathered in front of Narn, and Bradhinal, seeing Shumat's colours, made a premature sally, not knowing that Bolan, slowed by the small horses of the archers, was lagging well behind, nor that this was the morning Grenaspaluk had picked for an all-out assault on the city.

Though it meant separating from his new allies, the city infantry, Bradhinal launched a charge that easily broke through the nearest of the enemy, and made westward towards where Shumat was advancing cautiously through pastureland. But Grenaspaluk's main army, a packed mass, moved from south of the inlet, and Bradhinal halted his ride, to find supporting foot-soldiers had been pushed back or swept away, and between him and the city gates were five times his own numbers of enemy, with many bows. He was able to rescue part of the infantry, shepherding them to the mound where he had decided to take up his stand and await the arrival of Bolan with the main strength of cavalry.

Grenaspaluk had to take men from his attack on the city to watch both Bradhinal and the wary Shumat, and when that assault had been beaten back from the walls there was an odd lull, while the bandit captain brought all the rest of his men out of their encampment, gathering strength in front of Narn's gates. Though numerous, Grenaspaluk evidently did not trust his own horse for an attack against regular cavalry, merely using their mass as threat and barrier against any attempt by Bradhinal to relieve the city. He, the enemy captain, was easily identified as he commanded from the top of a hillock, a looming figure with a bellowing voice, watching all fights.

Shumat was first to move, starting a swerving cross-country run with the object of joining Bradhinal. Together their seven squadrons, all excellent lances, could mount a charge against the weight of enemy, and Grenaspaluk made an instant counter-move, wheeling fully half his forces to prevent any junction.

That was the moment when Bolan appeared at the brim of the Bowl of Narn, his squadrons already ordered for the charge; a messenger had let him know him battle had begun.

Telling this part Shumat could not keep still; his voice trembled and he made small, excited flicks with his hands. "He did it out of the manual. He had the slope, and started slow, a parade-ground front of twenty-four lances, right at the nearest flank of the enemy. At a hundred paces it was rolling thunder, then Bolan on that big grey of his went out ahead, and drove into the enemy before the squadrons struck. He was like a boar in a field of steel, and I lost sight of him. His men were fighting to catch him, and somehow he went right through the crowd, and came out at the far side, climbing the hillock where Grenaspaluk had his banner. Old Bolan tossed away his lance, which was slivers, drew his sword as if he was making salute — I'd swear he was smiling. He turned and skewered Grenaspaluk, and didn't know what he'd done — he admits it."

Then, Shumat said, Bradhinal came down from his mound to show others could do it, and Shumat joined with him. Fall of their leader had broken the spirit of the bandit armies, and when pikemen from the city made a new sortie it became a rout, with many enemy throwing down their weapons and giving themselves up. "Bolan? He saw we had it won, sat there on the hilltop — you know, Larghai in the tapestry at the Treasury. But don't let anyone tell you he can't ride, or fight, when it's there in front of him, with no room for what-ifs. You should have seen it; it was better than the *Song of Tales*."

But Shumat too had missed one of the decisive actions. Antrovai's company had been on the right of Bolan's charge, and the Under-Captain was clear of the main mass of enemy. As Bolan was downing Grenaspaluk, Antrovai saw the bandits had virtually emptied their settlement, protected to the landward by an earthwork with a single opening, leaving only a few men to guard their houses, their women, and their fighting ships. Not waiting for any orders Antrovai pulled out a pair of squadrons and outraced retreating enemy to the gateway, overwhelming its inadequate guard. One squadron turned to become defenders, but Antrovai swept on to waterside, where ships were being readied. One, having oarsmen aboard, managed to put out into the harbour, but pitch used for caulking was simmering over fires, and Antrovai's men made firebrands to set all the rest of the ships ablaze. With that fire red behind him, Antrovai returned to help hold the entrance. The exploit capped victory, but Antrovai was killed fighting in the gateway.

Though he would not say it, Dolvid thought Antrovai, in joining the campaign, had found everything he was looking for — a proper use for his talents, a big fight, a justification for his career; everything, including death.

He was among seven officers of half-squadron rank and above killed in the battle. For the numbers engaged, perhaps seven thousand on all sides, losses for Bolan's forces had been remarkably small, although most had some sort of wound, Shumat a small stab in the calf and a slash across the right knuckles. Bolan was untouched.

"He urgently wants your assistance. Not everyone in Narn wants to be governed by Loyal Elders, and he's going to have to sit in the high seat in their Hall of Wardens and render judgements, which he does not much fancy. We've saved the port from bandits, but not from poverty; it's a fishing village in the hulk of a city. Bolan's the one-armed man who won a longbow."

After the desolation of its former province the green of the Narn hinterland was startling. Odis Combe had trees, aspen and wild cherry, maple, hazel and black birch, and flowers mingled with the grasses, yet that still was a forbidding scene, black spars of rock thrusting up like threats; he was glad to pass through and climb out to scrubby pasture, the crests of the ridges scrubbed bare, a first glimpse of sea.

Coming to the lip of the Bowl of Narn was altogether different, sight of home after a long journey. Poplars marching, the breeze-stirred flicker of silvery oleaster; birds were everywhere, bees clambering over the blossoming hedgerows, a cup full of golden light, with varied greens of early summer, fresh scent of growing, pierced by the salt tang of ocean. Only as they rode down the wide-curving road, Shumat indicating places in his account of the battle, was it apparent this was largely a devastated land, with wrecked farmhouses, many burned out, neglected orchards chopped for firewood, farmlands gone to weeds. If the city were not half-empty its people would be more desperate; it would take more than one season to restore these growing-lands.

Grim granite mountains rose to the eastward, and seen against that background Narn at a distance was noble stone on its deep inlet. History and legend met and overlapped on this shore, where Odi Kukkuk as a boy met and wrestled down the Red Bull, and cut from its hide his leather armlet, emblem of his strength. Yuvakh came here two thousand years ago, and Larghai; Pir Kallikuk might have been born here. Gabhanil came here from across the Eastern Ocean not once but twice, wandering into the history and destiny of the realm. On that hillock, Bolan, ducking the sweep of an axe, placed his sword-point with unnatural calm to fell Grenaspaluk.

The cobbles of Narn were iron-tough. A hard-built city, and many buildings and stumps of buildings were there before Empire came, rebuilt and built on, but recognisable for their strangeness, forms of unfamiliar flowers showing just above cobbles, a row of oddly bulged pillars, stone surfaces never left plain, but restlessly carved in coils and windings. No one could say whether those earliest builders (who must have had good tools) had been destroyed by the Gabhanil when they came, or joined with them and intermarried till their own story was lost. Or perhaps they had come, built, and then gone back to a homeland in the remote East, where the grimacing beasts and writhing flowers they left as carvings were common as this realm's sheep and goats, the clover and hawthorn they munched.

The newer building was less interesting, but the Hall of Wardens on the central square was comical to Dolvid, a poor cousin to the Bronze Residence at Kadon Dinul, built in much the same period, but with masons and builders who aimed beyond their skills. The corner pillars leant outwards a little, perhaps because the crudely carved friezes had been made too large; there had once been a central cupola, but it had evidently caved in, and been roughly repaired with brickwork and slabs of stone. Bolan came out on the uneven steps to welcome Dolvid, accepted his congratulations in a preoccupied way, and before he had washed, changed, eaten or as much as relieved himself after his long ride, was thrusting documents at him for an opinion.

Most of them were claims, claims for compensation on cargoes lost or destroyed (some shipped while Dolvid was a pupil at the *Mankh'*), property-claims the Elders could not settle, claims against that very council for illegal appropriation. There were claims for back-wages from men who, though long living as ordinary townsfolk, had never formally been released from the *rabhsai*'s service, and land-claims for others who had been discharged; one man claimed the whole of Odis Combe as a lineal descendant of Odi Kukkuk; this much-thumbed petition was said to have been reappearing for a generation, and the petitioner, they were told, could often be seen strutting in a mangy bear-skin, offering to run a foot-race against the flight of an eagle, leap unscathed from Leaning Cliffs, satisfy six eager brides in a single night, or duplicate any other of his ancestor's celebrated feats.

Apart from this oddity, the common theme was absence of money, which also weakened drafts for a new constitution drawn up in the Council and elsewhere, all obviously regarding Kadon Dinul as a fountainhead of the wealth needed to bring prosperity back to Narn. There were soon many new claims against the captured treasury of Grenaspaluk, and there Dolvid foresaw a long battle. On one hand it was lawful prize, and

Bolan, after rendering a fourth part to the *rabhsai*, was entitled to one-seventh for his own, the rest to be shared with his army, according to rank, responsibility and merit. Dolvid agreed men who had endured hardship and danger were entitled to their reward; seeing the uncertainty of his future when the campaign was over he would not have minded a windfall himself. Yet the money and valuables had largely been extorted from the people they had been sent to relieve.

"Help has to be paid for. If these people had the guts to refuse to pay, or had fought to get back what Grenaspaluk took, we wouldn't have had to come here. Anyway, how can we judge which claims are true? Grenaspaluk didn't have Arvus keeping his accounts."

Moreover, there turned out to be claims on claims; some claimants were themselves accused of extortion and theft. "A part, at least," Dolvid ventured, "could be used for the city at large, to buy food for distribution. Their hunger will be starvation by next spring. They need seed and tools, building stuff to restart their farms, loans without interest."

Bolan made a face, but put off further discussion of those moneys to ask what opportunities Dolvid could see for profitable investment.

"No cargoes will be landed — " sensing Khelagh's money behind this — "unless merchants have capital."

Food and capital were indeed the questions, interwoven. Alarmed by rising prices, one of the first acts of the Loyal Elders on seizing power two years ago had been to fix the price of necessities, wheat flour then selling for three to five times its price at Kadon Dinul. A bold stroke, but not practicable, and the result had been to kill money as the city's medium of exchange. Except for irregular and inadequate distributions by the Council, flour or meat could be obtained only by those with fish or cloth or leather to barter with. The coming of Bolan's troops had begun the rebirth of money, not yet for foodstuffs. Women could be had for money, though most of them would rather be paid from the soldiers' rations, but merchants with no trust in the long road westward had stocks of goods to sell, jewels and fine metalware, pottery with a deeper glaze than any made in the Heartland, furs, articles of carved ivory and shaped wood hard as stone, all at bargain prices, sellers uncertain how long their luck would last. If the lands were kept peaceful some of these goods might start trickling west again, but though Dolvid saw lovely and curious things, he could not find the one commodity to perform the miracle, make Narn a needed part of the realm.

Viewing poverty and disrepair, Shumat had called the city worse than the lakeside encampment at Yuvakh Din, a dunghill. Most tumbledown of all was the waterfront with its idle, fouled wharves and empty warehouses, a forlorn relic of prosperous days, several wide spaces where landed goods would have been displayed and bid for, and of the booths surrounding them not one in ten was occupied, the rest shuttered and silent. Weathered signs gave a glimpse into a rich, alien past where there could be a merchant who sold only hot spices and another for sweet, a 'mother of princes' who used 'smoke-reading' to foretell futures, a hostelry offering girls in three different colours of skin, a shop for nothing but blue beads, another for fruit shown big as a child's head, with the look of a pine-cone. A few cookshops were still open, or had reopened when the troops came, and Dolvid sampled many new foods, mainly fish and shellfish, but made new with hot, sour or pungent spices. He tasted herring for the first time, hot and fatty, and there were huge sweet lobsters, prawns and oysters, delicate-fleshed flatfish of several kinds, and once a thick slice cut from a fish said to have a sword for snout.

In those cookshops, sharing his food in doorways of dilapidated warehouses open for the first time in years, sitting on a bollard at water's edge, he listened to many stories, sometimes told by men whose faces and accents came from distant countries, but more often by men and women of Narn, memories of when the port was thronged with seagoers from everywhere; tales of talking birds and lizards that could change their colours, of a nut the same size as the pine-fruit giving both meat and milk. He heard about an animal that changed itself to stone, a stone that became a winged beast, a plant which when burnt gave men the power of walking without touching ground. Everything went into his journals, not trying to guess what was true or how truth might be disguised; after the swallow-riders and Daënakh's find of bones he was not willing to call anything mere fable. Strangely, as in the weavings of poetry, truth that went beyond plain fact could be held by apparent absurdity, Pir Perus wrestling with the poppy-red sun, or tales he heard now, as with the men living behind the rising sun, whose all-father was a lamed potter turning the heavens on his wheel.

Meanwhile the Council of Elders, not all of them old, some very shrewd, were pressing for settlement of claims. Most were or had been merchants, and Dolvid found debating with men of business refreshingly straightforward, once understood they were out for all they could get. With them he negotiated a compromise he hoped Bolan would, if grudgingly, agree to: articles from Grenaspaluk's hoard, especially jewellery and furnishings, where ownership could be established, would be returned, and half-restitution paid in clear cases of outright theft. Where those making claims might in turn be liable to others, that money would be withheld pending later adjudication, and go to make up a fund for loans at token interest, especially to new or returning farmers. The rest, still a large sum, was lawful prize-money, but Dolvid credited the *rabhsai* with a generous gesture, saying Lambarr would wish his share, in this period of need, to be part of the money available to borrowers, who could repay him when their crops or their cargoes came in.

When he heard that part Bolan said he must be mad, but none of it mattered unless Narn the port could be made profitable. Shumat rode away, going back to Yuvakh Din to relieve the *Kímukan* Indhil, and stay on as acting-commander till Antrovai's successor was found. Dolvid did not envy his meeting with Antrovai's chilly wife, now widow, but Shumat was obviously looking forward to renewal of self-torture over Manda. He would less mind losing her, he confessed, but for knowing some other man would have her.

As he left with his squadron, Bolan muttered against staying here too long. "The Great Pledging is only a fortnight away. It could be done. We'd give them a show to shout for, hah?"

He meant the Pledging crowds, and almost seemed to be serious about the journey. Dolvid, dismayed, rather cunningly suggested that after such victories Bolan could raise his own crowds in the Avenue; his return would be all the more notable as an event in its own right. And his fame more lasting, he did not add, if Narn was not lost to the realm again in six months.

Bolan was attracted to the part of the argument he was allowed to hear, and they went back to judging cases, and discussing all the things that might make back their cost ten times over if brought to Kadon Dinul, wondering whether the Residence Quarter would make a fashion of the glazed pottery, or the tiny Narn octopus that reminded Dolvid of stirrup-leather soaked in fish-oil, but pickled (as it would have to be for the journey) was like tripe flavoured with anchovies. But it was nonsense to speak of rebuilding a great port around such trifling and uncertain trade. A few ships did come nosing into harbour, like cats wary of their reception, and overland news came from Tan Lughsai by way of Kadon Dinul, hailing Bolan's victories, confirming his permanent rank of full captain. He, frowning, did not appear ready to cope with eminence, and under clear skies of the Narn summer what they had left behind was immeasurably distant; they were held there by unchanging riddles, and the waste of Naëni muffled their calls for guidance. Perhaps after all they had ridden off the edge of the world.

End of the second book.

www.ingramcontent.com/pod-product-compliance
Lightning Source LLC
Chambersburg PA
CBHW031416240626
47154CB00001B/59